D0044773

THE TRIALS OF APOLLO

◄ 3 ►

THE BURNING MAZE

Also by Rick Riordan

PERCY JACKSON AND THE OLYMPIANS
Book One: *The Lightning Thief*
Book Two: *The Sea of Monsters*
Book Three: *The Titan's Curse*
Book Four: *The Battle of the Labyrinth*
Book Five: *The Last Olympian*

The Demigod Files

The Lightning Thief: The Graphic Novel
The Sea of Monsters: The Graphic Novel
The Titan's Curse: The Graphic Novel

Percy Jackson's Greek Gods
Percy Jackson's Greek Heroes
From Percy Jackson: Camp Half-Blood Confidential

THE KANE CHRONICLES
Book One: *The Red Pyramid*
Book Two: *The Throne of Fire*
Book Three: *The Serpent's Shadow*

The Red Pyramid: The Graphic Novel
The Throne of Fire: The Graphic Novel
The Serpent's Shadow: The Graphic Novel

From the Kane Chronicles: Brooklyn House Magicians' Manual

THE HEROES OF OLYMPUS
Book One: *The Lost Hero*
Book Two: *The Son of Neptune*
Book Three: *The Mark of Athena*
Book Four: *The House of Hades*
Book Five: *The Blood of Olympus*

The Demigod Diaries

The Lost Hero: The Graphic Novel
The Son of Neptune: The Graphic Novel

Demigods & Magicians

MAGNUS CHASE AND THE GODS OF ASGARD
Book One: *The Sword of Summer*
Book Two: *The Hammer of Thor*
Book Three: *The Ship of the Dead*

For Magnus Chase: Hotel Valhalla Guide to the Norse Worlds

THE TRIALS OF APOLLO
Book One: *The Hidden Oracle*
Book Two: *The Dark Prophecy*

RICK RIORDAN

3

THE BURNING MAZE

DISNEY • HYPERION
Los Angeles New York

 For information address Disney • Hyperion,
125 West End Avenue, New York, New York 10023.

First Edition, May 2018
1 3 5 7 9 10 8 6 4 2
FAC-020093-18075

Printed in the United States of America

This book is set in Danton, Gauthier FY/Fontspring;
Goudy Old Style, Goudy, Sabon/Monotype
Designed by Joann Hill

Library of Congress Cataloging-in-Publication Data
Names: Riordan, Rick, author.
Title: The burning maze / Rick Riordan.
Description: First edition. • Los Angeles ; New York : Disney-Hyperion, 2018.
• Series: The trials of Apollo ; book 3 • Summary: In response to the Dark
Prophecy, Leo flies ahead on Festus to warn the Roman camp, while Lester
and Meg must go through the Labyrinth to find the third emperor—and an
Oracle who speaks in word puzzles—somewhere in the American Southwest.
Identifiers: LCCN 2017059850 • ISBN 9781484746431 (hardback)
Subjects: LCSH: Apollo (Deity)—Juvenile fiction. • CYAC: Apollo
(Deity)—Fiction. • Gods, Greek—Fiction. • Oracles—Fiction. • Mythology,
Greek—Fiction. • BISAC: JUVENILE FICTION / Action & Adventure /
General. • JUVENILE FICTION / Legends, Myths, Fables / Greek & Roman.
• JUVENILE FICTION / Fantasy & Magic.
Classification: LCC PZ7.R4829 Bu 2018 • DDC [Fic]—dc23
LC record available at https://lccn.loc.gov/2017059850

Reinforced binding

Visit www.DisneyBooks.com
Follow @ReadRiordan

THIS LABEL APPLIES TO TEXT STOCK

To Melpomene, the Muse of Tragedy
I hope you're pleased with yourself

The Dark Prophecy

The words that memory wrought are set to fire,
Ere new moon rises o'er the Devil's Mount.
The changeling lord shall face a challenge dire,
Till bodies fill the Tiber beyond count.

Yet southward must the sun now trace its course,
Through mazes dark to lands of scorching death
To find the master of the swift white horse
And wrest from him the crossword speaker's breath.

To westward palace must the Lester go;
Demeter's daughter finds her ancient roots.
The cloven guide alone the way does know,
To walk the path in thine own enemy's boots.

When three are known and Tiber reached alive,
'Tis only then Apollo starts to jive.

1

Once was Apollo
Now a rat in the Lab'rinth
Send help. And cronuts

NO.

I refuse to share this part of my story. It was the lowest, most humiliating, most awful week in my four-thousand-plus years of life. Tragedy. Disaster. Heartbreak. I will not tell you about it.

Why are you still here? Go away!

But alas, I suppose I have no choice. Doubtless, Zeus *expects* me to tell you the story as part of my punishment.

It's not enough that he turned me, the once divine Apollo, into a mortal teenager with acne, flab, and the alias Lester Papadopoulos. It's not enough that he sent me on a dangerous quest to liberate five great ancient Oracles from a trio of evil Roman emperors. It's not even enough that he enslaved me—his *formerly favorite son*—to a pushy twelve-year-old demigod named Meg!

On top of all that, Zeus wants me to record my shame for posterity.

Very well. But I have warned you. In these pages, only suffering awaits.

Where to begin?

With Grover and Meg, of course.

For two days, we had traveled the Labyrinth—across pits of darkness and around lakes of poison, through dilapidated shopping malls with only discount Halloween stores and questionable Chinese food buffets.

The Labyrinth could be a bewildering place. Like a web of capillaries beneath the skin of the mortal world, it connected basements, sewers, and forgotten tunnels around the globe with no regard to the rules of time and space. One might enter the Labyrinth through a manhole in Rome, walk ten feet, open a door, and find oneself at a training camp for clowns in Buffalo, Minnesota. (Please don't ask. It was traumatic.)

I would have preferred to avoid the Labyrinth altogether. Sadly, the prophecy we'd received in Indiana had been quite specific: *Through mazes dark to lands of scorching death*. Fun! *The cloven guide alone the way does know.*

Except that our cloven guide, the satyr Grover Underwood, did not seem to know the way.

"You're lost," I said, for the fortieth time.

"Am not!" he protested.

He trotted along in his baggy jeans and green tie-dyed T-shirt, his goat hooves wobbling in his specially modified New Balance 520s. A red knit cap covered his curly hair. Why he thought this disguise helped him better pass for human, I couldn't say. The bumps of his horns were clearly visible beneath the hat. His shoes popped off his hooves several times a day, and I was getting tired of being his sneaker retriever.

He stopped at a T in the corridor. In either direction, rough-hewn stone walls marched into darkness. Grover tugged his wispy goatee.

"Well?" Meg asked.

Grover flinched. Like me, he had quickly come to fear Meg's displeasure.

Not that Meg McCaffrey *looked* terrifying. She was small for her age, with stoplight-colored clothes—green dress, yellow leggings, red high-tops—all torn and dirty thanks to our many crawls through narrow tunnels. Cobwebs streaked her dark pageboy haircut. The lenses of her cat-eye glasses were so grimy I couldn't imagine how she could see. In all, she looked like a kindergartner who had just survived a vicious playground brawl for possession of a tire swing.

Grover pointed to the tunnel on the right. "I—I'm pretty sure Palm Springs is that way."

"Pretty sure?" Meg asked. "Like last time, when we walked into a bathroom and surprised a Cyclops on the toilet?"

"That wasn't my fault!" Grover protested. "Besides, this direction *smells* right. Like . . . cacti."

Meg sniffed the air. "I don't smell cacti."

"Meg," I said, "the satyr is supposed to be our guide. We don't have much choice but to trust him."

Grover huffed. "Thanks for the vote of confidence. Your daily reminder: I didn't *ask* to be magically summoned halfway across the country and to wake up in a rooftop tomato patch in Indianapolis!"

Brave words, but he kept his eyes on the twin rings around Meg's middle fingers, perhaps worried she might summon her golden scimitars and slice him into rotisserie-style cabrito.

Ever since learning that Meg was a daughter of Demeter, the goddess of growing things, Grover Underwood had acted more intimidated by her than by me, a former Olympian deity. Life was not fair.

Meg wiped her nose. "Fine. I just didn't think we'd be wandering around down here for two days. The new moon is in—"

"Three more days," I said, cutting her off. "We know."

Perhaps I was too brusque, but I didn't need a reminder about the other part of the prophecy. While we traveled south to find the next Oracle, our friend Leo Valdez was desperately flying his bronze dragon toward Camp Jupiter, the Roman demigod training ground in Northern California, hoping to warn them about the fire, death, and disaster that supposedly faced them at the new moon.

I tried to soften my tone. "We have to assume Leo and the Romans can handle whatever's coming in the north. We have our own task."

"And plenty of our own fires." Grover sighed.

"Meaning what?" Meg asked.

As he had for the last two days, Grover remained evasive. "Best not to talk about it . . . here."

He glanced around nervously as if the walls might have ears, which was a distinct possibility. The Labyrinth was a living structure. Judging from the smells that emanated from some of the corridors, I was fairly sure it had a lower intestine at least.

Grover scratched his ribs. "I'll try to get us there fast, guys," he promised. "But the Labyrinth has a mind of its own. Last time I was here, with Percy . . ."

His expression turned wistful, as it often did when he referred to his old adventures with his best friend, Percy Jackson. I couldn't blame him. Percy was a handy demigod to have around. Unfortunately, he was not as easy to summon from a tomato patch as our satyr guide had been.

I placed my hand on Grover's shoulder. "We know you're doing your best. Let's keep going. And while you're sniffing for cacti, if you could keep your nostrils open for breakfast—perhaps coffee and lemon-maple cronuts—that would be great."

We followed our guide down the right-hand tunnel.

Soon the passage narrowed and tapered, forcing us to crouch and waddle in single file. I stayed in the middle, the safest place to be. You may not find that brave, but Grover was a lord of the Wild, a member of the satyrs' ruling Council of Cloven Elders. Allegedly, he had great powers, though I hadn't seen him use any yet. As for Meg, she could not only dual-wield golden scimitars, but also do amazing things with packets of gardening seeds, which she'd stocked up on in Indianapolis.

I, on the other hand, had grown weaker and more defenseless by the day. Since our battle with the emperor Commodus, whom I'd blinded with a burst of divine light, I had not been able to summon even the smallest bit of my former godly power. My fingers had grown sluggish on the fret board of my combat ukulele. My archery skills had deteriorated. I'd even missed a shot when I fired at that Cyclops on the toilet. (I'm not sure which of us had been more embarrassed.) At the same time, the waking visions that sometimes paralyzed me had become more frequent and more intense.

I hadn't shared my concerns with my friends. Not yet.

I wanted to believe my powers were simply recharging. Our trials in Indianapolis had nearly destroyed me, after all.

But there was another possibility. I had fallen from Olympus and crash-landed in a Manhattan dumpster in January. It was now March. That meant I had been human for about two months. It was possible that the longer I stayed mortal, the weaker I would become, and the harder it would be to get back to my divine state.

Had it been that way the last two times Zeus exiled me to earth? I couldn't remember. On some days, I couldn't even remember the taste of ambrosia, or the names of my sun-chariot horses, or the face of my twin sister, Artemis. (Normally I would've said that was a blessing, not remembering my sister's face, but I missed her terribly. Don't you *dare* tell her I said that.)

We crept along the corridor, the magical Arrow of Dodona buzzing in my quiver like a silenced phone, as if asking to be taken out and consulted.

I tried to ignore it.

The last few times I'd asked the arrow for advice, it had been unhelpful. Worse, it had been unhelpful in Shakespearean English, with more *thees*, *thous*, and *yea, verilys* than I could stomach. I'd never liked the '90s. (By which I mean the 1590s.) Perhaps I would confer with the arrow when we made it to Palm Springs. *If* we made it to Palm Springs . . .

Grover stopped at another T.

He sniffed to the right, then the left. His nose quivered like a rabbit that had just smelled a dog.

Suddenly he yelled "Back!" and threw himself into reverse. The corridor was so narrow he toppled into my lap, which forced me to topple into Meg's lap, who sat down hard with a startled grunt. Before I could complain that I don't *do* group massage, my ears popped. All the moisture was sucked out of the air. An acrid smell rolled over me—like fresh tar on an Arizona highway—and across the corridor in front of us roared a sheet of yellow fire, a pulse of pure heat that stopped as quickly as it had begun.

My ears crackled . . . possibly from the blood boiling in my head. My mouth was so dry it was impossible to swallow. I couldn't tell if I was trembling uncontrollably, or if all three of us were.

"Wh—what was that?" I wondered why my first instinct had been to say *who*. Something about that blast had felt horribly familiar. In the lingering bitter smoke, I thought I detected the stench of hatred, frustration, and hunger.

Grover's red knit hat steamed. He smelled of burnt goat hair. "That," he said weakly, "means we're getting close. We need to hurry."

"Like I've been *saying*," Meg grumbled. "Now get off." She kneed me in the butt.

I struggled to rise, at least as far as I could in the cramped tunnel. With the fire gone, my skin felt clammy. The corridor in front of us had gone dark and silent, as if it couldn't possibly have been a vent for hellfire, but I'd spent enough time in the sun chariot to gauge the heat of flames. If we'd been caught in that blast, we would've been ionized into plasma.

"We'll have to go left," Grover decided.

"Um," I said, "left is the direction from which the fire came."

"It's also the quickest way."

"How about backward?" Meg suggested.

"Guys, we're close," Grover insisted. "I can *feel* it. But we've wandered into *his* part of the maze. If we don't hurry—"

Screee!

The noise echoed from the corridor behind us. I wanted to believe it was some random mechanical sound the Labyrinth often generated: a metal door swinging on rusty hinges, or a battery-operated toy from the Halloween clearance store rolling into a bottomless pit. But the look on Grover's face told me what I already suspected: the noise was the cry of a living creature.

SCREEE! The second cry was angrier, and much closer.

I didn't like what Grover had said about us being in *his part of the maze*. Who was *his* referring to? I certainly didn't want to run into a corridor that had an insta-broil setting, but, on the other hand, the cry behind us filled me with terror.

"Run," Meg said.

"Run," Grover agreed.

We bolted down the left-hand tunnel. The only good news: it was slightly larger, allowing us to flee for our lives with more elbow room. At the next crossroads, we turned left again, then took an immediate right. We jumped a pit, climbed a staircase, and raced down another corridor, but the creature behind us seemed to have no trouble following our scent.

SCREEE! it cried from the darkness.

I knew that sound, but my faulty human memory couldn't place it. Some sort of avian creature. Nothing cute like a parakeet or a cockatoo. Something from the infernal regions—dangerous, bloodthirsty, very cranky.

We emerged in a circular chamber that looked like the bottom of a giant well. A narrow ramp spiraled up the side of the rough brick wall. What might be at the top, I couldn't tell. I saw no other exits.

SCREEE!

The cry grated against the bones of my middle ear. The flutter of wings echoed from the corridor behind us—or was I hearing *multiple* birds? Did these things travel in flocks? I had encountered them before. Confound it, I should *know* this!

"What now?" Meg asked. "Up?"

Grover stared into the gloom above, his mouth hanging open. "This doesn't make any sense. This shouldn't be here."

"Grover!" Meg said. "Up or no?"

"Yes, up!" he yelped. "Up is good!"

"No," I said, the back of my neck tingling with dread. "We won't make it. We need to block this corridor."

Meg frowned. "But—"

"Magic plant stuff!" I shouted. "Hurry!"

One thing I will say for Meg: when you need plant stuff done magically, she's your girl. She dug into the pouches on her belt, ripped open a packet of seeds, and flung them into the tunnel.

Grover whipped out his panpipe. He played a lively jig to encourage growth as Meg knelt before the seeds, her face scrunched in concentration.

Together, the lord of the Wild and the daughter of Demeter made a super gardening duo. The seeds erupted into tomato plants. Their stems grew, interweaving across the mouth of the tunnel. Leaves unfurled with ultra-speed. Tomatoes swelled into fist-size red fruits. The tunnel was almost closed off when a dark feathery shape burst through a gap in the net.

Talons raked my left cheek as the bird flew past, narrowly missing my eye. The creature circled the room, screeching in triumph, then settled on the spiral ramp ten feet above us, peering down with round gold eyes like searchlights.

An owl? No, it was twice as big as Athena's largest specimens. Its plumage glistened obsidian black. It lifted one leathery red claw, opened its golden beak, and, using its thick black tongue, licked the blood from its talons—*my* blood.

My sight grew fuzzy. My knees turned to rubber. I was dimly aware of other noises coming from the tunnel—frustrated shrieks, the flapping of wings as more demon birds battered against the tomato plants, trying to get through.

Meg appeared at my side, her scimitars flashing in

her hands, her eyes fixed on the huge dark bird above us. "Apollo, you okay?"

"Strix," I said, the name floating up from the recesses of my feeble mortal mind. "That thing is a strix."

"How do we kill it?" Meg asked. Always the practical one.

I touched the cuts on my face. I could feel neither my cheek nor my fingers. "Well, killing it could be a problem."

Grover yelped as the strixes outside screamed and threw themselves at the plants. "Guys, we've got six or seven more trying to get in. These tomatoes aren't going to hold them."

"Apollo, answer me right now," Meg ordered. "What do I need to do?"

I wanted to comply. Really, I did. But I was having trouble forming words. I felt as if Hephaestus had just performed one of his famous tooth extractions on me and I was still under the influence of his giggle nectar.

"K-killing the bird will curse you," I said finally.

"And if I *don't* kill it?" Meg asked.

"Oh, then it will d-disembowel you, drink your blood, and eat your flesh." I grinned, though I had a feeling I hadn't said anything funny. "Also, don't let a strix scratch you. It'll paralyze you!"

By way of demonstration, I fell over sideways.

Above us, the strix spread its wings and swooped down.

2

Now I'm a suitcase
Duct-taped to a satyr's back.
Worst. Morning. Ever.

"STOP!" GROVER YELPED. "We come in peace!"

The bird was not impressed. It attacked, only missing the satyr's face because Meg lashed out with her scimitars. The strix veered, pirouetting between her blades, and landed unscathed a little higher up the spiral ramp.

SCREE! the strix yelled, ruffling its feathers.

"What do you *mean* 'you need to kill us'?" Grover asked.

Meg scowled. "You can talk to it?"

"Well, yes," Grover said. "It's an animal."

"Why didn't you tell us what it was saying before now?" Meg asked.

"Because it was just yelling *scree*!" Grover said. "Now it's saying *scree* as in it needs to kill us."

I tried to move my legs. They seemed to have turned into sacks of cement, which I found vaguely amusing. I could still move my arms and had some feeling in my chest, but I wasn't sure how long that would last.

"Perhaps ask the strix *why* it needs to kill us?" I suggested.

"Scree!" Grover said.

I was getting tired of the strix language. The bird replied in a series of squawks and clicks.

Meanwhile, out in the corridor, the other strixes shrieked and bashed against the net of plants. Black talons and gold beaks poked out, snapping tomatoes into pico de gallo. I figured we had a few minutes at most until the birds burst through and killed us all, but their razor-sharp beaks sure were cute!

Grover wrung his hands. "The strix says he's been sent to drink our blood, eat our flesh, and disembowel us, not necessarily in that order. He says he's sorry, but it's a direct command from the emperor."

"Stupid emperors," Meg grumbled. "Which one?"

"I don't know," Grover said. "The strix just calls him *Scree*."

"You can translate *disembowel*," she noted, "but you can't translate the emperor's name?"

Personally, I was okay with that. Since leaving Indianapolis, I'd spent a lot of time mulling over the Dark Prophecy we had received in the Cave of Trophonius. We had already encountered Nero and Commodus, and I had a dreadful suspicion about the identity of the third emperor, whom we had yet to meet. At the moment, I didn't want confirmation. The euphoria of the strix venom was starting to dissipate. I was about to be eaten alive by a bloodsucking mega-owl. I didn't need any more reasons to weep in despair.

The strix dove at Meg. She dodged aside, whacking the flat of her blade against the bird's tail feathers as it rushed past, sending the unfortunate bird into the opposite wall, where it smacked face-first into the brick, exploding in a cloud of monster dust and feathers.

"Meg!" I said. "I told you not to kill it! You'll get cursed!"

"I didn't kill it. It committed suicide against that wall."

"I don't think the Fates will see it that way."

"Then let's not tell them."

"Guys?" Grover pointed to the tomato plants, which were rapidly thinning under the onslaught of claws and beaks. "If we can't kill the strixes, maybe we should strengthen this barrier?"

He raised his pipes and played. Meg turned her swords back into rings. She stretched her hands toward the tomato plants. The stems thickened and the roots struggled to take hold in the stone floor, but it was a losing battle. Too many strixes were now battering the other side, ripping through the new growth as fast as it emerged.

"No good." Meg stumbled back, her face beaded with sweat. "Only so much we can do without soil and sunlight."

"You're right." Grover looked above us, his eyes following the spiral ramp up into the gloom. "We're nearly home. If we can just get to the top before the strixes get through—"

"So we climb," Meg announced.

"Hello?" I said miserably. "Paralyzed former god here."

Grover grimaced at Meg. "Duct tape?"

"Duct tape," she agreed.

May the gods defend me from heroes with duct tape. And heroes *always* seem to have duct tape. Meg produced a roll from a pouch on her gardening belt. She propped me into a sitting position, back-to-back with Grover, then proceeded to loop tape under our armpits, binding me to the satyr as if I were a hiking pack.

With Meg's help, Grover staggered to his feet, jostling me around so I got random views of the walls, the floor, Meg's face, and my own paralyzed legs manspreading beneath me.

"Uh, Grover?" I asked. "Will you have enough strength to carry me all the way up?"

"Satyrs are great climbers," he wheezed.

He started up the narrow ramp, my paralyzed feet dragging behind us. Meg followed, glancing back every so often at the rapidly deteriorating tomato plants.

"Apollo," she said, "tell me about strixes."

I sifted through my brain, panning for useful nuggets among the sludge.

"They . . . they are birds of ill omen," I said. "When they show up, bad things happen."

"Duh," said Meg. "What else?"

"Er, they usually feed on the young and weak. Babies, old people, paralyzed gods . . . that sort of thing. They breed in the upper reaches of Tartarus. I'm only speculating here, but I'm pretty sure they don't make good pets."

"How do we drive them off?" she said. "If we can't kill them, how do we stop them?"

"I—I don't know."

Meg sighed in frustration. "Talk to the Arrow of Dodona. See if it knows anything. I'm going to try buying us some time."

She jogged back down the ramp.

Talking to the arrow was just about the *only* way my day could get worse, but I was under orders, and when Meg commanded me, I could not disobey. I reached over my shoulder, groped through my quiver, and pulled forth the magic missile.

"Hello, Wise and Powerful Arrow," I said. (Always best to start with flattery.)

TOOKEST THEE LONG ENOUGH, intoned the arrow. *FOR FORTNIGHTS UNTOLD HAVE I TRIED TO SPEAK WITH THEE.*

"It's been about forty-eight hours," I said.

VERILY, TIME DOTH CREEP WHEN ONE IS QUIVERED. THOU SHOULDST TRY IT AND SEEST HOW THOU LIKEST IT.

"Right." I resisted the urge to snap the arrow's shaft. "What can you tell me about strixes?"

I MUST SPEAK TO THEE ABOUT— HOLD THE PHONE. STRIXES? WHEREFORE TALKEST TO ME OF THOSE?

"Because they are about to killeth—to kill us."

FIE! groaned the arrow. *THOU SHOULDST AVOID SUCH DANGERS!*

"I would never have thought of that," I said. "Do you have any strix-pertinent information or not, O Wise Projectile?"

The arrow buzzed, no doubt trying to access Wikipedia. It denies using the Internet. Perhaps, then, it's just a coincidence the arrow is always more helpful when we are in an area with free Wi-Fi.

Grover valiantly lugged my sorry mortal body up the ramp. He huffed and gasped, staggering dangerously close to the edge. The floor of the room was now fifty feet below us—just far enough for a nice, lethal fall. I could see Meg down there pacing, muttering to herself and shaking out more packets of gardening seeds.

Above, the ramp seemed to spiral forever. Whatever waited for us at the top, assuming there *was* a top, remained lost in the darkness. I found it very inconsiderate that the Labyrinth did not provide an elevator, or at least a proper handrail. How were heroes with accessibility needs supposed to enjoy this death trap?

At last the Arrow of Dodona delivered its verdict: *STRIXES ART DANGEROUS.*

"Once again," I said, "your wisdom brings light to the darkness."

SHUT THEE UP, the arrow continued. *THE BIRDS CAN BE SLAIN, THOUGH THIS SHALT CURSE THE SLAYER AND CAUSETH MORE STRIXES TO APPEARETH.*

"Yes, yes. What else?"

"What's it saying?" Grover asked between gasps.

Among its many irritating qualities, the arrow spoke solely in my mind, so not only did I look like a crazy person when I conversed with it, but I had to constantly report its ramblings to my friends.

"It's still searching Google," I told Grover. "Perhaps, O Arrow, you could do a Boolean search, 'strix plus defeat.'"

I USE NOT SUCH CHEATS! the arrow thundered. Then it was silent long enough to type *strix + defeat.*

THE BIRDS MAY BE REPELLED WITH PIG ENTRAILS, it reported. *HAST THOU ANY?*

"Grover," I called over my shoulder, "would you happen to have any pig entrails?"

"*What?*" He turned, which was not an effective way of facing me, since I was duct-taped to his back. He almost scraped my nose off on the brick wall. "Why would I carry pig entrails? I'm a vegetarian!"

Meg clambered up the ramp to join us.

"The birds are almost through," she reported. "I tried different kinds of plants. I tried to summon Peaches. . . ." Her voice broke with despair.

Since entering the Labyrinth, she had been unable to summon her peach-spirit minion, who was handy in a fight but rather picky about when and where he showed up. I supposed that, much like tomato plants, Peaches didn't do well underground.

"Arrow of Dodona, what else?" I shouted at its point. "There has to be *something* besides pig intestines that will keep strixes at bay!"

WAIT, the arrow said. *HARK! IT APPEARETH THAT ARBUTUS SHALL SERVE*.

"*Our-butt-us* shall what?" I demanded.

Too late.

Below us, with a peal of bloodthirsty shrieks, the strixes broke through the tomato barricade and swarmed into the room.

3

Strixes do sucketh
Yea, verily I tell you
Much sucking is theirs

"HERE THEY COME!" MEG YELLED.

Honestly, whenever I wanted her to talk about something important, she shut up. But when we were facing an obvious danger, she wasted her breath yelling *Here they come*.

Grover increased his pace, showing heroic strength as he bounded up the ramp, hauling my flabby duct-taped carcass behind him.

Facing backward, I had a perfect view of the strixes as they swirled out of the shadows, their yellow eyes flashing like coins in a murky fountain. A dozen birds? More? Given how much trouble we'd had with a single strix, I didn't like our chances against an entire flock, especially since we were now lined up like juicy targets on a narrow, slippery ledge. I doubted Meg could help *all* the birds commit suicide by whacking them face-first into the wall.

"Arbutus!" I yelled. "The arrow said something about arbutus repelling strixes."

"That's a plant." Grover gasped for air. "I think I met an arbutus once."

"Arrow," I said, "what is an arbutus?"

I KNOW NOT! BECAUSE I WAS BORN IN A GROVE DOTH NOT MAKETH ME A GARDENER!

Disgusted, I shoved the arrow back into my quiver.

"Apollo, cover me." Meg thrust one of her swords into my hand, then rifled through her gardening belt, glancing nervously at the strixes as they ascended.

How Meg expected me to cover her, I wasn't sure. I was garbage at swordplay, even when I wasn't duct-taped to a satyr's back and facing targets that would curse anyone who killed them.

"Grover!" Meg yelled. "Can we figure out what type of plant an arbutus is?"

She ripped open a random packet and tossed seeds into the void. They burst like heated popcorn kernels and formed grenade-size yams with leafy green stems. They fell among the flock of strixes, hitting a few and causing startled squawking, but the birds kept coming.

"Those are tubers," Grover wheezed. "I think an arbutus is a fruit plant."

Meg ripped open a second seed packet. She showered the strixes with an explosion of bushes dotted with green fruits. The birds simply veered around them.

"Grapes?" Grover asked.

"Gooseberries," said Meg.

"Are you sure?" Grover asked. "The shape of the leaves—"

"Grover!" I snapped. "Let's restrict ourselves to military botany. What's a—? DUCK!"

Now, gentle reader, you be the judge. Was I asking the question *What's a duck?* Of course I wasn't. Despite Meg's later complaints, I was trying to warn her that the nearest strix was charging straight at her face.

She didn't understand my warning, which was *not my fault.*

I swung my borrowed scimitar, attempting to protect my young friend. Only my terrible aim and Meg's quick reflexes prevented me from decapitating her.

"Stop that!" she yelled, swatting the strix aside with her other blade.

"You said *cover me*!" I protested.

"I didn't mean—" She cried out in pain, stumbling as a bloody cut opened along her right thigh.

Then we were engulfed in an angry storm of talons, beaks, and black wings. Meg swung her scimitar wildly. A strix launched itself at my face, its claws about to rip my eyes out, when Grover did the unexpected: he screamed.

Why is that surprising? you may be asking. *When you're swarmed by entrail-devouring birds, it is a perfect time to scream.*

True. But the sound that came from the satyr's mouth was no ordinary cry.

It reverberated through the chamber like the shock wave of a bomb, scattering the birds, shaking the stones, and filling me with cold, unreasoning fear.

Had I not been duct-taped to the satyr's back, I would have fled. I would have jumped off the ledge just to get away from that sound. As it was, I dropped Meg's sword and clamped my hands over my ears. Meg, lying prone on the ramp, bleeding and no doubt already partially paralyzed by the strix's poison, curled into a ball and buried her head in her arms.

The strixes fled back down into the darkness.

My heart pounded. Adrenaline surged through me. I needed several deep breaths before I could speak.

"Grover," I said, "did you just summon Panic?"

I couldn't see his face, but I could feel him shaking. He lay down on the ramp, rolling to one side so I faced the wall.

"I didn't mean to." Grover's voice was hoarse. "Haven't done that in years."

"P-panic?" Meg asked.

"The cry of the lost god Pan," I said. Even saying his name filled me with sadness. Ah, what good times the nature god and I had had in ancient days, dancing and cavorting in the wilderness! Pan had been a first-class cavorter. Then humans destroyed most of the wilderness, and Pan faded into nothing. You humans. You're why we gods can't have nice things.

"I've never heard anyone but Pan use that power," I said. "How?"

Grover made a sound that was half sob, half sigh. "Long story."

Meg grunted. "Got rid of the birds, anyway." I heard her ripping fabric, probably making a bandage for her leg.

"Are you paralyzed?" I asked.

"Yeah," she muttered. "Waist down."

Grover shifted in our duct-tape harness. "I'm still okay, but exhausted. The birds will be back, and there's no way I can carry you up the ramp now."

I did not doubt him. The shout of Pan would scare away almost anything, but it was a taxing bit of magic. Every time Pan used it, he would take a three-day nap afterward.

Below us, the strixes' cries echoed through the Labyrinth. Their screeching already sounded like it was turning from fear—*Fly away!*—to confusion: *Why are we flying away?*

I tried to wriggle my feet. To my surprise, I could now feel my toes inside my socks.

"Can someone cut me loose?" I asked. "I think the poison is losing strength."

From her horizontal position, Meg used a scimitar to saw me out of the duct tape. The three of us lined up with our backs literally to the wall—three sweaty, sad, pathetic pieces of strix bait waiting to die. Below us, the squawking of the doom birds got louder. Soon they'd be back, angrier than ever. About fifty feet above us, just visible now in the dim glint of Meg's swords, our ramp dead-ended at a domed brick ceiling.

"So much for an exit," Grover said. "I thought for sure . . . This shaft looks so much like . . ." He shook his head, as if he couldn't bear to tell us what he'd hoped.

"I'm not dying here," Meg grumbled.

Her appearance said otherwise. She had bloody knuckles and skinned knees. Her green dress, a prized gift from Percy Jackson's mother, looked like it had been used as a saber-toothed tiger's scratching post. She had ripped off her left legging and used it to stanch the bleeding cut on her thigh, but the fabric was already soaked through.

Nevertheless, her eyes shone defiantly. The rhinestones still glittered on the tips of her cat-eye glasses. I'd learned never to count out Meg McCaffrey while her rhinestones still glittered.

She rummaged through her seed packages, squinting at the labels. "Roses. Daffodils. Squash. Carrots."

"No . . ." Grover bumped his fist against his forehead. "Arbutus is like . . . a flowering tree. Argh, I should *know* this."

I sympathized with his memory problems. I should have known *many* things: the weaknesses of strixes, the nearest secret exit from the Labyrinth, Zeus's private number so I could call him and plead for my life. But my mind was blank. My legs had begun to tremble—perhaps a sign I would soon be able to walk again—but this didn't cheer me up. I had nowhere to go, except to choose whether I wanted to die at the top of this chamber or the bottom.

Meg kept shuffling seed packets. "Rutabaga, wisteria, pyracantha, strawberries—"

"Strawberries!" Grover yelped so loudly I thought he was trying for another blast of Panic. "That's it! The arbutus is a strawberry tree!"

Meg frowned. "Strawberries don't *grow* on trees. They're genus *Fragaria*, part of the rose family."

"Yes, yes, I know!" Grover rolled his hands like he couldn't get the words out fast enough. "And Arbutus is in the heath family, but—"

"What are you two talking about?" I demanded. I wondered if they were sharing the Arrow of Dodona's Wi-Fi connection to look up information on botany.com. "We're about to die, and you're arguing about plant genera?"

"*Fragaria* might be close enough!" Grover insisted. "Arbutus fruit *looks* like strawberries. That's why it's called a strawberry tree. I met an arbutus dryad once. We got in this big argument about it. Besides, I specialize in strawberry-growing. All the satyrs from Camp Half-Blood do!"

Meg stared doubtfully at her packet of strawberry seeds. "I dunno."

Below us, a dozen strixes burst forth from the mouth of the tunnel, shrieking in a chorus of pre-disembowelment fury.

"TRY THE FRAGGLE ROCK!" I yelled.

"*Fragaria*," Meg corrected.

"WHATEVER!"

Rather than throwing her strawberry seeds into the void, Meg ripped open the packet and shook them out along the edge of the ramp with maddening slowness.

"Hurry." I fumbled for my bow. "We've got maybe thirty seconds."

"Hold on." Meg tapped out the last of the seeds.

"Fifteen seconds!"

"Wait." Meg tossed aside the packet. She placed her hands over the seeds like she was about to play the keyboard (which, by the way, she can't do well, despite my efforts to teach her).

"Okay," she said. "Go."

Grover raised his pipes and began a frantic version of "Strawberry Fields Forever" in triple time. I forgot about my bow and grabbed my ukulele, joining him in the song. I didn't know if it would help, but if I was going to get ripped apart, at least I wanted to go out playing the Beatles.

Just as the wave of strixes was about to hit, the seeds exploded like a battery of fireworks. Green streamers arced across the void, anchoring against the far wall and forming a row of vines that reminded me of the strings of a giant lute. The strixes could have easily flown through the gaps, but instead they went crazy, veering to avoid the plants and colliding with each other in midair.

Meanwhile, the vines thickened, leaves unfurled, white flowers bloomed, and strawberries ripened, filling the air with their sweet fragrance.

The chamber rumbled. Wherever the strawberry plants touched the stone, the brick cracked and dissolved, giving the strawberries an easier place to root.

Meg lifted her hands from her imaginary keyboard. "Is the Labyrinth . . . *helping*?"

"I don't know!" I said, strumming furiously on an F minor 7. "But don't stop!"

With impossible speed, the strawberries spread across the walls in a tide of green.

I was just thinking *Wow, imagine what the plants could do with sunlight!* when the domed ceiling cracked like an eggshell. Brilliant rays stabbed through the darkness. Chunks of rock rained down, smashing into the birds, punching through strawberry vines (which, unlike the strixes, grew back almost immediately).

As soon as the sunlight hit the birds, they screamed and dissolved into dust.

Grover lowered his panpipe. I set down my ukulele. We watched in amazement as the plants continued to grow, interlacing until a strawberry-runner trampoline stretched across the entire area of the room at our feet.

The ceiling had disintegrated, revealing a brilliant blue sky. Hot dry air wafted down like the breath from an open oven.

Grover raised his face to the light. He sniffled, tears glistening on his cheeks.

"Are you hurt?" I asked.

He stared at me. The heartbreak on his face was more painful to look at than the sunlight.

"The smell of warm strawberries," he said. "Like Camp Half-Blood. It's been so long. . . ."

I felt an unfamiliar twinge in my chest. I patted Grover's knee. I had not spent much time at Camp Half-Blood, the training ground for Greek demigods on Long Island, but I understood how he felt. I wondered how my children were doing there: Kayla, Will, Austin. I remembered sitting with them at the campfire, singing "My Mother Was a Minotaur" as we ate burnt marshmallows off a stick. Such perfect camaraderie is rare, even in an immortal life.

Meg leaned against the wall. Her complexion was pasty, her breathing ragged.

I dug through my pockets and found a broken square of ambrosia in a napkin. I did not keep the stuff for myself. In my mortal state, eating the food of the gods might cause me to spontaneously combust. But Meg, I had found, was not always good about taking her ambrosia.

"Eat." I pressed the napkin into her hand. "It'll help the paralysis pass more quickly."

She clenched her jaw, as if about to yell *I DON'T*

WANNA!, then apparently decided she liked the idea of having working legs again. She began nibbling on the ambrosia.

"What's up there?" she asked, frowning at the blue sky.

Grover brushed the tears from his face. "We've made it. The Labyrinth brought us right to our base."

"Our base?" I was delighted to learn we *had* a base. I hoped that meant security, a soft bed, and perhaps an espresso machine.

"Yeah." Grover swallowed nervously. "Assuming anything is left of it. Let's find out."

4

Welcome to my base
We have rocks, sand, and ruins
Did I mention rocks?

THEY TELL ME I REACHED THE SURFACE.

I don't remember.

Meg was partially paralyzed, and Grover had already carried me halfway up the ramp, so it seems wrong that I was the one who passed out, but what can I say? That Fm7 chord on "Strawberry Fields Forever" must have taken more out of me than I realized.

I *do* remember feverish dreams.

Before me rose a graceful olive-skinned woman, her long auburn hair gathered up in a donut braid, her sleeveless dress as light and gray as moth wings. She looked about twenty, but her eyes were black pearls—their hard luster formed over centuries, a defensive shell hiding untold sorrow and disappointment. They were the eyes of an immortal who had seen great civilizations fall.

We stood together on a stone platform, at the edge of what looked like an indoor swimming pool filled with lava. The air shimmered with heat. Ashes stung my eyes.

The woman raised her arms in a supplicating gesture. Glowing red iron cuffs shackled her wrists. Molten chains anchored her to the platform, though the hot metal did not seem to burn her.

"I am sorry," she said.

Somehow, I knew she wasn't speaking to me. I was only observing this scene through the eyes of someone else. She'd just delivered bad news to this other person, *crushing* news, though I had no idea what it was.

"I would spare you if I could," she continued. "I would spare *her*. But I cannot. Tell Apollo he must come. Only he can release me, though it is a . . ." She choked as if a shard of glass had wedged in her throat. "Four letters," she croaked. "Starts with *T*."

Trap, I thought. *The answer is* trap*!*

I felt briefly thrilled, the way you do when you're watching a game show and you know the answer. *If only I were the contestant*, you think, *I'd win all the prizes!*

Then I realized I didn't like this game show. Especially if the answer was *trap*. Especially if that trap was the grand prize waiting for me.

The woman's image dissolved into flames.

I found myself in a different place—a covered terrace overlooking a moonlit bay. In the distance, shrouded in mist, rose the familiar dark profile of Mount Vesuvius, but Vesuvius as it had been before the eruption of 79 CE blew its summit to pieces, destroying Pompeii and wiping out thousands of Romans. (You can blame Vulcan for that. He was having a *bad* week.)

The evening sky was bruised purple, the coastline lit only by firelight, the moon, and the stars. Under my feet, the terrace's mosaic floor glittered with gold and silver tiles, the sort of artwork very few Romans could afford. On the walls, multicolored frescoes were framed in silk draperies that had to have cost hundreds of thousands of denarii. I knew where I must be: an imperial villa, one of the many pleasure palaces that lined the Gulf of Naples in the early days of the empire. Normally such a place would have blazed with light throughout the night, as a show of power and opulence, but the torches on this terrace were dark, wrapped in black cloth.

In the shadow of a column, a slender young man stood facing the sea. His expression was obscured, but his posture spoke of impatience. He tugged on his white robes, crossed his arms over his chest, and tapped his sandaled foot against the floor.

A second man appeared, marching onto the terrace with the clink of armor and the labored breathing of a heavyset fighter. A praetorian guard's helmet hid his face.

He knelt before the younger man. "It is done, Princeps."

Princeps. Latin for *first in line* or *first citizen*—that lovely euphemism the Roman emperors used to downplay just how absolute their power was.

"Are you sure this time?" asked a young, reedy voice. "I don't want any more surprises."

The praetor grunted. "Very sure, Princeps."

The guard held out his massive hairy forearms. Bloody scratches glistened in the moonlight, as if desperate fingernails had raked his flesh.

"What did you use?" The younger man sounded fascinated.

"His own pillow," the big man said. "Seemed easiest."

The younger man laughed. "The old pig deserved it. I wait *years* for him to die, finally we announce he's kicked the *situla*, and he has the nerve to wake up again? I don't think so. Tomorrow will be a new, better day for Rome."

He stepped into the moonlight, revealing his face—a face I had hoped never to see again.

He was handsome in a thin, angular way, though his ears stuck out a bit too much. His smile was twisted. His eyes had all the warmth of a barracuda's.

Even if you do not recognize his features, dear reader, I am sure you have met him. He is the school bully too charming to get caught; the one who thinks up the cruelest pranks, has others carry out his dirty work, and still maintains a perfect reputation with the teachers. He is the boy who pulls the legs off insects and tortures stray animals, yet laughs with such pure delight he can almost convince you it is harmless fun. He's the boy who steals money from the temple collection plates, behind the backs of old ladies who praise him for being *such a nice young man*.

He is that person, that type of evil.

And tonight, he had a new name, which would *not* foretell a better day for Rome.

The praetorian guard lowered his head. "Hail, Caesar!"

I awoke from my dream shivering.

"Good timing," Grover said.

I sat up. My head throbbed. My mouth tasted like strix dust.

I was lying under a makeshift lean-to—a blue plastic tarp set on a hillside overlooking the desert. The sun was going down. Next to me, Meg was curled up asleep, her hand resting on my wrist. I suppose that was sweet, except I knew where her fingers had been. (Hint: In her nostrils.)

On a nearby slab of rock, Grover sat sipping water from his canteen. Judging from his weary expression, I guessed he had been keeping watch over us while we slept.

"I passed out?" I gathered.

He tossed me the canteen. "I thought *I* slept hard. You've been out for hours."

I took a drink, then rubbed the gunk from my eyes, wishing I could wipe the dreams from my head as easily: a woman chained in a fiery room, a trap for Apollo, a new Caesar with the pleasant smile of a fine young sociopath.

Don't think about it, I told myself. *Dreams aren't necessarily true.*

No, I answered myself. *Only the bad ones. Like those.*

I focused on Meg, snoring in the shade of our tarp. Her leg was freshly bandaged. She wore a clean T-shirt over her tattered dress. I tried to extricate my wrist from her grip, but she held on tighter.

"She's all right," Grover assured me. "At least physically. Fell asleep after we got you situated." He frowned. "She didn't seem happy about being here, though. Said she couldn't handle this place. Wanted to leave. I was afraid she'd jump back into the Labyrinth, but I convinced her she needed to rest first. I played some music to relax her."

I scanned our surroundings, wondering what had upset Meg so badly.

Below us stretched a landscape only slightly more hospitable than Mars. (I mean the planet, not the god, though

I suppose neither is much of a host.) Sun-blasted ocher mountains ringed a valley patchworked with unnaturally green golf courses, dusty barren flats, and sprawling neighborhoods of white stucco walls, red-tiled roofs, and blue swimming pools. Lining the streets, rows of listless palm trees stuck up like raggedy seams. Asphalt parking lots shimmered in the heat. A brown haze hung in the air, filling the valley like watery gravy.

"Palm Springs," I said.

I'd known the city well in the 1950s. I was pretty sure I'd hosted a party with Frank Sinatra just down the road there, by that golf course—but it felt like another life. Probably because it had been.

Now the area seemed much less welcoming—the temperature too scorching for an early spring evening, the air too heavy and acrid. Something was wrong, something I couldn't quite place.

I scanned our immediate surroundings. We were camped at the crest of a hill, the San Jacinto wilderness at our backs to the west, the sprawl of Palm Springs at our feet to the east. A gravel road skirted the base of the hill, winding toward the nearest neighborhood about half a mile below, but I could tell that our hilltop had once boasted a large structure.

Sunk in the rocky slope were a half dozen hollow brickwork cylinders, each perhaps thirty feet in diameter, like the shells of ruined sugar mills. The structures were of varying heights, in varying stages of disintegration, but their tops were all level with one another, so I guessed they must have been massive support columns for a stilt house. Judging from the detritus that littered the hillside—shards of glass, charred planks, blackened clumps of brick—I guessed that the house must have burned down many years before.

Then I realized: we must have *climbed out* of one of those cylinders to escape the Labyrinth.

I turned to Grover. "The strixes?"

He shook his head. "If any survived, they wouldn't risk the daylight, even if they could get through the strawberries. The plants have filled the entire shaft." He pointed to the farthest ring of brickwork, where we must have emerged. "Nobody's getting in or out that way anymore."

"But . . ." I gestured at the ruins. "Surely this isn't your *base?*"

I was hoping he would correct me. *Oh, no, our base is that nice house down there with the Olympic-size swimming pool, right next to the fifteenth hole!*

Instead, he had the nerve to look pleased. "Yeah. This place has powerful natural energy. It's a perfect sanctuary. Can't you feel the life force?"

I picked up a charred brick. "Life force?"

"You'll see." Grover took off his cap and scratched between his horns. "The way things have been, all the dryads have to stay dormant until sunset. It's the only way they can survive. But they'll be waking up soon."

The way things have been.

I glanced west. The sun had just dropped behind the mountains. The sky was marbled with heavy layers of red and black, more appropriate for Mordor than Southern California.

"What's going on?" I asked, not sure I wanted the answer.

Grover gazed sadly into the distance. "You haven't seen the news? Biggest forest fires in state history. On top of the drought, the heat waves, and the earthquakes." He shuddered. "Thousands of dryads have died. Thousands more have gone into hibernation. If these were just *normal* natural disasters, that would be bad enough, but—"

Meg yelped in her sleep. She sat up abruptly, blinking in confusion. From the panic in her eyes, I guessed her dreams had been even worse than mine.

"W-we're really here?" she asked. "I didn't dream it?"

"It's all right," I said. "You're safe."

She shook her head, her lips quivering. "No. No, I'm not."

With fumbling fingers, she removed her glasses, as if she might be able to handle her surroundings better if they were fuzzier. "I can't be here. Not again."

"Again?" I asked.

A line from the Indiana prophecy tugged at my memory: *Demeter's daughter finds her ancient roots*. "You mean you *lived* here?"

Meg scanned the ruins. She shrugged miserably, though whether that meant *I don't know* or *I don't want to talk about it*, I couldn't tell.

The desert seemed an unlikely home for Meg—a street kid from Manhattan, raised in Nero's royal household.

Grover tugged thoughtfully at his goatee. "A child of Demeter . . . That actually makes a lot of sense."

I stared at him. "In this place? A child of Vulcan, perhaps. Or Feronia, the wilderness goddess. Or even Mefitis, the goddess of poisonous gas. But Demeter? What is a child of Demeter supposed to grow here? Rocks?"

Grover looked hurt. "You don't understand. Once you meet everybody—"

Meg crawled out from beneath the tarp. She got unsteadily to her feet. "I have to leave."

"Hold on!" Grover pleaded. "We need your help. At least talk to the others!"

Meg hesitated. "Others?"

Grover gestured north. I couldn't see what he was pointing to until I stood up. Then I noticed, half-hidden behind the brick ruins, a row of six boxy white structures like . . . storage sheds? No. Greenhouses. The one nearest the ruins had melted and collapsed long ago, no doubt a victim of the fire. The second hut's corrugated polycarbonate walls and roof had fallen apart like a house of cards. But the other four looked intact. Clay flowerpots were stacked outside. The doors stood open. Inside, green plant matter pressed against the translucent walls—palm fronds like giant hands pushing to get out.

I didn't see how anything could live in this scalded barren wasteland, especially inside a greenhouse meant to keep the climate even warmer. I definitely didn't want to get any closer to those claustrophobic hot boxes.

Grover smiled encouragingly. "I'm sure everyone's awake by now. Come on, I'll introduce you to the gang!"

5

First-aid succulent,
Heal me of my many cuts!
(But no slime trail, please)

GROVER LED US to the first intact greenhouse, which exuded a smell like the breath of Persephone.

That's not a compliment. Miss Springtime used to sit next to me at family dinners, and she was not shy about sharing her halitosis. Imagine the odor of a bin full of wet mulch and earthworm poop. Yes, I just love spring.

Inside the greenhouse, the plants had taken over. I found that frightening, since most of them were cacti. By the doorway squatted a pineapple cactus the size of a cracker barrel, its yellow spines like shish-kebab skewers. In the back corner stood a majestic Joshua tree, its shaggy branches holding up the roof. Against the opposite wall bloomed a massive prickly pear, dozens of bristly paddles topped with purple fruit that looked delicious, except for the fact that each one had more spikes than Ares's favorite mace. Metal tables groaned under the weight of other succulents—pickleweed, spinystar, cholla, and dozens more I couldn't name. Surrounded by so many thorns and flowers, in such oppressive heat, I had a flashback to Iggy Pop's 2003 Coachella set.

"I'm back!" Grover announced. "And I brought friends!"

Silence.

Even at sunset, the temperature inside was so high, and the air so thick, I imagined I would die of heatstroke in approximately four minutes. And I was a former sun god.

At last the first dryad appeared. A chlorophyll bubble ballooned from the side of the prickly pear and burst into green mist. The droplets coalesced into a small girl with emerald skin, spiky yellow hair, and a fringe dress made entirely of cactus bristles. Her glare was almost as pointed as her dress. Fortunately, it was directed at Grover, not me.

"Where have you *been*?" she demanded.

"Ah." Grover cleared his throat. "I got called away. Magical summons. I'll tell you all about it later. But look, I brought Apollo! And Meg, daughter of Demeter!"

He showed off Meg like she was a fabulous prize on *The Price Is Right*.

"Hmph," said the dryad. "I suppose daughters of Demeter are okay. I'm Prickly Pear. Or Pear for short."

"Hi," Meg said weakly.

The dryad narrowed her eyes at me. Given her spiny dress, I hoped she wasn't a hugger. "You're Apollo as in *the god Apollo*?" she asked. "I don't believe it."

"Some days, neither do I," I admitted.

Grover scanned the room. "Where are the others?"

Right on cue, another chlorophyll bubble popped over one of the succulents. A second dryad appeared—a large young woman in a muumuu like the husk of an artichoke. Her hair was a forest of dark green triangles. Her face and arms glistened as if they'd just been oiled. (At least I hoped it was oil and not sweat.)

"Oh!" she cried, seeing our battered appearances. "Are you hurt?"

Pear rolled her eyes. "Al, knock it off."

"But they look hurt!" Al shuffled forward. She took my hand. Her touch was cold and greasy. "Let me take care of these cuts, at least. Grover, why didn't you *heal* these poor people?"

"I tried!" the satyr protested. "They just took a lot of damage!"

That could be my life motto, I thought: *He takes a lot of damage*.

Al ran her fingertips over my cuts, leaving trails of goo like slug tracks. It was not a pleasant sensation, but it did ease the pain.

"You're Aloe Vera," I realized. "I used to make healing ointments out of you."

She beamed. "He remembers me! Apollo remembers me!"

In the back of the room, a third dryad emerged from the trunk of the Joshua tree—a *male* dryad, which was quite rare. His skin was as brown as his tree's bark, his olive hair long and wild, his clothes weathered khaki. He might have been an explorer just returning from the outback.

"I'm Joshua," he said. "Welcome to Aeithales."

And at that moment, Meg McCaffrey decided to faint.

I could have told her that swooning in front of an attractive boy was *never* cool. The strategy hadn't worked for me *once* in thousands of years. Nevertheless, being a good friend, I caught her before she could nose-dive into the gravel.

"Oh, poor girl!" Aloe Vera gave Grover another critical

look. "She's exhausted and overheated. Haven't you let her rest?"

"She's been asleep all afternoon!"

"Well, she's dehydrated." Aloe put her hand on Meg's forehead. "She needs water."

Pear sniffed. "Don't we all."

"Take her to the Cistern," Al said. "Mellie should be awake by now. I'll be along in a minute."

Grover perked up. "Mellie's here? They made it?"

"They arrived this morning," said Joshua.

"What about the search parties?" Grover pressed. "Any word?"

The dryads exchanged troubled glances.

"The news isn't good," Joshua said. "Only one group has come back so far, and—"

"Excuse me," I pleaded. "I have no idea what any of you are talking about, but Meg is heavy. Where should I put her?"

Grover stirred. "Right. Sorry, I'll show you." He draped Meg's left arm over his shoulders, taking half her weight. Then he faced the dryads. "Guys, how about we all meet at the Cistern for dinner? We've got a lot to talk about."

Joshua nodded. "I'll alert the other greenhouses. And, Grover, you promised us enchiladas. Three days ago."

"I know." Grover sighed. "I'll get more."

Together, the two of us lugged Meg out of the greenhouse.

As we dragged her across the hillside, I asked Grover my most burning question: "Dryads eat enchiladas?"

He looked offended. "Of course! You expect them just to eat fertilizer?"

"Well . . . yes."

"Stereotyping," he muttered.

I decided that was my cue to change the subject.

"Did I imagine it," I asked, "or did Meg faint because she heard the name of this place? *Aeithales*. That's ancient Greek for *evergreen*, if I recall correctly."

It seemed an odd name for a place in the desert. Then again, no odder than dryads eating enchiladas.

"We found the name carved into the old doorsill," Grover said. "There's a lot we don't know about the ruins, but like I said, this site has a lot of nature energy. Whoever lived here and started the greenhouses . . . they knew what they were doing."

I wished I could say the same. "Weren't the dryads *born* in those greenhouses? Don't they know who planted them?"

"Most were too young when the house burned down," Grover said. "Some of the older plants might know more, but they've gone dormant. Or"—he nodded toward the destroyed greenhouses—"they're no longer with us."

We observed a moment of silence for the departed succulents.

Grover steered us toward the largest of the brick cylinders. Judging from its size and position in the center of the ruins, I guessed it must have once been the central support column for the structure. At ground level, rectangular openings ringed the circumference like medieval castle windows. We dragged Meg through one of these and found ourselves in a space very much like the well where we'd fought the strixes.

The top was open to the sky. A spiral ramp led downward, but fortunately only twenty feet before reaching the bottom. In the center of the dirt floor, like the hole in a giant donut, glittered a dark blue pool, cooling the air and making the space feel comfortable and welcoming. Around the pool lay a ring of sleeping bags. Blooming cacti overflowed from alcoves built into the walls.

The Cistern was not a fancy structure—nothing like the dining pavilion at Camp Half-Blood, or the Waystation in Indiana—but inside it I immediately felt better, safer. I understood what Grover had been talking about. This place resonated with soothing energy.

We got Meg to the bottom of the ramp without tripping and falling, which I considered a major accomplishment. We set her down on one of the sleeping bags, then Grover scanned the room.

"Mellie?" he called. "Gleeson? Are you guys here?"

The name Gleeson sounded vaguely familiar to me, but, as usual, I couldn't place it.

No chlorophyll bubbles popped from the plants. Meg turned on her side and muttered in her sleep . . . something about Peaches. Then, at the edge of the pond, wisps of white fog began to gather. They fused into the shape of a petite woman in a silvery dress. Her dark hair floated around her as if she were underwater, revealing her slightly pointed ears. In a sling over one shoulder she held a sleeping baby perhaps seven months old, with hooved feet and tiny goat horns on his head. His fat cheek was squished against his mother's clavicle. His mouth was a veritable cornucopia of drool.

The cloud nymph (for surely that's what she was) smiled at Grover. Her brown eyes were bloodshot from lack of sleep. She held one finger to her lips, indicating that she'd rather not wake the baby. I couldn't blame her. Satyr babies at that age are loud and rambunctious, and can teethe their way through several metal cans a day.

Grover whispered, "Mellie, you made it!"

"Grover, dear." She looked down at the sleeping form of Meg, then tilted her head at me. "Are you . . . Are you him?"

"If you mean Apollo," I said, "I'm afraid so."

Mellie pursed her lips. "I'd heard rumors, but I didn't believe them. You poor thing. How are you holding up?"

In times past, I would have scoffed at any nymph who dared to call me *poor thing*. Of course, few nymphs would have shown me such consideration. Usually they were too busy running away from me. Now, Mellie's show of concern caused a lump to form in my throat. I was tempted to rest my head on her other shoulder and sob out my troubles.

"I—I'm fine," I managed. "Thank you."

"And your sleeping friend here?" she asked.

"Just exhausted, I think." Though I wondered if that was the whole story with Meg. "Aloe Vera said she would be along in a few minutes to care for her."

Mellie looked worried. "All right. I'll make sure Aloe doesn't overdo it."

"Overdo it?"

Grover coughed. "Where's Gleeson?"

Mellie scanned the room, as if just realizing this Gleeson person was not present. "I don't know. As soon as we got here, I went dormant for the day. He said he was going into town to pick up some camping supplies. What time is it?"

"After sunset," Grover said.

"He should've been back by now." Mellie's form shimmered with agitation, becoming so hazy I was afraid the baby might fall right through her body.

"Gleeson is your husband?" I guessed. "A satyr?"

"Yes, Gleeson Hedge," Mellie said.

I remembered him then, vaguely—the satyr who had sailed with the demigod heroes of the *Argo II*. "Do you know where he went?"

"We passed an army-surplus store as we drove in, down the hill. He loves army-surplus stores." Mellie turned to Grover. "He may have just gotten distracted, but . . . I don't suppose you could go check on him?"

At that moment, I realized just how exhausted Grover Underwood must be. His eyes were even redder than Mellie's. His shoulders drooped. His reed pipes dangled listlessly from his neck. Unlike Meg and me, he hadn't slept since last night in the Labyrinth. He'd used the cry of Pan, gotten us to safety, then spent all day guarding us, waiting for the dryads to wake up. Now he was being asked to make another excursion to check on Gleeson Hedge.

Still, he mustered a smile. "Sure thing, Mellie."

She gave him a peck on the cheek. "You're the best lord of the Wild ever!"

Grover blushed. "Watch Meg McCaffrey until we get back, would you? Come on, Apollo. Let's go shopping."

6

Random plumes of fire
Ground squirrels nibble my nerves
I love the desert

EVEN AFTER FOUR THOUSAND YEARS, I could still learn important life lessons. For instance: Never go shopping with a satyr.

Finding the store took forever, because Grover kept getting sidetracked. He stopped to chat with a yucca. He gave directions to a family of ground squirrels. He smelled smoke and led us on a chase across the desert until he found a burning cigarette someone had dropped onto the road.

"This is how fires start," he said, then responsibly disposed of the cigarette butt by eating it.

I didn't see anything within a mile radius that could have caught fire. I was reasonably sure rocks and dirt were not flammable, but I never argue with people who eat cigarettes. We continued our search for the army-surplus store.

Night fell. The western horizon glowed—not with the usual orange of mortal light pollution, but with the ominous red of a distant inferno. Smoke blotted out the stars. The temperature barely cooled. The air still smelled bitter and *wrong*.

I remembered the wave of flames that had nearly incinerated us in the Labyrinth. The heat seemed to have had a personality—a resentful malevolence. I could imagine such waves coursing beneath the surface of the desert, washing through the Labyrinth, turning the mortal terrain above into an even more uninhabitable wasteland.

I thought about my dream of the woman in molten chains, standing on a platform above a pool of lava. Despite my fuzzy memories, I was sure that woman was the Erythraean Sibyl, the next Oracle we had to free from the emperors. Something told me she was imprisoned in the very center of . . . whatever was generating those subterranean fires. I did not relish the idea of finding her.

"Grover," I said, "in the greenhouse, you mentioned something about search parties?"

He glanced over, swallowing painfully, as if the cigarette butt were still stuck in his throat. "The heartiest satyrs and dryads—they've been fanning out across the area for months." He fixed his eyes on the road. "We don't have many searchers. With the fires and the heat, the cacti are the only nature spirits that can still manifest. So far, only a few have come back alive. The rest . . . we don't know."

"What are they are searching for?" I asked. "The source of the fires? The emperor? The Oracle?"

Grover's hoof-fitted shoes slipped and skidded on the gravel shoulder. "Everything is connected. It has to be. I didn't know about the Oracle until you told me, but if the emperor is guarding it, the maze is where he would put it. And the maze is the source of our fire problems."

"When you say *maze*," I said, "you mean the Labyrinth?"

"Sort of." Grover's lower lip trembled. "The network of tunnels under Southern California—we assume it's part of the larger Labyrinth, but something's been happening to it. It's like this section of the Labyrinth has been . . . infected. Like it has a fever. Fires have been gathering, strengthening. Sometimes, they mass and spew— There!"

He pointed south. A quarter mile up the nearest hill, a plume of yellow flame vented skyward like the fiery tip of a welding torch. Then it was gone, leaving a patch of molten rock. I considered what would've happened if I'd been standing there when the vent flared.

"That's not normal," I said.

My ankles felt wobbly, as if I were the one with fake feet.

Grover nodded. "We already had enough problems in California: drought, climate change, pollution, all the usual stuff. But those flames . . ." His expression hardened. "It's some kind of magic we don't understand. Almost a full year I've been out here, trying to find the source of the heat and shut it off. I've lost so many friends."

His voice was brittle. I understood about losing friends. Over the centuries, I'd lost many mortals who were dear to me, but at that moment, one in particular came to mind: Heloise the griffin, who had died at the Waystation, defending her nest, defending us all from the attack of Emperor Commodus. I remembered her frail body, her feathers disintegrating into a bed of catnip in Emmie's roof garden. . . .

Grover knelt and cupped his hand around a clump of weeds. The leaves crumbled.

"Too late," he muttered. "When I was a seeker, looking for Pan, at least I had hope. I thought I could find Pan and he'd save us all. Now . . . the god of the Wild is dead."

I scanned the glittering lights of Palm Springs, trying to imagine Pan in such a place. Humans had done quite a number on the natural world. No wonder Pan had faded and passed on. What remained of his spirit he'd left to his followers—the satyrs and dryads—entrusting them with his mission to protect the wild.

I could have told Pan that was a terrible idea. I once went on vacation and entrusted the realm of music to my follower Nelson Riddle. I came back a few decades later and found pop music infected with sappy violins and backup singers, and Lawrence Welk was playing accordion on prime-time television. *Never. Again.*

"Pan would be proud of your efforts," I told Grover.

Even to me that sounded halfhearted.

Grover rose. "My father and my uncle sacrificed their lives searching for Pan. I just wish we had more help carrying on his work. Humans don't seem to care. Even demigods. Even . . ."

He stopped himself, but I suspected he was about to say *Even gods*.

I had to admit he had a point.

Gods wouldn't normally mourn the loss of a griffin, or a few dryads, or a single ecosystem. *Eh,* we would think. *Doesn't concern me!*

The longer I was mortal, the more affected I was by even the smallest loss.

I hated being mortal.

We followed the road as it skirted the walls of a gated community, leading us toward the neon store signs in the distance. I watched where I put my feet, wondering with each step if a plume of fire might turn me into a Lester flambé.

"You said everything is connected," I recalled. "You think the third emperor created this burning maze?"

Grover glanced from side to side, as if the third emperor might jump out from behind a palm tree with an ax and a scary mask. Given my suspicions about the emperor's identity, that might not be too far-fetched.

"Yes," he said, "but we don't know how or why. We don't even know where the emperor's base is. As far as we can tell, he moves around constantly."

"And . . ." I swallowed, afraid to ask. "The emperor's identity?"

"All we know is that he uses the monogram *NH*," said Grover. "For Neos Helios."

A phantom ground squirrel gnawed its way up my spine. "Greek. Meaning *New Sun*."

"Right," Grover said. "Not a Roman emperor's name."

No, I thought. But it was one of his favorite titles.

I decided not to share that information; not here in the dark, with only a jumpy satyr for company. If I confessed what I now knew, Grover and I might break down and sob in each other's arms, which would be both embarrassing and unhelpful.

We passed the gates of the neighborhood: DESERT PALMS. (Had someone really gotten *paid* to think up that name?)

We continued to the nearest commercial street, where fast-food joints and gas stations shimmered.

"I hoped Mellie and Gleeson would have new information," Grover said. "They've been staying in LA with some demigods. I thought maybe they'd had more luck tracking down the emperor, or finding the heart of the maze."

"Is that why the Hedge family came to Palm Springs?" I asked. "To share information?"

"Partly." Grover's tone hinted at a darker, sadder reason behind Mellie and Gleeson's arrival, but I didn't press.

We stopped at a major intersection. Across the boulevard stood a warehouse store with a glowing red sign: MARCO'S MILITARY MADNESS! The parking lot was empty except for an old yellow Pinto parked near the entrance.

I read the store sign again. On second look, I realized the name was not MARCO. It was MACRO. Perhaps I'd developed a bit of demigod dyslexia simply from hanging around them too long.

Military Madness sounded like exactly the sort of place I didn't want to go. And Macro, as in *large worldview* or *computer program* or . . . something else. Why did that name unleash another herd of ground squirrels into my nervous system?

"It looks closed," I said dully. "Must be the wrong army-surplus store."

"No." Grover pointed to the Pinto. "That's Gleeson's car."

Of course it is, I thought. With my luck, how could it not be?

I wanted to run away. I did not like the way that giant red sign washed the asphalt in bloodstained light. But Grover Underwood had led us through the Labyrinth, and after all his talk about losing friends, I was not about to let him lose another.

"Well, then," I said, "let's go find Gleeson Hedge."

7

Family fun packs
Should be for frozen pizzas
Not for frag grenades

HOW HARD COULD IT BE to find a satyr in an army-surplus store?

As it turned out, quite hard.

Macro's Military Madness stretched on forever—aisle after aisle of equipment no self-respecting army would want. Near the entrance, a giant bin with a neon purple sign promised PITH HELMETS! BUY 3, GET 1 FREE! An endcap display featured a Christmas tree built of stacked propane tanks with garlands of blowtorch hoses, and a placard that read 'TIS ALWAYS THE SEASON! Two aisles, each a quarter mile long, were entirely devoted to camouflage clothing in every possible color: desert brown, forest green, arctic gray, and hot pink, just in case your spec-ops team needed to infiltrate a child's princess-themed birthday party.

Directory signs hung over each lane: HOCKEY HEAVEN, GRENADE PINS, SLEEPING BAGS, BODY BAGS, KEROSENE LAMPS, CAMPING TENTS, LARGE POINTY STICKS. At the far end of the store, perhaps half a day's hike away, a massive yellow banner screamed FIREARMS!!!

I glanced at Grover, whose face looked even paler under

the harsh fluorescents. “Should we start with the camping supplies?” I asked.

The corners of his mouth drifted downward as he scanned a display of rainbow-colored impaling spikes. “Knowing Coach Hedge, he’ll gravitate toward the guns.”

So we started our trek toward the distant promised land of FIREARMS!!!

I didn’t like the store’s too-bright lighting. I didn’t like the too-cheerful canned music, or the too-cold air-conditioning that made the place feel like a morgue.

The handful of employees ignored us. One young man was label-gunning 50% OFF stickers on a row of Porta-Poo™ portable toilets. Another employee stood unmoving and blank-faced at the express register, as if he had achieved boredom-induced nirvana. Each worker wore a yellow vest with the Macro logo on the back: a smiling Roman centurion making the *okay* sign.

I didn’t like that logo, either.

At the front of the store stood a raised booth with a supervisor’s desk behind a Plexiglas screen, like the warden’s post in a prison. An ox of a man sat there, his bald head gleaming, veins bulging on his neck. His dress shirt and yellow vest could barely contain his bulky arm muscles. His bushy white eyebrows gave him a startled expression. As he watched us walk past, his grin made my skin crawl.

“I don’t think we should be here,” I muttered to Grover.

He eyed the supervisor. “Pretty sure there are no monsters here or I’d smell them. That guy is human.”

This did not reassure me. Some of my least favorite

7

Family fun packs
Should be for frozen pizzas
Not for frag grenades

HOW HARD COULD IT BE to find a satyr in an army-surplus store?

As it turned out, quite hard.

Macro's Military Madness stretched on forever—aisle after aisle of equipment no self-respecting army would want. Near the entrance, a giant bin with a neon purple sign promised PITH HELMETS! BUY 3, GET 1 FREE! An endcap display featured a Christmas tree built of stacked propane tanks with garlands of blowtorch hoses, and a placard that read 'TIS ALWAYS THE SEASON! Two aisles, each a quarter mile long, were entirely devoted to camouflage clothing in every possible color: desert brown, forest green, arctic gray, and hot pink, just in case your spec-ops team needed to infiltrate a child's princess-themed birthday party.

Directory signs hung over each lane: HOCKEY HEAVEN, GRENADE PINS, SLEEPING BAGS, BODY BAGS, KEROSENE LAMPS, CAMPING TENTS, LARGE POINTY STICKS. At the far end of the store, perhaps half a day's hike away, a massive yellow banner screamed FIREARMS!!!

I glanced at Grover, whose face looked even paler under

the harsh fluorescents. "Should we start with the camping supplies?" I asked.

The corners of his mouth drifted downward as he scanned a display of rainbow-colored impaling spikes. "Knowing Coach Hedge, he'll gravitate toward the guns."

So we started our trek toward the distant promised land of FIREARMS!!!

I didn't like the store's too-bright lighting. I didn't like the too-cheerful canned music, or the too-cold air-conditioning that made the place feel like a morgue.

The handful of employees ignored us. One young man was label-gunning 50% OFF stickers on a row of Porta-Poo™ portable toilets. Another employee stood unmoving and blank-faced at the express register, as if he had achieved boredom-induced nirvana. Each worker wore a yellow vest with the Macro logo on the back: a smiling Roman centurion making the *okay* sign.

I didn't like that logo, either.

At the front of the store stood a raised booth with a supervisor's desk behind a Plexiglas screen, like the warden's post in a prison. An ox of a man sat there, his bald head gleaming, veins bulging on his neck. His dress shirt and yellow vest could barely contain his bulky arm muscles. His bushy white eyebrows gave him a startled expression. As he watched us walk past, his grin made my skin crawl.

"I don't think we should be here," I muttered to Grover.

He eyed the supervisor. "Pretty sure there are no monsters here or I'd smell them. That guy is human."

This did not reassure me. Some of my least favorite

8

We blow up some things
You thought all the things blew up?
No, we found more things

MOST SATYRS EXCEL AT RUNNING AWAY.

Gleeson Hedge, however, was not most satyrs. He grabbed a barrel brush from his cart, yelled "DIE!" and charged the three-hundred-pound manager.

Even the automatons were too surprised to react, which probably saved Hedge's life. I grabbed the satyr's collar and dragged him backward as the employees' first shots went wild, a barrage of bright orange discount stickers flying over our heads.

I pulled Hedge down the aisle as he launched a fierce kick, overturning his shopping cart at our enemies' feet. Another discount sticker grazed my arm with the force of an angry Titaness's slap.

"Careful!" Macro yelled at his men. "I need Apollo in one piece, not half-off!"

Gleeson clawed at the shelves, grabbed a demo-model Macro's Self-Lighting Molotov Cocktail™ (BUY ONE, GET TWO FREE!), and tossed it at the store employees with the battle cry "Eat surplus!"

Macro shrieked as the Molotov cocktail landed amid

people were human. Nevertheless, I followed Grover deeper into the store.

As he predicted, Gleeson Hedge was in the firearms section, whistling as he stuffed his shopping cart with rifle scopes and barrel brushes.

I saw why Grover called him *Coach*. Hedge wore bright blue double-weave polyester gym shorts that left his hairy goat legs exposed, a red baseball cap that perched between his small horns, a white polo shirt, and a whistle around his neck, as if he expected at any moment to be called in to referee a soccer game.

He looked older than Grover, judging from his sun-weathered face, but it was hard to be sure with satyrs. They matured at roughly half the speed of humans. I knew Grover was thirty-ish in people years, for instance, but only sixteen in satyr terms. The coach could have been anywhere between forty and a hundred in human time.

"Gleeson!" Grover called.

The coach turned and grinned. His cart overflowed with quivers, crates of ammo, and plastic-sealed rows of grenades that promised FUN FOR THE WHOLE FAMILY!!!

"Hey, Underwood!" he said. "Good timing! Help me pick some land mines."

Grover flinched. "Land mines?"

"Well, they're just empty casings," Gleeson said, gesturing toward a row of metal canisters that looked like canteens, "but I figured we could fill them with explosives and make them active again! You like the World War II models or the Vietnam-era kind?"

"Uh . . ." Grover grabbed me and shoved me forward. "Gleeson, this is Apollo."

Gleeson frowned. "Apollo . . . like *Apollo* Apollo?" He scanned me from head to toe. "It's even worse than we thought. Kid, you gotta do more core exercises."

"Thanks." I sighed. "I've never heard that before."

"I could whip you into shape," Hedge mused. "But first, help me out. Stake mines? Claymores? What do you think?"

"I thought you were buying camping supplies."

Gleeson arched his brow. "These *are* camping supplies. If I have to be outdoors with my wife and kid, holed up in that cistern, I'm going to feel a lot better knowing I'm armed to the teeth and surrounded by pressure-detonated explosives! I got a family to protect!"

"But . . ." I glanced at Grover, who shook his head as if to say *Don't even try*.

At this point, dear reader, you may be wondering *Apollo, why would you object? Gleeson Hedge has it right! Why mess around with swords and bows when you can fight monsters with land mines and machine guns?*

Alas, when one is fighting ancient forces, modern weapons are unreliable at best. The mechanisms of standard mortal-made guns and bombs tend to jam in supernatural situations. Explosions may or may not get the job done, and regular ammunition only serves to annoy most monsters. Some heroes do indeed use firearms, but their ammo must be crafted from magical metals—Celestial bronze, Imperial gold, Stygian iron, and so on.

Unfortunately, these materials are rare. Magically crafted bullets are finicky. They can be used only once

before disintegrating, whereas a sword made from magical metal will last for millennia. It's simply impractical to "spray and pray" when fighting a gorgon or a hydra.

"I think you already have a great assortment of supplies," I said. "Besides, Mellie is worried. You've been gone all day."

"No, I haven't!" Hedge protested. "Wait. What time is it?"

"After dark," Grover said.

Coach Hedge blinked. "Seriously? Ah, hockey pucks. I guess I spent too long in the grenade aisle. Well, fine. I suppose—"

"Excuse me," said a voice at my back.

The subsequent high-pitched yelp may have come from Grover. Or possibly me, who can be sure? I spun around to find that the huge bald man from the supervisor's booth had sneaked up behind us. This was quite a trick, since he was almost seven feet tall and must have weighed close to three hundred pounds. He was flanked by two employees, both staring impassively into space, holding label guns.

The manager grinned, his bushy white eyebrows creeping heavenward, his teeth the many colors of tombstone marble.

"I'm *so* sorry to interrupt," he said. "We don't get many celebrities and I just—I had to be sure. Are you Apollo? I mean . . . *the* Apollo?"

He sounded delighted by the possibility. I looked at my satyr companions. Gleeson nodded. Grover shook his head vigorously.

"And if I *were* Apollo?" I asked the manager.

"Oh, we'd comp your purchases!" the manager cried. "We'd roll out the red carpet!"

That was a dirty trick. I'd always been a sucker for the red carpet.

"Well, then, yes," I said, "I'm Apollo."

The manager squealed—a sound not unlike the Erymanthian Boar made that time I shot him in the hindquarters. "I *knew* it! I'm such a fan. My name is Macro. Welcome to my store!"

He glanced at his two employees. "Bring out the red carpet so we can roll Apollo up in it, will you? But first let's make the satyrs' deaths quick and painless. This is *such* an honor!"

The employees raised their labeling guns, ready to mark us down as clearance items.

"Wait!" I cried.

The employees hesitated. Up close, I could see how much they looked alike: the same greasy mops of dark hair, the same glazed eyes, the same rigid postures. They might have been twins, or—a horrible thought seeped into my brain—products of the same assembly line.

"I, um, er . . ." I said, poetic to the last. "What if I'm not really Apollo?"

Macro's grin lost some of its wattage. "Well, then, I'd have to kill you for disappointing me."

"Okay, I'm Apollo," I said. "But you can't just kill your customers. That's no way to run an army-surplus store!"

Behind me, Grover wrestled with Coach Hedge, who was desperately trying to claw open a family fun pack of

grenades while cursing the tamper-proof packaging.

Macro clasped his meaty hands. "I know it's terribly rude. I do apologize, Lord Apollo."

"So . . . you won't kill us?"

"Well, as I said, I won't kill *you*. The emperor has plans for you. He needs you alive!"

"Plans," I said.

I hated plans. They reminded me of annoying things like Zeus's once-a-century goal-setting meetings, or dangerously complicated attacks. Or Athena.

"B-but my friends," I stammered. "You can't kill the satyrs. A god of my stature can't be rolled up in a red carpet without my retinue!"

Macro regarded the satyrs, who were still fighting over the plastic-wrapped grenades.

"Hmm," said the manager. "I'm sorry, Lord Apollo, but you see, this may be my only chance to get back into the emperor's good graces. I'm fairly sure he won't want the satyrs."

"You mean . . . you're *out* of the emperor's good graces?"

Macro heaved a sigh. He began rolling up his sleeves as if he expected some hard, dreary satyr-murdering ahead. "I'm afraid so. I certainly didn't *ask* to be exiled to Palm Springs! Alas, the princeps is very particular about his security forces. My troops malfunctioned one too many times, and he shipped us out here. He replaced us with that horrible assortment of strixes and mercenaries and Big Ears. Can you believe it?"

I could neither believe it nor understand it. *Big ears?*

I examined the two employees, still frozen in place, label guns ready, eyes unfocused, faces expressionless.

"Your employees are automatons," I realized. "These are the emperor's former troops?"

"Alas, yes," Macro said. "They are *fully* capable, though. Once I deliver you, the emperor will surely see that and forgive me."

His sleeves were above his elbows now, revealing old white scars, as if his forearms had been clawed by a desperate victim many years ago. . . .

I remembered my dream of the imperial palace, the praetor kneeling before his new emperor.

Too late, I remembered the name of that praetor. "Naevius Sutorius Macro."

Macro beamed at his robotic employees. "I can't *believe* Apollo remembers me. This is such an honor!"

His robotic employees remained unimpressed.

"You killed Emperor Tiberius," I said. "Smothered him with a pillow."

Macro looked abashed. "Well, he was ninety percent dead already. I simply helped matters along."

"And you did it for"—an ice-cold burrito of dread sank into my stomach—"the next emperor. Neos Helios. It *is* him."

Macro nodded eagerly. "That's right! The one, the only Gaius Julius Caesar Augustus Germanicus!"

He spread his arms as if waiting for applause.

The satyrs stopped fighting. Hedge continued chewing on the grenade pack, though even his satyr teeth were having trouble with the thick plastic.

Grover backed away, putting the cart between himself and the store employees. "G-Gaius who?" He glanced at me. "Apollo, what does that mean?"

I gulped. "It means we run. Now!"

Hedge's scattered ammo boxes and, true to its advertising, burst into flames.

"Up and over!" Hedge tackled me around the waist. He slung me over his shoulder like a sack of soccer balls and scaled the shelves in an epic display of goat-climbing, leaping into the next aisle as crates of ammunition exploded behind us.

We landed in a pile of rolled-up sleeping bags.

"Keep moving!" Hedge yelled, as if the thought might not have occurred to me.

I scrambled after him, my ears ringing. From the aisle we'd just left, I heard bangs and screams as if Macro were running across a hot skillet strewn with popcorn kernels.

I saw no sign of Grover.

When we reached the end of the aisle, a store clerk rounded the corner, his label gun raised.

"Hi-YA!" Hedge executed a roundhouse kick on him.

This was a notoriously difficult move. Even Ares sometimes fell and broke his tailbone when practicing it in his dojo (witness the *Ares-so-lame* video that went viral on Mount Olympus last year, and which I absolutely was *not* responsible for uploading).

To my surprise, Coach Hedge executed it perfectly. His hoof connected with the clerk's face, knocking the automaton's head clean off. The body dropped to its knees and fell forward, wires sparking in its neck.

"Wow." Gleeson examined his hoof. "I guess that Iron Goat conditioning wax really works!"

The clerk's decapitated body gave me flashbacks to the Indianapolis *blemmyae*, who lost their fake heads with great regularity, but I had no time to dwell on the terrible past when I had such a terrible present to deal with.

Behind us, Macro called, "Oh, what have you done now?"

The manager stood at the far end of the lane, his clothes smeared with soot, his yellow vest peppered with so many holes it looked like a smoking piece of Swiss cheese. Yet somehow—just my luck—he appeared unharmed. The second store clerk stood behind him, apparently unconcerned that his robotic head was on fire.

"Apollo," Macro chided, "there's no point in fighting my automatons. This is a military-*surplus* store. I have fifty more just like these in storage."

I glanced at Hedge. "Let's get out of here."

"Yeah." Hedge grabbed a croquet mallet from a nearby rack. "Fifty may be too many even for me."

We skirted the camping tents, then zigzagged through Hockey Heaven, trying to make our way back to the store entrance. A few aisles away, Macro was shouting orders: "Get them! I'm not going to be forced to commit suicide again!"

"*Again?*" Hedge muttered, ducking under the arm of a hockey mannequin.

"He worked for the emperor." I panted, trying to keep up. "Old friends. But—*wheeze*—emperor didn't trust him. Ordered his arrest—*wheeze*—execution."

We stopped at an endcap. Gleeson peeked around the corner for signs of hostiles.

"So Macro committed suicide instead?" Hedge asked. "What a moron. Why's he working for this emperor again, if the guy wanted him killed?"

I wiped the sweat from my eyes. Honestly, why did mortal bodies have to sweat so much? "I imagine the emperor brought him back to life, gave him a second chance. Romans have strange ideas about loyalty."

Hedge grunted. "Speaking of which, where's Grover?"

"Halfway back to the Cistern, if he's smart."

Hedge frowned. "Nah. Can't believe he'd do that. Well . . ." He pointed ahead, where sliding glass doors led out to the parking lot. The coach's yellow Pinto was parked tantalizingly close—which is the first time *yellow*, *Pinto*, and *tantalizingly* have ever been used together in a sentence. "You ready?"

We charged the doors.

The doors did not cooperate. I slammed into one and bounced right off. Gleeson hammered at the glass with his croquet mallet, then tried a few Chuck Norris kicks, but even his Iron Goat–waxed hooves didn't leave a scratch.

Behind us, Macro said, "Oh, dear."

I turned, trying to suppress a whimper. The manager stood twenty feet away, under a whitewater raft that was suspended from the ceiling with a sign across its prow: BOATLOADS OF SAVINGS! I was beginning to appreciate why the emperor had ordered Macro arrested and executed. For such a big man, he was much too good at sneaking up on people.

"Those glass doors are bombproof," Macro said. "We have some for sale this week in our fallout shelter improvement department, but I suppose that wouldn't do you any good."

From various aisles, more yellow-vested employees converged—a dozen identical automatons, some covered in

Bubble Wrap as if they'd just broken out of storage. They formed a rough semicircle behind Macro.

I drew my bow. I fired a shot at Macro, but my hands shook so badly the arrow missed, embedding itself in an automaton's Bubble-Wrapped forehead with a crisp *pop!* The robot barely seemed to notice.

"Hmm." Macro grimaced. "You really are quite mortal, aren't you? I guess it's true what people say: 'Never meet your gods. They'll only disappoint you.' I just hope there's enough of you left for the emperor's magical friend to work with."

"Enough of m-me?" I stammered. "M-magical friend?"

I waited for Gleeson Hedge to do something clever and heroic. Surely he had a portable bazooka in the pocket of his gym shorts. Or perhaps his coach's whistle was magic. But Hedge looked as cornered and desperate as I felt, which wasn't fair. Cornered and desperate was *my* job.

Macro cracked his knuckles. "It's a shame, really. I'm much more loyal than *she* is, but I shouldn't complain. Once I bring you to the emperor, I'll be rewarded! My automatons will be given a second chance as the emperor's personal guard! After that, what do I care? The sorceress can take you into the maze and do her magic."

"H-her magic?"

Hedge hefted his croquet mallet. "I'll take out as many as I can," he muttered to me. "You find another exit."

I appreciated the sentiment. Unfortunately, I didn't think the satyr would be able to buy me much of a head start. Also, I didn't like the idea of returning to that kind, sleep-deprived cloud nymph, Mellie, and informing her that her husband had been killed by a squad of Bubble-Wrapped robots. Oh, my mortal sympathies *really* were getting the best of me!

"Who is this sorceress?" I demanded. "What—what does she intend to do with me?"

Macro's smile was cold and insincere. I had used that smile myself many times in the old days, whenever some Greek town prayed to me to save them from a plague and I had to break the news: *Gee, I'm sorry, but I* caused *that plague because I don't like you. Have a nice day!*

"You'll see soon enough," Macro promised. "I didn't believe her when she said you'd walk right into our trap, but here you are. She predicted that you wouldn't be able to resist the Burning Maze. Ah, well. Military Madness team members, kill the satyr and apprehend the former god!"

The automatons shuffled forward.

At the same moment, a blur of green, red, and brown near the ceiling caught my eye—a satyr-like shape leaping from the top of the nearest aisle, swinging off a fluorescent light fixture, and landing in the whitewater raft above Macro's head.

Before I could shout *Grover Underwood!* the raft landed on top of Macro and his minions, burying them under a boatload of savings. Grover leaped free, a paddle in his hand, and yelled, "Come on!"

The confusion allowed us a few moments to flee, but with the exit doors locked, we could only run deeper into the store.

"Nice one!" Hedge slapped Grover on the back as we raced through the camouflage department. "I knew you wouldn't leave us!"

"Yes, but there's no nature *anywhere* in here," Grover complained. "No plants. No dirt. No natural light. How are we supposed to fight in these conditions?"

"Guns!" Hedge suggested.

"That whole part of the store is on fire," Grover said, "thanks to a Molotov cocktail and some ammo boxes."

"Curses!" said the coach.

We passed a display of martial arts weapons, and Hedge's eyes lit up. He quickly exchanged his croquet mallet for a pair of nunchaku. "Now we're talking! You guys want some shurikens or a kusarigama?"

"I want to *run away*," Grover said, shaking his boat paddle. "Coach, you have to stop thinking about full-frontal assaults! You have a family!"

"Don't you think I know that?" Coach growled. "We *tried* settling down with the McLeans in LA. Look how well *that* turned out."

I guessed there was a story there—why they had come from LA, why Hedge sounded so bitter about it—but while fleeing from enemies in a surplus store was perhaps not the best time to talk about it.

"I suggest we find another exit," I said. "We can run away and argue about ninja weapons at the same time."

This compromise seemed to satisfy them both.

We sped past a display of inflatable swimming pools (How were those military surplus?), then turned a corner and saw in front of us, at the far rear corner of the building, a set of double doors labeled EMPLOYEES ONLY.

Grover and Hedge charged ahead, leaving me gasping in their wake. From somewhere nearby, Macro's voice called, "You can't escape, Apollo! I've already called the Horse. He'll be here any minute!"

The horse?

Why did that term send a B major chord of terror vibrating through my bones? I searched my jumbled memories for a clear answer but came up empty.

My first thought: Maybe "the Horse" was a nom de guerre. Perhaps the emperor employed an evil wrestler who wore a black satin cape, shiny spandex shorts, and a horse-head-shaped helmet.

My second thought: Why did Macro get to call for backup when I could not? Demigod communications had been magically sabotaged for months. Phones short-circuited. Computers melted. Iris-messages and magical scrolls failed to work. Yet our enemies seemed to have no trouble texting each other messages like *Apollo, my place. Where U @? Help me kill him!*

It wasn't fair.

Fair would have been me getting my immortal powers back and blasting our enemies to tiny pieces.

We burst through the EMPLOYEES ONLY doors. Inside was a storage room/loading bay filled with more Bubble-Wrapped automatons, all standing silent and lifeless like the crowd at one of Hestia's housewarming parties. (She may be the goddess of the family hearth, but the lady has no clue about how to throw a party.)

Gleeson and Grover ran past the robots and began tugging at the rolling metal garage door that sealed off the loading dock.

"Locked." Hedge whacked the door with his nunchaku.

I peered out the tiny plastic windows of the employee doors. Macro and his minions were barreling in our direction. "Run or stay?" I asked. "We're about to be cornered again."

"Apollo, what have you got?" Hedge demanded.

"What do you mean?"

"What's the ace up your sleeve? I did the Molotov cocktail. Grover dropped the boat. It's your turn. Godly fire, maybe? We could use some godly fire."

"I have *zero* godly fire up my sleeves!"

"We stay," Grover decided. He tossed me his boat paddle. "Apollo, block those doors."

"But—"

"Just keep Macro out!" Grover must have been taking assertiveness lessons from Meg. I jumped to comply.

"Coach," Grover continued, "can you play a song of opening for the loading-dock door?"

Hedge grunted. "Haven't done one of those in years, but I'll try. What'll *you* be doing?"

Grover studied the dormant automatons. "Something my friend Annabeth taught me. Hurry!"

I slipped the paddle through the door handles, then lugged over a tetherball pole and braced it against the door. Hedge began to trill a tune on his coach's whistle—"The Entertainer" by Scott Joplin. I'd never thought of the whistle as a musical instrument. Coach Hedge's performance did nothing to change my mind.

Meanwhile Grover ripped the plastic off the nearest automaton. He rapped his knuckles against its forehead, which made a hollow clang.

"Celestial bronze, all right," Grover decided. "This might work!"

"What are you going to do?" I demanded. "Melt them down for weapons?"

"No, activate them to work for us."

"They won't help *us*! They belong to Macro!"

Speak of the praetor: Macro pushed against the doors, rattling the paddle and the tetherball-pole brace. "Oh, come on, Apollo! Stop being difficult!"

Grover pulled the Bubble Wrap off another automaton. "During the Battle of Manhattan," he said, "when we were fighting Kronos, Annabeth told us about an override command written into the firmware of automatons."

"That's only for public statuary in Manhattan!" I said. "Every god who's *any* god knows that! You can't expect these things to respond to 'command sequence: Daedalus twenty-three'!"

Instantly, as in a scary episode of *Doctor Who*, the plastic-wrapped automatons snapped to attention and turned to face me.

"Yes!" Grover yelled gleefully.

I did not feel so gleeful. I'd just activated a room full of metal temp workers who were more likely to kill me than obey me. I had no idea how Annabeth Chase had figured out that the Daedalus command could be used on any automaton. Then again, she'd been able to redesign my palace on Mount Olympus with perfect acoustics and surround-sound speakers in the bathroom, so her cleverness shouldn't have surprised me.

Coach Hedge kept trilling Scott Joplin. The loading-bay

door didn't move. Macro and his men banged against my makeshift barricade, nearly making me lose my grip on the tetherball pole.

"Apollo, talk to the automatons!" Grover said. "They're waiting for *your* orders now. Tell them *begin Plan Thermopylae*!"

I didn't like being reminded of Thermopylae. So many brave and attractive Spartans had died in that battle defending Greece from the Persians. But I did as I was told. "Begin Plan Thermopylae!"

At that moment, Macro and his twelve servants busted through the doors—snapping the paddle, knocking aside the tetherball pole, and launching me into the midst of my new metal acquaintances.

Macro stumbled to a halt, six minions fanning out on either side. "What's this? Apollo, you can't activate my automatons! You haven't paid for them! Military Madness team members, apprehend Apollo! Tear the satyrs apart! Stop that infernal whistling!"

Two things saved us from instant death. First, Macro had made the mistake of issuing too many orders at once. As any maestro can tell you, a conductor should never simultaneously order the violins to speed up, the timpani to soften, and the brass to crescendo. You will end up with a symphonic train wreck. Macro's poor soldiers were left to decide for themselves whether they should first apprehend me, or tear apart the satyrs, or stop the whistling. (Personally, I would have gone after the whistler with extreme prejudice.)

The other thing that saved us? Rather than listening to

Macro, our new temp-worker friends began executing Plan Thermopylae. They shuffled forward, linking their arms and surrounding Macro and his companions, who awkwardly tried to get around their robotic colleagues and bumped into each other in confusion. (The scene was reminding me more of a Hestia housewarming by the second.)

"Stop this!" Macro shrieked. "I order you to stop!"

This only added to the confusion. Macro's faithful minions froze in their tracks, allowing our Daedalus-operated dudes to encircle Macro's group.

"No, not *you*!" Macro yelled to his minions. "*You* all don't stop! *You* keep fighting!" Which did nothing to clarify the situation.

The Daedalus dudes encircled their comrades, squeezing them in a massive group hug. Despite Macro's size and strength, he was trapped in the center, squirming and shoving uselessly.

"No! I can't—!" He spat Bubble Wrap from his mouth. "Help! The Horse can't see me like this!"

From deep in their chests, the Daedalus dudes began to emit a hum, like engines stuck in the wrong gear. Steam rose from the seams of their necks.

I backed away, as one does when a group of robots starts to steam. "Grover, what exactly *is* Plan Thermopylae?"

The satyr gulped. "Er, they're supposed to stand their ground so we can retreat."

"Then why are they steaming?" I asked. "Also, why are they starting to glow red?"

"Oh, dear." Grover chewed his lower lip. "They may have confused Plan Thermopylae with Plan Petersburg."

"Which means—?"

"They may be about to sacrifice themselves in a fiery explosion."

"Coach!" I yelled. "Whistle better!"

I threw myself at the loading-bay door, working my fingers under the bottom and lifting with all my pathetic mortal strength. I whistled along with Hedge's frantic tune. I even tap-danced a little, since that is well-known to speed up musical spells.

Behind us, Macro shrieked, "Hot! Hot!"

My clothes felt uncomfortably warm, as if I were sitting at the edge of a bonfire. After our experience with the wall of flames in the Labyrinth, I did not want to take my chances with a group hug/explosion in this small room.

"Lift!" I yelled. "Whistle!"

Grover joined in our desperate Joplin performance. Finally, the loading-bay door began to budge, creaking in protest as we raised it a few inches off the floor.

Macro's shrieking became unintelligible. The humming and heat reminded me of that moment just before my sun chariot would take off, blasting into the sky in a triumph of solar power.

"Go!" I yelled to the satyrs. "Both of you, roll under!"

I thought that was quite heroic of me—though to be honest, I half expected them to insist *Oh, no, please! Gods first!*

No such courtesy. The satyrs shimmied under the door, then held it from the other side while I tried to wriggle through the gap. Alas, I found myself stymied by my own accursed love handles. In short, I got stuck.

"Apollo, come on!" Grover yelled.

"I'm trying!"

"Suck it in, boy!" screamed the coach.

I'd never had a personal trainer before. Gods simply don't need someone yelling at them, shaming them into working harder. And honestly, who would want that job, knowing you could get zapped by lightning the first time you chided your client into doing an extra five push-ups?

This time, however, I was glad to be yelled at. The coach's exhortations gave me the extra burst of motivation I needed to squeeze my flabby mortal body through the gap.

No sooner had I gotten to my feet than Grover yelled, "Dive!"

We leaped off the edge of the loading dock as the steel door—which was apparently *not* bombproof—exploded behind us.

9

Collect call from Horse

Do you accept the charges?

Nay-ay-ay-ay-ay

OH, VILLAINY!

Please explain to me why I always end up falling into dumpsters.

I must confess, however, that this dumpster saved my life. Macro's Military Madness went up in a chain of explosions that shook the desert, rattling the flaps of the foul-smelling metal box that sheltered us. Sweating and shivering, barely able to breathe, the two satyrs and I huddled amid trash bags and listened to the pitter-patter of debris raining from the sky—an unexpected downpour of wood, plaster, glass, and sporting equipment.

After what seemed like years, I was about to risk speaking—something like *Get me out of here or I'm going to vomit*—when Grover clamped his hand over my mouth. I could barely see him in the dark, but he shook his head urgently, his eyes wide with alarm. Coach Hedge also looked tense. His nose quivered as if he smelled something even worse than the garbage.

Then I heard the *clop, clop, clop* of hooves against asphalt as they approached our hiding place.

A deep voice grumbled, "Well, this is just perfect."

An animal's muzzle snuffled the rim of our dumpster, perhaps smelling for survivors. For us.

I tried not to weep or wet my pants. I succeeded at one of those. I'll let you decide which.

The flaps of the dumpster remained closed. Perhaps the garbage and the burning warehouse masked our scent.

"Hey, Big C?" said the same deep voice. "Yeah. It's me."

From the lack of audible response, I guessed the newcomer was talking on the phone.

"Nah, the place is *gone*. I don't know. Macro must have—" He paused, as if the person on the other end had launched into a tirade.

"I know," said the newcomer. "Could've been a false alarm, but . . . Ah, nuts. Human police are on the way."

A moment after he said that, I heard the faint sound of sirens in the distance.

"I could search the area," the newcomer suggested. "Maybe check those ruins up the hill."

Hedge and Grover exchanged a worried look. Surely the ruins meant our sanctuary, currently housing Mellie, Baby Hedge, and Meg.

"I know you *think* you took care of it," said the newcomer. "But, look, that place is still dangerous. I'm telling you—" This time I could hear a faint, tinny voice raging on the other end of the line.

"Okay, C," said the newcomer. "Yes. Jupiter's jumpers, calm down! I'll just— Fine. Fine. I'm on my way back."

His exasperated sigh told me the call must have ended.

"Kid's gonna give me colic," the speaker grumbled aloud to himself.

Something slammed into the side of our dumpster, right next to my face. Then the hooves galloped away.

Several minutes passed before I felt safe enough even to look at the two satyrs. We silently agreed that we had to get out of the dumpster before we died of suffocation, heat-stroke, or the smell of my pants.

Outside, the alley was littered with smoking chunks of twisted metal and plastic. The warehouse itself was a blackened shell, flames still swirling within, adding more columns of smoke to the ash-choked night sky.

"W-who was that?" Grover asked. "He smelled like a guy on a horse, but . . ."

Coach Hedge's nunchaku clattered in his hands. "Maybe a centaur?"

"No." I put my hand on the dented metal side of the dumpster—which now bore the unmistakable impression of a shod hoof. "He was a horse. A talking horse."

The satyrs stared at me.

"All horses talk," Grover said. "They just talk in Horse."

"Wait." Hedge frowned at me. "You mean you *understood* the horse?"

"Yes," I said. "That horse spoke in English."

They waited for me to explain, but I couldn't make myself say more. Now that we were out of immediate danger, now that my adrenaline was ebbing, I found myself gripped by a cold, heavy despair. If I'd harbored any last hopes that I might be wrong about the enemy we were facing, those hopes had been torpedoed.

Gaius Julius Caesar Augustus Germanicus . . . strangely enough, that name could have applied to several famous ancient Romans. But the master of Naevius Sutorius Macro? *Big C? Neos Helios?* The only Roman emperor ever to possess a talking horse? That could mean only one person. One *terrible* person.

The flashing lights of emergency vehicles pulsed against the fronds of the nearest palm trees.

"We need to get out of here," I said.

Gleeson stared at the wreckage of the surplus store. "Yeah. Let's go around front, see if my car survived. I just wish I got some camping supplies out of this deal."

"We got something much worse." I took a shaky breath. "We got the identity of the third emperor."

The explosion hadn't scathed the coach's yellow 1979 Ford Pinto. Of course it hadn't. Such a hideous car couldn't be destroyed by anything less than a worldwide apocalypse. I sat in back, wearing a new pair of hot-pink camo pants we'd salvaged from the army surplus wreckage. I was in such a stupor, I barely remember going through the drive-through lane of Enchiladas del Rey and picking up enough combo plates to feed several dozen nature spirits.

Back at the hilltop ruins, we convened a council of the cacti.

The Cistern was packed with desert-plant dryads: Joshua Tree, Prickly Pear, Aloe Vera, and many more, all dressed in bristly clothes and doing their best not to poke each other.

Mellie fussed over Gleeson, one minute showering him with kisses and telling him how brave he was, the next minute punching him and accusing him of wanting her to raise Baby Hedge by herself as a widow. The infant—whose name, I learned, was Chuck—was awake and none too happy, kicking his little hooves into his father's stomach as Gleeson tried to hold him, tugging Hedge's goatee with his chubby little fists.

"On the bright side," Hedge told Mellie, "we got enchiladas and I scored some awesome nunchaku!"

Mellie gazed heavenward, perhaps wishing she could go back to her simple life as an unmarried cloud.

As for Meg McCaffrey, she had regained consciousness and looked as well as she ever looked—just slightly greasier thanks to the first-aid ministrations of Aloe Vera. Meg sat at the edge of the pool, trailing her bare feet in the water and stealing glances at Joshua Tree, who stood nearby, brooding handsomely in his khakis.

I asked Meg how she was feeling—because I am nothing if not thoughtful—but she waved me off, insisting she was fine. I think she was just embarrassed by my presence as she tried to discreetly ogle Joshua, which made me roll my eyes.

Girl, I see you, I felt like saying. *You are not subtle, and we really need to have a talk about crushing on dryads.*

I didn't want her to order me to slap myself, however, so I kept my mouth shut.

Grover distributed enchilada plates to everyone. He ate nothing himself—a sure sign of how nervous he felt—but paced the circumference of the pool, tapping his fingers against his reed pipes.

"Guys," he announced, "we've got problems."

I would not have imagined Grover Underwood as a leader. Nevertheless, as he spoke, all the other nature spirits gave him their full attention. Even Baby Chuck quieted down, tilting his head toward Grover's voice as if it was something interesting and possibly worth kicking.

Grover related everything that had happened to us since we'd met up in Indianapolis. He recounted our days in the Labyrinth—the pits and poison lakes, the sudden wave of fire, the flock of strixes, and the spiral ramp that had led us up to these ruins.

The dryads looked around nervously, as if imagining the Cistern filled with demonic owls.

"You sure we're safe?" asked a short plump girl with a lilting accent and red flowers in her hair (or perhaps sprouting from her hair).

"I don't know, Reba." Grover glanced at Meg and me. "This is Rebutia, guys. Reba, for short. She's a transplant from Argentina."

I waved politely. I'd never met an Argentinian cactus before, but I had a soft spot for Buenos Aires. You haven't really tangoed until you've tangoed with a Greek god at La Ventana.

Grover continued, "I don't think that exit from the maze has ever been there before. It's sealed now. I think the Labyrinth was helping us, bringing us home."

"*Helping us?*" Prickly Pear looked up from her cheese enchiladas. "The same Labyrinth harboring fires that are destroying the whole state? The same Labyrinth we've been exploring for months, trying to find the source of those fires, with no luck? The same Labyrinth that's swallowed a dozen of our search parties? What does it look like when the Labyrinth *isn't* helping us?"

The other dryads grumbled in agreement. Some bristled, literally.

Grover raised his hands for calm. "I know we're all worried and frustrated. But the Burning Maze isn't the entire Labyrinth. And at least now we have some idea *why* the emperor set it up the way he did. It's because of Apollo."

Dozens of cactus spirits turned to stare at me.

"Just to clarify," I said in a small voice, "it's not my *fault*. Tell them, Grover. Tell your very nice . . . very spiny friends it isn't my fault."

Coach Hedge grunted. "Well, it kind of *is*. Macro said the maze was a trap for you. Probably because of the Oracle thingie you're looking for."

Mellie's gaze ping-ponged between her husband and me. "Macro? Oracle thingie?"

I explained how Zeus had me traveling around the country, freeing ancient Oracles as part of my penance, because that's just the sort of horrible father he was.

Hedge then recounted our fun shopping expedition to Macro's Military Madness. When he got sidetracked talking about the various types of land mines he'd found, Grover intervened.

"So we exploded Macro," Grover summed up, "who was a Roman follower of this emperor. And he mentioned some kind of a sorceress who wants to . . . I dunno, do some evil magic on Apollo, I guess. And she's helping the emperor. And we think they put the next Oracle—"

"The Sibyl of Erythraea," I said.

"Right," Grover agreed. "We think they put her at the center of the maze as some sort of bait for Apollo. Also, there's a talking horse."

Mellie's face clouded over, which was unsurprising since she was a cloud. "All horses talk."

Grover explained what we'd heard in the dumpster. Then he backed up and explained why we'd been in a dumpster. Then he explained how I'd wet my pants and that was why I was wearing hot-pink camo.

"*Ohhh.*" All the dryads nodded, as if *this* was the real question that had been bothering them.

"Can we get back to the problem at hand?" I pleaded. "We have a common cause! You want the fires stopped. I have a quest to free the Erythraean Sibyl. Both those things require us to find the heart of the maze. That's where we'll find the source of the flames *and* the Sibyl. I just—I *know* it."

Meg studied me intently, as if trying to decide what embarrassing order she should give me: *Jump in the pool? Hug Prickly Pear? Find a shirt that matches your pants?*

"Tell me about the horse," she said.

Order received. I had no choice. "His name is Incitatus."

"And he talks," Meg said. "Like, in a way humans can understand."

"Yes, though normally he only speaks to the emperor. Don't ask me *how* he talks. Or where he came from. I don't know. He's a magical horse. The emperor trusts him, probably more than he trusts anyone. Back when the emperor ruled ancient Rome, he dressed Incitatus in senatorial purple, even tried to make him a consul. People thought the emperor was crazy, but he was never crazy."

Meg leaned over the pool, hunching her shoulders as if withdrawing into her mental shell. With Meg, emperors were always a touchy subject. Raised in Nero's household (though the terms *abused* and *gaslighted* were more accurate), she'd betrayed me to Nero at Camp Half-Blood before returning to me in Indianapolis—a subject we'd skirted without really addressing for a while. I did not blame the poor girl. Truly. But getting her to trust my friendship, to trust *anyone* after her stepfather, Nero, was like training a wild squirrel to eat out of one's hand. Any loud noise was liable to cause her to flee, or bite, or both.

(I realize that's not a fair comparison. Meg bites *much* harder than a wild squirrel.)

Finally she said, "That line from the prophecy: *The master of the swift white horse*."

I nodded. "Incitatus belongs to the emperor. Or perhaps *belong* isn't the right word. Incitatus is the right-hand horse to the man who now claims the western United States—Gaius Julius Caesar Germanicus."

This was the dryads' cue for a collective gasp of horror, and perhaps some ominous background music. Instead, blank faces greeted me. The only ominous background sound was Baby Chuck chewing the Styrofoam lid of his father's #3 dinner especial.

"This Gaius person," said Meg. "Is he famous?"

I stared at the dark waters of the pool. I almost wished Meg *would* order me to jump in and drown. Or force me to wear a shirt that matched my hot-pink pants. Either punishment would have been easier than answering her question.

"The emperor is better known by his childhood nickname," I said. "Which he despises, by the way. History remembers him as Caligula."

10

Cute kid you got there
With the itty-bitty boots
And murderous grin

DO YOU KNOW the name Caligula, dear reader?

If not, consider yourself lucky.

All around the Cistern, cactus dryads puffed out their spikes. Mellie's lower half dissolved into mist. Even Baby Chuck coughed up a piece of Styrofoam.

"*Caligula?*" Coach Hedge's eye twitched the same way it had when Mellie threatened to take away his ninja weapons. "Are you sure?"

I wished I wasn't. I wished I could announce that the third emperor was kindly old Marcus Aurelius, or noble Hadrian, or bumbling Claudius.

But Caligula . . .

Even for those who knew little about him, the name Caligula conjured the darkest, most depraved images. His reign was bloodier and more infamous than Nero's, who had grown up in awe of his wicked great-uncle Gaius Julius Caesar Germanicus.

Caligula: a byword for murder, torture, madness, excess. Caligula: the villainous tyrant against whom all other villainous tyrants were measured. Caligula: who had a worse branding problem than the Edsel, the Hindenburg, and the Chicago Black Sox put together.

Grover shuddered. "I've always hated that name. What does it mean, anyway? Satyr Killer? Blood Drinker?"

"Booties," I said.

Joshua's shaggy olive hair stood straight up, which Meg seemed to find fascinating.

"Booties?" Joshua glanced around the Cistern, perhaps wondering if he'd missed the joke. No one was laughing.

"Yes." I could still remember how cute little Caligula had looked in his miniature legionnaire's outfit when he accompanied his father, Germanicus, on military campaigns. Why were sociopaths always so *adorable* as children?

"His father's soldiers gave Caligula the nickname when he was a child," I said. "He wore teeny-weenie legionnaire's boots, *caligae*, and they thought that was hysterical. So they called him Caligula—*Little Boots*, or *Baby Shoes*, or *Booties*. Pick your translation."

Prickly Pear stabbed her fork into her enchiladas. "I don't care if the guy's name is Snookums McCuddleFace. How do we *beat* him and get our lives back to normal?"

The other cacti grumbled and nodded. I was starting to suspect that prickly pears were the natural agitators of the cactus world. Get enough of them together, and they would start a revolution and overthrow the animal kingdom.

"We have to be careful," I warned. "Caligula is a master at trapping his enemies. The old saying *Give them enough rope to hang themselves*? That was *made* for Caligula. He delights in his reputation as a madman, but it's just a cover. He's quite sane. He's also completely amoral, even worse than . . ."

I stopped myself. I'd been about to say *worse than Nero*, but how could I make such a claim in front of Meg, whose entire childhood had been poisoned by Nero and his alter ego, the Beast?

Careful, Meg, Nero would always say. *Don't misbehave or you'll wake the Beast. I love you dearly, but the Beast . . . Well, I would hate to see you do something wrong and get hurt.*

How could I quantify such villainy?

"Anyway," I said, "Caligula is smart, patient, and paranoid. If this Burning Maze is some elaborate trap, part of some bigger plan of his, it won't be easy to shut down. And beating him, even *finding* him, will be a challenge." I was tempted to add *Perhaps we don't want to find him. Perhaps we should run away.*

That wouldn't work for the dryads. They were rooted, quite literally, to the land in which they grew. Transplants like Reba were rare. Few nature spirits could survive being potted and transported to a new environment. Even if every dryad here managed to flee the fires of Southern California, thousands more would stay and burn.

Grover shuddered. "If *half* the stuff I've heard about Caligula is true . . ."

He paused, apparently realizing that everyone was watching him, gauging how much they should panic based on Grover's reactions. I, for one, did not want to be in the middle of a room filled with cacti that were running around screaming.

Fortunately, Grover kept his cool.

"Nobody is unbeatable," he declared. "Not Titans, giants, or gods—and *definitely* not some Roman emperor named Booties. This guy is causing Southern California to wither and die. He's behind the droughts, the heat, the fires. We *have* to find a way to stop him. Apollo, how did Caligula die the first time?"

I tried to remember. As usual, my mortal hard drive of a brain was shot full of holes, but I seemed to recall a dark tunnel packed with praetorian guards, crowding around the emperor, their knives flashing and glistening with blood.

"His own guards killed him," I said, "which I'm sure has made him even more paranoid. Macro mentioned that the emperor kept changing his personal guard. First automatons replaced the praetors. Then he changed them again to mercenaries and strixes and . . . big ears? I don't know what that means."

One of the dryads huffed indignantly. I guessed she was Cholla, since she looked like a cholla plant—wispy white hair, a fuzzy white beard, and large paddle-shaped ears covered with bristles. "No decent big-eared person would work for such a villain! What about other weaknesses? The emperor must have some!"

"Yeah!" Coach Hedge chimed in. "Is he scared of goats?"

"Is he allergic to cactus sap?" Aloe Vera asked hopefully.

"Not that I know of," I said.

The assembled dryads looked disappointed.

"You said you got a prophecy in Indiana?" Joshua asked. "Any clues there?"

His tone was skeptical, which I could understand. A

Hoosier prophecy just doesn't have the same ring to it as a *Delphic prophecy*.

"I have to find the *westward palace*," I said. "Which must mean Caligula's base."

"No one knows where that is," grumbled Pear.

Perhaps it was my imagination, but Mellie and Gleeson seemed to exchange an anxious look. I waited for them to say something else, but they did not.

"Also from the prophecy . . ." I continued. "I have to *wrest from him the crossword speaker's breath*. Meaning, I think, that I have to free the Erythraean Sibyl from his control."

"Does this Sibyl like crosswords?" Reba asked. "I like crosswords."

"The Oracle gave her prophecies in the form of word puzzles," I explained. "Like crosswords. Or acrostics. The prophecy also talks about Grover bringing us here, and a lot of terrible things that will happen at Camp Jupiter in the next few days—"

"The new moon," Meg muttered. "Coming very soon."

"Yes." I tried to contain my annoyance. Meg seemed to want me to be in two places at once, which would have been no problem for Apollo the god. For Lester the human, I could barely manage being in one place at once.

"There's another line," Grover remembered. "*Walk the path in thine own enemy's boots?* Could that have something to do with Caligula's booties?"

I imagined my ginormous sixteen-year-old feet crammed into a Roman toddler's military-issued leather baby shoes. My toes began to throb.

"I hope not," I said. "But if we could free the Sibyl from

the maze, I'm sure she would help us. I'd like to have more guidance before I charge off to confront Caligula in person."

Other things I would have liked: my godly powers back, the entire firearms department of Macro's Military Madness locked and loaded in the hands of a demigod army, an apology letter from my father, Zeus, promising never again to turn me into a human, and a bath. But, as they say, Lesters can't be choosers.

"That brings us back to where we started," Joshua said. "You need the Oracle freed. We need the fires shut off. To do that, we need to get through the maze, but nobody knows how."

Gleeson Hedge cleared his throat. "Maybe somebody does."

Never before had so many cacti stared at a satyr.

Cholla stroked her wispy white beard. "Who is this somebody?"

Hedge turned to his wife, as if to say *All you, sweetie*.

Mellie spent a few more microseconds pondering the night sky, and possibly her former life as a nebulous bachelorette.

"Most of you know we've been living with the McLeans," she said.

"As in Piper McLean," I explained, "daughter of Aphrodite."

I remembered her—one of the seven demigods who had sailed aboard the *Argo II*. In fact, I'd been hoping to call on her and her boyfriend, Jason Grace, while I was in Southern California, to see if they would defeat the emperor and free the Oracle for me.

Wait. Scratch that. I meant, of course, that I hoped they would *help me* do those things.

Mellie nodded. "I was Mr. McLean's personal assistant. Gleeson was a full-time stay-at-home father, doing a great job—"

"I was, wasn't I?" Gleeson agreed, giving Baby Chuck the chain of his nunchaku to teethe on.

"Until everything went wrong," Mellie said with a sigh.

Meg McCaffrey tilted her head. "What do you mean?"

"Long story," said the cloud nymph, in a tone that implied *I could tell you, but then I'd have to turn into a storm cloud and cry a lot and zap you with lightning and kill you*. "The point is, a couple of weeks ago, Piper had a dream about the Burning Maze. She thought she'd found a way to reach the center. She went exploring with . . . that boy, Jason."

That boy. My finely tuned senses told me Mellie was not happy with Jason Grace, son of Jupiter.

"When they came back . . ." Mellie paused, her lower half swirling in a corkscrew of cloud stuff. "They said they had failed. But I don't think that's the whole story. Piper hinted that they had encountered something down there that . . . rattled them."

The stone walls of the Cistern seemed to creak and shift in the cooling night air, as if sympathetically vibrating with the word *rattled*. I thought of my dream about the Sibyl in fiery chains, apologizing to someone after delivering terrible news: *I am sorry. I would spare you if I could. I would spare her*.

Had she been addressing Jason, or Piper, or both of them? If so, and if they had actually found the Oracle . . .

"We need to talk to those demigods," I decided.

Mellie lowered her head. "I can't take you. Going back . . . it would break my heart."

Hedge shifted Baby Chuck to his other arm. "Maybe I could—"

Mellie shot him a warning look.

"Yeah, I can't go either," Hedge muttered.

"I'll take you," Grover volunteered, though he looked more exhausted than ever. "I know where the McLean house is. Just, uh, maybe we can wait until the morning?"

A sense of relief washed over the assembled dryads. Their spikes relaxed. The chlorophyll came back into their complexions. Grover may not have solved their problems, but he had given them hope—at the very least, a sense that we could *do* something.

I gazed at the circle of hazy orange sky above the Cistern. I thought about the fires blazing to the west, and what might be going on up north at Camp Jupiter. Sitting at the bottom of a shaft in Palm Springs, unable to help the Roman demigods or even know what was happening to them, I could empathize with the dryads—rooted in place, watching in despair as the wildfires got closer and closer.

I didn't want to quash the dryads' newfound hopes, but I felt compelled to say, "There's more. Your sanctuary might not be safe for much longer."

I told them what Incitatus had said to Caligula on the phone. And no, I never thought I would be reporting on an eavesdropped conversation between a talking horse and a dead Roman emperor.

Aloe Vera trembled, shaking several highly medicinal triangle spikes from her hair. "H-how could they know about Aeithales? They've never bothered us here!"

Grover winced. "I don't know, guys. But . . . the horse did seem to imply that Caligula was the one who had destroyed it years ago. He said something like *I know you think you took care of it. But that place is still dangerous.*"

Joshua's bark-brown face turned even darker. "Doesn't make sense. Even *we* don't know what this place was."

"A house," Meg said. "A big house on stilts. These cisterns . . . they were support columns, geothermal cooling, water supply."

The dryads bristled all over again. They said nothing, waiting for Meg to continue.

She drew in her wet feet, making her look even more like a nervous squirrel ready to spring away. I remembered how she'd wanted to leave here as soon as we arrived, how she'd warned it wasn't safe. I recalled one line of the prophecy we hadn't yet discussed: *Demeter's daughter finds her ancient roots.*

"Meg," I said, as gently as I could, "how do you know this place?"

Her expression turned tense but defiant, as if she wasn't sure whether to burst into tears or fight me.

"Because it was my home," she said. "My dad built Aeithales."

11

No touchy the god
Unless your visions are good
And you wash your hands

YOU DON'T DO THAT.

You don't just announce that your dad built a mysterious house on a sacred spot for dryads, then get up and leave without an explanation.

So of course, that's what Meg did.

"See you in the morning," she announced to no one in particular.

She trudged up the ramp, still barefoot despite traipsing past twenty different species of cactus, and slipped into the dark.

Grover looked around at his assembled comrades. "Um, well, good meeting, everybody."

He promptly fell over, snoring before he hit the ground.

Aloe Vera gave me a concerned glance. "Should I go after Meg? She might need more aloe goo."

"I'll check on her," I promised.

The nature spirits began cleaning up their dinner trash (dryads are very conscientious about that sort of thing), while I went in search of Meg McCaffrey.

I found her five feet off the ground, perched on the rim

of the farthest brick cylinder, facing inward and staring into the shaft below. Judging from the warm strawberry fragrance wafting from the cracks in the stone, I guessed this was the same well we'd used to exit the Labyrinth.

"You're making me nervous," I said. "Would you come down?"

"No," she said.

"Of course not," I muttered.

I climbed up, despite the fact that scaling walls really wasn't in my skill set. (Oh, who am I kidding? In my present state, I didn't *have* a skill set.)

I joined Meg on the edge, dangling my feet over the abyss from which we'd escaped. . . . Had it really been only this morning? I couldn't see the net of strawberry plants below in the shadows, but their smell was powerful and exotic in the desert setting. Strange how a common thing can become uncommon in a new environment. Or in my case, how an uncommonly amazing god can become so very common.

The night sapped the color from Meg's clothes, making her look like a grayscale stoplight. Her runny nose glistened. Behind the grimy lenses of her glasses, her eyes were wet. She twisted one gold ring, then the other, as if adjusting knobs on an old-fashioned radio.

We'd had a long day. The silence between us felt comfortable, and I wasn't sure I could tolerate any further scary information about our Hoosier prophecy. On the other hand, I needed explanations. Before I went to sleep in this place again, I wanted to know how safe or unsafe it was, and whether I might wake up with a talking horse in my face.

My nerves were shot. I considered throttling my young

master and yelling *TELL ME NOW!*, but I decided that might not be sensitive to her feelings.

"Would you like to talk about it?" I asked gently.

"No."

Not a huge surprise. Even under the best of circumstances, Meg and conversation were awkward acquaintances.

"If Aeithales is the place mentioned in the prophecy," I said, "your ancient roots, then it might be important to know about it so . . . we can stay alive?"

Meg looked over. She didn't order me to leap into the strawberry pit, or even to shut up. Instead, she said, "Here," and grabbed my wrist.

I had become used to waking visions—being yanked backward down memory lane whenever godly experiences overloaded my mortal neurons. This was different. Rather than my own past, I found myself plunged into Meg McCaffrey's, seeing her memories from her point of view.

I stood in one of the greenhouses before the plants grew wild. Well-ordered rows of new cactus pups lined the metal shelves, each clay pot fitted with a digital thermometer and moisture gauge. Misting hoses and grow lights hovered overhead. The air was warm, but pleasantly so, and smelled of freshly turned earth.

Wet gravel crunched under my feet as I followed my father on his rounds—*Meg's* father, I mean.

From my vantage point as a tiny girl, I saw him smiling down at me. As Apollo I'd met him before in other visions—a middle-aged man with dark curly hair and a broad, freckled nose. I'd witnessed him in New York, giving Meg a red rose from her mother, Demeter. I'd also seen his dead body splayed on the steps of Grand Central Station, his chest a ruin of knife or claw marks, on the day Nero became Meg's stepfather.

In this memory of the greenhouse, Mr. McCaffrey didn't look much younger than in those other visions. The emotions I sensed from Meg told me she was about five years old, the same age she'd been when she and her father wound up in New York. But Mr. McCaffrey looked so much happier in this scene, so much more at ease. As Meg gazed into her father's face, I was overwhelmed by her pure joy and contentment. She was with Daddy. Life was wonderful.

Mr. McCaffrey's green eyes sparkled. He picked up a potted cactus pup and knelt to show Meg. "I call this one Hercules," he said, "because he can withstand *anything*!"

He flexed his arm and said, "GRRRR!" which sent little Meg into a fit of giggles.

"Er-klees!" she said. "Show me more plants!"

Mr. McCaffrey set Hercules back on the shelf, then held up one finger like a magician: *Watch this!* He dug into the pocket of his denim shirt and presented his cupped fist to Meg.

"Try to open it," he said.

Meg pulled at his fingers. "I can't!"

"You can. You're very strong. Try *really* hard!"

"GRRR!" said little Meg. This time she managed to open his hand, revealing seven hexagonal seeds, each the size of a nickel. Inside their thick green skins, the seeds glowed faintly, making them look like a fleet of tiny UFOs.

"Ooh," said Meg. "Can I eat them?"

Her father laughed. "No, sweetheart. These are very

special seeds. Our family has been trying to produce seeds like this for"—he whistled softly—"a *long* time. And when we plant them . . ."

"What?" Meg asked breathlessly.

"They will be very special," her dad promised. "Even stronger than Hercules!"

"Plant them now!"

Her father ruffled her hair. "Not yet, Meg. They're not ready. But when it's time, I'll need your help. We'll plant them together. Will you promise to help me?"

"I promise," she said, with all the solemnity of her five-year-old heart.

The scene shifted. Meg padded barefoot into the beautiful living room of Aeithales, where her father stood facing a wall of curved glass, overlooking the nighttime city lights of Palm Springs. He was talking on the phone, his back to Meg. She was supposed to be asleep, but something had woken her—maybe a bad dream, maybe the sense that Daddy was upset.

"No, I *don't* understand," he was saying into the phone. "You have no right. This property isn't . . . Yes, but my research can't . . . That's impossible!"

Meg crept forward. She loved being in the living room. Not just for the pretty view, but for the way the polished hardwood felt against her bare feet—smooth and cool and silky, like she was gliding across a living sheet of ice. She loved the plants Daddy kept on the shelves and in giant pots all around the room—cacti blooming in dozens of colors, Joshua trees that formed living columns, holding up the roof, growing *into* the ceiling and spreading across it in a web of fuzzy branches and green spiky clusters. Meg was too young to understand that Joshua trees weren't supposed to do that. It seemed completely reasonable to her that vegetation would weave together to help form the house.

Meg also loved the big circular well in the center of the room—the Cistern, Daddy called it—railed off for safety, but so wonderful for how it cooled the whole house and made the place feel safe and anchored. Meg loved to race down the ramp and dip her feet in the cool water of the pool at the bottom, though Daddy always said, *Don't soak too long! You might turn into a plant!*

Most of all, she loved the big desk where Daddy worked—the trunk of a mesquite tree that grew straight up through the floor and plunged back down again, like the coil of a sea serpent breaching the waves, leaving just enough of an arc to form the piece of furniture. The top of the trunk was smooth and level, a perfect work surface. Tree hollows provided cubbyholes for storage. Leafy sprigs curved up from the desktop, making a frame to hold Daddy's computer monitor. Meg had once asked if he'd hurt the tree when he carved the desk out of it, but Daddy had chuckled.

"No, sweetheart, I would never hurt the tree. Mesquite offered to shape herself into a desk *for* me."

This, too, did not seem unusual to five-year-old Meg—calling a tree *she*, talking to it the way you would speak to a person.

Tonight, though, Meg didn't feel so comfortable in the living room. She didn't like the way Daddy's voice was shaking. She reached his desk and found, instead of the usual seed packets and drawings and flowers, a stack of mail—typed letters, thick stapled documents, envelopes—all in dandelion yellow.

Meg couldn't read, but she didn't like those letters. They looked important and bossy and angry. The color hurt her eyes. It wasn't as nice as real dandelions.

"You don't understand," Daddy said into the phone. "This is more than my life's work. It's centuries. *Thousands* of years' work . . . I don't care if that sounds crazy. You can't just—"

He turned and froze, seeing Meg at his desk. A spasm crossed his face—his expression shifting from anger to fear to concern, then settling into a forced cheerfulness. He slipped his phone into his pocket.

"Hey, sweetheart," he said, his voice stretched thin. "Couldn't sleep, huh? Yeah, me neither."

He walked to the desk, swept the dandelion-yellow papers into a tree hollow, and offered Meg his hand. "Want to check the greenhouses?"

The scene changed again.

A jumbled, fragmentary memory: Meg was wearing her favorite outfit, a green dress and yellow leggings. She liked it because Daddy said it made her look like one of their greenhouse friends—a beautiful, growing thing. She stumbled down the driveway in the dark, following Daddy, her backpack stuffed with her favorite blanket because Daddy said they had to hurry. They could only take what they could carry.

They were halfway to the car when Meg stopped, noticing that the lights were on in the greenhouses.

"Meg," her father said, his voice as broken as the gravel under their feet. "Come on, sweetheart."

"But Er-klees," she said. "And the others."

"We can't bring them," Daddy said, swallowing back a sob.

Meg had never heard her father cry before. It made her feel like the earth was dropping out from underneath her.

"The magic seeds?" she asked. "We can plant them—where we're going?"

The idea of going somewhere else seemed impossible, scary. She'd never known any home but Aeithales.

"We can't, Meg." Daddy sounded like he could barely talk. "They have to grow *here*. And now . . ."

He looked back at the house, floating on its massive stone supports, its windows ablaze with gold light. But something was wrong. Dark shapes moved across the hillside—men, or something like men, dressed in black, encircling the property. And more dark shapes swirling overhead, wings blotting out the stars.

Daddy grabbed her hand. "No time, sweetheart. We have to leave. Now."

Meg's last memory of Aeithales: She sat in the back of her father's station wagon, her face and hands pressed against the rear window, trying to keep the lights of the house in view as long as possible. They'd driven only halfway down the hill when their home erupted in a blossom of fire.

I gasped, my senses suddenly yanked back to the present. Meg removed her hand from my wrist.

I stared at her in amazement, my sense of reality wobbling so much I was afraid I might fall into the strawberry pit. "Meg, how did you . . . ?"

She picked at a callus on her palm. "Dunno. Just needed to."

Such a very *Meg* answer. Still, the memories had been so painful and vivid they made my chest hurt, as if I'd been hit with a defibrillator.

How had Meg shared her past with me? I knew satyrs could create an empathy link with their closest friends. Grover Underwood had one with Percy Jackson, which he said explained why he sometimes got an inexplicable craving for blueberry pancakes. Did Meg have a similar talent, perhaps because we were linked as master and servant?

I didn't know.

I *did* know that Meg was hurting, much more than she expressed. The tragedies of her short life had started before her father's death. They had started here. These ruins were all that remained of a life that could have been.

I wanted to hug her. And believe me, that was not a feeling I had often. It was liable to result in an elbow to my rib cage or a sword hilt to my nose.

"Did you . . . ?" I faltered. "Did you have these memories all along? Do you know what your father was trying to do here?"

A listless shrug. She grabbed a handful of dust and trickled it into the pit as if sowing seeds.

"Phillip," Meg said, as if the name had just occurred to her. "My dad's name was Phillip McCaffrey."

The name made me think of the Macedonian king, father of Alexander. A good fighter, but *no* fun at all. Never any interest in music or poetry or even archery. With Philip it was all phalanxes, all the time. *Boring*.

"Phillip McCaffrey was a very good father," I said, trying to keep the bitterness out of my voice. I myself did not have much experience with good fathers.

"He smelled like mulch," Meg remembered. "In a good way."

I didn't know the difference between a good mulch smell and a bad mulch smell, but I nodded respectfully.

I gazed at the row of greenhouses—their silhouettes barely visible against the red-black night sky. Phillip McCaffrey had obviously been a talented man. Perhaps a botanist? Definitely a mortal favored by the goddess Demeter. How else could he have created a house like Aeithales, in a place with such natural power? What had he been working on, and what had he meant when he said his family had been doing the same research for thousands of years? Humans rarely thought in terms of millennia. They were lucky if they even knew the names of their great-grandparents.

Most important, what had happened to Aeithales, and why? Who had driven the McCaffreys from their home and forced them east to New York? That last question, unfortunately, was the only one I felt I could answer.

"Caligula did this," I said, gesturing at the ruined cylinders on the hillside. "That's what Incitatus meant when he said the emperor took care of this place."

Meg turned toward me, her face like stone. "We're

going to find out. Tomorrow. You, me, Grover. We'll find these people, Piper and Jason."

Arrows rattled in my quiver, but I couldn't be sure if it was the Arrow of Dodona buzzing for attention, or my own body trembling. "And if Piper and Jason don't know anything helpful?"

Meg brushed the dust from her hands. "They're part of the seven, right? Percy Jackson's friends?"

"Well . . . yes."

"Then they'll know. They'll help. We'll find Caligula. We'll explore this mazy place and free the Sibyl and stop the fires and whatever."

I admired her ability to summarize our quest in such eloquent terms.

On the other hand, I was not excited about exploring the mazy place, even if we had the help of two more powerful demigods. Ancient Rome had had powerful demigods too. Many of them tried to overthrow Caligula. All of them had died.

I kept coming back to my vision of the Sibyl, apologizing for her terrible news. Since when did an Oracle *apologize*?

I would spare you if I could. I would spare her.

The Sibyl had insisted I come to her rescue. Only I could free her, though it was a trap.

I never liked traps. They reminded me of my old crush Britomartis. Ugh, the number of Burmese tiger pits I'd fallen into for the sake of that goddess.

Meg swung her legs around. "I'm going to sleep. You should too."

She hopped off the wall and picked her way across the hillside, heading back toward the Cistern. Since she had not actually ordered me to go to sleep, I stayed on the ledge for a long time, staring down into the strawberry-clogged chasm below, listening for the fluttering wings of ill omen.

12

O, Pinto, Pinto!
Wherefore art thou puke yellow?
I'll hide in the back

GODS OF OLYMPUS, had I not suffered enough?

Driving from Palm Springs to Malibu with Meg and Grover would have been bad enough. Skirting wildfire evacuation zones and the LA morning rush hour made it worse. But did we *have* to make the journey in Gleeson Hedge's mustard-colored 1979 Ford Pinto coupe?

"Are you kidding?" I asked when I found my friends waiting with Gleeson at the car. "Don't any of the cacti own a better—I mean another vehicle?"

Coach Hedge glowered. "Hey, buddy, you should be grateful. This is a classic! Belonged to my granddaddy goat. I've kept it in *great* shape, so don't you guys *dare* wreck it."

I thought about my most recent experiences with cars: the sun chariot crashing nose-first into the lake at Camp Half-Blood; Percy Jackson's Prius getting wedged between two peach trees in a Long Island orchard; a stolen Mercedes swerving through the streets of Indianapolis, driven by a trio of demon fruit spirits.

"We'll take good care of it," I promised.

Coach Hedge conferred with Grover, making sure he knew how to find the McLean house in Malibu.

"The McLeans should still be there," Hedge mused. "At least, I hope so."

"What do you mean?" Grover asked. "Why would they *not* be there?"

Hedge coughed. "Anyway, good luck! Give Piper my best if you see her. Poor kid. . . ."

He turned and trotted back up the hill.

The inside of the Pinto smelled like hot polyester and patchouli, which brought back bad memories of disco-dancing with Travolta. (Fun fact: In Italian, his surname means *overwhelmed*, which perfectly describes what his cologne does.)

Grover took the wheel, since Gleeson trusted only him with the keys. (Rude.)

Meg rode shotgun, her red sneakers propped on the dashboard as she amused herself by growing bougainvillea vines around her ankles. She seemed in good spirits, considering last night's share session of childhood tragedy. That made one of us. I could barely think about the losses she'd suffered without blinking back tears.

Luckily, I had lots of room to cry in privacy, since I was stuck in the backseat.

We started west on Interstate 10. As we passed by Moreno Valley, it took me a while to realize what was wrong: rather than slowly changing to green, the landscape remained brown, the temperature oppressive, and the air dry and sour, as if the Mojave Desert had forgotten its boundaries and spread all the way to Riverside. To the north, the sky was a soupy haze, like the entire San Bernardino Forest was on fire.

By the time we reached Pomona and hit bumper-to-bumper traffic, our Pinto was shuddering and wheezing like a warthog with heatstroke.

Grover glanced in the rearview mirror at a BMW riding our tail.

"Don't Pintos explode if they're hit from behind?" he asked.

"Only sometimes," I said.

Back in my sun-chariot days, riding a vehicle that burst into flames was never something that bothered me, but after Grover brought it up, I kept looking behind me, mentally willing the BMW to back off.

I was in desperate need of breakfast—not just cold left-overs from last night's enchilada run. I would've smote a Greek city for a good cup of coffee and perhaps a nice long drive in the opposite direction from where we were going.

My mind began to drift. I didn't know if I was having actual waking dreams, shaken loose by my visions the day before, or if my consciousness was trying to escape the back-seat of the Pinto, but I found myself reliving memories of the Erythraean Sibyl.

I remembered her name now: Herophile, *friend of heroes*.

I saw her homeland, the Bay of Erythrae, on the coast of what would someday be Turkey. A crescent of wind-swept golden hills, studded with conifers, undulated down to the cold blue waters of the Aegean. In a small glen near the mouth of a cave, a shepherd in homespun wool knelt beside his wife, the naiad of a nearby spring, as she gave birth to their child. I will spare you the details, except for this: as the mother screamed in her final push, the child emerged from the womb not crying but *singing*—her beautiful voice filling the air with the sound of prophecies.

As you can imagine, that got my attention. From that moment on, the girl was sacred to Apollo. I blessed her as one of my Oracles.

I remembered Herophile as a young woman wandering the Mediterranean to share her wisdom. She sang to anyone who would listen—kings, heroes, priests of my temples. All struggled to transcribe her prophetic lyrics. Imagine having to commit the entire songbook of *Hamilton* to memory in a single sitting, without the ability to rewind, and you can appreciate their problem.

Herophile simply had too much good advice to share. Her voice was so enchanting, it was impossible for listeners to catch every detail. She couldn't control what she sang or when. She never repeated herself. You just had to be there.

She predicted the fall of Troy. She foresaw the rise of Alexander the Great. She advised Aeneas on where he should establish the colony that would one day become Rome. But did the Romans listen to all her advice, like *Watch out for emperors*, *Don't go crazy with the gladiator stuff*, or *Togas are not a good fashion statement*? No. No, they didn't.

For nine hundred years, Herophile roamed the earth. She did her best to help, but despite my blessings and occasional deliveries of pick-me-up flower arrangements, she became discouraged. Everyone she'd known in her youth was dead. She'd seen civilizations rise and fall. She'd heard too many priests and heroes say *Wait, what? Could you repeat that? Let me get a pencil.*

She returned home to her mother's hillside in Erythrae. The spring had dried up centuries before, and with it her mother's spirit, but Herophile settled in the nearby cave. She helped supplicants whenever they came to seek her wisdom, but her voice was never the same.

Gone was her beautiful singing. Whether she'd lost her confidence, or whether the gift of prophecy had simply changed into a different sort of curse, I couldn't be sure. Herophile spoke haltingly, leaving out important words that the listener would have to guess. Sometimes her voice failed altogether. In frustration, she scribbled lines on dried leaves, leaving them for the supplicant to arrange in the proper order to find meaning.

The last time I saw Herophile . . . yes, the year was 1509 CE. I'd coaxed her out of her cave for one last visit to Rome, where Michelangelo was painting her portrait on the ceiling of the Sistine Chapel. Apparently, she was being celebrated for some obscure prophecy long ago, when she'd predicted the birth of Jesus the Nazarene.

"I don't know, Michael," Herophile said, sitting next to him on his scaffold, watching him paint. "It's beautiful, but my arms are not that . . ." Her voice seized up. "Eight letters, starts with M."

Michelangelo tapped his paintbrush to his lips. "Muscular?"

Herophile nodded vigorously.

"I can fix that," Michelangelo promised.

Afterward, Herophile returned to her cave for good. I'll admit I lost track of her. I assumed she had faded away, like so many other ancient Oracles. Yet now here she was, in Southern California, at the mercy of Caligula.

I really should have kept sending those floral arrangements.

Now, all I could do was try to make up for my negligence. Herophile was *still* my Oracle, as much as Rachel Dare at Camp Half-Blood, or the ghost of poor Trophonius in Indianapolis. Whether it was a trap or not, I couldn't leave her in a chamber of lava, shackled with molten manacles. I began to wonder if maybe, just maybe, Zeus had been *right* to send me to earth, to correct the wrongs I had allowed to happen.

I quickly shoved that thought aside. No. This punishment was entirely unfair. Still, ugh. Is anything worse than realizing you might agree with your father?

Grover navigated around the northern edge of Los Angeles, through traffic that moved almost as slowly as Athena's brainstorming process.

I don't wish to be unfair to Southern California. When the place was not on fire, or trapped in a brown haze of smog, or rumbling with earthquakes, or sliding into the sea, or choked with traffic, there were things I liked about it: the music scene, the palm trees, the beaches, the nice days, the pretty people. Yet I understood why Hades had located the main entrance to the Underworld here. Los Angeles was a magnet for human aspirations—the perfect place for mortals to gather, starry-eyed with dreams of fame, then fail, die, and circle down the drain, flushed into oblivion.

There, you see? I can be a balanced observer!

Every so often I looked skyward, hoping to see Leo Valdez flying overhead on his bronze dragon, Festus. I wanted him to be carrying a large banner that said EVERYTHING'S COOL! The new moon wasn't for two more days, true, but maybe Leo had finished his rescue mission early! He could land on the highway, tell us that Camp Jupiter had been saved from whatever threat had faced them. Then he could ask Festus to blowtorch the cars in front of us to speed up our travels.

Alas, no bronze dragon circled above, though it would've been hard to spot. The entire sky was bronze colored.

"So, Grover," I said, after a few decades on the Pacific Coast Highway, "have you ever *met* Piper or Jason?"

Grover shook his head. "Seems strange, I know. We've all been in SoCal for so long. But I've been busy with the fires. Jason and Piper have been questing and going to school and whatever. I just never got the chance. Coach says they're . . . nice."

I got the feeling he'd been about to say something other than *nice*.

"Is there a problem we should know about?" I asked.

Grover drummed his fingers on the steering wheel. "Well . . . they've been under a lot of stress. First, they were looking for Leo Valdez. Then they did some other quests. Then things started to go bad for Mr. McLean."

Meg glanced up from braiding a bougainvillea. "Piper's dad?"

Grover nodded. "He's a famous actor, you know. Tristan McLean?"

A frisson of pleasure went up my back. I loved Tristan McLean in *King of Sparta.* And *Jake Steel 2: The Return of Steel.* For a mortal, that man had *endless* abs.

"How did things go badly?" I asked.

"You don't read celebrity news," Grover guessed.

Sad but true. With all my running around as a mortal, freeing ancient Oracles and fighting Roman megalomaniacs, I'd had zero time to keep up with juicy Hollywood gossip.

"Messy breakup?" I speculated. "Paternity suit? Did he say something horrible on Twitter?"

"Not exactly," Grover said. "Let's just . . . see how things are going when we get there. It might not be so bad."

He said that in the way people do when they expect it to be *exactly* that bad.

By the time we made it to Malibu, it was nearly lunchtime. My stomach was turning itself inside out from hunger and car sickness. Me, who used to spend all day cruising in the sun Maserati, *carsick.* I blamed Grover. He drove with a heavy hoof.

On the bright side, our Pinto had not exploded, and we found the McLean house without incident.

Set back from the winding road, the mansion at 12 Oro del Mar clung to rocky cliffs overlooking the Pacific. From street level, the only visible parts were the white stucco security walls, the wrought-iron gates, and an expanse of red-clay-tiled roofs.

The place would have radiated a sense of privacy and Zen tranquility if not for the moving trucks parked outside. The gates stood wide open. Troops of burly men were carting away sofas, tables, and large works of art. Pacing back and forth at the end of the driveway, looking bedraggled and stunned, as if he'd just walked away from a car wreck, was Tristan McLean.

His hair was longer than I'd seen it in the films. Silky black locks swept across his shoulders. He'd put on weight, so he no longer resembled the sleek killing machine he'd been in *King of Sparta*. His white jeans were smeared with soot. His black T-shirt was torn at the collar. His loafers looked like a pair of overbaked potatoes.

It didn't seem right, a celebrity of his caliber just standing in front of his Malibu house without any guards or personal assistants or adoring fans—not even a mob of paparazzi to snap embarrassing pictures.

"What's wrong with him?" I wondered.

Meg squinted through the windshield. "He looks okay."

"No," I insisted. "He looks . . . *average*."

Grover turned off the engine. "Let's go say hi."

Mr. McLean stopped pacing when he saw us. His dark brown eyes seemed unfocused. "Are you Piper's friends?"

I couldn't find my words. I made a gurgling sound I hadn't produced since I first met Grace Kelly.

"Yes, sir," said Grover. "Is she home?"

"Home . . ." Tristan McLean tasted the word. He seemed to find it bitter and without meaning. "Go on inside." He waved vaguely down the driveway. "I think she's . . ." His voice trailed off as he watched two movers carting away a large marble statue of a catfish. "Go ahead. Doesn't matter."

I wasn't sure if he was talking to us or to the movers,

but his defeated tone alarmed me even more than his appearance.

We made our way through a courtyard of sculpted gardens and sparkling fountains, through a double-wide entrance with polished oak doors, and into the house.

Red-Saltillo-tiled floors gleamed. Cream-white walls retained paler impressions where paintings had recently hung. To our right stretched a gourmet kitchen that even Edesia, the Roman goddess of banquets, would have adored. Before us spread a great room with a thirty-foot-high cedar-beamed ceiling, a massive fireplace, and a wall of sliding glass doors leading to a terrace with views of the ocean.

Sadly, the room was a hollowed-out shell: no furniture, no carpets, no artwork—just a few cables curling from the wall and a broom and dustpan leaning in one corner.

A room so impressive should not have been empty. It felt like a temple without statues, music, and gold offerings. (Oh, why did I torture myself with such analogies?)

Sitting on the fireplace surround, going through a stack of papers, was a young woman with coppery skin and layered dark hair. Her orange Camp Half-Blood T-shirt led me to assume I was looking at Piper, daughter of Aphrodite and Tristan McLean.

Our footsteps echoed in the vast space, but Piper did not look up as we approached. Perhaps she was too engrossed in her papers, or she assumed we were movers.

"You want me to get up *again*?" she muttered. "Pretty sure the fireplace is staying here."

"Ahem," I said.

Piper glanced up. Her multicolored irises caught the light like smoky prisms. She studied me as if not sure what she was looking at (oh, boy, did I know the feeling), then gave Meg the same confused once-over.

She fixed her eyes on Grover and her jaw dropped. "I—I know you," she said. "From Annabeth's photos. You're Grover!"

She shot to her feet, her forgotten papers spilling across the Saltillo tiles. "What's happened? Are Annabeth and Percy all right?"

Grover edged back, which was understandable given Piper's intense expression.

"They're fine!" he said. "At least, I assume they're fine. I haven't actually, um, seen them in a while, b-but I have an empathy link with Percy, so if he *wasn't* fine, I think I'd know—"

"Apollo." Meg knelt down. She picked up one of the fallen papers, her frown even more severe than Piper's.

My stomach completed its turn inside out. Why had I not noticed the color of the documents sooner? All of the papers—envelopes, collated reports, business letters—were dandelion yellow.

"'N.H. Financials,'" Meg read from the letterhead. "'Division of Triumvirate—'"

"Hey!" Piper swiped the paper from her hand. "That's private!" Then she faced me as if doing a mental rewind. "Wait. Did she just call you *Apollo*?"

"I'm afraid so." I gave her an awkward bow. "Apollo, god of poetry, music, archery, and many other important things, at your service, though my learner's permit reads Lester Papadopoulos."

She blinked. "What?"

"Also, this is Meg McCaffrey," I said. "Daughter of Demeter. She doesn't mean to be nosy. It's just that we've seen papers like these before."

Piper's gaze bounced from me to Meg to Grover. The satyr shrugged as if to say *Welcome to my nightmare*.

"You're going to have to rewind," Piper decided.

I did my best to give her the elevator-pitch summary: my fall to earth, my servitude to Meg, my two previous quests to free the Oracles of Dodona and Trophonius, my travels with Calypso and Leo Valdez. . . .

"LEO?" Piper grabbed my arms so hard I feared she would leave bruises. "He's *alive*?"

"Hurts," I whimpered.

"Sorry." She let go. "I need to know everything about Leo. Now."

I did my best to comply, fearing that she might physically pull the information from my brain otherwise.

"That little fire-flicker," she grumbled. "We search for months, and he just shows up at *camp*?"

"Yes," I agreed. "There is a waiting list of people who would like to hit him. We can fit you in sometime next fall. But right now, we need your help. We have to free a Sibyl from the emperor Caligula."

Piper's expression reminded me of a juggler's, trying to track fifteen different objects in the air at once.

"I knew it," she muttered. "I knew Jason wasn't telling me—"

Half a dozen movers suddenly lumbered through the front door, speaking in Russian.

Piper scowled. "Let's talk on the terrace," she said. "We can exchange bad news."

13

Don't move the gas grill
Meg is still playing with it
We are so KA-BOOM

OH, THE SCENIC OCEAN VISTA! Oh, the waves crashing against the cliffs below, and the gulls whirling overhead! Oh, the large, sweaty mover in a lounge chair, checking his texts!

The man looked up when we arrived on the terrace. He scowled, grudgingly got to his feet, and lumbered inside, leaving a mover-shaped perspiration stain on the fabric of the chair.

"If I still had my cornucopia," Piper said, "I'd shoot those guys with glazed hams."

My abdominal muscles twitched. I'd once been hit in the gut by a roasted boar shot from a cornucopia, when Demeter was especially angry with me . . . but that's another story.

Piper climbed the terrace fence and sat on top of it, facing us, her feet hooked around the rails. I supposed she'd perched there hundreds of times and no longer thought about the long drop. Far below, at the bottom of a zigzagging wooden stairway, a narrow strip of beach clung to the base of the cliffs. Waves crashed against jagged rocks. I decided not to join Piper on the railing. I wasn't afraid of heights, but I was definitely afraid of my own poor sense of balance.

Grover peered at the sweaty lounge chair—the only piece of furniture left on the deck—and opted to remain standing. Meg strolled over to a built-in stainless-steel gas grill and began playing with the knobs. I estimated we had about five minutes before she blew us all to bits.

"So." I leaned on the railing next to Piper. "You know of Caligula."

Her eyes shifted from green to brown, like tree bark aging. "I knew *someone* was behind our problems—the maze, the fires, this." She gestured through the glass doors at the empty mansion. "When we were closing the Doors of Death, we fought a lot of villains who'd come back from the Underworld. Makes sense an evil Roman emperor would be behind Triumvirate Holdings."

I guessed Piper was about sixteen, the same age as . . . no, I couldn't say *the same age as me*. If I thought in those terms, I would have to compare her perfect complexion to my own acne-scarred face, her finely chiseled nose to my bulbous wad of cartilage, her softly curved physique to mine, which was also softly curved but in all the wrong ways. Then I would have to scream *I HATE YOU!*

So young, yet she had seen so many battles. She said *when we were closing the Doors of Death* the way her high school peers might say *when we were swimming at Kyle's house*.

"We knew there was a burning maze," she continued. "Gleeson and Mellie told us about that. They said the satyrs and dryads . . ." She gestured at Grover. "Well, it's no secret you guys have been having a bad time with the drought and fires. Then I had some dreams. You know."

Grover and I nodded. Even Meg looked over from her dangerous experiments with outdoor cooking equipment and grunted sympathetically. We all knew that demigods couldn't take a catnap without being plagued by omens and portents.

"Anyway," Piper continued, "I thought we could find the heart of this maze. I figured whoever was responsible for making our lives miserable would be there, and we could send him or her back to the Underworld."

"When you say *we*," Grover asked, "you mean you and—?"

"Jason. Yes."

Her voice dipped when she spoke his name, the same way mine did when I was forced to speak the names *Hyacinthus* or *Daphne*.

"Something happened between you," I deduced.

She picked an invisible speck from her jeans. "It's been a tough year."

You're telling me, I thought.

Meg activated one of the barbecue burners, which flared blue like a thruster engine. "You guys break up or what?"

Leave it to McCaffrey to be tactless about love with a child of Aphrodite, while simultaneously starting a fire in front of a satyr.

"Please don't play with that," Piper asked gently. "And, yes, we broke up."

Grover bleated, "Really? But I heard—I thought—"

"You thought what?" Piper's voice remained calm

and even. "That we'd be together forever like Percy and Annabeth?" She stared into the empty house, not exactly as if she missed the old furniture, but as if she were imagining the space completely redone. "Things change. People change. Jason and me—we started out oddly. Hera kind of messed with our heads, made us think we shared a past we didn't share."

"Ah," I said. "That sounds like Hera."

"We fought the war against Gaia. Then we spent months searching for Leo. Then we tried to settle into school, and the moment I actually had some time to breathe . . ." She hesitated, searching each of our faces as if realizing she was about to share the real reasons, the *deeper* reasons, with people she barely knew. I remembered how Mellie had called Piper *poor girl*, and the way the cloud nymph had said Jason's name with distaste.

"Anyway," Piper said, "things change. But we're fine. He's fine. I'm fine. At least . . . I *was*, until this started." She gestured at the great room, where the movers were now lugging a mattress toward the front door.

I decided it was time to confront the elephant in the room. Or rather, the elephant on the terrace. Or rather, the elephant that would have been on the terrace had the movers not hauled him away.

"What happened exactly?" I asked. "What's in all those dandelion-colored documents?"

"Like this one," Meg said, pulling from her gardening belt a folded letter she must have filched from the great room. For a child of Demeter, she had sticky fingers.

"Meg!" I said. "That's not yours."

I may have been a little sensitive about stealing other people's mail. Once Artemis rifled through my correspondence and found some juicy letters from Lucrezia Borgia that she teased me about for decades.

"N.H. Financials," Meg persisted. "Neos Helios. Caligula, right?"

Piper dug her fingernails in the wooden rail. "Just get rid of it. Please."

Meg dropped the letter into the flames.

Grover sighed. "I could have eaten that for you. It's better for the environment, and stationery tastes great."

That got a thin smile from Piper.

"The rest is all yours," she promised. "As for what they say, it's all legal, legal, blah-blah, financial, boring, legal. Bottom line, my dad is ruined." She raised an eyebrow at me. "You really haven't seen any of the gossip columns? The magazine covers?"

"That's what *I* asked," Grover said.

I made a mental note to visit the nearest grocery store checkout lane and stock up on reading material. "I am woefully behind," I admitted. "When did this all start?"

"I don't even know," Piper said. "Jane, my dad's former personal assistant—she was in on it. Also his financial manager. His accountant. His film agent. This company Triumvirate Holdings . . ." Piper spread her hands, like she was describing a natural disaster that could not have been foreseen. "They went to a *lot* of trouble. They must have spent years and tens of millions of dollars to destroy everything my dad built—his credit, his assets, his reputation with the studios. All gone. When we hired Mellie . . . well, she was great. She was the first person to spot the trouble. She tried to help, but it was much too late. Now my dad is worse than broke. He's deeply in debt. He owes millions in taxes he didn't even know about. Best we can hope for is that he avoids jail time."

"That's horrible," I said.

And I meant it. The prospect of never seeing Tristan McLean's abs on the big screen again was a bitter disappointment, though I was too tactful to say this in front of his daughter.

"It's not like I can expect a lot of sympathy," Piper said. "You should see the kids at my school, smirking and talking about me behind my back. I mean, even more than usual. *Oh, boo-hoo. You lost all three of your houses.*"

"*Three* houses?" Meg asked.

I didn't see why that was surprising. Most minor deities and celebrities I knew had at least a dozen, but Piper's expression turned sheepish.

"I know it's ridiculous," she said. "They repo-ed ten cars. And the helicopter. They're foreclosing on this place at the end of the week and taking the airplane."

"You have an airplane." Meg nodded as if this at least made perfect sense. "Cool."

Piper sighed. "I don't care about the *stuff*, but the nice former park ranger who was our pilot is going to be out of a job. And Mellie and Gleeson had to leave. So did the house staff. Most of all . . . I'm worried about my dad."

I followed her gaze. Tristan McLean was now wandering

through the great room, staring at blank walls. I liked him better as an action hero. The role of broken man didn't suit him.

"He's been healing," Piper said. "Last year, a giant kidnapped him."

I shuddered. Being captured by giants could truly scar a person. Ares had been kidnapped by two of them, millennia ago, and he was never the same. Before, he had been arrogant and annoying. Afterward, he was arrogant, annoying, and brittle.

"I'm surprised your father's mind is still in one piece," I said.

The corners of Piper's eyes tightened. "When we rescued him from the giant, we used a potion to wipe his memory. Aphrodite said it was the only thing we could do for him. But now . . . I mean, how much trauma can one person take?"

Grover removed his cap and stared at it mournfully. Perhaps he was thinking reverent thoughts, or perhaps he was just hungry. "What will you do now?"

"Our family still has property," Piper said, "outside Tahlequah, Oklahoma—the original Cherokee allotment. End of the week, we're using our last flight on the airplane to go back home. This is one battle I guess your evil emperors won."

I didn't like the emperors being called *mine*. I didn't like the way Piper said *home*, as if she'd already accepted that she would live the rest of her life in Oklahoma. Nothing against Oklahoma, mind you. My pal Woody Guthrie hailed from

Okemah. But mortals from Malibu typically didn't see it as an upgrade.

Also, the idea of Tristan and Piper being forced to move east reminded me of the visions Meg had shown me last night: she and her father being pushed out of their home by the same boring dandelion-colored legal blah-blah, fleeing their burning house, and winding up in New York. Out of Caligula's frying pan, into Nero's fire.

"We can't let Caligula win," I told Piper. "You're not the only demigod he's targeted."

She seemed to absorb those words. Then she faced Meg, as if truly seeing her for the first time. "You too?"

Meg turned off the gas burner. "Yeah. My dad."

"What happened?"

Meg shrugged. "Long time ago."

We waited, but Meg had decided to be Meg.

"My young friend is a girl of few words," I said. "But with her permission . . . ?"

Meg did not order me to shut up or to jump off the terrace, so I recounted for Piper what I'd seen in McCaffrey's memories.

When I was done, Piper hopped down from the railing. She approached Meg, and before I could say *Watch out, she bites harder than a wild squirrel!* Piper wrapped her arms around the younger girl.

"I'm so sorry." Piper kissed the top of her head.

I waited nervously for Meg's golden scimitars to flash into her hands. Instead, after a moment of petrified surprise, Meg melted into Piper's hug. They stayed like that for a long time, Meg quivering, Piper holding her as if she were the demigod Comforter-in-Chief, her own troubles irrelevant next to Meg's.

Finally, with a sniffle/hiccup, Meg pulled away, wiping her nose. "Thanks."

Piper looked at me. "How long has Caligula been messing with demigods' lives?"

"Several thousand years," I said. "He and the other two emperors did not go back through the Doors of Death. They never really left the world of the living. They are basically minor gods. They've had millennia to build their secret empire, Triumvirate Holdings."

"So why us?" Piper said. "Why now?"

"In your case," I said, "I can only guess Caligula wants you out of the way. If you are distracted by your father's problems, you are no threat, especially if you're in Oklahoma, far from Caligula's territory. As for Meg and her dad . . . I don't know. He was involved in some sort of work Caligula found threatening."

"Something that would've helped the dryads," Grover added. "It *had* to be, based on where he was working, those greenhouses. Caligula ruined a man of nature."

Grover sounded as angry as I'd ever heard him. I doubted there was higher praise a satyr could give a human than calling him *a man of nature*.

Piper studied the waves on the horizon. "You think it's all connected. Caligula is working up to something—pushing out anyone who threatens him, starting this Burning Maze, destroying the nature spirits."

"And imprisoning the Oracle of Erythraea," I said. "As a trap. For me."

"But what does he want?" Grover demanded. "What's his endgame?"

Those were excellent questions. With Caligula, however, you almost never wanted the answers. They would make you cry.

"I'd like to ask the Sibyl," I said, "if anyone here knows how we might find her."

Piper pressed her lips together. "Ah. *That's* why you're here."

She looked at Meg, then at the gas grill, perhaps trying to decide what would be more dangerous—going on a quest with us, or remaining here with a bored child of Demeter.

"Let me get my weapons," Piper said. "We'll go for a ride."

14

Bedrossian Man

Bedrossian Man, runs as

Fast as . . . yoga pants

"DON'T JUDGE," Piper warned as she reemerged from her room.

I would not have dreamed of it.

Piper McLean looked fashionably ready for combat in her bright white Converses, distressed skinny jeans, leather belt, and orange camp tee. Braided down one side of her hair was a bright blue feather—a *harpy* feather, if I wasn't mistaken.

Strapped to her belt was a triangular-bladed dagger like the kind Greek women used to wear—a *parazonium*. Hecuba, future queen of Troy, sported one back when we were dating. It was mostly ceremonial, as I recalled, but very sharp. (Hecuba had a bit of a temper.)

Hanging from the other side of Piper's belt . . . Ah. I guessed *this* was the reason she felt self-conscious. Holstered to her thigh was a miniature quiver stocked with foot-long projectiles, their fletching made from fluffy thistles. Slung across her shoulder, along with a backpack, was a four-foot tube of river cane.

"A blowgun!" I cried. "I *love* blowguns!"

Not that I was an expert, mind you, but the blowgun *was* a missile weapon—elegant, difficult to master, and *very* sneaky. How could I not love it?

Meg scratched her neck. "Are blowguns Greeky?"

Piper laughed. "No, they're not Greeky. But they are Cherokee-y. My Grandpa Tom made this one for me a long time ago. He was always trying to get me to practice."

Grover's goatee twitched as if trying to free itself from his chin, Houdini-style. "Blowguns are really difficult to use. My Uncle Ferdinand had one. How good are you?"

"Not the best," Piper admitted. "Nowhere near as good as my cousin in Tahlequah; she's a tribal champion. But I've been practicing. Last time Jason and I were in the maze"—she patted her quiver—"these came in handy. You'll see."

Grover managed to contain his excitement. I understood his concern. In a novice's hands, a blowgun was more dangerous to allies than to enemies.

"And the dagger?" Grover asked. "Is that really—?"

"Katoptris," Piper said proudly. "Belonged to Helen of Troy."

I yelped. "You have Helen of Troy's dagger? Where did you *find* it?"

Piper shrugged. "In a shed at camp."

I felt like pulling out my hair. I remembered the day Helen had received that dagger as a wedding present. Such a *gorgeous* blade, held by the most beautiful woman ever to walk the earth. (No offense to the billions of other women out there who are also quite enchanting; I love you all.) And Piper had found this historically significant, well-crafted, powerful weapon in a *shed*?

Alas, time makes bric-a-brac of everything, no matter how important. I wondered if such a fate awaited me. In a thousand years, somebody might find me in a toolshed and say *Oh, look. Apollo, god of poetry. Maybe I can polish him up and use him.*

"Does the blade still show visions?" I asked.

"You know about that, huh?" Piper shook her head. "The visions stopped last summer. That wouldn't have anything to do with you getting kicked out of Olympus, would it, Mr. God of Prophecy?"

Meg sniffed. "Most things are his fault."

"Hey!" I said. "Er, moving right along, Piper, where exactly are you taking us? If all your cars have been repossessed, I'm afraid we're stuck with Coach Hedge's Pinto."

Piper smirked. "I think we can do better than that. Follow me."

She led us to the driveway, where Mr. McLean had resumed his duties as a dazed wanderer. He meandered around the drive, head bowed as if he were looking for a dropped coin. His hair stuck up in ragged rows where his fingers had raked through it.

On the tailgate of a nearby truck, the movers were taking their lunch break, casually eating off china plates that had no doubt been in the McLeans' kitchen not long before.

Mr. McLean looked up at Piper. He seemed unconcerned by her knife and blowgun. "Going out?"

"Just for a while." Piper kissed her father on the cheek. "I'll be back tonight. Don't let them take the sleeping bags, okay? You and I can camp out on the terrace. It'll be fun."

"All right." He patted her arm absently. "Good luck . . . studying?"

"Yep," Piper said. "Studying."

You have to love the Mist. You can stroll out of your house heavily armed, in the company of a satyr, a demigod, and a flabby former Olympian, and thanks to the Mist's perception-bending magic, your mortal father assumes you're going to a study group. *That's right, Dad. We need to go over some math problems that involve the trajectory of blowgun darts against moving targets.*

Piper led us across the street to the nearest neighbor's house—a Frankenstein's mansion of Tuscan tiles, modern windows, and Victorian gables that screamed *I have too much money and not enough taste! HELP!*

In the wraparound driveway, a heavyset man in athleisure-wear was just getting out of his white Cadillac Escalade.

"Mr. Bedrossian!" Piper called.

The man jumped, facing Piper with a look of terror. Despite his workout shirt, his ill-advised yoga pants, and his flashy running shoes, he looked like he'd been more *leisurely* than *athletic*. He was neither sweaty nor out of breath. His thinning hair made a perfect brushstroke of black grease across his scalp. When he frowned, his features gravitated toward the center of his face as if circling the twin black holes of his nostrils.

"P-Piper," he stammered. "What do you—?"

"I would *love* to borrow the Escalade, thank you!" Piper beamed.

"Uh, actually, this isn't—"

"This isn't a problem?" Piper supplied. "And you'd be delighted to lend it to me for the day? Fantastic!"

Bedrossian's face convulsed. He forced out the words, "Yes. Of course."

"Keys, please?"

Mr. Bedrossian tossed her the fob, then ran into his house as fast as his tight-fitting yoga pants would allow.

Meg whistled under her breath. "That was cool."

"What *was* that?" Grover asked.

"That," I said, "was charmspeaking." I reappraised Piper McLean, not sure if I should be impressed or if I should run after Mr. Bedrossian in a panic. "A rare gift among Aphrodite's children. Do you borrow Mr. Bedrossian's car a lot?"

Piper shrugged. "He's been an *awful* neighbor. He also has a dozen other cars. Believe me, we're not causing him any hardship. Besides, I usually bring back what I borrow. Usually. Shall we go? Apollo, you can drive."

"But—"

She smiled that sweetly scary *I-could-make-you-do-it* smile.

"I'll drive," I said.

We took the scenic coastal road south in the Bedrossian-mobile. Since the Escalade was only slightly smaller than Hephaestus's fire-breathing hydra tank, I had to be careful to avoid sideswiping motorcycles, mailboxes, small children on tricycles, and other annoying obstacles.

"Are we going to pick up Jason?" I asked.

Next to me in the passenger's seat, Piper loaded a dart into her blowgun. "No need. Besides, he's in school."

"*You're* not."

"I'm moving, remember? As of next Monday, I'm enrolled at Tahlequah High." She raised her blowgun like a champagne glass. "Go, Tigers."

Her words sounded strangely unironic. Again, I wondered how she could be so resigned to her fate, so ready to let Caligula expel her and her father from the life they had built here. But since she had a loaded weapon in her hand, I didn't challenge her.

Meg's head popped up between our seats. "We won't need your ex-boyfriend?"

I swerved and almost ran over someone's grandmother.

"Meg!" I chided. "Sit back and buckle up, please. Grover—" I glanced in the rearview mirror and saw the satyr chewing on a strip of gray fabric. "Grover, stop eating your seat belt. You're setting a bad example."

He spat out the strap. "Sorry."

Piper ruffled Meg's hair, then playfully pushed her into the backseat. "To answer your question, no. We'll be fine without Jason. I can show you the way into the maze. It was my dream, after all. This entrance is the one the emperor uses, so it *should* be the straightest shot to the center, where he's keeping your Sibyl."

"And when you went inside before," I said, "what happened?"

Piper shrugged. "The usual Labyrinth stuff—traps, changing corridors. Also some strange creatures. Guards. Hard to describe. And fire. Lots of that."

I remembered my vision of Herophile, raising her chained arms in the room of lava, apologizing to someone who wasn't me.

"You didn't actually find the Oracle?" I asked.

Piper was silent for half a block, gazing at flashes of ocean vista between houses. "I didn't. But there was a short time when we got separated, Jason and me. Now . . . I'm wondering if he told me everything that happened to him. I'm pretty sure he didn't."

Grover refastened his mangled seat belt. "Why would he lie?"

"That," Piper said, "is a very good question and a good reason to go back there without him. To see for myself."

I had a sense that Piper was holding back quite a bit herself—doubts, guesses, personal feelings, maybe what had happened to *her* in the Labyrinth.

Hooray, I thought. Nothing spices up a dangerous quest like personal drama between formerly romantically involved heroes who may or may not be telling each other (and me) the whole truth.

Piper directed me into downtown Los Angeles.

I considered this a bad sign. "Downtown Los Angeles" had always struck me as an oxymoron, like "hot ice cream" or "military intelligence." (Yes, Ares, that was an insult.)

Los Angeles was all about sprawl and suburbs. It wasn't meant to have a downtown, any more than pizza was meant to have mango chunks. Oh, sure, here and there among the dull gray government buildings and closed-up storefronts, parts of downtown had been revitalized. As we zigzagged through the surface streets, I spotted plenty of new condos, hip stores, and swanky hotels. But to me, all those efforts seemed about as effective as putting makeup on a Roman legionnaire. (And believe me, I'd tried.)

We pulled over near Grand Park, which was neither grand nor much of a park. Across the street rose an eight-story honeycomb of concrete and glass. I seemed to recall going there once, decades before, to register my divorce from Greta Garbo. Or was it Liz Taylor? I couldn't recall.

"The Hall of Records?" I asked.

"Yeah," Piper said. "But we're not going inside. Just park in the fifteen-minute loading zone over there."

Grover leaned forward. "What if we're not back in fifteen minutes?"

Piper smiled. "Then I'm sure the towing company will take good care of Mr. Bedrossian's Escalade."

Once on foot, we followed Piper to the side of the government complex, where she put her finger to her lips for quiet, then motioned for us to peek around the corner.

Running the length of the block was a twenty-foot-high concrete wall, punctuated by unremarkable metal doors that I assumed were service entrances. In front of one of those doors, about halfway down the block, stood a strange-looking guard.

Despite the warm day, he wore a black suit and tie. He was squat and burly, with unusually large hands. Wrapped around his head was something I couldn't quite figure out, like an extra-large Arabic kaffiyeh made of white fuzzy terry-cloth, which draped across his shoulders and hung halfway down his back. That alone might not have been so strange. He could have been a private security guard working for some Saudi oil tycoon. But why was he standing in an alley next to a nondescript metal door? And why was his face entirely covered in white fur—fur that exactly matched his headdress?

Grover sniffed the air, then pulled us back around the corner.

"That guy isn't human," he whispered.

"Give the satyr a prize," Piper whispered back, though I wasn't sure why we were being so quiet. We were half a block away, and there was plenty of street noise.

"What is he?" Meg asked.

Piper checked the dart in her blowgun. "That's a good question. But they can be *real* trouble if you don't take them by surprise."

"*They?*" I asked.

"Yeah." Piper frowned. "Last time, there were two. And they had black fur. Not sure how this one is different. But that door is the entrance to the maze, so we need to take him out."

"Should I use my swords?" Meg asked.

"Only if I miss." Piper took a few deep breaths. "Ready?"

I didn't imagine she would accept *no* as an answer, so I nodded along with Grover and Meg.

Piper stepped out, raised her blowgun, and fired.

It was a fifty-foot shot, at the edge of what I consider practical blowgun range, but Piper hit her target. The dart pierced the man's left trouser leg.

The guard looked down at the strange new accoutrement protruding from his thigh. The shaft's fletching matched his white fur perfectly.

Oh, great, I thought. *We just made him angry*.

Meg summoned her golden swords.

Grover fumbled for his reed pipes.

I prepared to run away screaming.

"Wait," Piper said.

The guard listed sideways, as if the whole city were tilting to starboard, then passed out cold on the sidewalk.

I raised my eyebrows. "*Poison?*"

"Grandpa Tom's special recipe," Piper said. "Now, come on. I'll show you what's *really* weird about Fuzz Face."

15

Grover leaves early
Grover is a smart satyr
Lester, not so much

"WHAT *IS* HE?" Meg asked again. "He's fun."

Fun would not have been my adjective of choice.

The guard lay sprawled on his back, his lips foaming, his half-lidded eyes twitching in a semiconscious state.

Each of his hands had eight fingers. That explained why they'd looked so large from a distance. Judging from the width of his black leather shoes, I guessed he had eight toes as well. He seemed young, no more than a teenager in human terms, but except for his forehead and cheeks, his whole face was covered in fine white fur that resembled the chest hair of a terrier.

The real conversation piece was his ears. What I had mistaken for a headdress had come unfurled, revealing two floppy ovals of cartilage, shaped like human ears but each the size of a beach towel, which told me immediately that the poor boy's middle school nickname would have been Dumbo. His ear canals were wide enough to catch baseballs, and stuffed with so much hair that Piper could have used it to fletch an entire quiverful of darts.

"Big Ears," I said.

"Duh," said Meg.

"No, I mean this must be one of the Big Ears that Macro spoke of."

Grover took a step back. "The creatures Caligula is using for his personal guard? Do they have to be so *scary-looking*?"

I walked a circle around the young humanoid. "Think how keen his hearing must be! And imagine all the guitar chords he could play with those hands. How have I never seen this species before? They would make the world's best musicians!"

"Hmm," Piper said. "I don't know about music, but they fight like you wouldn't believe. Two of them almost killed Jason and me, and we've fought a lot of different monsters."

I saw no weapons on the guard, but I could believe he was a tough fighter. Those eight-fingered fists could have done some damage. Still, it seemed a waste to train these creatures for war. . . .

"Unbelievable," I murmured. "After four thousand years, I am still discovering new things."

"Like how dumb you are," Meg volunteered.

"No."

"So you already knew that?"

"Guys," Grover interrupted. "What do we do with Big Ears?"

"Kill him," Meg said.

I frowned at her. "What happened to *He's fun*? What happened to *Everything alive deserves a chance to grow*?"

"He works for the emperors," she said. "He's a monster. He'll just dust back to Tartarus, right?"

Meg looked at Piper for confirmation, but she was busy scanning the street.

"Still seems odd there's only one guard," Piper mused. "And why is he so young? After we broke in once already, you'd think they'd put *more* guards on duty. Unless . . ."

She didn't finish the thought, but I heard it loud and clear: *Unless they want us to come in.*

I studied the guard's face, which was still twitching from the effects of the poison. Why did I have to think of his face as the fuzzy underside of a dog? It made killing him difficult.

"Piper, what does your poison do, exactly?"

She knelt and pulled out the dart. "Judging from how it worked on the other Big Ears, it will paralyze him for a long while but won't kill him. It's diluted coral-snake venom with a few special herbal ingredients."

"Remind me never to drink your herbal tea," Grover muttered.

Piper smirked. "We can just leave Big Ears. Doesn't seem right to dust him to Tartarus."

"Hmph." Meg looked unconvinced, but she flicked her twin blades, instantly snapping them back into golden rings.

Piper walked to the metal door. She pulled it open, revealing a rusty freight elevator with a single control lever and no gate.

"Okay, just so we're clear," Piper said, "I'll show you where Jason and I entered the maze, but I'm not doing the stereotypical Native American tracker thing. I don't know tracking. I'm not your guide."

We all readily agreed, as one does when delivered an ultimatum by a friend with strong opinions and poison darts.

"Also," she continued, "if any of you find the need for spiritual guidance on this quest, I am not here to provide that service. I'm not going to dispense bits of ancient Cherokee wisdom."

"Very well," I said. "Though as a former prophecy god, I enjoy bits of spiritual wisdom."

"Then you'll have to ask the satyr," Piper said.

Grover cleared his throat. "Um, recycling is good karma?"

"There you go," Piper said. "Everybody good? All aboard."

The interior of the elevator was poorly lit and smelled of sulfur. I recalled that Hades had an elevator in Los Angeles that led to the Underworld. I hoped Piper hadn't gotten her quests mixed up.

"Are you sure this thing goes to the Burning Maze?" I asked. "Because I didn't bring any rawhide chews for Cerberus."

Grover whimpered. "You *had* to mention Cerberus. That's *bad* karma."

Piper threw the switch. The elevator rattled and began to sink at the same speed as my spirits.

"This first part is all mortal," Piper assured us. "Downtown Los Angeles is riddled with abandoned subway tunnels, air-raid shelters, sewer lines. . . ."

"All my favorite things," Grover murmured.

"I don't really know the history," Piper said, "but Jason told me some of the tunnels were used by smugglers and partyers during Prohibition. Now you get taggers, runaways, homeless folks, monsters, government employees."

Meg's mouth twitched. "Government employees?"

"It's true," Piper said. "Some of the city workers use the tunnels to go from building to building."

Grover shuddered. "When they could just walk in the sunlight with nature? Repulsive."

Our rusty metal box rattled and creaked. Whatever was below would definitely hear us coming, especially if they had ears the size of beach towels.

After perhaps fifty feet, the elevator shuddered to a stop. Before us stretched a cement corridor, perfectly square and boring, lit by weak blue fluorescents.

"Doesn't seem so scary," said Meg.

"Just wait," Piper said. "The fun stuff is up ahead."

Grover fluttered his hands halfheartedly. "Yay."

The square corridor opened into a larger round tunnel, its ceiling lined with ducts and pipes. The walls were so heavily tagged they might have been an undiscovered Jackson Pollock masterpiece. Empty cans, dirty clothes, and mildewed sleeping bags littered the floor, filling the air with the unmistakable odor of a homeless camp: sweat, urine, and utter despair.

None of us spoke. I tried to breathe as little as possible until we emerged into an even larger tunnel, this one lined with rusty train tracks. Along the walls, pitted metal signs read HIGH VOLTAGE, NO ENTRY, and THIS WAY OUT.

Railroad gravel crunched under our feet. Rats scurried along the tracks, chittering at Grover as they passed.

"Rats," he whispered, "are *so* rude."

After a hundred yards, Piper led us into a side hallway, this one tiled in linoleum. Half-burned-out banks of fluorescents flickered overhead. In the distance, barely visible in the dim light, two figures were slumped together on the floor. I assumed they were homeless people until Meg froze. "Are those dryads?"

Grover yelped in alarm. "Agave? Money Maker?" He sprinted forward, the rest of us following at his heels.

Agave was an enormous nature spirit, worthy of her plant. Standing, she would have been at least seven feet tall, with blue-gray skin, long limbs, and serrated hair that must've been literally murder to shampoo. Around her neck, her wrists, and her ankles, she wore spiked bands, just in case anyone tried to intrude on her personal space. Kneeling next to her friend, Agave didn't look too bad until she turned, revealing her burns. The left side of her face was a mass of charred tissue and glistening sap. Her left arm was nothing but a desiccated brown curl.

"Grover!" she rasped. "Help Money Maker. Please!"

He knelt next to the stricken dryad.

I'd never heard of a money maker plant before, but I could see how she got her name. Her hair was a thick cluster of plaited disks like green quarters. Her dress was made of the same stuff, so she appeared to be clad in a shower of chlorophyll coinage. Her face might have once been beautiful, but now it was shriveled like a week-old party balloon. From the knees down, her legs were gone—burned away. She tried to focus on us, but her eyes were opaque green. When she moved, jade coins dropped from her hair and dress.

"Grover's here?" She sounded like she was breathing a mixture of cyanide gas and metal filings. "Grover . . . we got so close."

The satyr's lower lip trembled. His eyes rimmed with tears. "What happened? How—?"

"Down there," said Agave. "Flames. She just came out of nowhere. Magic—" She began coughing up sap.

Piper peered warily down the corridor. "I'm going to scout ahead. Be right back. I do *not* want to be caught by surprise."

She dashed off down the hall.

Agave tried to speak again but fell over sideways. Somehow, Meg caught her and propped her up without getting impaled. She touched the dryad's shoulder, muttering under her breath *Grow, grow, grow*. Cracks began to mend in Agave's charred face. Her breathing eased. Then Meg turned to Money Maker. She placed her hand on the dryad's chest, then recoiled as more jade petals shook loose.

"I can't do much for her down here," Meg said. "They both need water and sunlight. Right *now*."

"I'll get them to the surface," Grover said.

"I'll help," Meg said.

"No."

"Grover—"

"No!" His voice cracked. "Once I'm outside, I can heal them as well as you can. This is *my* search party, here on *my* orders. It's my responsibility to help them. Besides, your quest is down here with Apollo. You really want him going on without you?"

I thought this was an excellent point. I would need Meg's help.

Then I noticed the way they were both looking at me, as if they doubted my abilities, my courage, my capacity to finish this quest without a twelve-year-old girl holding my hand.

They were right, of course, but that made it no less embarrassing.

I cleared my throat. "Well, I'm sure if I *had* to . . ."

Meg and Grover had already lost interest in me, as if my feelings were not their primary concern. (I know. I couldn't believe it either.) Together they helped Agave to her feet.

"I'm fine," Agave insisted, tottering dangerously. "I can walk. Just get Money Maker."

Gently, Grover picked her up.

"Careful," Meg warned. "Don't shake her or she'll lose all her petals."

"Don't shake Money Maker," Grover said. "Got it. Good luck!"

Grover hurried into the darkness with the two dryads just as Piper returned.

"Where are they going?" she asked.

Meg explained.

Piper's frown deepened. "I hope they get out okay. If that guard wakes up . . ." She let the thought expire. "Anyway, we'd better keep going. Stay alert. Heads on a swivel."

Short of injecting myself with pure caffeine and electrifying my underwear, I wasn't sure how I could possibly be more alert or swivel-headed, but Meg and I followed Piper down the grim fluorescent hall.

Another thirty yards, and the corridor opened into a vast space that looked like . . .

"Wait," I said. "Is this an underground parking garage?"

It certainly seemed so, except for the complete absence of cars. Stretching into the darkness, the polished cement floor was painted with yellow directional arrows and rows of empty grid spaces. Lines of square pillars supported the ceiling twenty feet above. Posted on some of them were signs like: HONK. EXIT. YIELD TO LEFT.

In a car-crazy town like LA, it seemed odd that anyone would abandon a usable parking garage. Then again, I supposed street meters sounded pretty good when your other option was a creepy maze frequented by taggers, dryad search parties, and government workers.

"This is the place," Piper said. "Where Jason and I got separated."

The smell of sulfur was stronger here, mixed with a sweeter fragrance . . . like cloves and honey. It made me edgy, reminding me of something I couldn't quite place—something dangerous. I resisted the urge to run.

Meg wrinkled her nose. "Pee-yoo."

"Yeah," Piper agreed. "That smell was here last time. I thought it meant . . ." She shook her head. "Anyway, right about here, a wall of flames came roaring out of nowhere. Jason ran right. I ran left. I'm telling you—that heat seemed malevolent. It was the most intense fire I've ever felt, and I've fought Enceladus."

I shivered, remembering that giant's fiery breath. We used to send him boxes of chewable antacids for Saturnalia, just to make him mad.

"And after you and Jason got separated?" I asked.

Piper moved to the nearest pillar. She ran her hand along the letters of a YIELD sign. "I tried to find him, of course. But he just disappeared. I searched for a long time. I was pretty freaked-out. I wasn't going to lose another . . ."

She hesitated, but I understood. She had already suffered the loss of Leo Valdez, who until recently she had assumed dead. She wasn't going to lose another friend.

"Anyway," she said, "I started smelling that fragrance. That kind of clove scent?"

"It's distinctive," I agreed.

"Yucky," Meg corrected.

"It started to get really strong," Piper said. "I'll be honest, I got scared. Alone, in the dark, I panicked. I left." She grimaced. "Not very heroic, I know."

I wasn't going to criticize, given the fact that my knees were presently knocking together the Morse code message *RUN AWAY!*

"Jason showed up later," Piper said. "Simply walked out of the exit. He wouldn't talk about what had happened. He just said going back in the maze wouldn't accomplish anything. The answers were elsewhere. He said he wanted to look into some ideas and get back to me." She shrugged. "That was two weeks ago. I'm still waiting."

"He found the Oracle," I guessed.

"That's what I'm wondering. Maybe if we go that way"—Piper pointed to the right—"we'll find out."

None of us moved. None of us yelled *Hooray!* and skipped merrily into the sulfur-infused darkness.

My thoughts spun so rapidly I wondered if my head actually *was* on a swivel.

Malevolent heat, as if it had a personality. The nickname of the emperor: Neos Helios, the New Sun, Caligula's bid to brand himself as a living god. Something Naevius Macro had said: *I just hope there's enough of you left for the emperor's magical friend to work with.*

And that fragrance, clove and honey . . . like an ancient perfume, combined with sulfur.

"Agave said 'she just came out of nowhere,'" I recalled.

Piper's hand tightened on the hilt of her dagger. "I was hoping I misheard that. Or maybe by *she*, she meant Money Maker."

"Hey," Meg said. "Listen."

It was difficult over the loud swiveling of my head and the electricity crackling in my underwear, but finally I heard it: the clatter of wood and metal, echoing in the darkness, and the hiss and scrape of large creatures moving at a fast pace.

"Piper," I said, "what did that perfume remind you of? Why did it scare you?"

Her eyes now looked as electric blue as her harpy feather. "An—an old enemy, somebody my mom warned me I would see again someday. But she couldn't possibly be—"

"A sorceress," I guessed.

"Guys," Meg interrupted.

"Yeah." Piper's voice turned cold and heavy, as if she was just realizing how much trouble we were actually in.

"A sorceress from Colchis," I said. "A grandchild of Helios, who drove a chariot."

"Pulled by dragons," Piper said.

"Guys," Meg said, more urgently, "we need to hide."

Too late, of course.

The chariot rattled around the corner, pulled by twin golden dragons that spewed yellow fumes from their nostrils like sulfur-fueled locomotives. The driver had not changed since I'd last seen her, a few thousand years ago. She was still dark-haired and regal, her black silk dress rippling around her.

Piper pulled her knife. She stepped into view. Meg followed her lead, summoning her swords and standing shoulder to shoulder with the daughter of Aphrodite. I, foolishly, stood at their side.

"Medea." Piper spat out the word with as much venom and force as she would a dart from her blowgun.

The sorceress pulled the reins, bringing her chariot to a halt. Under different circumstances, I might have enjoyed the surprised look on her face, but it didn't last long.

Medea laughed with genuine pleasure. "Piper McLean, you darling girl." She turned her dark rapacious gaze on me. "This is Apollo, I take it? Oh, you've saved me so much time and trouble. And after we're done, Piper, you'll make a lovely snack for my dragons!"

16

Let's charmspeak battle
You are ugly and you suck
The end. Do I win?

SUN DRAGONS . . . I hate them. And I was a sun god.

As dragons go, they aren't particularly large. With a little lubrication and muscle, you can stuff one inside a mortal recreational vehicle. (And I have done so. You should have seen the look on Hephaestus's face when I asked him to go inside the Winnebago to check the brake pedal.)

But what they lack in size, sun dragons make up for in viciousness.

Medea's twin pets snarled and snapped, their fangs like porcelain in the fiery kilns of their mouths. Heat rippled off their golden scales. Their wings, folded against their backs, flashed like solar panels. Worst of all were their glowing orange eyes. . . .

Piper shoved me, breaking my gaze. "Don't stare," she warned. "They'll paralyze you."

"I know that," I muttered, though my legs had been in the process of turning to rock. I'd forgotten I wasn't a god anymore. I was no longer immune to little things like sun dragons' eyes and, you know, getting killed.

Piper elbowed Meg. "Hey. You too."

Meg blinked, coming out of her stupor. "What? They're pretty."

"Thank you, my dear!" Medea's voice turned gentle and soothing. "We haven't formerly met. I'm Medea. And you're obviously Meg McCaffrey. I've heard so much about you." She patted the chariot rail next to her. "Come up, darling. You needn't fear me. I'm friends with your stepfather. I'll take you to him."

Meg frowned, confused. The points of her swords dipped. "What?"

"She's charmspeaking." Piper's voice hit me like a glass of ice water in the face. "Meg, don't listen to her. Apollo, you neither."

Medea sighed. "Really, Piper McLean? Are we going to have another charmspeak battle?"

"No need," Piper said. "I'd just win again."

Medea curled her lip in a good imitation of her sun dragons' snarls. "Meg belongs with her stepfather." She swept a hand toward me as if pushing away some trash. "Not with this sorry excuse for a god."

"Hey!" I protested. "If I had my powers—"

"But you don't," Medea said. "Look at yourself, Apollo. Look what your father has done to you! Not to worry, though. Your misery is at an end. I'll squeeze out whatever power is left and put it to good use!"

Meg's knuckles turned white on the grips of her swords. "What does she mean?" she muttered. "Hey, Magic Lady, what do you mean?"

The sorceress smiled. She no longer wore the crown of her birthright as princess of Colchis, but at her throat a golden pendant still gleamed—the crossed torches of Hecate. "Shall I tell her, Apollo, or should you? Surely you know why I've brought you here."

Why she had brought me here.

As if each step I'd taken since climbing out of that dumpster in Manhattan had been preordained, orchestrated by her . . . The problem was: I found that entirely plausible. This sorceress had destroyed kingdoms. She had betrayed her own father by helping the original Jason steal the Golden Fleece. She had killed her own brother and chopped him to bits. She had murdered her own children. She was the most brutal and power-hungry of Hecate's followers, and also the most formidable. Not only that, but she was a demigod of ancient blood, the granddaughter of Helios himself, former Titan of the sun.

Which meant . . .

It all came to me at once, a realization so horrible my knees buckled.

"Apollo!" Piper barked. "Get up!"

I tried. I really did. My limbs would not cooperate. I hunched over on all fours and exhaled an undignified moan of pain and terror. I heard a *clap-clap-clap* and wondered if the moorings that anchored my mind to my mortal skull had finally snapped.

Then I realized Medea was giving me a polite round of applause.

"There it is." She chuckled. "It took you a while, but even *your* slow brain got there eventually."

Meg grabbed my arm. "You're not giving in, Apollo," she ordered. "Tell me what's going on."

She hauled me to my feet.

I tried to form words, to comply with her demand for an explanation. I made the mistake of looking at Medea, whose eyes were as transfixing as her dragons'. In her face, I saw the vicious glee and bright violence of Helios, her grandfather, as he had been in his glory days—before he faded into oblivion, before I took his place as master of the sun chariot.

I remembered how the emperor Caligula had died. He'd been on the verge of leaving Rome, planning to sail to Egypt and make a new capital there, in a land where people understood about living gods. He had meant to *make* himself a living god: Neos Helios, the New Sun—not just in name, but *literally*. That's why his praetors were so anxious to kill him on the evening before he left the city.

What's his endgame? Grover had asked.

My satyr spiritual advisor had been on the right track.

"Caligula's always had the same goal," I croaked. "He wants to be the center of creation, the new god of the sun. He wants to supplant me, the way I supplanted Helios."

Medea smiled. "And it really couldn't happen to a nicer god."

Piper shifted. "What do you mean . . . *supplant?*"

"Replace!" Medea said, then began counting on her fingers as if giving cooking tips on daytime television. "First, I extract every bit of Apollo's immortal essence—which isn't much at the moment, so that won't take long. Then, I'll add his essence to what I already have cooking, the leftover power of my dearly departed grandfather."

"Helios," I said. "The flames in the maze. I—I recognized his anger."

"Well, Grandpa's a bit cranky." Medea shrugged. "That happens when your life force fades to practically nothing, then your granddaughter summons you back a little at a time, until you're a lovely raging firestorm. I wish you could suffer as Helios has suffered—howling for millennia in a state of semiconsciousness, just aware enough of what you've lost to feel the pain and resentment. But alas, we don't have that much time. Caligula is anxious. I'll take what's left of you and Helios, invest that power in my friend the emperor, and voilà! A new god of the sun!"

Meg grunted. "That's dumb," she said, as if Medea had suggested a new rule for hide-and-seek. "You can't do that. You can't just destroy a god and make a new one!"

Medea didn't bother answering.

I knew that what she described was *entirely* possible. The emperors of Rome had made themselves semidivine simply by instituting worship among the populace. Over the centuries, several mortals had made themselves gods, or were promoted to godhood by the Olympians. My father, Zeus, had made Ganymede an immortal simply because he was cute and knew how to serve wine!

As for destroying gods . . . most of the Titans had been slain or banished thousands of years ago. And I was standing here now, a mere mortal, stripped of all godliness for the *third time*, simply because Daddy wanted to teach me a lesson.

For a sorceress of Medea's power, such magic was within reach, provided her victims were weak enough to be overcome—such as the remnants of a long-faded Titan, or a sixteen-year-old fool named Lester who had strolled right into her trap.

"You would destroy your own grandfather?" I asked.

Medea shrugged. "Why not? You gods are all family, but you're constantly trying to kill each other."

I hate it when evil sorceresses have a point.

Medea extended her hand toward Meg. "Now, my dear, hop up here with me. Your place is with Nero. All will be forgiven, I promise."

Charmspeak flowed through her words like Aloe Vera's gel—slimy and cold but somehow soothing. I didn't see how Meg could possibly resist. Her past, her stepfather, especially the Beast—they were never far from her mind.

"Meg," Piper countered, "don't let either of us tell you what to do. Make up your own mind."

Bless Piper's intuition, appealing to Meg's stubborn streak. And bless Meg's willful, weed-covered little heart. She interposed herself between me and Medea. "Apollo's *my* dumb servant. You can't have him."

The sorceress sighed. "I appreciate your courage, dear. Nero told me you were special. But my patience has limits. Shall I give you a taste of what you are dealing with?"

Medea lashed her reins, and the dragons charged.

17

Phil and Don are dead
Bye-bye, love and happiness
Hello, headlessness

I ENJOY RUNNING PEOPLE OVER in a chariot as much as the next deity, but I did *not* like the idea of being the guy run over.

As the dragons barreled toward us, Meg stood her ground, which was either admirable or suicidal. I tried to decide whether to cower behind her or leap out of the way—both options less admirable but also less suicidal—when the choice became irrelevant. Piper threw her dagger, impaling the left dragon's eye.

Left Dragon shrieked in pain, pushed against Right Dragon, and sent the chariot veering off course. Medea barreled past us, just out of reach of Meg's swords, and disappeared into the darkness while screaming insults at her pets in ancient Colchian—a language no longer spoken, but which featured twenty-seven different words for *kill* and not a single way to say *Apollo rocks*. I hated the Colchians.

"You guys okay?" Piper asked. The tip of her nose was sunburn red. The harpy feather smoldered in her hair. Such things happened during close encounters with superheated lizards.

"Fine," Meg grumbled. "I didn't even get to stab anything."

I gestured at Piper's empty knife sheath. "Nice shot."

"Yeah, now if I only had more daggers. Guess I'm back to using blowgun darts."

Meg shook her head. "Against those dragons? Did you see their armored hides? I'll take them with my swords."

In the distance, Medea continued yelling, trying to get her beasts under control. The harsh creak of wheels told me the chariot was turning for another pass.

"Meg," I said, "it'll only take Medea one charm-spoken word to defeat you. If she says *stumble* at the right moment . . ."

Meg glowered at me, as if it were *my* fault the sorceress could charmspeak. "Can we shut up Magic Lady somehow?"

"It would be easier to cover your ears," I suggested.

Meg retracted her blades. She rummaged through her supplies while the rumble of the chariot's wheels got faster and closer.

"Hurry," I said.

Meg ripped open a pack of seeds. She sprinkled some in each of her ear canals, then pinched her nose and exhaled. Tufts of bluebonnets sprouted from her ears.

"That's interesting," Piper said.

"WHAT?" Meg shouted.

Piper shook her head. *Never mind.*

Meg offered us bluebonnet seeds. We both declined. Piper, I guessed, was naturally resistant to other charm-speakers. As for me, I did not intend to get close enough to be Medea's primary target. Nor did I have Meg's weakness—a conflicted desire, misguided but powerful, to please her stepfather and reclaim some semblance of home and family—which Medea could and would exploit. Besides, the idea of walking around with lupines sticking out of my ears made me queasy.

"Get ready," I warned.

"WHAT?" Meg asked.

I pointed at Medea's chariot, now charging toward us out of the gloom. I traced my finger across my throat, the universal sign for *kill that sorceress and her dragons*.

Meg summoned her swords.

She charged the sun dragons as if they were not ten times her size.

Medea yelled with what sounded like real concern, "Move, Meg!"

Meg charged on, her festive ear protection bouncing up and down like giant blue dragonfly wings. Just before a head-on collision, Piper shouted, "DRAGONS, HALT!"

Medea countered, "DRAGONS, GO!"

The result: chaos not seen since Plan Thermopylae.

The beasts lurched in their harnesses, Right Dragon charging forward, Left Dragon stopping completely. Right stumbled, pulling Left forward so the two dragons crashed together. The yoke twisted and the chariot toppled sideways, throwing Medea across the pavement like a cow from a catapult.

Before the dragons could recover, Meg plunged in with her double blades. She beheaded Left and Right, releasing from their bodies a blast of heat so intense my sinuses sizzled.

Piper ran forward and yanked her dagger from the dead dragon's eye.

"Good job," she told Meg.

"WHAT?" Meg asked.

I emerged from behind a cement column, where I had courageously taken cover, waiting in case my friends required backup.

Pools of dragon blood steamed at Meg's feet. Her lupine ear accessories smoked, and her cheeks were burned, but otherwise she looked unharmed. The heat radiating from the sun dragon bodies had already started to cool.

Thirty feet away, in a COMPACT CAR ONLY spot, Medea struggled to her feet. Her dark braided hairdo had come undone, spilling down one side of her face like oil from a punctured tanker. She staggered forward, baring her teeth.

I slung my bow from my shoulder and fired a shot. My aim was decent, but even for a mortal, my strength was feeble. Medea flicked her fingers. A gust of wind sent my arrow spinning into the dark.

"You killed Phil and Don!" snarled the sorceress. "They've been with me for millennia!"

"WHAT?" Meg asked.

With a wave of her hand, Medea summoned a stronger blast of air. Meg flew across the parking garage, crashed into the pillar, and crumpled, her swords clattering against the asphalt.

"Meg!" I tried to run to her, but more wind swirled around me, caging me in a vortex.

Medea laughed. "Stay right there, Apollo. I'll get to you in a moment. Don't worry about Meg. The descendants of

Plemnaeus are of hardy stock. I won't kill her unless I have to. Nero wants her alive."

The descendants of Plemnaeus? I wasn't sure what that meant, or how it applied to Meg, but the thought of her being returned to Nero made me struggle harder.

I threw myself against the miniature cyclone. The wind shoved me back. If you've ever held your hand out the window of the sun Maserati as it speeds across the sky, and felt the force of a thousand-mile-an-hour wind shear threatening to rip your immortal fingers off, I'm sure you can relate.

"As for you, Piper . . ." Medea's eyes glittered like black ice. "You remember my aerial servants, the *venti*? I could simply have one throw you against a wall and break every bone in your body, but what fun would that be?" She paused and seemed to consider her words. "Actually, that would be a lot of fun!"

"Too scared?" Piper blurted out. "Of facing me yourself, woman to woman?"

Medea sneered. "Why do heroes always do that? Why do they try to taunt me into doing something foolish?"

"Because it usually works," Piper said sweetly. She crouched with her blowgun in one hand and her knife in the other, ready to lunge or dodge as needed. "You keep saying you're going to kill me. You keep telling me how powerful you are. But I keep beating you. I don't see a powerful sorceress. I see a lady with two dead dragons and a bad hairdo."

I understood what Piper was doing, of course. She was giving us time—for Meg to regain consciousness, and for me to find a way out of my personal tornado prison.

Neither event seemed likely. Meg lay motionless where she had fallen. Try as I might, I could not body-slam my way through the swirling ventus.

Medea touched her crumbling hairdo, then pulled her hand away.

"You've never beaten me, Piper McLean," she growled. "In fact, you did me a favor by destroying my home in Chicago last year. If not for that, I wouldn't have found my new friend here in Los Angeles. Our goals align very well indeed."

"Oh, I bet," Piper said. "You and Caligula, the most twisted Roman emperor in history? A match made in Tartarus. In fact, that's where I'm going to send you."

On the other side of the chariot wreckage, Meg McCaffrey's fingers twitched. Her bluebonnet earplugs shivered as she took a deep breath. I had never been so glad to see wildflowers tremble in someone's ears!

I pushed my shoulder against the wind. I still couldn't break through, but the barrier seemed to be softening, as if Medea was losing focus on her minion. Venti were fickle spirits. Without Medea keeping it on task, the air servant was likely to lose interest and fly off to find some nice pigeons or airplane pilots to harass.

"Brave words, Piper," said the sorceress. "Caligula wanted to kill you and Jason Grace, you know. It would have been simpler. But I convinced him it would be better to let you suffer in exile. I liked the idea of you and your formerly famous father stuck on a dirt farm in Oklahoma, both of you slowly going mad with boredom and hopelessness."

Piper's jaw muscles tensed. Suddenly she reminded me

of her mother, Aphrodite, whenever someone on earth compared their own beauty to hers. "You're going to regret letting me live."

"Probably." Medea shrugged. "But it has been fun watching your world fall apart. As for Jason, that lovely boy with the name of my former husband—"

"What about him?" Piper demanded. "If you've hurt him—"

"Hurt him? Not at all! I imagine he's in school right now, listening to some boring lecture, or writing an essay, or whatever dreary work mortal teenagers do. The last time you two were in the maze . . ." She smiled. "Yes, of course I know about that. We granted him access to the Sibyl. That's the only way to find her, you know. I have to *allow* you to reach the center of the maze—unless you're wearing the emperor's shoes, of course." Medea laughed, as if the idea amused her. "And really, they wouldn't go with your outfit."

Meg tried to sit up. Her glasses had slipped sideways and were hanging from the tip of her nose.

I elbowed my cyclone cage. The wind was definitely swirling more slowly now.

Piper gripped her knife. "What did you do to Jason? What did the Sibyl say?"

"She only told him the truth," Medea said with satisfaction. "He wanted to know how to find the emperor. The Sibyl told him. But she told him a bit *more* than that, as Oracles often do. The truth was enough to break Jason Grace. He won't be a threat to anyone now. Neither will you."

"You're going to pay," Piper said.

"Lovely!" Medea rubbed her hands. "I'm feeling generous, so I'll grant your request. A duel just between us, woman to woman. Choose your weapon. I'll choose mine."

Piper hesitated, no doubt remembering how the wind had knocked my arrow aside. She shouldered her blowgun, leaving herself armed with just her dagger.

"A pretty weapon," Medea said. "Pretty like Helen of Troy. Pretty like you. But, woman to woman, let me give you some advice. *Pretty* can be useful. *Powerful* is better. For my weapon, I choose Helios, the Titan of the sun!"

She lifted her arms, and fire erupted around her.

18

Whoa, there, Medea
Don't be all up in my face
With your hot granddad

RULE OF DUELING ETIQUETTE: When choosing a weapon for single combat, you should *absolutely not* choose to wield your grandfather.

I was no stranger to fire.

I had fed nuggets of molten gold to the sun horses with my bare hands. I'd gone swimming in the calderas of active volcanoes. (Hephaestus does throw a great pool party.) I had withstood the fiery breath of giants, dragons, and even my sister before she'd brushed her teeth in the morning. But none of those horrors could compare to the pure essence of Helios, former Titan of the sun.

He had not always been hostile. Oh, he was fine in his glory days! I remembered his beardless face, eternally young and handsome, his curly dark hair crowned with a golden diadem of fire that made him too bright to look upon for more than an instant. In his flowing golden robes, his burning scepter in hand, he would stroll through the halls of Olympus, chatting and joking and flirting shamelessly.

Yes, he was a Titan, but Helios had supported the gods during our first war with Kronos. He had fought at our sides against the giants. He possessed a kind and generous aspect—*warm*, as one would expect from the sun.

But gradually, as the Olympians gained power and fame among human worshippers, the memory of the Titans faded. Helios appeared less and less often in the halls of Mount Olympus. He became distant, angry, fierce, withering—all those *less* desirable solar qualities.

Humans began to look at me—brilliant, golden, and shining—and associate me with the sun. Can you blame them?

I never asked for the honor. One morning I simply woke up and found myself the master of the sun chariot, along with all my other duties. Helios faded to a dim echo, a whisper from the depths of Tartarus.

Now, thanks to his evil sorceress granddaughter, he was back. Sort of.

A white-hot maelstrom roared around Medea. I felt Helios's anger, his scorching temper that used to scare the daylights out of me. (Ew, bad pun. Sorry.)

Helios had never been a god of all trades. He was not like me, with many talents and interests. He did *one* thing with dedication and piercing focus: he drove the sun. Now, I could feel how bitter he was, knowing that his role had been assumed by *me*, a mere dabbler in solar matters, a weekend sun-chariot driver. For Medea, gathering his power from Tartarus had not been difficult. She had simply called on his resentment, his desire for revenge. Helios was *burning* to destroy me, the god who had eclipsed him. (Ew, there's another one.)

Piper McLean ran. This was not a matter of bravery

or cowardice. A demigod's body simply wasn't designed to endure such heat. Had she stayed in Medea's proximity, Piper would have burst into flames.

The only positive development: my ventus jailer vanished, most likely because Medea couldn't focus on both him and Helios. I stumbled toward Meg, yanked her to her feet, and dragged her away from the growing firestorm.

"Oh, no, Apollo," Medea called out. "No running away!"

I pulled Meg behind the nearest cement column and covered her as a curtain of flame sliced across the garage—sharp and fast and deadly, sucking the air from my lungs and setting my clothes on fire. I rolled instinctively, desperately, and crawled behind the next column over, smoking and dizzy.

Meg staggered to my side. She was steaming and red but still alive, her toasted lupines stubbornly rooted in her ears. I had shielded her from the worst of the heat.

From somewhere across the parking garage, Piper's voice echoed, "Hey, Medea! Your aim sucks!"

I peeked around the column as Medea turned toward the sound. The sorceress stood fixed in place, encircled in fire, releasing slices of white heat in every direction like spokes from the center of a wheel. One wave blasted in the direction of Piper's voice.

A moment later, Piper called, "Nope! Getting colder!"

Meg shook my arm. "WHAT DO WE DO?"

My skin felt like a cooked sausage casing. Blood sang in my veins, the lyrics being *HOT, HOT, HOT!*

I knew I would die if I suffered even another glancing

blast from that fire. But Meg was right. We had to do something. We couldn't let Piper take all the (quite literal) heat.

"Come out, Apollo!" Medea taunted. "Say hello to your old friend! Together you will fuel the New Sun!"

Another curtain of heat flashed past, a few columns away. The essence of Helios did not roar or dazzle with many colors. It was ghostly white, almost transparent, but it would kill us as fast as exposure to a nuclear core. (Public safety announcement: Reader, do *not* go to your local nuclear power plant and stand in the reactor chamber.)

I had no strategy to defeat Medea. I had no godly powers, no godly wisdom, nothing but a terrified feeling that, if I survived this, I would need another set of pink camo pants.

Meg must have seen the hopelessness in my face.

"ASK THE ARROW!" she yelled. "I WILL KEEP MAGIC LADY DISTRACTED!"

I hated that idea. I was tempted to yell back *WHAT?*

Before I could, Meg darted off.

I fumbled for my quiver and pulled forth the Arrow of Dodona. "O Wise Projectile, we need help!"

IS'T HOT IN HITHER? the arrow asked. *OR IS'T JUST ME?*

"We have a sorceress throwing Titan heat around!" I yelled. "Look!"

I wasn't sure if the arrow had magical eyes, or radar, or some other way to sense its environment, but I stuck its point around the corner of the pillar, where Piper and Meg were now playing a deadly game of chicken—fried chicken—with Medea's blasts of grandfather fire.

HAST YON WENCH A BLOWGUN? the arrow demanded.

"Yes."

FIE! A BOW AND ARROWS ART FAR SUPERIOR!

"She's half-Cherokee," I said. "It's a traditional Cherokee weapon. Now can you *please* tell me how to defeat Medea?"

HMM, the arrow mused. *THOU MUST USE THE BLOWGUN.*

"But you just said—"

REMIND ME NOT! 'TIS BITTER TO SPEAK OF! THOU HAST THY ANSWER!

The arrow went silent. The one time I *wanted* it to elaborate, the arrow shut up. Naturally.

I shoved it back in my quiver and ran to the next column, taking cover under a sign that read HONK!

"Piper!" I yelled.

She glanced over from five pillars away. Her face was pulled in a tight grimace. Her arms looked like cooked lobster shells. My medical mind told me she had a few hours at best before heatstroke set in—nausea, dizziness, unconsciousness, probably death. But I focused on the *few hours* part. I needed to believe we would live long enough to die from such causes.

I mimed shooting a blowgun, then pointed in Medea's direction.

Piper stared at me like I was crazy. I couldn't blame her. Even if Medea didn't bat away the dart with a gust of wind, the missile would never make it through that swirling wall of heat. I could only shrug and mouth the words *Trust me. I asked my arrow.*

What Piper thought of that, I couldn't tell, but she unslung her blowgun.

Meanwhile, across the parking garage, Meg taunted Medea in typical Meg fashion.

"DUMMY!" she yelled.

Medea sent out a vertical blade of heat, though judging from her aim, she was trying to scare Meg rather than kill her.

"Come out and stop this foolishness, dear!" she called, filling her words with concern. "I don't want to hurt you, but the Titan is hard to control!"

I ground my teeth. Her words were a little too close to Nero's mind games, holding Meg in check with the threat of his alter ego, the Beast. I just hoped Meg couldn't hear a word through her smoldering wildflower earbuds.

While Medea had her back turned, looking for Meg, Piper stepped into the open.

She took her shot.

The dart flew straight through the wall of fire and speared Medea between the shoulder blades. How? I can only speculate. Perhaps, being a Cherokee weapon, it was not subject to the rules of Greek magic. Perhaps, just as Celestial bronze will pass straight through regular mortals, not recognizing them as legitimate targets, the fires of Helios could not be bothered to disintegrate a puny blowgun dart.

Whatever the case, the sorceress arched her back and screamed. She turned, glowering, then reached behind her and pulled out the missile. She stared at it incredulously. "A *blowgun dart?* Are you kidding me?"

The fires continued to swirl around her, but none shot

toward Piper. Medea staggered. Her eyes crossed.

"And it's *poison?*" The sorceress laughed, her voice tinged with hysteria. "You would try to poison *me*, the world's foremost expert on poisons? There is no poison I can't cure! You cannot—"

She dropped to her knees. Green spittle flew from her mouth. "Wh-what is this concoction?"

"Compliments of my Grandpa Tom," Piper said. "Old family recipe."

Medea's complexion turned as pale as the fire. She forced out a few words, interspersed with gagging. "You think . . . changes anything? My power . . . doesn't summon Helios. . . . I hold him back!"

She fell over sideways. Rather than dissipating, the cone of fire swirled even more furiously around her.

"Run," I croaked. Then I yelled for all I was worth, "RUN NOW!"

We were halfway back to the corridor when the parking lot behind us went supernova.

19

In my underclothes
Slathered with grease. Really not
As fun as it sounds

I AM NOT SURE HOW we got out of the maze.

Lacking any evidence to the contrary, I will credit my own courage and fortitude. Yes, that must have been it. Having escaped the worst of the Titan's heat, I bravely supported Piper and Meg and exhorted them to keep going. Smoking and half-conscious but still alive, we stumbled through the corridors, retracing our steps until we arrived at the freight elevator. With one last heroic burst of strength, I flipped the lever and we ascended.

We spilled into the sunlight—*regular* sunlight, not the vicious zombie sunlight of a quasi-dead Titan—and collapsed on the sidewalk. Grover's shocked face hovered over me.

"Hot," I whimpered.

Grover pulled out his panpipe. He began to play, and I lost consciousness.

In my dreams, I found myself at a party in ancient Rome. Caligula had just opened his newest palace at the base of the Palatine Hill, making a daring architectural statement by knocking out the back wall of the Temple of Castor and

Pollux and using it as his front entrance. Since Caligula considered himself a god, he saw no problem with this, but the Roman elites were horrified. This was sacrilege akin to setting up a big-screen TV on a church altar and having a Super Bowl party with communion wine.

That didn't stop the crowd from attending the festivities. Some gods had even shown up (in disguise). How could we resist such an audacious, blasphemous party with free appetizers? Throngs of costumed revelers moved through vast torchlit halls. In every corner, musicians played songs from across the empire: Gaul, Hispania, Greece, Egypt.

I myself was dressed as a gladiator. (Back then, with my godly physique, I could totally pull that off.) I mingled with senators who were disguised as slave girls, slave girls who were disguised as senators, a few unimaginative toga ghosts, and a couple of enterprising patricians who had crafted the world's first two-man donkey costume.

Personally, I did not mind the sacrilegious temple/palace. It wasn't *my* temple, after all. And in those first years of the Roman Empire, I found the Caesars refreshingly risqué. Besides, why should we gods punish our biggest benefactors?

When the emperors expanded their power, they expanded *our* power. Rome had spread our influence across a huge part of the world. Now we Olympians were the gods of the empire! Move over, Horus. Forget about it, Marduk. The Olympians were ascendant!

We weren't about to mess with success just because the emperors got big-headed, especially when they modeled their arrogance after ours.

I wandered the party incognito, enjoying being among all the pretty people, when he finally appeared: the young emperor himself, in a golden chariot pulled by his favorite white stallion, Incitatus.

Flanked by praetorian guards—the only people not in costume—Gaius Julius Caesar Germanicus was buck naked, painted in gold from head to foot, with a spiky crown of sun rays across his brow. He was pretending to be *me*, obviously. But when I saw him, my first feeling wasn't anger. It was admiration. This beautiful, shameless mortal pulled off the role perfectly.

"I am the New Sun!" he announced, beaming at the crowd as if his smile were responsible for all the warmth in the world. "I am Helios. I am Apollo. I am Caesar. You may now bask in my light!"

Nervous applause from the crowd. Should they grovel? Should they laugh? It was always hard to tell with Caligula, and if you got it wrong, you usually died.

The emperor climbed down from his chariot. His horse was led to the hors d'oeuvres table while Caligula and his guards made their way through the crowd.

Caligula stopped and shook hands with a senator dressed as a slave. "You look lovely, Cassius Agrippa! Will you be my slave, then?"

The senator bowed. "I am your loyal servant, Caesar."

"Excellent!" Caligula turned to his guards. "You heard the man. He is now my slave. Take him to my slave master. Confiscate all his property and money. Let his family go free, though. I'm feeling generous."

The senator spluttered, but he could not form the words to protest. Two guards hustled him away as Caligula called after him, "Thank you for your loyalty!"

The crowd shifted like a herd of cattle in a thunderstorm. Those who had been surging forward, anxious to catch the emperor's eye and perhaps win his favor, now tried their best to melt into the pack.

"It's a bad night," some whispered in warning to their colleagues. "He's having a bad night."

"Marcus Philo!" cried the emperor, cornering a poor young man who had been attempting to hide behind the two-man donkey. "Come out here, you scoundrel!"

"Pr-Princeps," the man stuttered.

"I *loved* the satire you wrote about me," Caligula said. "My guards found a copy of it in the Forum and brought it to my attention."

"S-sire," said Philo. "It was only a weak jest. I didn't mean—"

"Nonsense!" Caligula smiled at the crowd. "Isn't Philo great, everybody? Didn't you like his work? The way he described me as a rabid dog?"

The crowd was on the verge of full panic. The air was so full of electricity, I wondered if my father was there in disguise.

"I promised that poets would be free to express themselves!" Caligula announced. "No more paranoia like in old Tiberius's reign. I *admire* your silver tongue, Philo. I think *everyone* should have a chance to admire it. I will reward you!"

Philo gulped. "Thank you, lord."

"Guards," said Caligula, "take him away. Pull his tongue out, dip it in molten silver, and display it in the Forum where everyone can admire it. Really, Philo—wonderful work!"

Two praetorians hauled away the screaming poet.

"And you there!" Caligula called.

Only then did I realize the crowd had ebbed around me, leaving me exposed. Suddenly, Caligula was in my face. His beautiful eyes narrowed as he studied my costume, my godly physique.

"I don't recognize you," he said.

I wanted to speak. I knew that I had nothing to fear from Caesar. If worse came to worst, I could simply say *Bye!* and vanish in a cloud of glitter. But, I have to admit, in Caligula's presence, I was awestruck. The young man was wild, powerful, unpredictable. His audacity took my breath away.

At last, I managed a bow. "I am a mere actor, Caesar."

"Oh, indeed!" Caligula brightened. "And you play the gladiator. Would you fight to the death in my honor?"

I silently reminded myself that I was immortal. It took a little convincing. I drew my gladiator's sword, which was nothing but a costume blade of soft tin. "Point me to my opponent, Caesar!" I scanned the audience and bellowed, "I will destroy anyone who threatens my lord!"

To demonstrate, I lunged and poked the nearest praetorian guard in the chest. My sword bent against his breastplate. I held aloft my ridiculous weapon, which now resembled the letter Z.

A dangerous silence followed. All eyes fixed on Caesar.

Finally, Caligula laughed. "Well done!" He patted my shoulder, then snapped his fingers. One of his servants shuffled forward and handed me a heavy pouch of gold coins.

Caligula whispered in my ear, "I feel safer already."

The emperor moved on, leaving onlookers laughing with relief, some casting envious glances at me as if to ask *What is your secret?*

After that, I stayed away from Rome for decades. It was a rare man who could make a god nervous, but Caligula unsettled me. He almost made a better Apollo than I did.

My dream changed. I saw Herophile again, the Sibyl of Erythraea, reaching out her shackled arms, her face lit red by the roiling lava below.

"Apollo," she said, "it won't seem worth it to you. I'm not sure it is myself. But you must come. You must hold them together in their grief."

I sank into the lava, Herophile still calling my name as my body broke and crumbled into ash.

I woke up screaming, lying on top of a sleeping bag in the Cistern.

Aloe Vera hovered over me, her prickly triangles of hair mostly snapped off, leaving her with a glistening buzz cut.

"You're okay," she assured me, putting her cool hand against my fevered forehead. "You've been through a lot, though."

I realized I was wearing only my underwear. My entire body was beet maroon, slathered in aloe. I couldn't breathe through my nose. I touched my nostrils and discovered I had been fitted with small green aloe nose plugs.

I sneezed them out.

"My friends?" I asked.

Aloe moved aside. Behind her, Grover Underwood sat cross-legged between Piper's and Meg's sleeping bags, both girls fast asleep. Like me, they had been slathered with goo. It was a perfect opportunity to take a picture of Meg with green plugs sticking out of her nostrils, for blackmail purposes, but I was too relieved that she was alive. Also, I didn't have a phone.

"Will they be all right?" I asked.

"They were in worse shape than you," Grover said. "It was touch and go for a while, but they'll pull through. I've been feeding them nectar and ambrosia."

Aloe smiled. "Also, my healing properties are *legendary*. Just wait. They'll be up and walking around by dinner."

Dinner . . . I looked at the dark orange circle of sky above. Either it was late afternoon, or the wildfires were closer, or both.

"Medea?" I asked.

Grover frowned. "Meg told me about the battle before she passed out, but I don't know what happened to the sorceress. I never saw her."

I shivered in my aloe gel. I wanted to believe Medea had died in the fiery explosion, but I doubted we could be so lucky. Helios's fire hadn't seemed to bother her. Maybe she was naturally immune. Or maybe she had worked some protective magic on herself.

"Your dryad friends?" I asked. "Agave and Money Maker?"

Aloe and Grover exchanged a sorrowful look.

"Agave might pull through," said Grover. "She went dormant as soon as we got her back to her plant. But Money Maker . . ." He shook his head.

I had barely met the dryad. Still, the news of her death hit me hard. I felt as if *I* were dropping green leaf-coins from my body, shedding essential pieces of myself.

I thought about Herophile's words in my dream: *It won't seem worth it to you. I'm not sure it is myself. But you must come. You must hold them together in their grief.*

I feared that Money Maker's death was only one small part of the grief that awaited us.

"I'm sorry," I said.

Aloe patted my greasy shoulder. "It isn't your fault, Apollo. By the time you found her, she was too far gone. Unless you'd had . . ."

She stopped herself, but I knew what she'd intended to say: *Unless you'd had your godly healing powers*. A lot would have been different if I'd been a god, not a pretender in this pathetic Lester Papadopoulos disguise.

Grover touched the blowgun at Piper's side. The river-cane tube had been badly charred, pitted with burn holes that would probably make it unusable.

"Something else you should know," he said. "When Agave and I carried Money Maker out of the maze? That big-eared guard, the guy with the white fur? He was gone."

I considered this. "You mean he died and disintegrated? Or he got up and walked away?"

"I don't know," Grover said. "Does either seem likely?"

Neither did, but I decided we had bigger problems to think about.

"Tonight," I said, "when Piper and Meg wake up, we need to have another meeting with your dryad friends. We're going to put this Burning Maze out of business, once and for all."

20

O Muse, let us now
Sing in praise of botanists!
They do plant stuff. Yay.

OUR COUNCIL OF WAR was more like a council of wincing.

Thanks to Grover's magic and Aloe Vera's constant sliming (I mean *attention*), Piper and Meg regained consciousness. By dinnertime, the three of us could wash, get dressed, and even walk around without screaming too much, but we still hurt a great deal. Every time I stood up too fast, tiny golden Caligulas danced before my eyes.

Piper's blowgun and quiver—both heirlooms from her grandfather—were ruined. Her hair was singed. Her burned arms, glistening with aloe, looked like newly glazed brick. She called her father to warn him she would be spending the night with her study group, then settled into one of the Cistern's brickwork alcoves with Mellie and Hedge, who kept urging her to drink more water. Baby Chuck sat in Piper's lap, staring enraptured at her face as if it were the most amazing thing in the world.

As for Meg, she sat glumly by the pool, her feet in the water, a plate of cheese enchiladas in her lap. She wore a baby blue T-shirt from Macro's Military Madness featuring a smiling cartoon AK-47 with the caption: SHOOTIE'S JUNIOR MARKSMAN CLUB! Next to her sat Agave, looking dejected, though a new green spike had started to grow where her withered arm had fallen off. Her dryad friends kept coming by, offering her fertilizer and water and enchiladas, but Agave shook her head glumly, staring at the collection of fallen money maker petals in her hand.

Money Maker, I was told, had been planted on the hillside with full dryad honors. Hopefully, she would be reincarnated as a beautiful new succulent, or perhaps a white-tailed antelope squirrel. Money Maker had always loved those.

Grover looked exhausted. Playing all the healing music had taken its toll, not to mention the stress of driving back to Palm Springs at unsafe speeds in the borrowed/slightly stolen Bedrossian-mobile with five critical burn victims.

Once we had all gathered—condolences exchanged, enchiladas eaten, aloe slimed—I began the meeting.

"All of this," I announced, "is my fault."

You can imagine how difficult this was for me to say. The words simply had not been in the vocabulary of Apollo. I half hoped the collected dryads, satyrs, and demigods would rush to reassure me that I was blameless. They did not.

I forged on. "Caligula's goal has always been the same: to make himself a god. He saw his ancestors immortalized after their deaths: Julius, Augustus, even disgusting old Tiberius. But Caligula didn't want to wait for death. He was the first Roman emperor who wanted to be a *living* god."

Piper looked up from playing with the baby satyr. "Caligula kind of *is* a minor god now, right? You said he and the two other emperors have been around for thousands of years. So he got what he wanted."

"Partly," I agreed. "But being a *minor* anything isn't enough for Caligula. He always dreamed of replacing one of the Olympians. He toyed with the idea of becoming the new Jupiter or Mars. In the end, he set his sights on being"—I swallowed the sour taste from my mouth—"the new me."

Coach Hedge scratched his goatee. (Hmm. If a goat wears a goatee, is it a man-tee?) "So, what? Caligula kills you, puts on a *Hi, I'm Apollo!* name tag, and walks into Olympus hoping nobody notices?"

"It would be worse than killing me," I said. "He would *consume* my essence, along with the essence of Helios, to make himself the new sun god."

Prickly Pear bristled. "The other Olympians would just *allow* this?"

"The Olympians," I said bitterly, "allowed Zeus to strip me of my powers and toss me to earth. They've done half of Caligula's job *for* him. They won't interfere. As usual, they'll expect heroes to set things right. If Caligula *does* become the new sun god, I will be gone. Permanently gone. That's what Medea has been preparing for with the Burning Maze. It's a giant cooking pot for sun-god soup."

Meg wrinkled her nose. "Gross."

For once, I was in total agreement with her.

Standing in the shadows, Joshua Tree crossed his arms. "So the fires of Helios—that's what's killing our land?"

I spread my hands. "Well, humans aren't helping. But

on top of the usual pollution and climate change, yes, the Burning Maze was the tipping point. Everything that's left of the Titan Helios is now coursing through this section of the Labyrinth under Southern California, slowly turning the top side into a fiery wasteland."

Agave touched the side of her scarred face. When she looked up at me, her stare was as pointed as her collar. "If Medea succeeds, will all the power go into Caligula? Will the maze stop burning and killing us?"

I had never considered cacti a particularly vicious life-form, but as the other dryads studied me, I could imagine them tying me up with a ribbon and a large card that said FOR CALIGULA, FROM NATURE and dropping me on the emperor's doorstep.

"Guys, that won't help," Grover said. "Caligula's responsible for what's happening to us right now. He doesn't care about nature spirits. You really want to give him the full power of a sun god?"

The dryads muttered in reluctant agreement. I made a mental note to send Grover a nice card on Goat Appreciation Day.

"So what do we do?" asked Mellie. "I don't want my son growing up in a burning wasteland."

Meg took off her glasses. "We kill Caligula."

It was jarring, hearing a twelve-year-old girl speak so matter-of-factly about assassination. Even more jarring, I was tempted to agree with her.

"Meg," I said, "that may not be possible. You remember Commodus. He was the weakest of the three emperors, and the best we could do was force him out of Indianapolis. Caligula will be much more powerful, more deeply entrenched."

"Don't care," she muttered. "He hurt my dad. He did . . . all this." She gestured around at the old cistern.

"What do you mean *all this?*" Joshua asked.

Meg shot a look at me as if to say *Your turn.*

Once again, I explained what I had seen in Meg's memories—Aeithales as it had once been, the legal and financial pressure Caligula must have used to shut down Phillip McCaffrey's work, the way Meg and her father had been forced to flee just before the house was firebombed.

Joshua frowned. "I remember a saguaro named Hercules from the first greenhouse. One of the few who survived the house fire. Old, tough dryad, always in pain from his burns, but he kept clinging to life. He used to talk about a little girl who lived in the house. He said he was waiting for her to return." Joshua turned to Meg in amazement. "That was *you?*"

Meg brushed a tear from her cheek. "He didn't make it?"

Josh shook his head. "He died a few years ago. I'm sorry."

Agave took Meg's hand. "Your father was a great hero," she said. "Clearly, he was doing his best to help plants."

"He was a . . . botanist," Meg said, pronouncing the word as if she'd just remembered it.

The dryads lowered their heads. Hedge and Grover removed their hats.

"I wonder what your dad's big project was," Piper said, "with those glowing seeds. What did Medea call you . . . a descendant of Plemnaeus?"

The dryads let out a collective gasp.

"Plemnaeus?" asked Reba. "*The* Plemnaeus? Even in Argentina, we know of him!"

I stared at her. "You do?"

Prickly Pear snorted. "Oh, come on, Apollo! You're a god. Surely you know of the great hero Plemnaeus!"

"Um . . ." I was tempted to blame my faulty mortal memory, but I was pretty sure I had never heard the name, even when I was a god. "What monster did he slay?"

Aloe edged away from me, as if she did not want to be in the line of fire when the other dryads shot their spines at me.

"Apollo," Reba chided, "a healer god should know better."

"Er, of course," I agreed. "But, um, who exactly—?"

"Typical," Pear muttered. "The killers are remembered as heroes. The growers are forgotten. Except by us nature spirits."

"Plemnaeus was a Greek king," Agave explained. "A noble man, but his children were born under a curse. If any of them cried even once during their infancy, they would die instantly."

I wasn't sure how that made Plemnaeus noble, but I nodded politely. "What happened?"

"He appealed to Demeter," said Joshua. "The goddess herself raised his next son, Orthopolis, so that he would live. In gratitude, Plemnaeus built a temple to Demeter. Ever since, his offspring have dedicated themselves to Demeter's work. They have always been great agriculturalists and botanists."

Agave squeezed Meg's hand. "I understand now why your father was able to build Aeithales. His work must have been special indeed. Not only did he come from a long line of Demeter's heroes, he attracted the personal attention of the goddess, your mother. We are honored that you've come home."

"Home," agreed Prickly Pear.

"Home," Joshua echoed.

Meg blinked back tears.

This seemed like an excellent time for a song circle. I imagined the dryads putting their spiky arms around one another and swaying as they sang "In the Garden." I was even willing to provide ukulele music.

Coach Hedge brought us back to harsh reality.

"That's great." He gave Meg a respectful nod. "Kid, your dad must have been something. But unless he was growing some kind of secret weapon, I don't know how it helps us. We've still got an emperor to kill and a maze to destroy."

"Gleeson . . ." Mellie chided.

"Hey, am I wrong?"

No one challenged him.

Grover stared disconsolately at his hooves. "What do we do, then?"

"We stick to the plan," I said. The certainty in my voice seemed to surprise everyone. It definitely surprised me. "We find the Sibyl of Erythraea. She's more than just bait. She's the key to everything. I'm sure of it."

Piper cradled Baby Chuck as he grabbed for her harpy feather. "Apollo, we tried navigating the maze. You saw what happened."

"Jason Grace made it through," I said. "He found the Oracle."

Piper's expression darkened. "Maybe. But even if you believe Medea, Jason only found the Oracle because Medea *wanted* him to."

"She mentioned there was another way to navigate the maze," I said. "The emperor's shoes. Apparently, they let Caligula walk through safely. We need those shoes. That's what the prophecy meant: *walk the path in thine own enemy's boots*."

Meg wiped her nose. "So you're saying we need to find Caligula's place and steal his shoes. While we're there, can't we just kill him?"

She asked this casually, like *Can we stop by Target on the way home?*

Hedge wagged his finger at McCaffrey. "See, now *that's* a plan. I like this girl."

"Friends," I said, wishing I had some of Piper's charm-speaking skills, "Caligula's been alive for thousands of years. He's a minor god. We don't know *how* to kill him so he stays dead. We also don't know how to destroy the maze, and we certainly don't want to make things worse by unleashing all that godly heat into the upper world. Our priority has to be the Sibyl."

"Because it's *your* priority?" Pear grumbled.

I resisted the urge to yell *Duh!*

"Either way," I said, "to learn the emperor's location, we need to consult Jason Grace. Medea told us the Oracle gave him information on how to find Caligula. Piper, will you take us to Jason?"

Piper frowned. Baby Chuck had her finger in his tiny fist and was moving it dangerously close to his mouth.

"Jason's living at a boarding school in Pasadena," she said at last. "I don't know if he'll listen to me. I don't know if he'll help. But we can try. My friend Annabeth always says information is the most powerful weapon."

Grover nodded. "I never argue with Annabeth."

"It's settled, then," I said. "Tomorrow we continue our quest by busting Jason Grace out of school."

21

When life gives you seeds
Plant them in dry rocky soil
I'm an optimist

I SLEPT POORLY.

Are you shocked? I was shocked.

I dreamed of my most famous Oracle, Delphi, though alas, it was not during the good old days when I would have been welcomed with flowers, kisses, candy, and my usual VIP table at Chez Oracle.

Instead, it was modern Delphi—devoid of priests and worshippers, filled instead with the hideous stench of Python, my old enemy, who had reclaimed his ancient lair. His rotten-egg/rancid-meat smell was impossible to forget.

I stood deep in the caverns, where no mortal ever trod. In the distance, two voices conversed, their bodies lost in the swirling volcanic vapors.

"It's under control," said the first, in the high nasal tones of Emperor Nero.

The second speaker growled, a sound like a chain pulling an ancient roller coaster uphill.

"Very little has been *under control* since Apollo fell to earth," said Python.

His cold voice sent ripples of revulsion through my

body. I couldn't see him, but I could imagine his baleful amber eyes flecked with gold, his enormous dragon form, his wicked claws.

"You have a great opportunity," Python continued. "Apollo is weak. He is mortal. He is accompanied by your own stepdaughter. How is it that he is not yet dead?"

Nero's voice tightened. "We had a difference of opinion, my colleagues and I. Commodus—"

"Is a fool," Python hissed, "who only cares about spectacle. We both know that. And your great-uncle, Caligula?"

Nero hesitated. "He insisted . . . He has need of Apollo's power. He wants the former god to meet his fate in a very, ah, particular way."

Python's massive bulk shifted in the darkness—I heard his scales rubbing against the stone. "I know Caligula's plan. I wonder who is controlling whom? You have assured me—"

"Yes," Nero snapped. "Meg McCaffrey *will* come back to me. She will serve me yet. Apollo will die, as I promised."

"If Caligula succeeds," Python mused, "then the balance of power will change. I would prefer to back *you*, of course, but if a new sun god rises in the west—"

"You and I have a deal," Nero snarled. "You support me once the Triumvirate controls—"

"—all means of prophecy," Python agreed. "But it does not as yet. You lost Dodona to the Greek demigods. The Cave of Trophonius has been destroyed. I understand the Romans have been alerted to Caligula's plans for Camp Jupiter. I have no wish to rule the world alone. But if you fail me, if I have to kill Apollo myself—"

"I will hold up my side of the bargain," Nero said. "You hold up yours."

Python rasped in an evil approximation of a laugh. "We will see. The next few days should be very instructive."

I woke with a gasp.

I found myself alone and shivering in the Cistern. Piper's and Meg's sleeping bags were empty. Above, the sky shone a brilliant blue. I wanted to believe this meant the wildfires had been brought under control. More likely it meant the winds had simply shifted.

My skin had healed overnight, though I still felt like I'd been dipped in liquid aluminum. With a minimum of grimacing and yelping, I managed to get dressed, get my bow, quiver, and ukulele, and climb the ramp to the hillside.

I spotted Piper at the base of the hill, talking with Grover at the Bedrossian-mobile. I scanned the ruins and saw Meg crouching by the first collapsed greenhouse.

Thinking of my dream, I burned with anger. Had I still been a god, I would have roared my displeasure and cracked a new Grand Canyon across the desert. As it was, I could only clench my fists until my nails cut my palms.

It was bad enough that a trio of evil emperors wanted my Oracles, my life, my very essence. It was bad enough that my ancient enemy Python had retaken Delphi and was waiting for my death. But the idea of Nero using Meg as a pawn in this game . . . No. I told myself I would never let Nero get Meg in his clutches again. My young friend was strong. She was striving to break free of her stepfather's vile influence. She and I had been through too much together for her to go back.

Still, Nero's words unsettled me: *Meg McCaffrey will come back to me. She will serve me yet.*

I wondered . . . if my own father, Zeus, appeared to me just then and offered me a way back to Olympus, what price would I be willing to pay? Would I leave Meg to her fate? Would I abandon the demigods and satyrs and dryads who had become my comrades? Would I forget about all the terrible things Zeus had done to me over the centuries and swallow my pride, just so I could regain my place in Olympus, knowing full well I would still be under Zeus's thumb?

I tamped down those questions. I wasn't sure I wanted to know the answers.

I joined Meg at the collapsed greenhouse. "Good morning."

She did not look up. She'd been digging through the wreckage. Half-melted polycarbonate walls had been turned over and tossed aside. Her hands were dirty from clawing at the soil. Near her sat a grimy glass peanut butter jar, the rusty lid removed and lying next to it. Cupped in her palm were some greenish pebbles.

I sucked in my breath.

No, they weren't pebbles. In Meg's hand lay seven coin-size hexagons—green seeds exactly like the ones in the memories she'd shared.

"How?" I asked.

She glanced up. She wore teal camouflage today, which made her look like an entirely different dangerous and scary little girl. Someone had cleaned her glasses (Meg never did), so I could see her eyes. They glinted as hard and clear as the rhinestones in her frames.

"The seeds were buried," she said. "I . . . had a dream about them. The saguaro Hercules did it, put them in that jar right before he died. He was saving the seeds . . . for me, for when it was time."

I wasn't sure what to say. *Congratulations. What nice seeds*. Honestly, I didn't know much about how plants grew. I did notice, however, that the seeds weren't glowing as they had in Meg's memories.

"Do you think they're still, uh, good?" I asked.

"Going to find out," she said. "Going to plant them."

I looked around at the desert hillside. "You mean here? Now?"

"Yep. It's time."

How could she know that? I also didn't see how planting a few seeds would make a difference when Caligula's maze was causing half of California to burn.

On the other hand, we were off on another quest today, hoping to find Caligula's palace, with no guarantee we would come back alive. I supposed there was no time like the present. And if it made Meg feel better, why not?

"How can I help?" I asked.

"Poke holes." Then she added, as if I might need extra guidance, "In the dirt."

I accomplished this with an arrow tip, making seven small impressions in the barren, rocky soil. I couldn't help thinking that these seed holes didn't look like very comfortable places to grow.

While Meg placed her green hexagons in their new homes, she directed me to get water from the Cistern's well.

"It has to be from there," she warned. "A big cupful."

A few minutes later I returned with a Big Hombre–size plastic cup from Enchiladas del Rey. Meg drizzled the water over her newly planted friends.

I waited for something dramatic to happen. In Meg's presence, I'd gotten used to chia seed explosions, demon peach babies, and instant walls of strawberries.

The dirt did not move.

"Guess we wait," Meg said.

She hugged her knees and scanned the horizon.

The morning sun blazed in the east. It had risen today, as always, but no thanks to me. It didn't care if I was driving the sun chariot, or if Helios was raging in the tunnels under Los Angeles. No matter what humans believed, the cosmos kept turning, and the sun stayed on course. Under different circumstances, I would have found that reassuring. Now I found the sun's indifference both cruel and insulting. In only a few days, Caligula might become a solar deity. Under such villainous leadership, you might think the sun would refuse to rise or set. But shockingly, disgustingly, day and night would continue as they always had.

"Where is she?" Meg asked.

I blinked. "Who?"

"If my family is so important to her, thousands of years of blessings, or whatever, why hasn't she ever . . . ?"

She waved at the vast desert, as if to say *So much real estate, so little Demeter*.

She was asking why her mother had never appeared

to her, why Demeter had allowed Caligula to destroy her father's work, why she'd let Nero raise her in his poisonous imperial household in New York.

I couldn't answer Meg's questions. Or rather, as a former god, I could think of several possible answers, but none that would make Meg feel better: *Demeter was too busy watching the crop situation in Tanzania. Demeter got distracted inventing new breakfast cereals. Demeter forgot you existed.*

"I don't know, Meg," I admitted. "But this . . ." I pointed at the seven tiny wet circles in the dirt. "This is the sort of thing your mother would be proud of. Growing plants in an impossible place. Stubbornly insisting on creating life. It's ridiculously optimistic. Demeter would approve."

Meg studied me as if trying to decide whether to thank me or hit me. I'd gotten used to that look.

"Let's go," she decided. "Maybe the seeds will sprout while we're gone."

The three of us piled into the Bedrossian-mobile: Meg, Piper, and me.

Grover had decided to stay behind—supposedly to rally the demoralized dryads, but I think he was simply exhausted from his series of near-death excursions with Meg and me. Coach Hedge volunteered to accompany us, but Mellie quickly un-volunteered him. As for the dryads, none seemed anxious to be our plant shields after what had happened to Money Maker and Agave. I couldn't blame them.

At least Piper agreed to drive. If we got pulled over for possession of a stolen vehicle, she could charmspeak her way out of being arrested. With my luck, I would spend all day in jail, and Lester's face would *not* look good in a mug shot.

We retraced our route from yesterday—the same heat-blasted terrain, the same smoke-stained skies, the same clogged traffic. Living the California dream.

None of us felt much like talking. Piper kept her eyes fixed on the road, probably thinking about a reunion she did not want with an ex-boyfriend she had left on awkward terms. (Oh, boy, I could relate.)

Meg traced the swirls on her teal camo pants. I imagined she was reflecting on her father's final botany project and why Caligula had found it so threatening. It seemed unbelievable that Meg's entire life had been altered by seven green seeds. Then again, she was a child of Demeter. With the goddess of plants, insignificant-looking things could be very significant.

The smallest seedlings, Demeter often told me, *grow into century oaks*.

As for me, I had no shortage of problems to think about.

Python awaited. I knew instinctively that I would have to face him one day. If by some miracle I survived the emperors' various plots on my life, if I defeated the Triumvirate and freed the four other Oracles and single-handedly set everything right in the mortal world, I would *still* have to find a way to wrest control of Delphi from my most ancient enemy. Only then might Zeus let me become a god again. Because Zeus was just that awesome. Thanks, Dad.

In the meantime, I had to deal with Caligula. I would have to foil his plan to make me the secret ingredient in his sun-god soup. And I would have to do this while having no godly powers at my disposal. My archery skills had deteriorated. My singing and playing weren't worth olive pits. Divine strength? Charisma? Light? Fire power? All gauges read EMPTY.

My most humiliating thought: Medea would capture me, try to strip away my divine power, and find I didn't have any left.

What is this? she would scream. *There's nothing here but Lester!*

Then she would kill me anyway.

As I contemplated these happy possibilities, we wound our way through the Pasadena Valley.

"I've never liked this city," I murmured. "It makes me think of game shows, tawdry parades, and drunk washed-up starlets with spray-on tans."

Piper coughed. "FYI, Jason's mom was from here. She died here, in a car accident."

"I'm sorry. What did she do?"

"She was a drunk washed-up starlet with a spray-on tan."

"Ah." I waited for the sting of embarrassment to fade. It took several miles. "So why would Jason want to go to school here?"

Piper gripped the wheel. "After we broke up, he transferred to an all-boys boarding school up in the hills. You'll see. I guess he wanted something different, something quiet and out-of-the-way. No drama."

"He'll be happy to see *us*, then," Meg muttered, staring out the window.

We made our way into the hills above town, the houses getting more and more impressive as we gained altitude.

Even in Mansion Land, though, trees had started to die. Manicured lawns were turning brown around the edges. When water shortages and above-average temperatures affected the upscale neighborhoods, you *knew* things were serious. The rich and the gods were always the last to suffer.

At the crest of a hill stood Jason's school—a sprawling campus of blond-brick buildings interlaced with garden courtyards and walkways shaded by acacia trees. The sign in front, done in subtle bronze letters on a low brick wall, read: EDGARTON DAY AND BOARDING SCHOOL.

We parked the Escalade on a nearby residential street, using the Piper McLean if-it's-towed-we'll-just-borrow-another-car strategy.

A security guard stood at the front gates of the school, but Piper told him we were allowed to go inside, and the guard, with a look of great confusion, agreed that we were allowed to go inside.

The classrooms all opened onto the courtyards. Student lockers lined the breezeways. It was not a school design that would have worked in, say, Milwaukee during blizzard season, but in Southern California it spoke to just how much the locals took their mild, consistent weather for granted. I doubted the buildings even had air-conditioning. If Caligula continued cooking gods in his Burning Maze, the Edgarton school board might have to rethink that.

Despite Piper's insistence that she had distanced herself from Jason's life, she had his schedule memorized. She led us right to his fourth-period classroom. Peering through the windows, I saw a dozen students—all young men in blue blazers, dress shirts, red ties, gray slacks, and shiny shoes, like junior business executives. At the front of the class, in a director's chair, a bearded teacher in a tweed suit was reading from a paperback copy of *Julius Caesar*.

Ugh. Bill Shakespeare. I mean, yes, he was good. But even *he* would've been horrified at the number of hours mortals spent drilling his plays into the heads of bored teenagers, and the sheer number of pipes, tweed jackets, marble busts, and bad dissertations even his *least* favorite plays had inspired. Meanwhile, Christopher Marlowe got the short end of the Elizabethan stick. Kit had been *much* more gorgeous.

But I digress.

Piper knocked on the door and poked her head in. Suddenly the young men no longer looked bored. Piper said something to the teacher, who blinked a few times, then waved *go ahead* to a young man in the middle row.

A moment later, Jason Grace joined us in the breezeway.

I had only seen him a few times before—once when he was a praetor at Camp Jupiter; once when he had visited Delos; then shortly afterward, when we had fought side by side against the giants at the Parthenon.

He'd fought well enough, but I can't say that I'd paid him any special attention. In those days, I was still a god. Jason was just another hero in the *Argo II*'s demigod crew.

Now, in his school uniform, he looked quite impressive. His blond hair was cropped short. His blue eyes flashed behind a pair of black-rimmed glasses. Jason closed the classroom door behind him, tucked his books under his arm, and forced a smile, a little white scar twitching at the corner of his lip. "Piper. Hey."

I wondered how Piper managed to look so calm. I'd gone through many complicated breakups. They never got easier, and Piper didn't have the advantage of being able to turn her ex into a tree or simply wait until his short mortal life was over before returning to earth.

"Hey, yourself," she said, just a hint of strain in her voice. "This is—"

"Meg McCaffrey," Jason said. "And Apollo. I've been waiting for you guys."

He didn't sound terribly excited about it. He said it the way someone might say *I've been waiting for the results from my emergency brain scan*.

Meg sized up Jason as if she found his glasses far inferior to her own. "Yeah?"

"Yeah." Jason peered down the breezeway in each direction. "Let's go back to my dorm room. We're not safe out here."

22

For my school project
I made this pagan temple
Monopoly board

WE HAD TO GET PAST a teacher and two hall monitors, but thanks to Piper's charmspeak, they all agreed that it was perfectly normal for the four of us (including two females) to stroll into the dormitory during classroom hours.

Once we reached Jason's room, Piper stopped at the door. "Define *not safe*."

Jason peered over her shoulder. "Monsters have infiltrated the faculty. I'm keeping an eye on the humanities teacher. Pretty sure she's an empousa. I already had to slay my AP Calculus teacher, because he was a blemmyae."

Coming from a mortal, such talk would have been labeled homicidally paranoid. Coming from a demigod, it was a description of an average week.

"Blemmyae, huh?" Meg reappraised Jason, as if deciding that his glasses might not be so bad. "I hate blemmyae."

Jason smirked. "Come on in."

I would've called his room *spartan*, but I had seen the bedrooms of actual Spartans. They would have found Jason's dorm ridiculously comfortable.

The fifty-foot-square space had a bookcase, a bed, a desk, and a closet. The only luxury was an open window that looked out across the canyons, filling the room with the warm scent of hyacinth. (Did it *have* to be hyacinth? My heart always breaks when I smell that fragrance, even after thousands of years.)

On Jason's wall hung a framed picture of his sister Thalia smiling at the camera, a bow slung across her back, her short dark hair blown sideways by the wind. Except for her dazzling blue eyes, she looked nothing like her brother.

Then again, neither of them looked anything like me, and as the son of Zeus, I was technically their brother. And I had flirted with Thalia, which . . . Eww. Curse you, Father, for having so many children! It made dating a true minefield over the millennia.

"Your sister says hello, by the way," I said.

Jason's eyes brightened. "You saw her?"

I launched into an explanation of our time in Indianapolis: the Waystation, the emperor Commodus, the Hunters of Artemis rappelling into the football stadium to rescue us. Then I backed up and explained the Triumvirate, and all the miserable things that had happened to me since emerging from that Manhattan dumpster.

Meanwhile, Piper sat cross-legged on the floor, her back against the wall, as far as possible from the more comfortable sitting option of the bed. Meg stood at Jason's desk, examining some sort of school project—foam core studded with little plastic boxes, perhaps to represent buildings.

When I casually mentioned that Leo was alive and well

and presently on a mission to Camp Jupiter, all the electrical outlets in the room sparked. Jason looked at Piper, stunned.

"I know," she said. "After all we went through."

"I can't even . . ." Jason sat heavily on his bed. "I don't know whether to laugh or yell."

"Don't limit yourself," grumbled Piper. "Do both."

Meg called from the desk, "Hey, what is this?"

Jason flushed. "A personal project."

"It's Temple Hill," Piper offered, her tone carefully neutral. "At Camp Jupiter."

I took a closer look. Piper was right. I recognized the layout of the temples and shrines where Camp Jupiter demigods honored the ancient deities. Each building was represented by a small plastic box glued to the board, the names of the shrines hand-labeled on the foam core. Jason had even marked lines of elevation, showing the hill's topographical levels.

I found my temple: APOLLO, symbolized by a red plastic building. It was not nearly as nice as the real thing, with its golden roof and platinum filigree designs, but I didn't want to be critical.

"Are these Monopoly houses?" Meg asked.

Jason shrugged. "I kinda used whatever I had—the green houses and red hotels."

I squinted at the board. I hadn't descended in glory to Temple Hill for quite some time, but the display seemed more crowded than the actual hill. There were at least twenty small tokens I didn't recognize.

I leaned in and read some of the handwritten labels. "Kymopoleia? My goodness, I haven't thought about her in centuries! Why did the Romans build her a shrine?"

"They haven't yet," Jason said. "But I made her a promise. She . . . helped us out on our voyage to Athens."

The way he said that, I decided he meant *she agreed not to kill us*, which was much more in keeping with Kymopoleia's character.

"I told her I'd make sure none of the gods and goddesses were forgotten," Jason continued, "either at Camp Jupiter or Camp Half-Blood. I'd see to it they *all* had some sort of shrine at both camps."

Piper glanced at me. "He's done a ton of work on his designs. You should see his sketchbook."

Jason frowned, clearly unsure whether Piper was praising him or criticizing him. The smell of burning electricity thickened in the air.

"Well," he said at last, "the designs won't win any awards. I'll need Annabeth to help with the actual blueprints."

"Honoring the gods is a noble endeavor," I said. "You should be proud."

Jason did not look proud. He looked worried. I remembered what Medea had said about the Oracle's news: *The truth was enough to break Jason Grace*. He did not appear to be broken. Then again, I did not appear to be Apollo.

Meg leaned closer to the display. "How come Potina gets a house but Quirinus gets a hotel?"

"There's not really any logic to it," Jason admitted. "I just used the tokens to mark positions."

I frowned. I'd been fairly sure I'd gotten a hotel, as

opposed to Ares's house, because I was more important.

Meg tapped her mother's token. "Demeter is cool. You should put the cool gods next to her."

"Meg," I chided, "we can't arrange the gods by *coolness*. That would lead to too many fights."

Besides, I thought, *everyone would want to be next to me*. Then I wondered bitterly if that would still be true when and if I made it back to Olympus. Would my time as Lester mark me forever as an immortal dweeb?

"Anyway," Piper interrupted. "The reason we came: the Burning Maze."

She didn't accuse Jason of holding back information. She didn't tell him what Medea had said. She simply studied his face, waiting to see how he would respond.

Jason laced his fingers. He stared at the sheathed *gladius* propped against the wall next to a lacrosse stick and a tennis racket. (These fancy boarding schools really offered the full range of extracurricular options.)

"I didn't tell you everything," he admitted.

Piper's silence felt more powerful than her charmspeaking.

"I—I reached the Sibyl," Jason continued. "I can't even explain *how*. I just stumbled into this big room with a pool of fire. The Sibyl was . . . standing across from me, on this stone platform, her arms chained with some fiery shackles."

"Herophile," I said. "Her name is Herophile."

Jason blinked, as if he could still feel the heat and cinders of the room.

"I wanted to free her," he said. "Obviously. But she told me it wasn't possible. It had to be . . ." He gestured at me. "She told me it was a trap. The whole maze. For Apollo. She told me you'd eventually come find me. You and her—Meg. Herophile said there was nothing I could do except give you help if you asked for it. She said to tell you, Apollo—you have to rescue her."

I knew all this, of course. I had seen and heard as much in my dreams. But hearing it from Jason, in the waking world, made it worse.

Piper rested her head against the wall. She stared at a water stain on the ceiling. "What else did Herophile say?"

Jason's face tightened. "Pipes—Piper, look, I'm sorry I didn't tell you. It's just—"

"What else did she say?" Piper repeated.

Jason looked at Meg, then at me, maybe for moral support.

"The Sibyl told me where I could find the emperor," he said. "Well, more or less. She said Apollo would need the information. He would need . . . a pair of shoes. I know that doesn't make much sense."

"I'm afraid it does," I said.

Meg ran her fingers along the plastic rooftops of the map. "Can we kill the emperor while we're stealing his shoes? Did the Sibyl say anything about that?"

Jason shook his head. "She just said that Piper and I . . . we couldn't do anything more by ourselves. It had to be Apollo. If we tried . . . it would be too dangerous."

Piper laughed drily. She raised her hands as if making an offering to the water stain.

"Jason, we've been through literally *everything* together. I can't even count how many dangers we've faced, how many times we've almost died. Now you're telling me you lied to me to, what, protect me? To keep me from going after Caligula?"

"I knew you would have done it," he murmured. "No matter what the Sibyl said."

"Then that would've been *my* choice," Piper said. "Not yours."

He nodded miserably. "And I would've insisted on going with you, no matter the risk. But the way things have been between us . . ." He shrugged. "Working as a team has been hard. I thought—I decided to wait until Apollo found me. I messed up, not telling you. I'm sorry."

He stared at his Temple Hill display, as if trying to figure out where to place a shrine to the god of feeling horrible about failed relationships. (Oh, wait. He already had one. It was for Aphrodite, Piper's mom.)

Piper took a deep breath. "This isn't about you and me, Jason. Satyrs and dryads are dying. Caligula's planning to turn himself into a new sun god. Tonight's the new moon, and Camp Jupiter is facing some kind of huge threat. Meanwhile, Medea is in that maze, throwing around Titan fire—"

"*Medea?*" Jason sat up straight. The lightbulb in his desk lamp burst, raining glass across his diorama. "Back up. What's Medea got to do with this? What do you mean about the new moon and Camp Jupiter?"

I thought Piper might refuse to share the information, just for spite, but she didn't. She gave Jason the lowdown about the Indiana prophecy that predicted bodies filling the Tiber. Then she explained Medea's cooking project with her grandfather.

Jason looked like our father had just hit him with a thunderbolt. "I had no idea."

Meg crossed her arms. "So, you going to help us or what?"

Jason studied her, no doubt unsure what to make of this scary little girl in teal camouflage.

"Of—of course," he said. "We'll need a car. And I'll need an excuse to leave campus." He looked hopefully at Piper.

She got to her feet. "Fine. I'll go talk to the office. Meg, come with me, just in case we run into that empousa. We'll meet you boys at the front gate. And Jason—?"

"Yeah?"

"If you're holding anything else back—"

"Right. I—I get it."

Piper turned and marched out of the room. Meg gave me a look like *You sure about this?*

"Go on," I told her. "I'll help Jason get ready."

Once the girls had left, I turned to confront Jason Grace, one son of Zeus/Jupiter to another.

"All right," I said. "What did the Sibyl *really* tell you?"

23

It's a beautiful
Day in the neighborhood— Wait
Actually, it's not

JASON TOOK HIS TIME RESPONDING.

He removed his jacket, hung it in the closet. He undid his tie and folded it over the coat hook. I had a flashback to my old friend Fred Rogers, the children's television host, who radiated the same calm centeredness when hanging up his work clothes. Fred used to let me crash on his sofa whenever I'd had a hard day of poetry-godding. He'd offer me a plate of cookies and a glass of milk, then serenade me with his songs until I felt better. I was especially fond of "It's You I Like." Oh, I missed that mortal!

Finally, Jason strapped on his gladius. With his glasses, dress shirt, slacks, loafers, and sword, he looked less like Mister Rogers and more like a well-armed paralegal.

"What makes you think I'm holding back?" he asked.

"Please," I said. "Don't try to be evasively prophetic with the god of evasive prophecies."

Jason sighed. He rolled up his shirtsleeves, revealing the Roman tattoo on the inside of his forearm—the lightning bolt emblem of our father. "First of all, it wasn't exactly a prophecy. It was more like a series of quiz show questions."

"Yes. Herophile delivers information that way."

"And you know how prophecies are. Even when the Oracle is friendly, they can be hard to interpret."

"Jason . . ."

"Fine," he relented. "The Sibyl said . . . She told me if Piper and I went after the emperor, one of us would die."

Die. The word landed between us with a thud, like a large, gutted fish.

I waited for an explanation. Jason stared at his foam core Temple Hill as if trying to bring it to life by sheer force of will.

"Die," I repeated.

"Yeah."

"Not *disappear*, not *wouldn't come back*, not *suffer defeat*."

"Nope. *Die*. Or more accurately, *three letters, starts with* D."

"Not *dad*, then," I suggested. "Or *dog*."

One fine blond eyebrow crept above the rim of his glasses. "*If you seek out the emperor, one of you will dog?* No, Apollo, the word was *die*."

"Still, that could mean many things. It could mean a trip to the Underworld. It could mean a death such as Leo suffered, where you pop right back to life. It could mean—"

"Now *you're* being evasive," Jason said. "The Sibyl meant death. Final. Real. No replays. You had to be there. The way she said it. Unless you happen to have an extra vial of the physician's cure in your pockets . . ."

He knew very well I did not. The physician's cure, which had brought Leo Valdez back to life, was only available from my son Asclepius, god of medicine. And since Asclepius wanted to avoid an all-out war with Hades, he rarely gave out free samples. As in never. Leo had been the first lucky recipient in four thousand years. He would likely be the last.

"Still . . ." I fumbled for alternate theories and loopholes. I hated thinking of permanent death. As an immortal, I was a conscientious objector. As good as your afterlife experience might be (and most of them were *not* good), life was better. The warmth of the actual sun, the vibrant colors of the upper world, the cuisine . . . really, even Elysium had nothing to compare.

Jason's stare was unrelenting. I suspected that in the weeks since his talk with Herophile, he had run every scenario. He was well past the *bargaining* stage in dealing with this prophecy. He had accepted that death meant death, the way Piper McLean had accepted that Oklahoma meant Oklahoma.

I didn't like that. Jason's calmness again reminded me of Fred Rogers, but in an exasperating way. How could anyone be so accepting and levelheaded all the time? Sometimes I just wanted him to get mad, to scream and throw his loafers across the room.

"Let's assume you're correct," I said. "You didn't tell Piper the truth because—?"

"You know what happened to her dad." Jason studied the calluses on his hands, proof he had not let his sword skills atrophy. "Last year when we saved him from the fire giant on Mount Diablo . . . Mr. McLean's mind wasn't in good shape. Now, with all the stress of the bankruptcy and everything else, can you imagine what would happen if he lost his daughter too?"

I recalled the disheveled movie star wandering his driveway, searching for imaginary coins. "Yes, but you can't *know* how the prophecy will unfold."

"I can't let it unfold with Piper dying. She and her dad are scheduled to leave town at the end of the week. She's actually . . . I don't know if *excited* is the right word, but she's relieved to get out of LA. Ever since I've known her, the thing she's wanted most is more time with her dad. Now they have a chance to start over. She can help her dad find some peace. Maybe find some peace herself."

His voice caught—perhaps with guilt, or regret, or fear.

"You wanted to get her safely out of town," I deduced. "Then you planned to find the emperor yourself."

Jason shrugged. "Well, with you and Meg. I knew you'd be coming to find me. Herophile said so. If you'd just waited another week—"

"Then what?" I demanded. "You would've let us lead you cheerily off to your death? How would *that* have affected Piper's peace of mind, once she found out?"

Jason's ears reddened. It struck me just how young he was—no more than seventeen. Older than my mortal form, yes, but not by much. This young man had lost his mother. He had survived the harsh training of Lupa the wolf goddess. He'd grown up with the discipline of the Twelfth Legion at Camp Jupiter. He'd fought Titans and giants. He'd helped save the world at least twice. But by mortal standards, he was barely an adult. He wasn't old enough to vote or drink.

Despite all his experiences, was it fair of me to expect him to think logically, and consider everyone else's feelings with perfect clarity, while pondering his own death?

I tried to soften my tone. "You don't want Piper to die. I understand that. She wouldn't want *you* to die. But avoiding prophecies never works. And keeping secrets from friends, especially deadly secrets . . . that *really* never works. It'll be our job to face Caligula together, steal that homicidal maniac's shoes, and get away *without* any five-letter words that start with *D*."

The scar ticked at the corner of Jason's mouth. "Donut?"

"You're horrible," I said, but some of the tension dissolved between my shoulder blades. "Are you ready?"

He glanced at the photo of his sister Thalia, then at the model of Temple Hill. "If anything happens to me—"

"Stop."

"If it does, if I can't keep my promise to Kymopoleia, would you take my mock-up design to Camp Jupiter? The sketchbooks for new temples at both camps—they're right there on the shelf."

"You'll take them yourself," I insisted. "Your new shrines will honor the gods. It's too worthy a project not to succeed."

He picked a shard of lightbulb glass off the roof of the Zeus hotel token. "*Worthy* doesn't always matter. Like what happened to you. Have you talked to Dad since . . . ?"

He had the decency not to elaborate: *Since you landed in the garbage as a flabby sixteen-year-old with no redeeming qualities*.

I swallowed back the taste of copper. From the depths

of my small mortal mind, my father's words rumbled: *YOUR FAULT. YOUR PUNISHMENT.*

"Zeus hasn't spoken to me since I became mortal," I said. "Before that, my memory is fuzzy. I remember the battle last summer at the Parthenon. I remember Zeus zapping me. After that, until the moment I woke up plummeting through the sky in January—it's a blank."

"I know *that* feeling, having six months of your life taken away." He gave me a pained look. "I'm sorry I couldn't do more."

"What could you have done?"

"I mean at the Parthenon. I tried to talk sense into Zeus. I told him he was wrong to punish you. He wouldn't listen."

I stared at him blankly, whatever remained of my natural eloquence clogged in my throat. Jason Grace had done *what*?

Zeus had many children, which meant I had many half brothers and half sisters. Except for my twin, Artemis, I'd never felt close to any of them. Certainly, I'd *never* had a brother defend me in front of Father. My Olympian brethren were more likely to deflect Zeus's fury by yelling *Apollo did it!*

This young demigod had stood up for me. He'd had no reason to do so. He barely knew me. Yet he'd risked his own life and faced the wrath of Zeus.

My first thought was to scream *ARE YOU INSANE?*

Then more appropriate words came to me. "Thank you."

Jason took me by the shoulders—not out of anger, or in a clinging way, but as a brother. "Promise me one thing. Whatever happens, when you get back to Olympus, when you're a god again, *remember*. Remember what it's like to be human."

A few weeks ago, I would have scoffed. *Why would I want to remember any of this?*

At best, if I were lucky enough to reclaim my divine throne, I would recall this wretched experience like a scary B-movie that had finally ended. I would walk out of the cinema into the sunlight, thinking *Phew! Glad that's over*.

Now, however, I had some inkling of what Jason meant. I had learned a lot about human frailty and human strength. I felt . . . different toward mortals, having been one of them. If nothing else, it would provide me with some excellent inspiration for new song lyrics!

I was reluctant to promise anything, though. I was already living under the curse of *one* broken oath. At Camp Half-Blood, I had rashly sworn on the River Styx not to use my archery or music skills until I was a god again. Then I had quickly reneged. Ever since, my skills had deteriorated.

I was sure the vengeful spirit of the River Styx wasn't done with me. I could almost feel her scowling at me from the Underworld: *What right do you have to promise anything to anyone, oath-breaker?*

But how could I not try? It was the least I could do for this brave mortal who had stood up for me when no one else would.

"I promise," I told Jason. "I will try my utmost to remember my human experience, as long as *you* promise to tell Piper the truth about the prophecy."

Jason patted my shoulders. "Deal. Speaking of which, the girls are probably waiting."

"One more thing," I blurted out. "About Piper. It's just . . . you seem like such a good power couple. Did you really—did you break up with her to make it easier for her to leave LA?"

Jason stared at me with those azure eyes. "Did she tell you that?"

"No," I admitted. "But Mellie seemed, ah, *upset* with you."

Jason considered. "I'm okay with Mellie blaming me. It's probably better."

"Do you mean it's not true?"

In Jason's eyes, I saw just a hint of desolation—like wildfire smoke momentarily obliterating a blue sky. I remembered Medea's words: *The truth was enough to break Jason Grace.*

"Piper ended it," he said quietly. "That was months ago, way before the Burning Maze. Now, come on. Let's go find Caligula."

24

Ah, Santa Barbara!
Famed for surfing! Fish tacos!
And crazy Romans!

ALAS FOR US AND MR. BEDROSSIAN, there was no sign of the Cadillac Escalade on the street where we'd parked.

"We've been towed," Piper announced casually, as if this was a regular occurrence for her.

She returned to the school's front office. A few minutes later, she emerged from the front gates driving Edgarton's green-and-gold van.

She rolled down the window. "Hey, kids. Want to go on a field trip?"

As we pulled away, Jason glanced nervously in the passenger-side rearview mirror, perhaps worried the security guard would give chase and demand we get signed permission slips before leaving campus to kill a Roman emperor. But no one followed us.

"Where to?" Piper asked when we reached the highway.

"Santa Barbara," Jason said.

Piper frowned, as if this answer was only slightly more surprising than *Uzbekistan*. "Okay."

She followed the signs for Highway 101 West.

For once, I hoped traffic would be jammed. I was not in a hurry to see Caligula. Instead, the roads were nearly empty. It was like the Southern California freeway system had heard me complaining and was now out for revenge.

Oh, go right ahead, Apollo! Highway 101 seemed to say. *We estimate an easy commute to your humiliating death!*

Next to me in the backseat, Meg drummed her fingers on her knees. "How much farther?"

I was only vaguely familiar with Santa Barbara. I hoped Jason would tell us it was far away—just past the North Pole, maybe. Not that I wanted to be stuck in a van with Meg that long, but at least then we could stop by Camp Jupiter and pick up a squadron of heavily armed demigods.

"About two hours," Jason said, dashing my hopes. "Northwest, along the coast. We're going to Stearns Wharf."

Piper turned to him. "You've been there?"

"I . . . Yeah. Just scouting the place with Tempest."

"Tempest?" I asked.

"His horse," Piper said, then to Jason: "You went scouting there alone?"

"Well, Tempest is a ventus," Jason said, ignoring Piper's question.

Meg stopped drumming her knees. "Like those windy things Medea had?"

"Except Tempest is friendly," Jason said. "I kind of . . . not tamed him, exactly, but we made friends. He'll show up when I call, usually, and let me ride him."

"A wind horse." Meg pondered the idea, no doubt weighing its merits against her own demonic diaper-wearing peach baby. "I guess that's cool."

"Back to the question," Piper said. "Why did you decide to scout Stearns Wharf?"

Jason looked so uncomfortable I feared he might blow out the van's electrical systems.

"The Sibyl," he said at last. "She told me I would find Caligula there. It's one of the places where he stops."

Piper tilted her head. "Where he *stops*?"

"His palace isn't a palace, exactly," Jason said. "We're looking for a boat."

My stomach dropped out and took the nearest exit back toward Palm Springs. "Ah," I said.

"*Ah?*" Meg asked. "Ah, what?"

"Ah, that makes sense," I said. "In ancient times, Caligula was notorious for his pleasure barges—huge floating palaces with bathhouses, theaters, rotating statues, racetracks, thousands of slaves. . . ."

I remembered how disgusted Poseidon had been, watching Caligula tootle around the Bay of Baiae, though I think Poseidon was just jealous *his* palace didn't have rotating statues.

"Anyway," I said, "that explains why you've had trouble locating him. He can move from harbor to harbor at will."

"Yeah," Jason agreed. "When I scouted, he wasn't there. I guess the Sibyl meant I'd find him at Stearns Wharf when I was *supposed* to find him. Which, I guess, is today." He shifted in his seat, leaning as far away as possible from Piper. "Speaking of the Sibyl . . . there's another detail I didn't share with you about the prophecy."

He told Piper the truth about the three-letter word that began with *D* and was not *dog*.

She took the news surprisingly well. She did not hit him. She didn't raise her voice. She merely listened, then remained silent for another mile or so.

At last, she shook her head. "That's quite a detail."

"I should've told you," Jason said.

"Um, yeah." She twisted the steering wheel exactly the way one would break the neck of a chicken. "Still . . . if I'm being honest? In your position, I might've done the same thing. I wouldn't want you to die either."

Jason blinked. "Does that mean you're not mad?"

"I'm furious."

"Oh."

"Furious, but also empathetic."

"Right."

It struck me how easily they talked together, even about difficult things, and how well they seemed to understand each other. I remembered Piper saying how frantic she'd been when she got separated from Jason in the Burning Maze—how she couldn't bear to lose another friend.

I wondered again what was behind their breakup.

People change, Piper had said.

Full points for vagueness, girl, but I wanted the *dirt*.

"So," she said. "Any other surprises? Any more tiny details you forgot?"

Jason shook his head. "I think that's it."

"Okay," Piper said. "Then we go to the wharf. We find this boat. We find Caligula's magic booties, and we kill him if we get the chance. But we *don't* let each other die."

"Or let *me* die," Meg added. "Or even Apollo."

"Thank you, Meg," I said. "My heart is as warm as a partially thawed burrito."

"No problem." She picked her nose, just in case she died and never got another chance. "How do we know which is the right boat?"

"I have a feeling we'll know," I said. "Caligula was never subtle."

"Assuming the boat is there this time," Jason said.

"It'd better be," said Piper. "Otherwise I stole this van and got you out of your afternoon physics lecture for nothing."

"Darn," Jason said.

They shared a guarded smile, a sort of *Yes, things are still weird between us, but I don't intend on letting you die today* look.

I hoped our expedition would go as smoothly as Piper had described. I suspected our odds were better of winning the Mount Olympus Mega-God Lottery. (The most I ever got was five drachmas on a scratcher card once.)

We drove in silence along the seaside highway.

To our left, the Pacific glittered. Surfers plied the waves. Palm trees bent in the breeze. To our left, the hills were dry and brown, littered with the red flowers of heat-distressed azaleas. Try as I might, I could not help thinking of those crimson swathes as the spilled blood of dryads, fallen in battle. I remembered our cactus friends back at the Cistern, bravely and stubbornly clinging to life. I remembered Money Maker, broken and burned in the maze under Los Angeles. For their sake, I *had* to stop Caligula. Otherwise . . . No. There could be no *otherwise*.

Finally, we reached Santa Barbara, and I saw why Caligula might like the place.

If I squinted, I could imagine I was back in the Roman resort town of Baiae. The curve of the coastline was almost the same—as well as the golden beaches, the hills dotted with upscale stucco and red-tiled homes, the pleasure craft moored in the harbor. The locals even had the same sun-baked, pleasantly dazed expressions, as if they were biding their time between morning surf sessions and afternoon golf.

The biggest difference: Mount Vesuvius did not rise in the distance. But I had a feeling another presence loomed over this lovely little town—just as dangerous and volcanic.

"He'll be here," I said, as we parked the van on Cabrillo Boulevard.

Piper arched her eyebrows. "Are you sensing a disturbance in the Force?"

"Please," I muttered. "I'm sensing my usual bad luck. In a place this harmless-looking, there's no way we will *not* find trouble."

We spent the afternoon canvassing the Santa Barbara waterfront, from the East Beach to the breakwater jetties. We disrupted a flock of pelicans in the saltwater marsh. We woke some napping sea lions on the fishing dock. We jostled through roving hordes of tourists on Stearns Wharf. In the harbor, we found a virtual forest of single-mast boats, along with some luxury yachts, but none seemed large or gaudy enough for a Roman emperor.

Jason even flew over the water for aerial reconnaissance.

When he came back, he reported no suspicious vessels on the horizon.

"Were you on your horse, Tempest, just then?" Meg asked. "I couldn't tell."

Jason smiled. "Nah, I don't call Tempest unless it's an emergency. I was just flying around on my own, manipulating the wind."

Meg pouted, considering the pockets of her gardening belt. "I can summon yams."

At last we gave up searching and grabbed a table at a beachside café. The grilled fish tacos were worthy of an ode by the Muse Euterpe herself.

"I don't mind giving up," I admitted, spooning some spicy seviche into my mouth, "if it comes with dinner."

"This is just a break," Meg warned. "Don't get comfortable."

I wished she hadn't phrased that as an order. It made it difficult for me to sit still for the rest of my meal.

We sat at the café, enjoying the breeze, the food, and the iced tea until the sun dipped to the horizon, turning the sky Camp Half-Blood orange. I allowed myself to hope that I'd been mistaken about Caligula's presence. We'd come here in vain. Hooray! I was about to suggest heading back to the van, perhaps finding a hotel so I wouldn't have to crash in a sleeping bag at the bottom of a desert well again, when Jason rose from our picnic-table bench.

"There." He pointed out to sea.

The ship seemed to materialize from the sun's glare, the way my sun chariot used to whenever I pulled into the

Stables of Sunset at the end of a long day's ride. The yacht was a gleaming white monstrosity with five decks above the waterline, its tinted black windows like elongated insect eyes. As with all big ships, it was difficult to judge its size from a distance, but the fact that it had *two* onboard helicopters, one aft and one forward, plus a small submarine locked in a crane on the starboard side, told me this was not an average pleasure craft. Perhaps there were bigger yachts in the mortal world, but I guessed not many.

"That *has* to be it," Piper said. "What now? You think it will dock?"

"Hold on," Meg said. "Look."

Another yacht, identical to the first, resolved out of the sunlight about a mile to the south.

"That must be a mirage, right?" Jason asked uneasily. "Or a decoy?"

Meg grunted in dismay, pointing out to sea yet again.

A third yacht shimmered into existence, halfway between the first two.

"This is crazy," Piper said. "Each one of those boats has to cost millions."

"Half a billion," I corrected. "Or more. Caligula was never shy about spending money. He is part of the Triumvirate. They've been accumulating wealth for centuries."

Another yacht popped onto the horizon as if coming out of sunshine warp, then another. Soon there were dozens—a loose armada strung across the mouth of the harbor like a string being fitted on a bow.

"No way." Piper rubbed her eyes. "This *has* to be an illusion."

"It's not." My heart sank. I'd seen this sort of display before.

As we watched, the line of super-yachts maneuvered closer together, anchoring themselves stern to bow, forming a glittering, floating blockade from Sycamore Creek all the way to the marina—a mile long at least.

"The Bridge of Boats," I said. "He's done it again."

"*Again?*" Meg asked.

"Caligula—back in ancient times." I tried to control the quavering in my voice. "When he was a boy, he received a prophecy. A Roman astrologer told him he had as much chance of becoming emperor as he did of riding a horse across the Bay of Baiae. In other words, it was impossible. But Caligula *did* become emperor. So he ordered the construction of a fleet of super-yachts"—I gestured feebly at the armada in front of us—"like this. He lined the boats up across the Bay of Baiae, forming a massive bridge. Then he rode across it on his horse. It was the biggest floating construction project ever attempted. Caligula couldn't even swim. That didn't faze him. He was determined to thumb his nose at fate."

Piper steepled her hands over her mouth. "The mortals have to see this, right? He can't just cut off all boat traffic in and out of the harbor."

"Oh, the mortals notice," I said. "Look."

Smaller boats began to gather around the yachts, like flies drawn to a sumptuous feast. I spotted two Coast Guard vessels, several local police boats, and dozens of inflatable dinghies with outboard motors, manned by dark-clad men with guns—the emperor's private security, I guessed.

"They're *helping*," Meg murmured, a hard edge to her voice. "Even Nero never . . . He paid off the police, had lots of mercenaries, but he never showed off *this* much."

Jason gripped the hilt of his gladius. "Where do we even start? How do we find Caligula in all of that?"

I didn't want to find Caligula at all. I wanted to run. The idea of death, *permanent* death with five whole letters and a *d* at the beginning, suddenly seemed very close. But I could feel my friends' confidence wavering. They needed a plan, not a screaming, panicking Lester.

I pointed toward the center of the floating bridge. "We start in the middle—the weakest point of a chain."

25

All in the same boat
Wait. Two of us disappeared.
Half in the same boat

JASON GRACE RUINED that perfectly good line.

As we tromped toward the surf, he sidled up next to me and murmured, "It's not true, you know. The middle of a chain has the same tensile strength as everywhere else, assuming force is applied equally along the links."

I sighed. "Are you making up for missing your physics lecture? You know what I meant!"

"I actually don't," he said. "Why attack in the middle?"

"Because . . . I don't know!" I said. "They won't be expecting it?"

Meg stopped at the water's edge. "Looks like they're expecting anything."

She was right. As the sunset faded to purple, the yachts lit up like giant Fabergé eggs. Spotlights swept the sky and sea as if advertising the biggest waterbed-mattress sale in history. Dozens of small patrol boats crisscrossed the harbor, just in case any Santa Barbara locals (Santa Barbarians?) had the nerve to try using their own coast.

I wondered if Caligula always had this much security, or if he was expecting us. By now he certainly knew we'd blown up Macro's Military Madness. He'd also probably heard about our fight with Medea in the maze, assuming the sorceress had survived.

Caligula also had the Sibyl of Erythraea, which meant he had access to the same information Herophile had given Jason. The Sibyl might not *want* to help an evil emperor who kept her in molten shackles, but she couldn't refuse any earnest petitioner posing direct questions. Such was the nature of oracular magic. I imagined the best she could do was give her answers in the form of *really* difficult crossword-puzzle clues.

Jason studied the sweep of the searchlights. "I could fly you guys over, one at a time. Maybe they won't see us."

"I think we should avoid flying, if possible," I said. "And we should find a way over there before it gets much darker."

Piper pushed her windblown hair from her face. "Why? Darkness gives us better cover."

"Strixes," I said. "They become active about an hour after sundown."

"Strixes?" Piper asked.

I recounted our experience with the birds of doom in the Labyrinth. Meg offered helpful editorial comments like *yuck*, *uh-huh*, and *Apollo's fault.*

Piper shuddered. "In Cherokee stories, owls are bad news. They tend to be evil spirits or spying medicine men. If these strixes are like giant bloodsucking owls . . . yeah, let's not meet them."

"Agreed," Jason said. "But how do we get to the ships?"

Piper stepped into the waves. "Maybe we ask for a lift."

She raised her arms and waved at the nearest dinghy,

about fifty yards out, as it swept its light across the beach.

"Uh, Piper?" Jason asked.

Meg summoned her swords. "It's fine. When they get close, I'll take them out."

I stared at my young master. "Meg, those are *mortals*. First of all, your swords will not work on them. Second, they don't understand whom they're working for. We can't—"

"They're working for the B—the bad man," she said. "Caligula."

I noticed her slip of the tongue. I had a feeling she'd been about to say: *working for the Beast*.

She put away her blades, but her voice remained cold and determined. I had a sudden horrible image of McCaffrey the Avenger assaulting the boat with nothing but her fists and packets of gardening seeds.

Jason looked at me as if to ask *Do you need to tie her down, or should I?*

The dinghy veered toward us. Aboard sat three men in dark fatigues, Kevlar vests, and riot helmets. One in back operated the outboard motor. One in front manned the searchlight. The one in the middle, no doubt the friendliest, had an assault rifle propped on his knee.

Piper waved and smiled at them. "Meg, don't attack. I've got this. All of you, give me some space to work, please. I can charm these guys better if you're not glowering behind me."

This was not a difficult request. The three of us backed away, though Jason and I had to drag Meg.

"Hello!" Piper called as the boat came closer. "Don't shoot! We're friendly!"

The boat ran aground with such speed I thought it might keep driving right onto Cabrillo Boulevard. Mr. Searchlight jumped out first, surprisingly agile for a guy in body armor. Mr. Assault Rifle followed, providing cover while Mr. Engine cut the outboard motor.

Searchlight sized us up, his hand on his sidearm. "Who are you?"

"I'm Piper!" said Piper. "You don't need to call this in. And you definitely don't need to train that rifle on us!"

Searchlight's face contorted. He started to match Piper's smile, then seemed to remember that his job required him to glower. Assault Rifle did not lower his gun. Engine reached for his walkie-talkie.

"IDs," barked Searchlight. "All of you."

Next to me, Meg tensed, ready to become McCaffrey the Avenger. Jason tried to look inconspicuous, but his dress shirt crackled with static electricity.

"Sure!" Piper agreed. "Although I have a much better idea. I'm just going to reach in my pocket, okay? Don't get excited."

She pulled out a wad of cash—maybe a hundred dollars total. For all I knew, it represented the last of the McLean fortune.

"My friends and I were talking," Piper continued, "about how *hard* you guys work, how difficult it must be patrolling the harbor! We were sitting over there at that café, eating these incredible fish tacos, and we thought, *Hey, those guys deserve a break. We should buy them dinner!*"

Searchlight's eyes seemed to become unmoored from his brain. "Dinner break . . . ?"

"Absolutely!" Piper said. "You can put down that heavy gun, toss that walkie-talkie away. Heck, you can just leave everything with us. We'll watch it while you eat. Grilled snapper, homemade corn tortillas, seviche salsa." She glanced back at us. "Amazing food, right, guys?"

We mumbled our assent.

"Yum," Meg said. She excelled at one-syllable answers.

Assault Rifle lowered his gun. "I could use some fish tacos."

"We've been working hard," Engine agreed. "We deserve a dinner break."

"Exactly!" Piper pressed the money into Searchlight's hand. "Our treat. Thank you for your service!"

Searchlight stared at the wad of cash. "But we're really not supposed to—"

"Eat with all that gear on?" Piper suggested. "You're absolutely right. Just throw it all in the boat—the Kevlar, the guns, your cell phones. That's right. Get comfortable!"

It took several more minutes of cajoling and lighthearted banter, but finally the three mercenaries had stripped down to just their commando pajamas. They thanked Piper, gave her a hug for good measure, then jogged off to assault the beachside café.

As soon as they were gone, Piper stumbled into Jason's arms.

"Whoa, you okay?" he asked.

"F-fine." She pushed away awkwardly. "Just harder charming a whole group. I'll be okay."

"That was impressive," I said. "Aphrodite herself could not have done better."

Piper didn't look pleased by my comparison. "We should hurry. The charm won't last."

Meg grunted. "Still would've been easier to kill—"

"Meg," I chided.

"—to beat them unconscious," she amended.

"Right." Jason cleared his throat. "Everybody in the boat!"

We were thirty yards offshore when we heard the mercenaries shouting, "Hey! Stop!" They ran into the surf, holding half-eaten fish tacos and looking confused.

Fortunately, Piper had taken all their weapons and communications devices.

She gave them a friendly wave and Jason gunned the outboard motor.

Jason, Meg, and I rushed to put on the guards' Kevlar vests and helmets. This left Piper in civilian clothes, but since she was the only one capable of bluffing her way through a confrontation, she let us have all the fun playing dress-up.

Jason made a perfect mercenary. Meg looked ridiculous—a little girl swimming in her father's Kevlar. I didn't look much better. The body armor chafed around my middle. (Curse you, un-combat-worthy love handles!) The riot helmet was as hot as an Easy-Bake oven, and the visor kept falling down, perhaps anxious to hide my acne-riddled face.

We tossed the guns overboard. That may sound foolish, but as I've said, firearms are fickle weapons in the hands of demigods. They would work on mortals, but no matter what Meg said, I didn't want to go around mowing down regular humans.

I had to believe that if these mercenaries truly understood whom they were serving, they too would throw down their arms. Surely humans would not blindly follow such an evil man of their own free will—I mean, except for the few hundred exceptions I could think of from human history. . . . But not Caligula!

As we approached the yachts, Jason slowed, matching our speed to that of the other patrol vessels.

He angled toward the nearest yacht. Up close, it towered above us like a white steel fortress. Purple and gold running lights glowed just below the water's surface so the vessel seemed to float on an ethereal cloud of Imperial Roman power. Painted along the prow of the ship, in black letters taller than me, was the name IVLIA DRVSILLA XXVI.

"Julia Drusilla the Twenty-Sixth," Piper said. "Was she an empress?"

"No," I said, "the emperor's favorite sister."

My chest tightened as I remembered that poor girl—so pretty, so agreeable, so incredibly out of her depth. Her brother Caligula had doted on her, idolized her. When he became emperor, he insisted she share his every meal, witness his every depraved spectacle, partake in all his violent revels. She had died at twenty-two—crushed by the suffocating love of a sociopath.

"She was probably the only person Caligula ever cared about," I said. "But why this boat is numbered twenty-six, I don't know."

"Because that one is twenty-five." Meg pointed to the next ship in line, its stern resting a few feet from our prow. Sure enough, painted across the back was IVLIA DRVSILLA XXV.

"I bet the one behind us is number twenty-seven."

"Fifty super-yachts," I mused, "all named for Julia Drusilla. Yes, that sounds like Caligula."

Jason scanned the side of the hull. There were no ladders, no hatches, no conveniently labeled red buttons: PRESS HERE FOR CALIGULA'S SHOES!

We didn't have much time. We had made it inside the perimeter of patrol vessels and searchlights, but each yacht surely had security cameras. It wouldn't be long before someone wondered why our little dinghy was floating beside *XXVI*. Also, the mercenaries we'd left on the beach would be doing their best to attract their comrades' attention. Then there were the flocks of strixes that I imagined would be waking up any minute, hungry and alert for any sign of disembowel-able intruders.

"I'll fly you guys up," Jason decided. "One at a time."

"Me first," Piper said. "In case someone needs charming."

Jason turned and let Piper lock her arms around his neck, as if they'd done this countless times before. The winds kicked up around the dinghy, ruffling my hair, and Jason and Piper floated up the side of the yacht.

Oh, how I envied Jason Grace! Such a simple thing it was to ride the winds. As a god, I could have done it with half my manifestations tied behind my back. Now, stuck in my pathetic body complete with love handles, I could only dream of such freedom.

"Hey." Meg nudged me. "Focus."

I gave her an indignant harrumph. "I am *pure* focus. I might, however, ask where *your* head is."

She scowled. "What do you mean?"

"Your rage," I said. "The number of times you've talked about killing Caligula. Your willingness to . . . beat his mercenaries unconscious."

"They're the enemy."

Her tone was as sharp as scimitars, giving me fair warning that if I continued with this topic, she might add my name to her Beat Unconscious list.

I decided to take a lesson from Jason—to navigate toward my target at a slower, less direct angle.

"Meg, have I ever told you about the first time I became mortal?"

She peered from under the rim of her ridiculously large helmet. "You messed up or something?"

"I . . . Yes. I messed up. My father, Zeus, killed one of my favorite sons, Asclepius, for bringing people back from the dead without permission. Long story. The point is . . . I was furious with Zeus, but he was too powerful and scary for me to fight. He would've vaporized me. So I took my revenge out in another way."

I peered at the top of the hull. I saw no sign of Jason or Piper. Hopefully that meant they had found Caligula's shoes and were just waiting for a clerk to bring them a pair in the right size.

"Anyway," I continued, "I couldn't kill Zeus. So I found the guys who had made his lightning bolts, the Cyclopes. I killed *them* in revenge for Asclepius. As punishment, Zeus made me mortal."

Meg kicked me in the shin.

"Ow!" I yelped. "What was that for?"

"For being dumb," she said. "Killing the Cyclopes was dumb."

I wanted to protest that this had happened thousands of years ago, but I feared it might just earn me another kick.

"Yes," I agreed. "It was dumb. But my point is . . . I was projecting my anger onto someone else, someone safer. I think you might be doing the same thing now, Meg. You're raging at Caligula because it's safer than raging at your stepfather."

I braced my shins for more pain.

Meg stared down at her Kevlar-coated chest. "That's not what I'm doing."

"I don't blame you," I hastened to add. "Anger is *good*. It means you're making progress. But be aware that you might be angry right now at the wrong person. I don't want you charging blindly into battle against this particular emperor. As hard as it is to believe, he is even more devious and deadly than Ne—the Beast."

She clenched her fists. "I told you, I'm not doing that. You don't know. You don't get it."

"You're right," I said. "What you had to endure in Nero's house . . . I can't imagine. No one should suffer like that, but—"

"Shut up," she snapped.

So, of course, I did. The words I'd been planning to say avalanched back down my throat.

"You don't know," she said again. "This Caligula guy did *plenty* to my dad and me. I can be mad at him if I want. I'll kill him if I can. I'll . . ." She faltered, as if struck by a sudden thought. "Where's Jason? He should be back by now."

I glanced up. I would have screamed if my voice were working. Two large dark figures dropped toward us in a controlled, silent descent on what appeared to be parasails. Then I realized those were not parasails—they were *giant ears*. In an instant, the creatures were upon us. They landed gracefully on either end of our dinghy, their ears folding around them, their swords at our throats.

The creatures looked very much like the Big Ear guard Piper had hit with her dart at the entrance to the Burning Maze, except these were older and had black fur. Their blades were blunt-tipped with serrated double edges, equally suited for bashing or hacking. With a jolt, I recognized the weapons as khandas, from the Indian subcontinent. I would have been pleased with myself for remembering such an obscure fact, had I not at that moment had a khanda's serrated edge across my jugular vein.

Then I had another flash of recollection. I remembered one of Dionysus's many drunken stories about his military campaigns in India—how he had come across a vicious tribe of demi-humans with eight fingers, huge ears, and furry faces. Why couldn't I have thought of that sooner? What had Dionysus told me about them . . . ? Ah, yes. His exact words were: *Never*, ever *try to fight them*.

"You're *pandai*," I managed to croak. "That's what your race is called."

The one next to me bared his beautiful white teeth. "Indeed! Now be nice little prisoners and come along. Otherwise your friends are dead."

26

Oh, Florence and Grunk
La-di-da, something, something
I'll get back to you

PERHAPS JASON, the physics expert, could explain to me how pandai flew. I didn't get it. Somehow, even while carrying us, our captors managed to launch themselves skyward with nothing but the flapping of their tremendous lobes. I wished Hermes could see them. He would never again brag about being able to wiggle his ears.

The pandai dropped us unceremoniously on the starboard deck, where two more of their kind held Jason and Piper at arrow-point. One of those guards appeared smaller and younger than the others, with white fur instead of black. Judging from the sour look on his face, I guessed he was the same guy Piper had shot down with Grandpa Tom's special recipe in downtown Los Angeles.

Our friends were on their knees, their hands zip-tied behind their backs, their weapons confiscated. Jason had a black eye. The side of Piper's head was matted with blood.

I rushed to her aid (being the good person I was) and poked at her cranium, trying to determine the extent of her injury.

"Ow," she muttered, pulling away. "I'm fine."

"You could have a concussion," I said.

Jason sighed miserably. "That's supposed to be *my* job. I'm always the one who gets knocked in the head. Sorry, guys. Things didn't exactly go as planned."

The largest guard, who had carried me aboard, cackled with glee. "The girl tried to charmspeak us! *Pandai*, who hear every nuance of speech! The boy tried to fight us! *Pandai*, who train from birth to master every weapon! Now you will all die!"

"Die! Die!" barked the other pandai, though I noticed the white-furred youngster did not join in. He moved stiffly, as if his poison-darted leg still bothered him.

Meg glanced from enemy to enemy, probably gauging how fast she could take them all down. The arrows pointed at Jason and Piper's chests made for tricky calculations.

"Meg, don't," Jason warned. "These guys—they're ridiculously good. And fast."

"Fast! Fast!" the pandai barked in agreement.

I scanned the deck. No additional guards were running toward us, no searchlights were trained on our position. No horns blared. Somewhere inside the boat, gentle music played—not the sort of sound track one might expect during an incursion.

The pandai had not raised a general alarm. Despite their threats, they had not yet killed us. They'd even gone to the trouble of zip-tying Piper's and Jason's hands. Why?

I turned to the largest guard. "Good sir, are you the panda in charge?"

He hissed. "The singular form is *pandos*. I *hate* being called a *panda*. Do I *look* like a panda?"

I decided not to answer that. "Well, Mr. Pandos—"

"My name is Amax," he snapped.

"Of course. Amax." I studied his majestic ears, then hazarded an educated guess. "I imagine you hate people eavesdropping on you."

Amax's furry black nose twitched. "Why do you say this? What did you overhear?"

"Nothing!" I assured him. "But I bet you have to be careful. Always other people, other pandai snooping into your business. That's—that's why you haven't raised an alarm yet. You *know* we're important prisoners. You want to keep control of the situation, without anyone else taking the credit for your good work."

The other pandai grumbled.

"Vector, on boat twenty-five, is *always* spying," the dark-furred archer muttered.

"Taking credit for our ideas," said the second archer. "Like Kevlar ear armor."

"Exactly!" I said, trying to ignore Piper, who was incredulously mouthing the words *Kevlar ear armor?* "Which is why, uh, before you do anything rash, you're going to want to hear what I have to say. In private."

Amax snorted. "Ha!"

His comrades echoed him: "HA-HA!"

"You just lied," Amax said. "I could hear it in your voice. You're afraid. You're bluffing. You have nothing to say."

"*I* do," Meg countered. "I'm Nero's stepdaughter."

Blood rushed into Amax's ears so rapidly I was surprised he didn't faint.

The shocked archers lowered their weapons.

"Timbre! Crest!" Amax snapped. "Keep those arrows steady!" He glowered at Meg. "You seem to be telling the truth. What is Nero's stepdaughter doing here?"

"Looking for Caligula," Meg said. "So I can kill him."

The pandai's ears rippled in alarm. Jason and Piper looked at each other as if thinking *Welp. Now we die.*

Amax narrowed his eyes. "You say you are from Nero. Yet you want to kill our master. This does not make sense."

"It's a juicy story," I promised. "With lots of secrets, twists, and turns. But if you kill us, you'll never hear it. If you take us to the emperor, someone *else* will torture it out of us. We would gladly tell you everything. You captured us, after all. But isn't there somewhere more private we can talk, so no one will overhear?"

Amax glanced toward the ship's bow, as if Vector might already be listening in. "You seem to be telling the truth, but there's so much weakness and fear in your voice, it's hard to be sure."

"Uncle Amax." The white-haired pandos spoke for the first time. "Perhaps the pimply boy has a point. If it's valuable information—"

"Silence, Crest!" snapped Amax. "You've already disgraced yourself once this week."

The pandos leader pulled more zip ties from his belt. "Timbre, Peak, bind the pimply boy and the stepdaughter of Nero. We will take them all below, interrogate them ourselves, and *then* hand them over to the emperor!"

"Yes! Yes!" barked Timbre and Peak.

So it was that three powerful demigods and one former major Olympian god were led as prisoners into a superyacht by four fuzzy creatures with ears the size of satellite dishes. Not my finest hour.

Since I had reached peak humiliation, I assumed Zeus would pick that moment to recall me to the heavens and the other gods would spend the next hundred years laughing at me.

But no. I remained fully and pathetically Lester.

The guards hustled us to the aft deck, which featured six hot tubs, a multicolored fountain, and a flashing gold and purple dance floor just waiting for partyers to arrive.

Affixed to the stern, a red-carpeted ramp jutted across the water, connecting our boat to the prow of the next yacht. I guessed all the boats were linked this way, making a road across Santa Barbara Harbor, just in case Caligula decided to do a golf-cart drive-through.

Rising amidships, the upper decks gleamed with dark-tinted windows and white walls. Far above, the conning tower sprouted radar dishes, satellite antennae, and two billowing pennants: one with the imperial eagle of Rome, the other with a golden triangle on a field of purple, which I supposed was the logo for Triumvirate Holdings.

Two more guards flanked the heavy oak doors that led inside. The guy on the left looked like a mortal mercenary, with the same black pajamas and body armor as the gentlemen we'd sent on the wild fish-taco chase. The guy on the right was a Cyclops (the huge single eye gave him away). He also smelled like a Cyclops (wet wool socks) and dressed like a Cyclops (denim cutoffs, torn black T-shirt, and a large wooden club).

The human mercenary frowned at our merry band of captors and prisoners.

"What's all this?" he asked.

"Not your concern, Florence," Amax growled. "Let us through!"

Florence? I might have snickered, except Florence weighed three hundred pounds, had knife scars across his face, and *still* had a better name than Lester Papadopoulos.

"Regulations," Florence said. "You got prisoners, I have to call it in."

"Not yet, you won't." Amax spread his ears like the hood of a cobra. "This is *my* ship. *I'll* tell you when to call it in—*after* we interrogate these intruders."

Florence frowned at his Cyclops partner. "What do you think, Grunk?"

Now, Grunk—that was a good Cyclops name. I didn't know if Florence realized he was working with a Cyclops. The Mist could be unpredictable. But I immediately formulated the premise for an action-adventure buddy-comedy series, *Florence and Grunk*. If I survived captivity, I'd have to mention it to Piper's father. Perhaps he could help me schedule some lunches and pitch the idea. Oh, gods . . . I had been in Southern California too long.

Grunk shrugged. "It's Amax's ears on the line if the boss gets mad."

"Okay." Florence waved us through. "You all have fun."

I had little time to appreciate the opulent interior—the

solid-gold fixtures, the luxurious Persian carpets, the million-dollar works of art, the plush purple furniture I was pretty sure had come from Prince's estate sale.

We saw no other guards or crew, which seemed strange. Then again, I supposed that, even with *Caligula's* resources, finding enough personnel to man fifty super-yachts at once might be difficult.

As we walked through a walnut-paneled library hung with masterpiece paintings, Piper caught her breath. She pointed her chin toward a Joan Miró abstraction.

"That came from my dad's house," she said.

"When we get out of here," Jason muttered, "we'll take it with us."

"I *heard* that." Peak jabbed his sword hilt into Jason's ribs.

Jason stumbled against Piper, who stumbled into a Picasso. Seeing an opportunity, Meg surged forward, apparently meaning to tackle Amax with all one hundred pounds of her weight. Before she took two steps, an arrow sprouted from the carpet at her feet.

"Don't," said Timbre. His vibrating bowstring was the only evidence he'd made the shot. He had drawn and fired so fast even *I* couldn't believe it.

Meg backed away. "Fine. Jeez."

The pandai herded us into a forward lounge. Along the front wrapped a one-hundred-and-eighty-degree glass wall overlooking the prow. Off to starboard, the lights of Santa Barbara twinkled. In front of us, yachts twenty-five through one made a glittering necklace of amethyst, gold, and platinum across the dark water.

The sheer extravagance of it all hurt my brain, and normally I was all about extravagance.

The pandai arranged four plush chairs in a row and shoved us into them. As interrogation rooms went, it wasn't bad. Peak paced behind us, sword at the ready in case anyone required decapitation. Timbre and Crest lurked on either flank, their bows down, but arrows nocked. Amax pulled up a chair and sat facing us, spreading his ears around him like a king's robe.

"This place is private," he announced. "Talk."

"First," I said, "I must know why you're not followers of Apollo. Such great archers? The finest hearing in the world? Eight fingers on each hand? You would be natural musicians! We seem *made* for each other!"

Amax studied me. "You are the former god, eh? They told us about you."

"I am Apollo," I confirmed. "It's not too late to pledge me your loyalty."

Amax's mouth quivered. I hoped he was on the verge of crying, perhaps throwing himself at my feet and begging my forgiveness.

Instead, he howled with laughter. "What do we need with Olympian gods? Especially gods who are pimply boys with no power?"

"But there's so much I could teach you!" I insisted. "Music! Poetry! I could teach you how to write haikus!"

Jason looked at me and shook his head vigorously, though I had no idea why.

"Music and poetry hurt our ears," Amax complained. "We have no need of them!"

"I like music," Crest murmured, flexing his fingers. "I can play a little—"

"Silence!" Amax yelled. "You can play *silence* for once, worthless nephew!"

Aha, I thought. Even among the pandai there were frustrated musicians. Amax suddenly reminded me of my father, Zeus, when he came storming down the hallway on Mount Olympus (literally storming, with thunder, lightning, and torrential rain) and ordered me to stop playing my infernal zither music. A totally unfair demand. Everyone *knows* 2:00 a.m. is the optimal time to practice the zither.

I might have been able to sway Crest to our side . . . if only I'd had more time. And if he weren't in the company of three older and larger pandai. And if we hadn't started our acquaintance with Piper shooting him in the leg with a poisoned dart.

Amax reclined in his cushy purple throne. "We pandai are mercenaries. We *choose* our masters. Why would we pick a washed-up god like you? Once, we served the kings of India! Now we serve Caligula!"

"Caligula! Caligula!" Timbre and Peak cried. Again, Crest was conspicuously quiet, frowning at his bow.

"The emperor trusts only us!" Timbre bragged.

"Yes," Peak agreed. "Unlike those Germani, *we* never stabbed him to death!"

I wanted to point out that this was a fairly low bar for loyalty, but Meg interrupted.

"The night is young," she said. "We could all stab him together."

Amax sneered. "I am still waiting, daughter of Nero, to

hear your juicy story about why you wish to kill our master. You'd better have good information. And lots of twists and turns! Convince me you are worth bringing to Caesar alive, rather than as dead bodies, and perhaps I'll get a promotion tonight! I will *not* be passed over again for some idiot like Overdrive on boat three, or Wah-Wah on boat forty-three."

"Wah-Wah?" Piper made a sound between a hiccup and a giggle, which may have been the effect of her bashed head. "Are you guys *all* named after guitar pedals? My dad has a collection of those. Well . . . he *had* a collection."

Amax scowled. "Guitar pedals? I don't know what that means! If you are making fun of our culture—"

"Hey," Meg said. "You wanna hear my story or not?"

We all turned to her.

"Um, Meg . . . ?" I asked. "Are you sure?"

The pandai no doubt picked up on my nervous tone, but I couldn't help it. First of all, I had no idea what Meg could possibly say that would increase our chances of survival. Second, knowing Meg, she would say it in ten words or less. Then we'd all be dead.

"I got twists and turns." She narrowed her eyes. "But are you *sure* we're alone, Mr. Amax? No one else is listening?"

"Of course not!" said Amax. "This ship is *my* base. That glass is fully soundproofed." He gestured dismissively at the ship in front of us. "Vector won't hear a word!"

"What about Wah-Wah?" Meg asked. "I know he's on boat forty-three with the emperor, but if his spies are nearby—"

"Ridiculous!" Amax said. "The emperor isn't on boat forty-three!"

Timbre and Peak snickered.

"Boat forty-three is the emperor's *footwear* boat, silly girl," said Peak. "An important assignment, yes, but not the throne-room boat."

"Right," Timbre said. "That's Reverb's boat, number twelve—"

"*Silence!*" Amax snapped. "Enough delays, girl. Tell me what you know, or die."

"Okay," Meg leaned forward as if to impart a secret. "Twists and turns."

Her hands shot forward, suddenly and inexplicably free of the zip tie. Her rings flashed as she threw them, turning into scimitars as they hurtled toward Amax and Peak.

27

I can kill you all
Or I can sing you Joe Walsh
Really, it's your choice

THE CHILDREN OF DEMETER are all about flowers. Amber waves of grain. Feeding the world and nurturing life.

They also excel at planting scimitars in the chests of their enemies.

Meg's Imperial gold blades found their targets. One hit Amax with such force he exploded in a cloud of yellow dust. The other cut through Peak's bow, embedding itself in his sternum and causing him to disintegrate inward like sand through an hourglass.

Crest fired his bow. Fortunately for me, his aim was off. The arrow buzzed past my face, the fletching scraping my chin, and impaled itself in my chair.

Piper kicked back in her seat, knocking into Timbre so his sword swing went wild. Before he could recover and decapitate her, Jason got overexcited.

I say that because of the lightning. The sky outside flashed, the curved wall of glass shattered, and tendrils of electricity wrapped around Timbre, frying him into an ash pile.

Effective, yes, but not the sort of stealth we'd been hoping for.

"Oops," said Jason.

With a horrified whimper, Crest dropped his bow. He staggered backward, struggling to draw his sword. Meg yanked her first scimitar from Amax's dust-covered chair and marched toward him.

"Meg, wait!" I said.

She glared at me. "What?"

I tried to raise my hands in a placating gesture, then remembered they were tied behind my back.

"Crest," I said, "there's no shame in surrender. You are not a fighter."

He gulped. "Y-you don't know me."

"You're holding your sword backward," I pointed out. "So unless you intend to stab yourself . . ."

He fumbled to correct the situation.

"Fly!" I pleaded. "This doesn't have to be your fight. Get out of here! Become the musician you want to see in the world!"

He must have heard the earnestness in my voice. He dropped his sword and jumped through the gaping hole in the glass, ear-sailing into the darkness.

"Why'd you let him go?" Meg demanded. "He'll warn everybody."

"I don't think so," I said. "Also, it doesn't matter. We just announced ourselves with a literal thunderbolt."

"Yeah, sorry," Jason said. "Sometimes that just happens."

Lightning strikes seemed like the sort of power he really

needed to get under control, but we had no time to argue about it. As Meg cut our zip ties, Florence and Grunk charged into the room.

Piper yelled, "Stop!"

Florence tripped and face-planted on the carpet, his rifle spraying a full clip sideways, shooting off the legs of a nearby sofa.

Grunk raised his club and charged. I instinctively pulled my bow, nocked an arrow, and let it fly—straight into the Cyclops's eye.

I was stunned. I'd actually hit my target!

Grunk fell to his knees, keeled over sideways, and began to disintegrate, putting an end to my plans for a cross-species buddy comedy.

Piper walked up to Florence, who was groaning with a broken nose.

"Thanks for stopping," she said, then gagged him and trussed his wrists and ankles with his own zip ties.

"Well, that was interesting." Jason turned to Meg. "And what you did? Incredible. Those pandai—when I tried to fight them, they disarmed me like it was child's play, but *you*, with those swords . . ."

Meg's cheeks reddened. "It was no big deal."

"It was a *very* big deal." Jason faced me. "So what now?"

A muted voice buzzed in my head. *NOW, THE VILE ROGUE APOLLO SHALT REMOVE ME FROM THIS MONSTER'S EYE POSTHASTE!*

"Oh, dear." I had done what I'd always feared, and sometimes dreamed of. I had mistakenly used the Arrow of

Dodona in combat. Its sacred point now quivered in the eye socket of Grunk, who had been reduced to nothing but his skull—a spoil of war, I supposed.

"Very sorry," I said, pulling the arrow free.

Meg snorted. "Is that—?"

"The Arrow of Dodona," I said.

AND MINE FURY IS BOUNDLESS! the arrow intoned. *THOU SHOOTEST ME FORTH TO SLAY THY FOES AS IF I WAST A MERE ARROW!*

"Yes, yes, I apologize. Now hush, please." I turned to my comrades. "We need to move quickly. The security forces will be coming."

"Emperor Stupid is on boat twelve," Meg said. "That's where we go."

"But the shoe boat," I said, "is forty-three, which is in the opposite direction."

"What if Emperor Stupid is *wearing* his shoes?" she asked.

"Hey." Jason pointed at the Arrow of Dodona. "That's the mobile source of prophecy you were telling us about, right? Maybe you should ask it."

I found that an annoyingly reasonable suggestion. I raised the arrow. "You heard them, O Wise Arrow. Which way do we go?"

THOU TELLEST ME TO HUSH, THEN THOU ASKETH ME FOR WISDOM? OH, FIE! OH, VILLAINY! BOTH DIRECTIONS MUST THOU PURSUE, IF THOU WOULDST SEE SUCCESS. BUT BEWARE. I SEE GREAT PAIN, GREAT SUFFERING. SACRIFICE MOST BLOODY!

"What did he say?" Piper demanded.

Oh, reader, I was so tempted to lie! I wanted to tell my friends that the arrow was in favor of returning to Los Angeles and booking rooms at a five-star hotel.

I caught Jason's eyes. I remembered how I had exhorted him to tell Piper the truth about the Sibyl's prophecy. I decided I could do no less.

I related what the arrow had said.

"So we split up?" Piper shook her head. "I hate this plan."

"Me too," Jason said. "Which means it's probably the right move."

He knelt and retrieved his gladius from the dust-pile remains of Timbre. Then he tossed the dagger Katoptris to Piper.

"I'm going after Caligula," he said. "Even if the shoes aren't there, maybe I can buy you guys some time, distract the security forces."

Meg picked up her other scimitar. "I'll come with you."

Before I could argue, she took a flying leap out of the broken window—which was a pretty good metaphor for her general approach to life.

Jason gave Piper and me one last worried look. "You two be careful."

He jumped after Meg. Almost immediately, gunfire erupted on the foredeck below.

I grimaced at Piper. "Those two were our *fighters*. We shouldn't have let them go together."

"Don't underestimate my fighting skill," Piper said. "Now let's go shoe-shopping."

She waited only long enough for me to clean and bandage her wounded head in the nearest restroom. Then she donned Florence's combat helmet and off we went.

I soon realized Piper didn't need to rely on charmspeak to persuade people. She carried herself with confidence, striding from ship to ship like she was supposed to be there. The yachts were lightly guarded—perhaps because most of the pandai and strixes had already flown over to check out the lightning strike on ship twenty-six. The few mortal mercenaries we passed gave Piper no more than a brief glance. Since I followed in her wake, they ignored me too. I supposed if they were used to working side by side with Cyclopes and Big Ears, they could overlook a couple of teenagers in riot gear.

Boat twenty-eight was a floating water park, with multilevel swimming pools connected by waterfalls, slides, and transparent tubes. A lonely lifeguard offered us a towel as we walked by. He looked sad when we didn't take one.

Boat twenty-nine: a full-service spa. Steam poured from every open porthole. On the aft deck, an army of bored-looking masseuses and cosmeticians stood ready, just in case Caligula decided to drop by with fifty friends for a shiatsu and mani-pedi party. I was tempted to stop, just for a quick shoulder massage, but since Piper, daughter of Aphrodite, marched right past without a glance at the offerings, I decided not to embarrass myself.

Boat thirty was a literal moveable feast. The entire ship seemed designed to provide an all-you-can-eat twenty-four-hour buffet, which no one was partaking in. Chefs stood by. Waiters waited. New dishes were brought out and old ones removed. I suspected the uneaten food, enough to feed the greater Los Angeles area, would be dumped overboard. Typical Caligula extravagance. Your ham sandwich tastes *so* much better when you know hundreds of identical sandwiches have been thrown away as your chefs waited for you to get hungry.

Our good luck failed on boat thirty-one. As soon as we crossed the red-carpeted ramp onto the bow, I knew we were in trouble. Groups of off-duty mercenaries lounged here and there, talking, eating, checking their cell phones. We got more frowns, more questioning looks.

From the tension in Piper's posture, I could tell she sensed the problem too. But before I could say *Gosh, Piper, I think we've stumbled into Caligula's floating barracks and we're about to die*, she forged ahead, doubtless deciding it would be as dangerous to backtrack as to bluff our way through.

She was wrong.

On the aft deck, we found ourselves in the middle of a Cyclops/mortal volleyball game. In a sand-filled pit, half a dozen hairy Cyclopes in swim trunks battled it out with half a dozen equally hairy mortals in combat pants. Around the edges of the game, more off-duty mercenaries were barbecuing steaks on a grill, laughing, sharpening knives, and comparing tattoos.

At the grill, a double-wide dude with a flattop haircut and a chest tattoo that read MOTHER spotted us and froze. "Hey!"

The volleyball game stopped. Everyone on deck turned and glowered at us.

Piper pulled off her helmet. "Apollo, back me up!"

I feared she might pull a Meg and charge into battle. In that case, *backing her up* would mean getting ripped limb from limb by sweaty ex-military types, which was *not* on my bucket list.

Instead, Piper began to sing.

I wasn't sure what surprised me more: Piper's beautiful voice, or the tune she chose.

I recognized it immediately: "Life of Illusion" by Joe Walsh. The 1980s were something of a blur to me, but that song I remembered—1981, the very beginning of MTV. Oh, the lovely videos I'd produced for Blondie and the Go-Gos! The amount of hairspray and leopard-print Spandex we had used!

The crowd of mercenaries listened in confused silence. Should they kill us now? Should they wait for us to finish? It wasn't every day someone serenaded you with Joe Walsh in the middle of a volleyball game. I'm sure the mercenaries were a little fuzzy on the proper etiquette.

After a couple of lines, Piper gave me a sharp glance like *A little help?*

Ah, she wanted me to back her up with *music*!

With great relief, I whipped out my ukulele and played along. In truth, Piper's voice needed no help. She belted out the lyrics with passion and clarity—a shock wave of emotion that was more than a heartfelt performance, more than charmspeak.

She moved through the crowd, singing of her own illusionary life. She inhabited the song. She invested the words with pain and sorrow, turning Walsh's peppy tune into a melancholy confessional. She spoke of breaking through walls of confusion, of enduring the little surprises nature had thrown at her, of jumping to conclusions about who she was.

She didn't change the lyrics. Nevertheless, I felt her story in every line: her struggle as the neglected child of a famous movie star; her mixed feelings about discovering she was a daughter of Aphrodite; most hurtful of all, her realization that the supposed love of her life, Jason Grace, was not someone she wanted to be with romantically. I didn't understand it all, but the power of her voice was undeniable. My ukulele responded. My chords turned more resonant, my riffs more soulful. Every note I played was a cry of sympathy for Piper McLean, my own musical skill amplifying hers.

The guards became unfocused. Some sat down, cradling their heads in their hands. Some stared into space and let their steaks burn on the grill.

None of them stopped us as we crossed the aft deck. None followed us across the bridge to boat thirty-two. We were halfway across that yacht before Piper finished her song and leaned heavily against the nearest wall. Her eyes were red, her face hollowed out with emotion.

"Piper?" I stared at her in amazement. "How did you—?"

"Shoes now," she croaked. "Talk later."

She stumbled on.

28

Apollo, disguised
As Apollo, disguised as . . .
Nah. Too depressing.

WE SAW NO SIGN that the mercenaries were pursuing us. How could they? Even hardened warriors could not be expected to give chase after such a performance. I imagined they were sobbing in each other's arms, or rifling through the yacht for extra boxes of tissues.

We made our way through the thirties of Caligula's super-yacht chain, using stealth when necessary, mostly relying on the apathy of the crew members we encountered. Caligula had always inspired fear in his servants, but that didn't equate to loyalty. No one asked us any questions.

On boat forty, Piper collapsed. I rushed to help, but she pushed me away.

"I'm okay," she muttered.

"You are not okay," I said. "You probably have a concussion. You just worked a powerful bit of musical charm. You need a minute to rest."

"We don't *have* a minute."

I was fully aware of that. Sporadic bursts of gunfire still crackled over the harbor from the direction we had come.

The harsh *scree* of strixes pierced the night sky. Our friends were buying us time, and we had none to waste.

This was also the night of the new moon. Whatever plans Caligula had for Camp Jupiter, far to the north, they were happening now. I could only hope Leo had reached the Roman demigods, and that they could fend off whatever evil came their way. Being powerless to help them was a terrible feeling. It made me anxious not to waste a moment.

"Nevertheless," I told Piper, "I *really* don't have time for you to die on me, or go into a coma. So you *will* take a moment to sit. Let's get out of the open."

Piper was too weak to protest much. In her present condition, I doubted she could have charmspoken her way out of a parking ticket. I carried her inside yacht forty, which turned out to be dedicated to Caligula's wardrobe.

We passed room after room filled with clothes—suits, togas, armor, dresses (why not?), and a variety of costumes from pirate to Apollo to panda bear. (Again, why not?)

I was tempted to dress up as Apollo, just to feel sorry for myself, but I didn't want to take the time to apply the gold paint. Why did mortals always think I was gold? I mean, I *could* be gold, but the shininess detracted from my naturally amazing looks. Correction: my *former* naturally amazing looks.

Finally we found a dressing room with a couch. I moved a pile of evening dresses, then ordered Piper to sit. I pulled out a crushed square of ambrosia and ordered her to eat it. (My goodness, I could be bossy when I had to be. At least that was one godly power I hadn't lost.)

While Piper nibbled her divine energy bar, I stared glumly at the racks of bespoke finery. "Why can't the shoes be here? This is his wardrobe boat, after all."

"Come on, Apollo." Piper winced as she shifted on the cushions. "Everybody knows you need a separate super-yacht just for shoes."

"I can't tell if you're joking."

She picked up a Stella McCartney dress—a lovely low-cut number in scarlet silk. "Nice." Then she pulled out her knife, gritting her teeth from the effort, and slit the gown right down the front.

"That felt good," she decided.

It seemed pointless to me. You couldn't hurt Caligula by ruining his things. He had *all* the things. Nor did it seem to make Piper any happier. Thanks to the ambrosia, her color was better. Her eyes were not as dulled with pain. But her expression remained stormy, like her mother's whenever she heard someone praise Scarlett Johansson's good looks. (Tip: *Never* mention Scarlett Johansson around Aphrodite.)

"The song you sang to the mercenaries," I ventured, "'Life of Illusion.'"

The corners of Piper's eyes tightened, as if she'd known this conversation was coming but was too tired to deflect it. "It's an early memory. Right after my dad got his first big acting break, he was blasting that song in the car. We were driving to our new house, the place in Malibu. He was singing to me. We were both so happy. I must have been . . . I don't know, in kindergarten?"

"But the way you sang it. You seemed to be talking about yourself, why you broke up with Jason?"

She studied her knife. The blade remained blank, devoid of visions.

"I tried," she murmured. "After the war with Gaea, I convinced myself everything would be perfect. For a while, a few months maybe, I thought it was. Jason's great. He's my closest friend, even more than Annabeth. But"—she spread her hands—"whatever I thought was there, my happily-ever-after . . . it just wasn't."

I nodded. "Your relationship was born in crisis. Such romances are difficult to sustain once the crisis is over."

"It wasn't just that."

"A century ago, I dated Grand Duchess Tatiana Romanov," I recalled. "Things were great between us during the Russian Revolution. She was so stressed, so scared, she really needed me. Then the crisis passed, and the magic just wasn't there anymore. Wait, actually, that could've been because she was shot to death along with the rest of her family, but still—"

"It was me."

My thoughts had been drifting through the Winter Palace, through the acrid gun smoke and bitter cold of 1917. Now I snapped back to the present. "What do you mean it was you? You mean you realized you didn't love Jason? That's no one's fault."

She grimaced, as if I still hadn't grasped what she meant . . . or perhaps she wasn't sure herself.

"I know it's nobody's fault," she said. "I *do* love him. But . . . like I told you, Hera forced us together—the marriage goddess, arranging a happy couple. My memories of starting to date Jason, our first few months together, were a total illusion. Then, as soon as I found *that* out, before I could even process what it meant, Aphrodite claimed me. My mom, the goddess of love."

She shook her head in dismay. "Aphrodite pushed me into thinking I was . . . that I needed to . . ." She sighed. "Look at me, the great charmspeaker. I don't even have words. Aphrodite expects her daughters to wrap men around our little fingers, break their hearts, et cetera."

I remembered the many times Aphrodite and I had fallen out. I was a sucker for romance. Aphrodite always had fun sending tragic lovers my way. "Yes. Your mother has definite ideas about how romance should be."

"So if you take *that* away," Piper said, "the goddess of marriage pushing me to settle down with a nice boy, the goddess of love pushing me to be the perfect romantic lady or whatever—"

"You're wondering who you are without all that pressure."

She stared at the remains of the scarlet evening dress. "For the Cherokee, like traditionally speaking? Your heritage comes from your mom's side. The clan she comes from is the clan you come from. The dad's side doesn't really count." She let out a brittle laugh. "Which means, technically, I'm not Cherokee. I don't belong to any of the seven main clans, because my mom is a Greek goddess."

"Ah."

"So, I mean, do I even have *that* to define myself? The last few months I've been trying to learn more about my heritage. Picking up my granddad's blowgun, talking to my dad about family history to take his mind off stuff. But what if I'm not *any* of the things I've been told I am? I have to figure out who I am."

"Have you come to any conclusions?"

She brushed her hair behind her ear. "I'm in process."

I could appreciate that. I, too, was in process. It was painful.

A line from the Joe Walsh song reverberated in my head. "'Nature loves her little surprises,'" I said.

Piper snorted. "She sure does."

I stared at the rows of Caligula's outfits—everything from wedding gowns to Armani suits to gladiator armor.

"It's been my observation," I said, "that you humans are more than the sum of your history. You can choose how much of your ancestry to embrace. You can overcome the expectations of your family and your society. What you cannot do, and should never do, is try to be someone other than yourself—Piper McLean."

She gave me a wry smile. "That's nice. I like that. You're sure you're not the god of wisdom?"

"I applied for the job," I said, "but they gave it to someone else. Something about inventing olives." I rolled my eyes.

Piper burst out laughing, which made me feel as if a good strong wind had finally blown all the wildfire smoke out of California. I grinned in response. When was the last time I'd had such a positive exchange with an equal, a friend, a kindred soul? I could not recall.

"All right, O Wise One." Piper struggled to her feet. "We'd better go. We've got a lot more boats to trespass on."

Boat forty-one: Lingerie department. I will spare you the frilly details.

Boat forty-two: a regular super-yacht, with a few crew members who ignored us, two mercenaries whom Piper charmed into jumping overboard, and a two-headed man whom I shot in the groin (by pure luck) and made disintegrate.

"Why would you put a regular boat between your clothes boats and your shoe boat?" Piper wondered. "That's just bad organization."

She sounded remarkably calm. My own nerves were starting to fray. I felt like I was splitting into pieces, the way I used to when several dozen Greek cities all prayed for me to manifest my glorious self at the same time in different places. It's *so* annoying when cities don't coordinate their holy days.

We crossed the port side, and I caught a glimpse of movement in the sky above us—a pale gliding shape much too big to be a seagull. When I looked again, it was gone.

"I think we're being followed," I said. "Our friend Crest."

Piper scanned the night sky. "What do we do about it?"

"I'd recommend nothing," I said. "If he wanted to attack us or raise the alarm, he could've already done it."

Piper did not look happy about our big-eared stalker, but we kept moving.

At last we reached *Julia Drusilla XLIII*, the fabled ship of shoes.

This time, thanks to the tip-off from Amax and his men, we expected pandai guards, led by the fearsome Wah-Wah. We were better prepared to deal with them.

As soon as we stepped onto the foredeck, I readied my

ukulele. Piper said very quietly, "Wow, I hope nobody overhears our secrets!"

Instantly, four pandai came running—two from the port side and two from starboard, all stumbling over each other to get to us first.

As soon as I could see the whites of their tragi, I strummed a C minor 6 tritone chord at top volume, which to creatures with such exquisite hearing must have felt like getting Q-tipped with live electric wires.

The pandai screeched and fell to their knees, giving Piper time to disarm them and zip-tie them thoroughly. Once they were properly hog-tied, I stopped my torturous ukulele assault.

"Which of you is Wah-Wah?" I demanded.

The pandos on the far left snarled, "Who wants to know?"

"Hello, Wah-Wah," I said. "We're looking for the emperor's magical shoes—you know, the ones that let him navigate the Burning Maze. You could save us a lot of time by telling us where they are on board."

He thrashed and cursed. "Never!"

"Or," I said, "I'll let my friend Piper do the searching, while I stay here and serenade you with my out-of-tune ukulele. Are you familiar with 'Tiptoe through the Tulips' by Tiny Tim?"

Wah-Wah spasmed with terror. "Deck two, port side, third door!" he spluttered. "Please, no Tiny Tim! No Tiny Tim!"

"Enjoy your evening," I said.

We left them in peace and went to find some footwear.

29

A horse is a horse
Of course, of course, and no one
Can— RUN! HE'LL KILL YOU!

A FLOATING MANSION full of shoes. Hermes would have been in paradise.

Not that he was the *official* god of shoes, mind you, but as patron deity of travelers, he was the closest thing we Olympians had. Hermes's collection of Air Jordans was unrivaled. He had closets full of winged sandals, rows of patent leather, racks of blue suede, and don't get me started on his roller skates. I still have nightmares about him skating through Olympus with his big hair and gym shorts and high striped socks, listening to Donna Summer on his Walkman.

As Piper and I made our way to deck two, port side, we passed illuminated podiums displaying designer pumps, a hallway lined floor-to-ceiling with shelves of red leather boots, and one room with nothing but soccer cleats, for reasons I couldn't fathom.

The room Wah-Wah had directed us to seemed to be more about quality than quantity.

It was the size of a goodly apartment, with windows that overlooked the sea so the emperor's prize shoes could have a nice view. In the middle of the room, a comfortable pair of couches faced a coffee table with a collection of exotic bottled waters, just in case you got thirsty and needed to rehydrate between putting on the left shoe and the right.

As for the shoes themselves, along the fore and aft walls were rows of . . .

"Whoa," Piper said.

I thought that summed it up rather well: rows of *whoa.*

On one pedestal sat a pair of Hephaestus's battle boots—huge contraptions with spiked heels and toes, built-in chain-mail socks, and laces that were tiny bronze automaton serpents to prevent unauthorized wearers.

On another pedestal, in a clear acrylic box, a pair of winged sandals fluttered around, trying to escape.

"Could those be the ones we need?" Piper asked. "We could fly right through the maze."

The idea was appealing, but I shook my head. "Winged shoes are tricky. If we put them on and they're enchanted to take us to the wrong place—"

"Oh, right," Piper said. "Percy told me about a pair that almost . . . uh, never mind."

We examined the other pedestals. Some held shoes that were merely one-of-a-kind: platform boots studded with diamonds, dress shoes made from the skin of the now extinct Dodo (rude!), or a pair of Adidas signed by all the players of the 1987 LA Lakers.

Other shoes were magical, and labeled as such: a pair of slippers woven by Hypnos to give pleasant dreams and deep sleep; a pair of dancing shoes fashioned by my old friend Terpsichore, the Muse of dance. I'd only seen a few of those over the years. Astaire and Rogers both had a pair.

So did Baryshnikov. Then there was a pair of Poseidon's old loafers, which would ensure perfect beach weather, good fishing, gnarly waves, and excellent tanning. Those loafers sounded pretty good to me.

"There." Piper pointed to an old pair of leather sandals casually tossed in the corner of the room. "Can we assume the least likely shoes are actually the most likely?"

I didn't like that assumption. I preferred it when the most likely to be popular or wonderful or talented turned out to be the one who *was* the most popular, wonderful, or talented, because that was normally me. Still, in this case, I thought Piper might be right.

I knelt next to the sandals. "These are caligae. Legionnaire's shoes."

I hooked one finger and lifted the shoes by the straps. There wasn't much to them—just leather soles and laces, worn soft and darkened with age. They looked like they'd seen many marches, but they'd been kept well-oiled and lovingly maintained through the centuries.

"Caligae," Piper said. "Like Caligula."

"Exactly," I agreed. "These are the adult version of the little booties that gave Gaius Julius Caesar Germanicus his childhood nickname."

Piper wrinkled her nose. "Can you sense any magic?"

"Well, they're not buzzing with energy," I said. "Or giving me flashbacks of stinky feet, or compelling me to put them on. But I think they're the right shoes. These are his namesake. They carry his power."

"Hmm. I suppose if you can talk to an arrow, you can read a pair of sandals."

"It's a gift," I agreed.

She knelt next to me and took one of the sandals. "This won't fit me. Way too big. They look about your size."

"Are you implying I have big feet?"

Her smile flickered. "These look almost as uncomfortable as the shoes of shame—this horrible white pair of nurse's shoes we had back in the Aphrodite cabin. You'd have to wear them as punishment if you did something bad."

"That sounds like Aphrodite."

"I got rid of them," she said. "But these . . . I suppose as long as you don't mind putting your feet where Caligula's feet have been—"

"DANGER!" cried a voice behind us.

Sneaking up behind someone and yelling *danger* is an excellent way to make them simultaneously leap, spin, and fall on their butts, which is what Piper and I did.

In the doorway stood Crest, his white fur matted and dripping as if he'd flown through Caligula's swimming pool. His eight-fingered hands wrapped around the door frame on either side. His chest heaved. His black suit was torn to pieces.

"Strixes," he panted.

My heart leaped into my nasal cavity. "Are they following you?"

He shook his head, his ears rippling like startled squids. "I think I evaded them, but—"

"Why are you here?" Piper demanded, her hand going to her dagger.

The look in Crest's eyes was a mixture of panic and

hunger. He pointed to my ukulele. "You can show me how to play?"

"I . . . yes," I said. "Though a guitar might be better, given the size of your hands."

"That chord," he said. "The one that made Wah-Wah screech. I want it."

I rose slowly, so as not to startle him further. "Knowledge of the C minor 6 tri-chord is an awesome responsibility. But, yes, I could show you."

"And you." He looked at Piper. "The way you sing. Can you teach me?"

Piper's hand dropped from her hilt. "I—I guess I could try, but—"

"Then we must leave now!" Crest said. "They have already captured your friends!"

"*What?*" Piper got to her feet. "Are you sure?"

"The scary girl. The lightning boy. Yes."

I swallowed back my despair. Crest had given a flawless description of Meg and Jason. "Where?" I asked. "Who has them?"

"*Him*," Crest said. "The emperor. His people will be here soon. We must fly! Be the musicians in the world!"

Under different circumstances, I would have considered this excellent advice, but not with our friends captured. I wrapped up the emperor's sandals and stuffed them into the bottom of my quiver. "Can you take us to our friends?"

"No!" Crest wailed. "You will die! The sorceress—"

Why did Crest not hear the enemies sneaking up behind him? I don't know. Perhaps Jason's lightning had left a ringing in his ears. Perhaps he was too distressed, too focused on us to guard his own back.

Whatever the case, Crest hurtled forward, crashing face-first into the box with the winged sandals. He collapsed on the carpet, the freed flying shoes kicking him repeatedly about the head. On his back glistened two deep impressions in the shape of horse hooves.

In the doorway stood a majestic white stallion, his head just clearing the top of the frame. In a flash, I realized why the emperor's yachts had such tall ceilings, wide hallways and doorways: they were designed to accommodate this horse.

"Incitatus," I said.

He locked eyes with me as no horse should be able to do—his huge brown pupils glinting with malicious awareness. "Apollo."

Piper looked stunned, as one does when encountering a talking horse on a shoe yacht.

She began to say, "What the—?"

Incitatus charged. He trampled straight over the coffee table and head-butted Piper against the wall with a sickening crunch. Piper dropped to the carpet.

I rushed toward her, but the horse slammed me away. I landed on the nearest sofa.

"Well, now." Incitatus surveyed the damage—the overturned pedestals and destroyed coffee table; broken bottles of exotic spring water seeping into the carpet; Crest groaning on the floor, the flying shoes still kicking him; Piper unmoving, blood trickling from her nose; and me on the sofa, cradling my bruised ribs.

"Sorry to intrude on your intrusion," he said. "I had to knock the girl out quickly, you understand. I don't like charmspeak."

His voice was the same as I'd heard while hiding in the dumpster behind Macro's Military Madness—deep and world-weary, tinged with annoyance, as if he'd seen every possible stupid thing bipeds could do.

I stared in horror at Piper McLean. She didn't appear to be breathing. I remembered the words of the Sibyl . . . especially that terrible word that began with *D*.

"You—you killed her," I stammered.

"Did I?" Incitatus nuzzled Piper's chest. "Nah. Not yet, but soon enough. Now come along. The emperor wants to see you."

30

I'll never leave you
Love will keep us together
Or glue. Glue works too

SOME OF MY BEST FRIENDS are magic horses.

Arion, the swiftest steed in the world, is my cousin, though he rarely comes to family dinners. The famous winged Pegasus is also a cousin—once removed, I think, since his mother was a gorgon. I'm not sure how that works. And, of course, the sun horses were my favorite steeds—though, thankfully, none of them talked.

Incitatus, however?

I didn't like him much.

He was a beautiful animal—tall and muscular, his coat gleaming like a sunlit cloud. His silky white tail swished behind him as if daring any flies, demigods, or other pests to approach his hindquarters. He wore neither tack nor saddle, though golden horseshoes gleamed on his hooves.

His very majesty grated on me. His jaded voice made me feel small and unimportant. But what I really hated were his eyes. Horse eyes should not be so cold and intelligent.

"Climb on," he said. "My boy is waiting."

"Your *boy*?"

He bared his marble-white teeth. "You know who I mean. Big C. Caligula. The New Sun who's gonna eat you for breakfast."

I sank deeper into the sofa cushions. My heart pounded. I had seen how fast Incitatus could move. I didn't like my chances against him alone. I would never be able to fire an arrow or strum a tune before he kicked my face in.

This would have been an excellent time for a surge of godly strength, so I could throw the horse out the window. Alas, I felt no such energy within me.

Nor could I expect any backup. Piper groaned, twitching her fingers. She looked half-conscious at best. Crest whimpered and tried to curl into a ball to escape the bullying of the winged shoes.

I rose from the couch, clenched my hands into fists, and forced myself to look Incitatus in the eye.

"I'm still the god Apollo," I warned. "I've faced two emperors already. I beat them both. Don't test me, horse."

Incitatus snorted. "Whatever, *Lester*. You're getting weaker. We've been keeping an eye on you. You've got hardly anything left. Now quit stalling."

"And how will you force me to come with you?" I demanded. "You can't pick me up and throw me on your back. You have no hands! No opposable thumbs! That was your fatal mistake!"

"Yeah, well, I could just kick you in the face. Or . . ." Incitatus nickered—a sound like someone calling their dog.

Wah-Wah and two of his guards slunk into the room. "You called, Lord Stallion?"

The horse grinned at me. "I don't need opposable

thumbs when I've got servants. Granted, they're *lame* servants that I had to chew free from their own zip ties—"

"Lord Stallion," Wah-Wah protested. "It was the ukulele! We couldn't—"

"Load 'em up," Incitatus ordered, "before you put me in a bad mood."

Wah-Wah and his helpers threw Piper across the horse's back. They forced me to climb up behind her, then they bound my hands once again—this time in front, at least, so I could better keep my balance.

Finally, they pulled Crest to his feet. They wrangled the physically abusive winged shoes back into their box, zip-tied Crest's hands, and force-marched him in front of our grim little parade. We made our way up to the deck, me ducking under every lintel, and retraced our path across the floating bridge of super-yachts.

Incitatus trotted along at an easy pace. Whenever we passed mercenaries or crew members, they knelt and lowered their heads. I wanted to believe they were honoring me, but I suspected they were honoring the horse's ability to bash their heads in if they didn't show proper respect.

Crest stumbled. The other pandai hauled him to his feet and prodded him along. Piper kept slipping off the stallion's back, but I did my best to keep her in place.

Once she muttered, "Uhn-fu."

Which might have meant *Thank you* or *Untie me* or *Why does my mouth taste like a horseshoe?*

Her dagger, Katoptris, was in easy reach. I stared at the hilt, wondering if I could draw it quickly enough to cut myself free, or plunge it into the horse's neck.

"I wouldn't," Incitatus said.

I stiffened. "What?"

"Use the knife. That'd be a bad move."

"Are—are you a mind-reader?"

The horse scoffed. "I don't need to read minds. You know how much you can tell from somebody's body language when they're riding your back?"

"I—I can't say that I've had the experience."

"Well, I could tell what you were planning. So don't. I'd have to throw you off. Then you and your girlfriend would probably crack your heads and die—"

"She's not my girlfriend!"

"—and Big C would be annoyed. He wants you to die in a certain way."

"Ah." My stomach felt as bruised as my ribs. I wondered if there was a special term for motion sickness while riding a horse on a boat. "So, when you said Caligula would *eat me for breakfast*—"

"Oh, I didn't mean that literally."

"Thank the gods."

"I meant the sorceress Medea will put you in chains and flay your human form to extract whatever remains of your godly essence. Then Caligula will consume your essence—yours and Helios's both—and make himself the new god of the sun."

"Oh." I felt faint. I assumed I still had *some* godly essence inside me—some tiny spark of my former awesomeness that allowed me to remember who I was and what I had once been capable of. I didn't want those last vestiges of divinity taken away, especially if the process involved flaying. The idea made my stomach churn. I hoped Piper wouldn't mind terribly if I threw up on her. "You—you seem like a reasonable horse, Incitatus. Why are you helping someone as volatile and treacherous as Caligula?"

Incitatus whinnied. "Volatile, schmolatile. The boy listens to me. He needs me. Doesn't matter how violent or unpredictable he may seem to others. I can keep him under control, use him to push through my agenda. I'm backing the right horse."

He didn't seem to recognize the irony of a horse backing the right horse. Also, I was surprised to hear that Incitatus *had* an agenda. Most equine agendas were fairly straightforward: food, running, more food, a good brushing. Repeat as desired.

"Does Caligula know that you're, ah, using him?"

"Of course!" said the horse. "Kid's not stupid. Once he gets what he wants, well . . . then we part ways. I intend to overthrow the human race and institute a government by the horses, for the horses."

"You . . . what?"

"You think equine self-governance is any crazier than a world ruled by the Olympian gods?"

"I never thought about it."

"You wouldn't, would you? You, with your bipedal arrogance! *You* don't spend your life with humans constantly expecting to *ride* you or have you pull their carts. Ah, I'm wasting my breath. You won't be around long enough to see the revolution."

Oh, reader, I can't express to you my terror—not at the idea of a horse revolution, but at the thought that my life was about to end! Yes, I know mortals face death, too, but it's *worse* for a god, I tell you! I'd spent millennia knowing I was immune to the great cycle of life and death. Then suddenly I find out—*LOL, not so much!* I was going to be flayed and consumed by a man who took his cues from a militant talking horse!

As we progressed down the chain of super-yachts, we saw more and more signs of recent battle. Boat twenty looked like it had been struck repeatedly with lightning. Its superstructure was a charred, smoking ruin, the blackened upper decks spackled with fire-extinguisher foam.

Boat eighteen had been converted into a triage center. The wounded were sprawled everywhere, groaning from bashed heads, broken limbs, bleeding noses, and bruised groins. Many of their injuries were at knee level or below—just where Meg McCaffrey liked to kick. A flock of strixes wheeled overhead, screeching hungrily. Perhaps they were just on guard duty, but I got the feeling they were waiting to see which of the wounded did not pull through.

Boat fourteen was Meg McCaffrey's coup de grace. Boston ivy had engulfed the entire yacht, including most of the crew, who were stitched to the walls by a thick web of crawlers. A cadre of horticulturists—no doubt called up from the botanical gardens on boat sixteen—were now trying to free their comrades using clippers and weed-whackers.

I was heartened to see that our friends had made it this far and caused so much damage. Perhaps Crest had been mistaken about them being captured. Surely two capable demigods like Jason and Meg would have managed to escape if they got cornered. I was counting on it, since I now needed them to rescue me.

But what if they could not? I racked my brain for clever ideas and devious schemes. Rather than racing, my mind moved at a wheezing jog.

I managed to come up with phase one of my master plan: I would escape without getting myself killed, then free my friends. I was hard at work on phase two—*how do I do that?*—when I ran out of time. Incitatus crossed to the deck of *Julia Drusilla XII*, cantered through a set of double golden doors, and carried us down a ramp into the ship's interior, which contained a single massive room—the audience chamber of Caligula.

Entering this space was like plunging down the throat of a sea monster. I'm sure the effect was intentional. The emperor wanted you to feel a sense of panic and helplessness.

You have been swallowed, the room seemed to say. *Now you will be digested.*

No windows here. The fifty-foot-high walls screamed with garishly painted frescoes of battles, volcanoes, storms, wild parties—all images of power gone amok, boundaries erased, nature overturned.

The tiled floor was a similar study in chaos—intricate, nightmarish mosaics of the gods being devoured by various monsters. Far above, the ceiling was painted black, and dangling from it were golden candelabras, skeletons in cages, and bare swords that hung by the thinnest of cords and looked ready to impale anyone below.

I found myself tilting sideways on Incitatus's back, trying

to find my equilibrium, but it was impossible. The chamber offered no safe place to rest my gaze. The rocking of the yacht didn't help.

Standing guard along the length of the throne room were a dozen pandai—six to port and six to starboard. They held gold-tipped spears and wore golden chain mail from head to foot, including giant metal flaps over their ears that, when struck, must have given them terrible tinnitus.

At the far end of the room, where the boat's hull narrowed to a point, the emperor had set his dais—putting his back to the corner like any good paranoid ruler. Before him swirled two columns of wind and debris that I couldn't quite make sense of—some sort of ventus performance art?

At the emperor's right hand stood another pandos dressed in the full regalia of a praetorian commander—Reverb, I guessed, captain of the guard. To the emperor's left stood Medea, her eyes gleaming with triumph.

The emperor himself was much as I remembered—young and lithe, handsome enough, though his eyes were too far apart, his ears too prominent (but not in comparison to the pandai), his smile too thin.

He was dressed in white slacks, white boat shoes, a striped blue-and-white shirt, a blue blazer, and a captain's hat. I had a horrible flashback to 1975, when I'd made the mistake of blessing Captain and Tennille with their hit single "Love Will Keep Us Together." If Caligula was the Captain, that made Medea *Tennille*, which felt wrong on so many levels. I tried to push the thought from my mind.

As our procession approached the throne, Caligula

leaned forward and rubbed his hands, as if the next course of his dinner had just arrived.

"Perfect timing!" he said. "I've been having the most fascinating conversation with your friends."

My friends?

Only then did my brain allow me to process what was inside the swirling columns of wind.

In one hovered Jason Grace. In the other, Meg McCaffrey. Both struggled helplessly. Both screamed without making a sound. Their tornado prisons whirled with glittering shrapnel—tiny pieces of Celestial bronze and Imperial gold that sliced at their clothes and skin, slowly cutting them to pieces.

Caligula rose, his placid brown eyes fixed on me. "Incitatus, this can't actually be him, can it?"

"Afraid so, pal," said the horse. "May I present the pathetic excuse for a god, Apollo, also known as Lester Papadopoulos."

The stallion knelt on his forelegs, spilling Piper and me onto the floor.

31

I give you my heart
I mean metaphorically
Put away that knife

I COULD THINK OF MANY NAMES to call Caligula. *Pal* was not one of them.

Nevertheless, Incitatus seemed perfectly at home in the emperor's presence. He trotted to starboard, where two pandai began brushing his coat while a third knelt to offer him oats from a golden bucket.

Jason Grace lashed out in his wind tunnel of shrapnel, trying to break free. He cast a distressed look at Piper and yelled something I couldn't hear. In the other wind column, Meg floated with her arms and legs crossed, scowling like an angry genie, ignoring the bits of metal cutting her face.

Caligula stepped down from his dais. He strolled between the wind columns with a jaunty lilt in his step, no doubt the effect of wearing a yacht-captain outfit. He stopped a few feet in front of me. In his open palm, he bounced two small bits of gold—Meg McCaffrey's rings.

"This must be the lovely Piper McLean." He frowned down at her, as if just realizing she was barely conscious. "Why is she like this? I can't taunt her in this condition. Reverb!"

The praetor commander snapped his fingers. Two guards shuffled forward and dragged Piper to her feet. One waved a small bottle under her nose—smelling salts, perhaps, or some vile magical equivalent of Medea's.

Piper's head snapped back. A shudder ran through her body, then she pushed the pandai away.

"I'm fine." She blinked at her surroundings, saw Jason and Meg in their wind columns, then glared at Caligula. She struggled to pull her knife, but her fingers didn't seem to work. "I'll *kill* you."

Caligula chuckled. "That would be amusing, my love. But let's not kill each other quite yet, eh? Tonight, I have other priorities."

He beamed at me. "Oh, Lester. What a *gift* Jupiter has given me!" He walked a circuit around me, running his fingertips along my shoulders as if checking for dust. I suppose I should have attacked him, but Caligula radiated such cool confidence, such a powerful aura that it befuddled my mind.

"Not much left of your godliness, is there?" he said. "Don't worry. Medea will coax it out of you. Then I'll take revenge on Zeus *for* you. Have some comfort in that."

"I—I don't want revenge."

"Of course you do! It will be wonderful, just wait and see. . . . Well, actually, you'll be dead, but you'll have to trust me. I'll make you proud."

"Caesar," Medea called from her side of the dais, "perhaps we could begin soon?"

She did her best to hide it, but I heard the strain in her voice. As I'd seen in the parking garage of death, even

Medea had her limits. Keeping Meg and Jason in twin tornadoes must have required a great deal of her strength. She couldn't possibly maintain her ventus prisons *and* do whatever magic she needed to de-god me. If only I could figure out how to exploit that weakness . . .

Annoyance flickered across Caligula's face. "Yes, yes, Medea. In a moment. First, I must greet my loyal servants. . . ." He turned to the pandai who'd accompanied us from the ship of shoes. "Which of you is Wah-Wah?"

Wah-Wah bowed, his ears spreading across the mosaic floor. "H-here, sire."

"Served me well, have you?"

"Yes, sire!"

"Until today."

The pandos looked like he was trying to swallow Tiny Tim's ukulele. "They—they tricked us, lord! With horrible music!"

"I see," Caligula said. "And how do you intend to make this right? How can I be sure of your loyalty?"

"I—I pledge you my heart, sire! Now and always! My men and I—" He clamped his huge hands over his mouth.

Caligula smiled blandly. "Oh, Reverb?"

His praetor commander stepped forward. "Lord?"

"You heard Wah-Wah?"

"Yes, lord," Reverb agreed. "His heart is yours. And also his men's hearts."

"Well, then." Caligula flicked his fingers in a vague *go away* gesture. "Take them outside and collect what is mine."

The throne-room guards from the port side marched

forward and seized Wah-Wah and his two lieutenants by the arms.

"No!" Wah-Wah screamed. "No, I—I didn't mean—!"

He and his men thrashed and sobbed, but it was no use. The golden-armored pandai dragged them away.

Reverb gestured at Crest, who stood trembling and whimpering next to Piper. "What about this one, sire?"

Caligula narrowed his eyes. "Remind me why this one has white fur?"

"He's young, sire," Reverb said, not a trace of sympathy in his voice. "Our people's fur darkens with age."

"I see." Caligula stroked Crest's face with the back of his hand, causing the young pandos to whimper even louder. "Leave him. He's amusing, and he seems harmless enough. Now shoo, Commander. Bring me those hearts."

Reverb bowed and hurried after his men.

My pulse hammered in my temples. I wanted to convince myself things were not so bad. Half the emperor's guards and their commander had just left. Medea was under the strain of controlling two venti. That meant only six elite pandai, a killer horse, and an immortal emperor to deal with. Now was the optimal time for me to execute my clever plan . . . if only I had one.

Caligula stepped to my side. He threw his arm around me like an old friend. "You see, Apollo? I'm not *crazy*. I'm not *cruel*. I just take people at their word. If you promise me your life, or your heart, or your wealth . . . then you should *mean* it, don't you think?"

My eyes watered. I was too afraid to blink.

"Your friend Piper, for instance," Caligula said. "She wanted to spend time with her dad. She resented his career. So, guess what? I took that career away! If she'd just gone to Oklahoma with him, like they'd planned, she could've gotten what she wanted! But does she thank me? No. She comes here to kill me."

"I *will*," Piper said, her voice a bit steadier. "Take my word on that."

"Exactly my point," Caligula said. "No gratitude."

He patted me on the chest, sending starbursts of pain across my bruised ribs. "And Jason Grace? He wants to be a priest or something, build shrines to the gods. Fine! I *am* a god. I have no problem with that! Then he comes here to wreck my yachts with lightning. Is that priestlike behavior? I don't think so."

He strolled toward the swirling columns of wind. This left his back exposed, but neither Piper nor I moved to attack him. Even now, recalling it, I cannot tell you why. I felt so powerless, as if I were caught in a vision that had happened centuries before. For the first time, I sensed what it would be like if the Triumvirate controlled every Oracle. They would not just foresee the future—they would shape it. Their every word would become inexorable destiny.

"And this one." Caligula studied Meg McCaffrey. "Her father once swore he wouldn't rest until he reincarnated the blood-born, the silver wives! Can you *believe* it?"

Blood-born. Silver wives. Those words sent a jolt through my nervous system. I felt I should know what they meant, how they related to the seven green seeds Meg had planted on the hillside. As usual, my human brain screamed in protest as I attempted to dredge the information from its depths. I could almost see the annoying FILE NOT FOUND message flashing behind my eyes.

Caligula grinned. "Well, of course I took Dr. McCaffrey at his word! I burned his stronghold to the ground. But honestly, I thought I was quite generous to let him and his daughter live. Little Meg had a wonderful life with my nephew Nero. If she'd just kept her promises to him . . ." He wagged his finger disapprovingly at her.

On the starboard side of the room, Incitatus looked up from his golden oat bucket and belched. "Hey, Big C? Great speech and all. But shouldn't we kill the two in the whirlwinds so Medea can turn her attention to flaying Lester alive? I really want to see that."

"Yes, please," Medea agreed, her teeth clenched.

"NO!" Piper shouted. "Caligula, let my friends go."

Unfortunately, she could barely stand up straight. Her voice shook.

Caligula chuckled. "My love, I've been trained to resist charmspeak by Medea herself. You'll have to do better than that if—"

"Incitatus," Piper called, her voice a little stronger, "kick Medea in the head."

Incitatus flared his nostrils. "I think I'll kick Medea in the head."

"No, you won't!" Medea shrieked in a sharp burst of charmspeak. "Caligula, silence the girl!"

Caligula strode over to Piper. "Sorry, love."

He backhanded her across the mouth so hard she turned a full circle before collapsing.

"OHHH!" Incitatus whinnied with pleasure. "Good one!"

I broke.

Never had I felt such rage. Not when I destroyed the entire family of Niobids for their insults. Not when I fought Heracles in the chamber of Delphi. Not even when I struck down the Cyclopes who had made my father's murderous lightning.

I decided at that moment Piper McLean would not die tonight. I charged Caligula, intent on wrapping my hands around his neck. I wanted to strangle him to death, if only to wipe that smug smile off his face.

I felt sure my godly power would return. I would rip the emperor apart in my righteous fury.

Instead, Caligula pushed me to the floor with hardly a glance.

"Please, Lester," he said. "You're embarrassing yourself."

Piper lay shivering as if she were cold.

Crest crouched nearby, trying in vain to cover his massive ears. No doubt he was regretting his decision to follow his dream of taking music lessons.

I fixed my eyes on the twin cyclones, hoping that Jason and Meg had somehow escaped. They had not, but strangely, as if by silent agreement, they seemed to have switched roles.

Rather than raging in response to Piper being struck, Jason now floated deathly still, his eyes closed, his face like stone. Meg, on the other hand, clawed at her ventus cage, screaming words I couldn't hear. Her clothes were in tatters. Her face was crosshatched with a dozen bleeding cuts, but she didn't seem to care. She kicked and punched and threw packets of seeds into the maelstrom, causing festive bursts of pansies and daffodils among the shrapnel.

By the imperial dais, Medea had turned pale and sweaty. Countering Piper's charmspeak must have taxed her, but that gave me no comfort.

Reverb and his guards would soon be back, bearing the hearts of the emperor's enemies.

A cold thought flooded through me. *The hearts of his enemies*.

I felt as if *I* had been backhanded. The emperor needed me alive, at least for the moment. Which meant my only leverage . . .

My expression must have been priceless. Caligula burst out laughing.

"Apollo, you look like someone stepped on your favorite lyre!" He tutted. "You think you've had it bad? I grew up as a hostage in my Uncle Tiberius's palace. Do you have *any* idea how evil that man was? I woke up every day expecting to be assassinated, just like the rest of my family. I became a consummate actor. Whatever Tiberius needed me to be, I was. And *I survived*. But you? Your life has been golden from start to finish. You don't have the stamina to be mortal."

He turned to Medea. "Very well, sorceress! You may turn your little blenders up to *puree* and kill the two prisoners. Then we will deal with Apollo."

Medea smiled. "Gladly."

"Wait!" I screamed, pulling an arrow from my quiver.

The emperor's remaining guards leveled their spears, but the emperor shouted, "HOLD!"

I didn't try to draw my bow. I didn't attack Caligula. Instead, I turned the arrow inward and pressed the point against my chest.

Caligula's smile evaporated. He examined me with thinly veiled contempt. "Lester . . . what are you doing?"

"Let my friends go," I said. "All of them. Then you can have me."

The emperor's eyes gleamed like a strix's. "And if I don't?"

I summoned my courage, and issued a threat I never could have imagined in my previous four thousand years of life. "I'll kill myself."

32

Don't make me do it
I'm crazy, I'll do it, I'll—
Ow, that really hurt

OH, NO, THOU SHALT NOT, buzzed a voice in my head.

My noble gesture was ruined when I realized I had, once again, drawn the Arrow of Dodona by mistake. It shook violently in my hand, no doubt making me look even more terrified than I was. Nevertheless, I held it fast.

Caligula narrowed his eyes. "You would never. You don't have a self-sacrificing instinct in your body!"

"Let them go." I pressed the arrow against my skin, hard enough to draw blood. "Or you'll never be the sun god."

The arrow hummed angrily, *KILLETH THYSELF WITH SOME OTHER PROJECTILE, KNAVE. OF COMMON MURDER WEAPONS, I AM NONE!*

"Oh, Medea," Caligula called over his shoulder, "if he kills himself in this fashion, can you still do your magic?"

"You *know* I can't," she complained. "It's a complicated ritual! We can't have him murdering himself in some sloppy way before I'm prepared."

"Well, that's mildly annoying." Caligula sighed. "Look, Apollo, you can't expect this will have a happy ending. I am not Commodus. I'm not playing a game. Be a nice boy and let Medea kill you in the correct way. Then I'll give these others a painless death. That's my best offer."

I decided Caligula would make a terrible car salesman.

Next to me, Piper shivered on the floor, her neural pathways probably overloaded by trauma. Crest had wrapped himself in his own ears. Jason continued to meditate in his cone of swirling shrapnel, though I couldn't imagine he would achieve nirvana under those circumstances.

Meg yelled and gesticulated at me, perhaps telling me not to be a fool and put down the arrow. I took no pleasure in the fact that, for once, I couldn't hear her orders.

The emperor's guards stayed where they were, gripping their spears. Incitatus munched his oats like he was at the movies.

"Last chance," Caligula said.

Somewhere behind me, at the top of the ramp, a voice called, "My lord!"

Caligula looked over. "What is it, Flange? I'm a little busy here."

"N-news, my lord."

"Later."

"Sire, it's about the northern attack."

I felt a surge of hope. The assault on New Rome was happening tonight. I didn't have the good hearing of a pandos, but the hysterical urgency in Flange's tone was unmistakable. He was *not* bringing the emperor good news.

Caligula's expression soured. "Come here, then. And don't touch the idiot with the arrow."

The pandos Flange shuffled past me and whispered something in the emperor's ear. Caligula may have considered himself a consummate actor, but he didn't do a good job of hiding his disgust.

"How disappointing." He tossed Meg's golden rings aside like they were worthless pebbles. "Your sword, please, Flange."

"I—" Flange fumbled for his khanda. "Y-yes, lord."

Caligula examined the blunt serrated blade, then returned it to its owner with vicious force, plunging it into the poor pandos's gut. Flange howled as he crumbled to dust.

Caligula faced me. "Now, where were we?"

"Your northern attack," I said. "Didn't go so well?"

It was foolish of me to goad him, but I couldn't help it. At that moment, I wasn't any more rational than Meg McCaffrey—I just wanted to hurt Caligula, to smash everything he owned to dust.

He waved aside my question. "Some jobs I have to do myself. That's fine. You'd think a *Roman* demigod camp would obey orders from a *Roman* emperor, but alas."

"The Twelfth Legion has a long history of supporting *good* emperors," I said. "And of deposing bad ones."

Caligula's left eye twitched. "Oh, Boost, where are you?"

On the port side, one of the horse-groomer pandai dropped his brush in alarm. "Yes, lord?"

"Take your men," Caligula said. "Spread the word. We break formation immediately and sail north. We have unfinished business in the Bay Area."

"But, sire . . ." Boost looked at me, as if deciding whether I was enough of a threat to warrant leaving the emperor without his remaining guards. "Yes, sire."

The rest of the pandai shuffled off, leaving Incitatus without anyone to hold his golden oat bucket.

"Hey, C," said the stallion. "Aren't you putting the cart before the horse? Before we head off to war, you've got to finish your business with Lester."

"Oh, I will," Caligula promised. "Now, Lester, we both know you're not going to—"

He lunged with blinding speed, making a grab for the arrow. I'd been anticipating that. Before he could stop me, I cleverly plunged the arrow into my chest. Ha! That would teach Caligula to underestimate me!

Dear reader, it takes a great deal of willpower to intentionally harm yourself. And not the *good* kind of willpower—the stupid, reckless kind you should *never* try to summon, even in an effort to save your friends.

As I stabbed myself, I was shocked by the sheer amount of pain I experienced. Why did killing yourself have to *hurt* so much?

My bone marrow turned to lava. My lungs filled with hot wet sand. Blood soaked my shirt and I fell to my knees, gasping and dizzy. The world spun around me as if the entire throne room had become a giant ventus prison.

VILLAINY! The Arrow of Dodona's voice buzzed in my mind (and now also in my chest). *THOU DIDST* NOT *JUST IMPALE ME HEREIN! O, VILE, MONSTROUS FLESH!*

A distant part of my brain thought it was unfair for him

to complain, since I was the one dying, but I couldn't have spoken even if I'd wanted to.

Caligula rushed forward. He grabbed the shaft of the arrow, but Medea yelled, "Stop!"

She ran across the throne room and knelt at my side.

"Pulling out the arrow could make matters worse!" she hissed.

"He stabbed himself in the chest," Caligula said. "How can it be worse?"

"Fool," she muttered. I wasn't sure whether the comment was directed at me or Caligula. "I don't want him to bleed out." She removed a black silk bag from her belt, pulled out a stoppered glass vial, and shoved the bag at Caligula. "Hold this."

She uncorked the vial and poured its contents over the entry wound.

COLD! complained the Arrow of Dodona. *COLD! COLD!*

Personally, I didn't feel a thing. The searing pain had become a dull, throbbing ache throughout my whole body. I was pretty sure that was a bad sign.

Incitatus trotted over. "Whoa, he really did it. That's a horse of a different color."

Medea examined the wound. She cursed in ancient Colchian, calling into question my mother's past romantic relationships.

"This idiot can't even *kill* himself right," grumbled the sorceress. "It appears that, somehow, he missed his heart."

'TWAS ME, WITCH! the arrow intoned from within my rib cage. *DOST THOU THINK I WOULD FAIN ALLOW*

MYSELF TO BE EMBEDDED IN THE DISGUSTING HEART OF LESTER? I DODGED AND WEAVED!

I made a mental note to either thank or break the Arrow of Dodona later, whichever made the most sense at the time.

Medea snapped her fingers at the emperor. "Hand me the red vial."

Caligula scowled, clearly not used to playing surgical nurse. "I never rummage through a woman's purse. Especially a sorceress's."

I thought this was the surest sign yet that he was perfectly sane.

"If you want to be the sun god," Medea snarled, "do it!"

Caligula found the red vial.

Medea coated her right hand with the gooey contents. With her left, she grabbed the Arrow of Dodona and yanked it from my chest.

I screamed. My vision went dark. My left pectorals felt like they were being excavated with a drill bit. When I regained my sight, I found the arrow wound plugged with a thick red substance like the wax of a letter seal. The pain was horrible, unbearable, but I could breathe again.

If I hadn't been so miserable, I might have smiled in triumph. I had been counting on Medea's healing powers. She was almost as skilled as my son Asclepius, though her bedside manner was not as good, and her cures tended to involve dark magic, vile ingredients, and the tears of small children.

I had not, of course, expected Caligula to let my friends

go. But I had hoped, with Medea distracted, she might lose control of her venti. And so she did.

That moment is fixed in my mind: Incitatus peering down at me, his muzzle flecked with oats; the sorceress Medea examining my wound, her hands sticky with blood and magic paste; Caligula standing over me, his splendid white slacks and shoes freckled with my blood; and Piper and Crest on the floor nearby, their presence momentarily forgotten by our captors. Even Meg seemed frozen within her churning prison, horrified by what I had done.

That was the last moment before everything went wrong, before our great tragedy unspooled—when Jason Grace thrust out his arms, and the cages of wind exploded.

33

No good news awaits
I warned you right at the start
Turn away, reader

ONE TORNADO can ruin your whole day.

I'd seen the sort of devastation Zeus could wreak when he got angry at Kansas. So I was not surprised when the two shrapnel-filled wind spirits ripped through the *Julia Drusilla XII* like chain saws.

We all should have died in the blast. Of that I'm certain. But Jason channeled the explosion up, down, and sideways in a two-dimensional wave—blasting through the port and starboard walls; bursting through the black ceiling that showered us with golden candelabras and swords; jackhammering through the mosaic floor into the bowels of the ship. The yacht groaned and shook—metal, wood, and fiberglass snapping like bones in the mouth of a monster.

Incitatus and Caligula stumbled in one direction, Medea in the other. None of them suffered so much as a scratch. Meg McCaffrey, unfortunately, was on Jason's left. When the venti exploded, she flew sideways through a newly made rent in the wall and disappeared into the dark.

I tried to scream. I think it came out as more of a death

rattle, though. With the explosion ringing in my ears, I couldn't be sure.

I could barely move. There was no chance I could go after my young friend. I cast around desperately and fixed my gaze on Crest.

The young pandos's eyes were so wide they almost matched his ears. A golden sword had fallen from the ceiling and impaled itself in the tile floor between his legs.

"Rescue Meg," I croaked, "and I will teach you how to play any instrument you wish."

I didn't know how even a pandos could hear me, but Crest seemed to. His expression changed from shock to reckless determination. He scrambled across the tilting floor, spread his ears, and leaped into the rift.

The break in the floor began to widen, cutting us off from Jason. Ten-foot-tall waterfalls poured in from the damaged hull to port and starboard—washing the mosaic floors in dark water and flotsam, spilling into the widening chasm in the center of the room. Below, broken machinery steamed. Flames guttered as seawater filled the hold. Above, lining the edges of the shattered ceiling, pandai appeared, screaming and drawing weapons—until the sky lit up and tendrils of lightning blasted the guards into dust.

Jason stepped out of the smoke on the opposite side of the throne room, his gladius in his hand.

Caligula snarled. "You're one of those Camp Jupiter brats, aren't you?"

"I'm Jason Grace," he said. "Former praetor of the Twelfth Legion. Son of Jupiter. Child of Rome. But I belong to both camps."

"Good enough," Caligula said. "I'll hold *you* responsible for Camp Jupiter's treason tonight. Incitatus!"

The emperor snatched up a golden spear that was rolling across the floor. He vaulted onto his stallion's back, charged the chasm, and leaped it in a single bound. Jason threw himself aside to avoid getting trampled.

From somewhere to my left came a howl of anger. Piper McLean had risen. Her lower face was a nightmare—her swollen upper lip split across her teeth, her jaw askew, a trickle of blood coming from the edge of her mouth.

She charged Medea, who turned just in time to catch Piper's fist in her nose. The sorceress stumbled, pinwheeling her arms as Piper pushed her over the edge of the chasm. The sorceress disappeared into the churning soup of burning fuel and seawater.

Piper shouted at Jason. She might have been saying *COME ON!* But all that came out was a guttural cry.

Jason was a little busy. He dodged Incitatus's charge, parrying Caligula's spear with his sword, but he was moving slowly. I could only guess how much energy he'd expended controlling the winds and the lightning.

"Get out of here!" he called to us. "Go!"

An arrow sprouted from his left thigh. Jason grunted and stumbled. Above us, more pandai had gathered, despite the threat of severe thunderstorms.

Piper yelled in warning as Caligula charged again. Jason just managed to roll aside. He made a grabbing gesture at the air, and a gust of wind yanked him aloft. Suddenly he sat astride a miniature storm cloud with four funnel clouds for legs and a mane that crackled with lightning—Tempest, his ventus steed.

He rode against Caligula, jousting sword versus spear. Another arrow took Jason in the upper arm.

"I told you this isn't a game!" yelled Caligula. "You don't walk away from me alive!"

Below, an explosion rocked the ship. The room split farther apart. Piper staggered, which probably saved her life; three arrows hit the spot where she'd been standing.

Somehow, she pulled me to my feet. I was clutching the Arrow of Dodona, though I had no memory of picking it up. I saw no sign of Crest, or Meg, or even Medea. An arrow sprouted from the toe of my shoe. I was in so much pain already I couldn't tell if it had pierced my foot or not.

Piper tugged at my arm. She pointed to Jason, her words urgent but unintelligible. I wanted to help him, but what could I do? I'd just stabbed myself in the chest. I was pretty sure that if I sneezed too hard, I would displace the red plug in my wound and bleed to death. I couldn't draw a bow or even strum a ukulele. Meanwhile, on the broken roof line above us, more and more pandai appeared, eager to help me commit arrowcide.

Piper was no better off. The fact that she was on her feet at all was a miracle—the sort of miracle that comes back to kill you later when the adrenaline wears off.

Nevertheless, how could we leave?

I watched in horror as Jason and Caligula fought, Jason bleeding from arrows in each limb now, yet somehow still able to raise his sword. The space was too small for two men on horses, yet they circled one another, trading blows. Incitatus kicked at Tempest with his golden-shod front hooves. The ventus responded with bursts of electricity that scorched the stallion's white flanks.

As the former praetor and the emperor charged past each other, Jason met my eyes across the ruined throne room. His expression told me his plan with perfect clarity. Like me, he had decided that Piper McLean would not die tonight. For some reason, he had decided that I must live too.

He yelled again, "GO! Remember!"

I was slow, dumbstruck. Jason held my gaze a fraction of a second too long, perhaps to make sure that last word sank in: *remember*—the promise he had extracted from me a million years ago this morning, in his Pasadena dorm room.

While Jason's back was turned, Caligula wheeled about. He threw his spear, driving its point between Jason's shoulder blades. Piper screamed. Jason stiffened, his blue eyes wide in shock.

He slumped forward, wrapping his arms around Tempest's neck. His lips moved, as if he was whispering something to his steed.

Carry him away! I prayed, knowing that no god would listen. *Please, just let Tempest get him to safety!*

Jason toppled from his steed. He hit the deck facedown, the spear still in his back, his gladius clattering from his hand.

Incitatus trotted up to the fallen demigod. Arrows continued to rain around us.

Caligula stared at me across the chasm—giving me the

same displeased scowl my father used to before inflicting one of his punishments: *Now look what you've made me do.*

"I warned you," Caligula said. Then he glanced at the pandai above. "Leave Apollo alive. He's no threat. But kill the girl."

Piper howled, shaking with impotent rage. I stepped in front of her and waited for death, wondering with cold detachment where the first arrow might strike. I watched as Caligula plucked out his spear, then drove it again into Jason's back, removing any last hope that our friend might still be alive.

As the pandai drew their bows and took aim, the air crackled with charged ozone. The winds swirled around us. Suddenly Piper and I were whisked from the burning shell of the *Julia Drusilla XII* on the back of Tempest—the ventus carrying out Jason's last orders to get us safely away, whether we wanted it or not.

I sobbed in despair as we shot across the surface of Santa Barbara Harbor, the sounds of explosions still rumbling behind us.

34

Surfing accident
My new euphemism for
Worst evening ever

FOR THE NEXT FEW HOURS, my mind deserted me.

I do not remember Tempest dropping us on the beach, though he must have done so. I recall moments of Piper yelling at me, or sitting in the surf shuddering with dry sobs, or uselessly clawing gobs of wet sand and throwing them at the waves. A few times, she slapped away the ambrosia and nectar I tried to give her.

I remember slowly pacing the thin stretch of beach, my feet bare, my shirt cold from the seawater. The plug of healing goo throbbed in my chest, leaking a little blood from time to time.

We were no longer in Santa Barbara. There was no harbor, no string of super-yachts, just the dark Pacific stretching before us. Behind us loomed a dark cliff. A zigzag of wooden stairs led up toward the lights of a house at the top.

Meg McCaffrey was there too. Wait. When did Meg arrive? She was thoroughly drenched, her clothes shredded, her face and arms a war zone of bruises and cuts. She sat next to Piper, sharing ambrosia. I suppose *my* ambrosia wasn't good enough. The pandos Crest squatted some distance away at the base of the cliff, eyeing me hungrily as if waiting for his first music lesson to begin. The pandos must have done what I'd asked. Somehow, he'd found Meg, pulled her from the sea, and flown her here . . . wherever *here* was.

The thing I remember most clearly is Piper saying *He's not dead.*

She said this over and over, as soon as she could manage the words, once the nectar and ambrosia tamed the swelling around her mouth. She still looked awful. Her upper lip needed stitches. She would definitely have a scar. Her jaw, chin, and lower lip were one gigantic eggplant-colored bruise. I suspected her dentist bill would be hefty. Still, she forced out the words with steady determination. "He's not dead."

Meg held her shoulder. "Maybe. We'll find out. You need to rest and heal."

I stared incredulously at my young master. "*Maybe?* Meg, you didn't see what happened! He . . . Jason . . . the spear—"

Meg glared at me. She did not say *Shut up*, but I heard the order loud and clear. On her hands, her gold rings glinted, though I didn't know how she could have retrieved them. Perhaps, like so many magic weapons, they automatically returned to their owner if lost. It would be like Nero to give his stepdaughter such clingy gifts.

"Tempest will find Jason," Meg insisted. "We just have to wait."

Tempest . . . right. After the ventus had brought Piper and me here, I vaguely remembered Piper harassing the spirit, using garbled words and gestures to order him back to the yachts to find Jason. Tempest had raced off across the surface of the sea like an electrified waterspout.

Now, staring at the horizon, I wondered if I could dare hope for good news.

My memories from the ship were coming back, piecing themselves together into a fresco more horrible than anything painted on Caligula's walls.

The emperor had warned me: *This is not a game*. He was indeed not Commodus. As much as Caligula loved theatrics, he would never mess up an execution by adding glitzy special effects, ostriches, basketballs, race cars, and loud music. Caligula did not *pretend* to kill. He killed.

"He's not dead." Piper repeated her mantra, as if trying to charmspeak herself as well as us. "He's gone through too much to die now, like that."

I wanted to believe her.

Sadly, I had witnessed tens of thousands of mortal deaths. Few of them had any meaning. Most were untimely, unexpected, undignified, and at least slightly embarrassing. The people who deserved to die took forever to do so. Those who deserved to live always went too soon.

Falling in combat against an evil emperor in order to save one's friends . . . that seemed all too plausible a death for a hero like Jason Grace. He'd *told* me what the Erythraean Sibyl said. If I hadn't asked him to come with us—

Don't blame yourself, said Selfish Apollo. *It was his choice*.

It was my *quest!* said Guilty Apollo. *If not for me, Jason would be safe in his dorm room, sketching new shrines for obscure minor deities! Piper McLean would be unharmed, spending time with her father, preparing for a new life in Oklahoma.*

Selfish Apollo had nothing to say to this, or he kept it selfishly to himself.

I could only watch the sea and wait, hoping that Jason Grace would come riding out of the darkness alive and well.

At last, the smell of ozone laced the air. Lightning flashed across the surface of the water. Tempest charged ashore, a dark form laid across his back like a saddlebag.

The wind horse knelt. He gently spilled Jason onto the sand. Piper shouted and ran to his side. Meg followed. The most horrible thing was the momentary look of relief on their faces, before it was crushed.

Jason's skin was the color of blank parchment, speckled with slime, sand, and foam. The sea had washed away the blood, but his school dress shirt was stained as purple as a senatorial sash. Arrows protruded from his arms and legs. His right hand was fixed in a pointing gesture, as if he were still telling us to go. His expression didn't seem tortured or scared. He looked at peace, as if he'd just managed to fall asleep after a hard day. I didn't want to wake him.

Piper shook him and sobbed, "JASON!" Her voice echoed from the cliffs.

Meg's face settled into a hard scowl. She sat back on her haunches and looked up at me. "Fix him."

The force of the command pulled me forward, made me kneel at Jason's side. I put my hand on Jason's cold forehead, which only confirmed the obvious. "Meg, I cannot fix death. I wish I could."

"There's always a way," Piper said. "The physician's cure! Leo took it!"

I shook my head. "Leo had the cure ready at the moment he died," I said gently. "He went through many hardships in advance to get the ingredients. Even then, he needed Asclepius to make it. That wouldn't work here, not for Jason. I'm so sorry, Piper. It's too late."

"No," she insisted. "No, the Cherokee always taught . . ." She took a shaky breath, as if steeling herself for the pain of speaking so many words. "One of the most important stories. Back when man first started destroying nature, the animals decided he was a threat. They all vowed to fight back. Each animal had a different way to kill humans. But the plants . . . they were kind and compassionate. They vowed the *opposite*—that they'd each find their own way to protect people. So, there's a plant cure for everything, whatever disease or poison or wound. *Some* plant has the cure. You just have to know which one!"

I grimaced. "Piper, that story holds a great deal of wisdom. But even if I were still a god, I couldn't offer you a remedy to bring back the dead. If such a thing existed, Hades would never allow its use."

"The Doors of Death, then!" she said. "*Medea* came back that way! Why not Jason? There's always a way to cheat the system. Help me!"

Her charmspeak washed over me, as powerful as Meg's order. Then I looked at Jason's peaceful expression.

"Piper," I said, "you and Jason fought to *close* the Doors of Death. Because you knew it was not right to let the dead back into the world of the living. Jason Grace struck me as many things, but he wasn't a cheater. Would he want you to rend the heavens and the earth and the Underworld to bring him back?"

Her eyes flashed angrily. "You don't care because you're a god. You'll go back to Olympus after you free the Oracles, so what does it matter? You're using us to get what you want, like all the other gods."

"Hey," Meg said, gently but firmly. "That won't help."

Piper pressed a hand on Jason's chest. "What did he die for, Apollo? A pair of *shoes?*"

A jolt of panic almost blew out my chest plug. I'd entirely forgotten about the shoes. I tugged the quiver from my back and turned it upside down, shaking out the arrows.

The rolled-up sandals of Caligula tumbled onto the beach.

"They're here." I scooped them up, my hands trembling. "At least—at least we have them."

Piper let out a broken sob. She stroked Jason's hair. "Yeah, yeah, that's great. You can go see your Oracle now. The Oracle that got him KILLED!"

Somewhere behind me, partway up the cliff, a man's voice cried out, "Piper?"

Tempest fled, bursting into wind and raindrops.

Hurrying down the cliffside stairs, in plaid pajama pants and a white T-shirt, came Tristan McLean.

Of course, I realized. Tempest had brought us to the McLean house in Malibu. Somehow, he had known to come here. Piper's father must have heard her cries all the way from the top of the cliff.

He ran toward us, his flip-flops slapping against his soles, sand spraying around the cuffs of his pants, his shirt rippling in the wind. His dark disheveled hair blew in his eyes, but it did not hide his look of alarm.

"Piper, I was waiting for you!" he called. "I was on the terrace and—"

He froze, first seeing his daughter's brutalized face, then the body lying on the sand.

"Oh, no, no." He rushed to Piper. "What—what is—? Who—?"

Having assured himself that Piper was not in imminent danger of dying, he knelt next to Jason and put his hand against the boy's neck, checking for a pulse. He put his ear to Jason's mouth, checking for breath. Of course, he found none.

He looked at us in dismay. He did a double take when he noticed Crest crouched nearby, his massive white ears spread around him.

I could almost feel the Mist swirling around Tristan McLean as he attempted to decipher what he was seeing, trying to put it into a context his mortal brain could understand.

"Surfing accident?" he ventured. "Oh, Piper, you *know* those rocks are dangerous. Why didn't you *tell* me—? How did—? Never mind. Never mind." With shaking hands, he dug his phone from the pocket of his pajama pants and dialed 9-1-1.

The phone squealed and hissed.

"My phone isn't—I—I don't understand."

Piper broke down in sobs, pressing herself to her father's chest.

At that moment, Tristan McLean should have broken once and for all. His life had fallen apart. He'd lost everything he'd worked for his entire career. Now, finding his daughter injured and her former boyfriend dead on the beach of his foreclosed property—surely, that was enough to make anyone's sanity crumble. Caligula would have another reason to celebrate a good night of sadistic work.

Instead, human resilience surprised me once again. Tristan McLean's expression turned steely. His focus cleared. He must have realized his daughter needed him and he couldn't afford to indulge in self-pity. He had one important role left to play: the role of her father.

"Okay, baby," he said, cradling her head. "Okay, we'll—we'll figure this out. We'll get through it."

He turned and pointed at Crest, still lurking near the cliff. "You."

Crest hissed at him like a cat.

Mr. McLean blinked, his mind doing a hard reset.

He pointed at me. "You. Take the others up to the house. I'm going to stay with Piper. Use the landline in the kitchen. Call nine-one-one. Tell them . . ." He looked at Jason's broken body. "Tell them to get here right away."

Piper looked up, her eyes swollen and red. "And, Apollo? Don't come back. You hear me? Just—just go."

"Pipes," her father said. "It's not their—"

"GO!" she screamed.

As we made our way up the rickety stairs, I wasn't sure which felt heavier: my exhausted body, or the cannonball of grief and guilt that had settled in my chest. All the way to the house, I heard Piper's sobs echoing off the dark cliffs.

35

If you give a pan-
dos a ukulele, he
Will want lessons. DON'T.

THE NEWS SIMPLY WENT from bad to worse.

Neither Meg nor I could make the landline function. Whatever curse afflicted demigod use of communications, it prevented us from getting a dial tone.

In desperation, I asked Crest to try. For him, the phone worked fine. I took that as a personal affront.

I told him to dial 9-1-1. After he failed repeatedly, it dawned on me that he was trying to punch in IX-I-I. I showed him how to do it correctly.

"Yes," he said to the operator. "There is a dead human on the beach. He requires help. . . . The address?"

"Twelve Oro del Mar," I said.

Crest repeated this. "That is correct. . . . Who am I?" He hissed and hung up.

That seemed like our cue to leave.

Misery upon misery: Gleeson Hedge's 1979 Ford Pinto was still parked in front of the McLean house. Lacking a better option, I was forced to drive it back to Palm Springs. I still felt terrible, but the magic sealant Medea had used on my chest seemed to be mending me, slowly and painfully, like an army of little demons with staple guns running around in my rib cage.

Meg rode shotgun, filling the car with a smell like smoky sweat, damp clothes, and burning apples. Crest sat in the backseat with my combat ukulele, picking and strumming, though I had yet to teach him any chords. As I'd anticipated, the fret board was much too small for his eight-fingered hand. Every time he played a bad combination of notes (which was every time he played) he hissed at the instrument, as if he might be able to intimidate it into cooperating.

I drove in a daze. The farther we got from Malibu, the more I found myself thinking, *No. Surely that didn't happen. Today must have been a bad dream. I did not just watch Jason Grace die. I did not just leave Piper McLean sobbing on that beach. I would never allow something like that to happen. I'm a good person!*

I did not believe myself.

Rather, I was the sort of person who deserved to be driving a yellow Pinto in the middle of the night with a grumpy, raggedy girl and a hissing, ukulele-obsessed pandos for company.

I wasn't even sure why we were returning to Palm Springs. What good would it do? Yes, Grover and our other friends were expecting us, but all we had to offer them was tragic news and an old pair of sandals. Our goal was in downtown Los Angeles: the entrance to the Burning Maze. To make sure Jason's death was not in vain, we should have been driving straight there to find the Sibyl and free her from her prison.

Ah, but who was I kidding? I was in no shape to do anything. Meg wasn't much better off. The best I could hope for was to make it to Palm Springs without dozing at the wheel. Then I could curl up at the bottom of the Cistern and cry myself to sleep.

Meg propped her feet on the dashboard. Her glasses had snapped in half, but she continued to wear them like skewed aviator goggles.

"Give her time," she told me. "She's angry."

For a moment, I wondered if Meg was speaking of herself in the third person. That's all I needed. Then I realized she meant Piper McLean. In her own way, Meg was trying to comfort me. The terrifying marvels of the day would never cease.

"I know," I said.

"You tried to kill yourself," she noted.

"I—I thought it would . . . distract Medea. It was a mistake. It's all my fault."

"Nah. I get it."

Was Meg McCaffrey forgiving me? I swallowed back a sob.

"Jason made a choice," she said. "Same as you. Heroes have to be ready to sacrifice themselves."

I felt unsettled . . . and not just because Meg had used such a long sentence. I didn't like her definition of heroism. I'd always thought of a hero as someone who stood on a parade float, waved at the crowd, tossed candy, and basked in the adulation of the commoners. But sacrificing yourself? No. That would *not* be one of my bullet points for a hero-recruitment brochure.

Also, Meg seemed to be calling *me* a hero, putting me in the same category as Jason Grace. That didn't feel right. I made a much better god than a hero. What I'd told Piper was true about the finality of death. Jason would not be coming back. If I perished here on earth, I would not be getting a do-over either. I could never face that idea as calmly as Jason had. I had stabbed myself in the chest fully expecting that Medea would heal me, if only so she could flay me alive a few minutes later. I was a coward that way.

Meg picked at a callus on her palm. "You were right. About Caligula. Nero. Why I was so angry."

I glanced over. Her face was taut with concentration. She'd said the emperors' names with a strange detachment, as if she were examining deadly virus samples on the other side of a glass wall.

"And how do you feel now?" I asked.

Meg shrugged. "The same. Different. I don't know. When you cut the roots off a plant? That's how I feel. It's hard."

Meg's jumbled comments made sense to me, which wasn't a good sign for my sanity. I thought about Delos, the island of my birth, which had floated on the sea without roots until my mother, Leto, settled on it to give birth to my sister and me.

It was difficult for me to imagine the world before I was born, to imagine Delos as a place adrift. My home had literally grown roots because of my existence. I had never been unsure of who I was, or who my parents were, or where I was from.

Meg's Delos had never stopped drifting. Could I blame her for being angry?

"Your family is ancient," I noted. "The line of Plemnaeus gives you a proud heritage. Your father was doing important work at Aeithales. The blood-born, the silver wives . . . whatever those seeds are that you planted, they terrified Caligula."

Meg had so many new cuts on her face it was difficult to tell whether or not she was frowning. "And if I can't get those seeds to grow?"

I didn't hazard an answer. I could not handle any more thoughts of failure tonight.

Crest poked his head between the seats. "Can you show me the C minor six tri-chord now?"

Our reunion in Palm Springs was not a happy one.

Just from our condition, the dryads on duty could tell we brought bad news. It was two in the morning, but they gathered the entire population of the greenhouses in the Cistern, along with Grover, Coach Hedge, Mellie, and Baby Chuck.

When Joshua Tree saw Crest, the dryad scowled. "Why have you brought this creature into our midst?"

"More importantly," Grover said, "where are Piper and Jason?"

He met my gaze, and his composure collapsed like a tower of cards. "Oh, no. No."

We told them our story. Or rather, I did. Meg sat at the edge of the pond and stared desolately into the water. Crest crawled into one of the niches and wrapped his ears around himself like a blanket, cradling my ukulele the same way Mellie cradled Baby Chuck.

My voice broke several times as I described Jason's final battle. His death finally became real to me. I gave up any hope that I would wake from this nightmare.

I expected Gleeson Hedge to explode, to start swinging his bat at everything and everyone. But like Tristan McLean, he surprised me. The satyr became still and calm, his voice unnervingly even.

"I was the kid's protector," he said. "I should've been there."

Grover tried to console him, but Hedge raised a hand. "Don't. Just don't." He faced Mellie. "Piper's gonna need us."

The cloud nymph brushed away a tear. "Yes. Of course."

Aloe Vera wrung her hands. "Should I go, too? Maybe there's something I can do." She looked at me suspiciously. "Did you *try* aloe vera on this Grace boy?"

"I fear he is truly dead," I said, "beyond even the powers of aloe."

She looked unconvinced, but Mellie squeezed her shoulder. "You're needed here, Aloe. Heal Apollo and Meg. Gleeson, get the diaper bag. I'll meet you at the car."

With Baby Chuck in her arms, she floated up and out of the Cistern.

Hedge snapped his fingers at me. "Pinto keys."

I tossed them. "Please don't do anything rash. Caligula is . . . You can't—"

Hedge stopped me with a cold stare. "I've got Piper to take care of. That's my priority. I'll leave the rash stuff to other people."

I heard the bitter accusation in his voice. Coming from Coach Hedge, that seemed deeply unfair, but I didn't have the heart to protest.

Once the Hedge family was gone, Aloe Vera fussed over Meg and me, smearing goo on our injuries. She tutted at the red plug in my chest and replaced it with a lovely green spike from her hair.

The other dryads seemed at a loss for what to do or say. They stood around the pond, waiting and thinking. I supposed, as plants, they were comfortable with long silences.

Grover Underwood sat down heavily next to Meg. He moved his fingers over the holes of his reed pipes.

"Losing a demigod . . ." He shook his head. "That's the worst thing that can happen to a protector. Years ago, when I thought I'd lost Thalia Grace . . ." He stopped himself, then slumped under the weight of despair. "Oh, Thalia. When she hears about this . . ."

I didn't think I could feel any worse, but this idea sent a few more razor blades circulating through my chest. Thalia Grace had saved my life in Indianapolis. Her fury in combat had been rivaled only by the tenderness with which she spoke of her brother. I felt that *I* should be the one to break the news to her. On the other hand, I did not want to be in the same state when she heard it.

I looked around at my dejected comrades. I remembered the Sibyl's words in my dream: *It won't seem worth it to you. I'm not sure it is myself. But you must come. You must hold them together in their grief*. Now I understood. I wished I didn't. How could I hold together a whole Cistern full of prickly dryads when I couldn't even hold *myself* together?

Nevertheless, I lifted the ancient pair of caligae we'd retrieved from the yachts. "At least we have these. Jason gave his life for us to have a chance at stopping Caligula's plans. Tomorrow, I'll wear these into the Burning Maze. I'll find a way to free the Oracle and stop the fires of Helios."

I thought that was a pretty good pep talk—designed to restore confidence and reassure my friends. I left out the part about not having a clue how to accomplish any of it.

Prickly Pear bristled, which she did with consummate skill. "You're in no shape to do anything. Besides, Caligula will know what you're planning. He'll be waiting and ready this time."

"She's right," Crest said from his niche.

The dryads frowned at him.

"Why is he even here?" Cholla demanded.

"Music lessons," I said.

That earned me several dozen confused looks.

"Long story," I said. "But Crest risked his life for us on the yachts. He saved Meg. We can trust him." I looked at the young pandos and hoped my assessment was correct. "Crest, is there anything you can tell us that might help?"

Crest wrinkled his fuzzy white nose (which did not at all make him look cute or make me want to cuddle him). "You cannot use the main entrance downtown. They will be waiting."

"We got past *you*," Meg said.

Crest's giant ears turned pink around the edges. "That

was different," he muttered. "My uncle was punishing me. It was the lunch shift. *No one* ever attacks during the lunch shift."

He glared at me like I should've known this. "They will have more fighters now. And traps. The horse might even be there. He can move very fast. Just one phone call and he can arrive."

I remembered how quickly Incitatus had shown up at Macro's Military Madness, and how viciously he'd fought aboard the shoe ship. I was not anxious to face him again.

"Is there another way in?" I asked. "Something, I don't know, less dangerous and conveniently close to the Oracle's room?"

Crest hugged his ukulele (*my* ukulele) tighter. "There is one. I know it. Others don't."

Grover tilted his head. "I have to say, that sounds a little *too* convenient."

Crest made a sour face. "I like exploring. Nobody else does. Uncle Amax—he always said I was a daydreamer. But when you explore, you find things."

I couldn't argue with that. When I explored, I tended to find dangerous things that wanted to kill me. I doubted tomorrow would be any different.

"Could you lead us to this secret entrance?" I asked.

Crest nodded. "Then you will have a chance. You can sneak in, get to the Oracle before the guards find you. Then you can come out and give me music lessons."

The dryads stared at me, their expressions unhelpfully blank, as if thinking *Hey, we can't tell you how to die. That's your choice.*

"We'll do it," Meg decided for me. "Grover, you in?"

Grover sighed. "Of course. But first, you two need sleep."

"And healing," Aloe added.

"And enchiladas?" I requested. "For breakfast?"

On that point, we reached consensus.

So, having enchiladas to look forward to—and also a likely fatal trip through the Burning Maze—I curled up in my sleeping bag and passed out.

36

A suspended fourth
The kind of chord you play just
Before suddenly—

I WOKE COVERED IN GOO and with aloe spikes (yet again) in my nostrils.

On the bright side, my ribs no longer felt like they were filled with lava. My chest had healed, leaving only a puckered scar where I'd impaled myself. I'd never had a scar before. I wished I could see it as a badge of honor. Instead, I feared that now, whenever I looked down, I would remember the worst night of my life.

At least I had slept deeply with no dreams. That aloe vera was good stuff.

The sun blazed directly above. The Cistern was empty except for me and Crest, who snored in his niche, clutching his ukulele teddy bear. Someone, probably hours ago, had left a breakfast enchilada plate with a Big Hombre soda next to my sleeping bag. The food had cooled to lukewarm. The ice in the soda had melted. I didn't care. I ate and drank ravenously. I was grateful for the hot salsa that cleared the smell of burning yachts out of my sinuses.

Once I de-slimed myself and washed in the pond, I dressed in a fresh set of Macro's camouflage—arctic white, because there was such a demand for that in the Mojave Desert.

I shouldered my quiver and bow. I tied Caligula's shoes to my belt. I considered trying to take the ukulele from Crest but decided to let him keep it for now, since I did not want to get my hands bitten off.

Finally, I climbed into the oppressive Palm Springs heat.

Judging from the angle of the sun, it must have been about three in the afternoon. I wondered why Meg had let me sleep so late. I scanned the hillside and saw no one. For a guilty moment, I imagined that Meg and Grover had been unable to wake me and had gone by themselves to take care of the maze.

Darn it! I could say when they returned. *Sorry, guys! And I was all ready too!*

But no. Caligula's sandals dangled from my belt. They wouldn't have left without those. I also doubted they'd have forgotten Crest, since he was the only one who knew the supersecret entrance to the maze.

I caught a flicker of movement—two shadows moving behind the nearest greenhouse. I approached and heard voices in earnest conversation: Meg and Joshua.

I wasn't sure whether to let them be or to march over and shout Meg, *this is no time to flirt with your yucca boyfriend!*

Then I realized they were talking about climates and growing seasons. Ugh. I stepped into view and found them studying a line of seven young saplings that had sprouted from the rocky soil . . . in the exact spots where Meg had planted her seeds only yesterday.

Joshua spied me immediately, a sure sign that my arctic camouflage was working.

"Well. He's alive." He didn't sound particularly thrilled about this. "We were just discussing the new arrivals."

Each sapling rose about three feet high, its branches white, its leaves pale-green diamonds that looked much too delicate for the desert heat.

"Those are ash trees," I said, dumbfounded.

I knew a lot about ash trees. . . . Well, more than I knew about most trees, anyway. Long ago, I had been called Apollo Meliai, Apollo of the Ash Trees, because of a sacred grove I owned in . . . oh, where was it? Back then I had so many vacation properties I couldn't keep them all straight.

My mind began to whirl. The word *meliai* meant something besides just *ash trees*. It had special significance. Despite being planted in a completely hostile climate, these young plants radiated strength and energy even I could sense. They'd grown overnight into healthy saplings. I wondered what they might look like tomorrow.

Meliai . . . I turned the word over in my mind. What had Caligula said? *Blood-born. Silver wives.*

Meg frowned. She looked much better this morning—back in her stoplight-colored clothes that had been miraculously patched and laundered. (I suspected the dryads, who are great with fabrics.) Her cat-eye glasses had been repaired with blue electrical tape. The scars on her arms and face had faded into faint white streaks like meteor trails across the sky.

"I still don't get it," she said. "Ash trees don't grow in the desert. Why was my dad experimenting with ash?"

"The Meliai," I said.

Joshua's eyes glittered. "That was my thought, too."

"The who?" Meg asked.

"I believe," I said, "that your father was doing more than simply researching a new, hardy plant strain. He was trying to re-create . . . or rather *reincarnate* an ancient species of dryad."

Was it my imagination, or did the young trees rustle? I restrained the urge to step back and run away. They were only saplings, I reminded myself. Nice, harmless baby plants that did not have any intention of murdering me.

Joshua knelt. In his khaki safari clothes, with his tousled gray-green hair, he looked like a wild-animal expert who was about to point out some deadly species of scorpion for the TV audience. Instead he touched the branches of the nearest sapling, then quickly removed his hand.

"Could it be?" he mused. "They're not conscious yet, but the power I sense . . ."

Meg crossed her arms and pouted. "Well, I wouldn't have planted them here if I'd known they were important ash trees or whatever. Nobody *told* me."

Joshua gave her a dry smile. "Meg McCaffrey, if these *are* the Meliai, they will survive even in this harsh climate. They were the very first dryads—seven sisters born when the blood of murdered Ouranos fell upon the soil of Gaea. They were created at the same time as the Furies, and with the same great strength."

I shuddered. I did not like the Furies. They were ugly, ill-tempered, and had bad taste in music. "The blood-born," I said. "That's what Caligula called them. And the *silver wives*."

"Mmm." Joshua nodded. "According to legend, the Meliai married humans who lived during the Silver Age, and gave birth to the race of the Bronze Age. But we all make mistakes."

I studied the saplings. They didn't look much like the mothers of Bronze Age humanity. They didn't look like the Furies, either.

"Even for a skilled botanist like Dr. McCaffrey," I said, "even with the blessing of Demeter . . . is reincarnating such powerful beings *possible?*"

Joshua swayed pensively. "Who can say? It seems the family of Plemnaeus was pursuing this goal for millennia. No one would be better suited. Dr. McCaffrey perfected the seeds. His daughter planted them."

Meg blushed. "I don't know. Whatever. Seems weird."

Joshua regarded the young ash trees. "We will have to wait and see. But imagine seven primordial dryads, beings of great power, bent on the preservation of nature and the destruction of any who would threaten it." His expression turned unusually warlike for a flowering plant. "Surely Caligula would see that as a major threat."

I couldn't argue. Enough of a threat to burn down a botanist's house and send him and his daughter straight into the arms of Nero? Probably.

Joshua rose. "Well, I must go dormant. Even for me, the daylight hours are taxing. We will keep an eye on our seven new friends. Good luck on your quest!"

He burst into a cloud of yucca fiber.

Meg looked disgruntled, probably because I had interrupted their flirty talk about climate zones.

"Ash trees," she grumbled. "And I planted them in the desert."

"You planted them where they needed to be," I said. "If these truly are the Meliai"—I shook my head in amazement—"they responded to *you*, Meg. You brought back a life force that has been absent for millennia. That is awe-inspiring."

She looked over. "Are you making fun of me?"

"No," I assured her. "You are your mother's child, Meg McCaffrey. You are quite impressive."

"Hmph."

I understood her skepticism.

Demeter was rarely described as *impressive*. Too often, the goddess got ridiculed for not being interesting or powerful enough. Like plants, Demeter worked slowly and quietly. Her designs grew over the course of centuries. But when those designs came to fruition (bad fruit pun, sorry), they could be extraordinary. Like Meg McCaffrey.

"Go wake up Crest," Meg told me. "I'll meet you down at the road. Grover's getting us a car."

Grover was almost as good as Piper McLean at procuring luxury vehicles. He had found us a red Mercedes XLS, which I normally would not have complained about—except it was the exact same make and model that Meg and I had driven from Indianapolis to the Cave of Trophonius.

I'd like to tell you I didn't believe in bad omens. But since I was the god of omens . . .

At least Grover agreed to drive. The winds had shifted south, filling the Morongo Valley with wildfire smoke and clogging traffic even more than usual. The afternoon sun filtered through the red sky like a baleful eye.

I feared the sun might look that hostile for the rest of eternity if Caligula became the new solar god . . . but no, I couldn't think like that.

If Caligula came into possession of the sun chariot, there was no telling what horrible things he would do to trick out his new ride: sequencers, under-carriage lighting, a horn that played the riff from "Low Rider" . . . Some things could not be tolerated.

I sat in the backseat with Crest and did my best to teach him basic ukulele chords. He was a quick learner, despite the size of his hands, but he grew impatient with the major chords and wanted to learn more exotic combinations.

"Show me the suspended fourth again," he said. "I like that."

Of course he would like the most unresolved chords.

"We should buy you a large guitar," I urged once more. "Or even a lute."

"You play ukulele," he said. "I will play ukulele."

Why did I always attract such stubborn companions? Was it my winning, easygoing personality? I didn't know.

When Crest concentrated, his expression reminded me strangely of Meg's—such a young face, yet so intent and serious, as if the fate of the world depended on this chord being played correctly, this packet of seeds being planted, this bag of rotten produce being thrown into the face of this particular street thug.

Why that similarity should make me fond of Crest, I wasn't sure, but it struck me how much he had lost since yesterday—his job, his uncle, almost his life—and how much he had risked coming with us.

"I never said how sorry I was," I ventured, "about your Uncle Amax."

Crest sniffed the ukulele fret board. "Why would you be sorry? Why would I?"

"Uh . . . It's just, you know, an expression of courtesy . . . when you kill someone's relatives."

"I never liked him," Crest said. "My mother sent me to him, said he would make me a *real* pandos warrior." He strummed his chord but got a diminished seventh by mistake. He looked pleased with himself. "I do not want to be a warrior. What is your job?"

"Er, well, I'm the god of music."

"Then that is what I shall be. A god of music."

Meg glanced back and smirked.

I tried to give Crest an encouraging smile, but I hoped he would not ask to flay me alive and consume my essence. I already had a waiting list for that. "Well, let's master these chords first, shall we?"

We traced our way north of LA, through San Bernardino, then Pasadena. I found myself gazing up at the hills where we'd visited the Edgarton School. I wondered what the faculty would do when they found Jason Grace missing, and when they discovered that their school van had been commandeered and abandoned at the Santa Barbara waterfront. I thought of Jason's diorama of Temple Hill on his desk, the sketchbooks that waited on his shelf. It seemed unlikely I would live long enough to keep my promise to him, to bring his plans safely to the two camps. The thought of failing him yet again hurt my heart even worse than Crest's attempt at a G-flat minor 6.

Finally Crest directed us south on Interstate 5, toward the city. We took the Crystal Springs Drive exit and plunged into Griffith Park with its winding roads, rolling golf courses, and thick groves of eucalyptus.

"Farther," Crest said. "The second right. Up that hill."

He guided us onto a gravel service road not designed for a Mercedes XLS.

"It's up there." Crest pointed into the woods. "We must walk."

Grover pulled over next to a stand of yuccas, who for all I knew were friends of his. He checked out the trailhead, where a small sign read OLD LOS ANGELES ZOO.

"I know this place." Grover's goatee quivered. "I hate this place. Why would you bring us here?"

"Told you," Crest said. "Maze entrance."

"But . . ." Grover gulped, no doubt weighing his natural aversion to places that caged animals against his desire to destroy the Burning Maze. "All right."

Meg seemed happy enough, all things considered. She breathed in the what-passed-in-LA-for-fresh air and even did a few tentative cartwheels as we made our way up the trail.

We climbed to the top of the ridge. Below us spread the ruins of a zoo—overgrown sidewalks, crumbling cement walls, rusty cages, and man-made caves filled with debris.

Grover hugged himself, shivering despite the heat. "The humans abandoned this place decades ago when they built their new zoo. I can still feel the emotions of the animals that were kept here—their sadness. It's horrible."

"Down here!" Crest spread his ears and sailed over the ruins, landing in a deep grotto.

Not having flight-worthy ears, the rest of us had to pick and climb our way through the tangled terrain. At last we joined Crest at the bottom of a grimy cement bowl covered with dried leaves and litter.

"A bear pit?" Grover turned pale. "Ugh. Poor bears."

Crest pressed his eight-fingered hands against the back wall of the enclosure. He scowled. "This is not right. It should be here."

My spirits sank to a new low. "You mean your secret entrance is gone?"

Crest hissed in frustration. "I should not have mentioned this place to Screamer. Amax must have heard us talking. He sealed it somehow."

I was tempted to point out that it was *never* a good idea to share your secrets with someone named Screamer, but Crest looked like he felt bad enough already.

"What now?" Meg asked. "Use the downtown exit?"

"Too dangerous," Crest said. "There *must* be a way to open this!"

Grover was so twitchy I wondered if he had a squirrel in his pants. He looked like he wanted very much to give up and run from this zoo as fast as possible. Instead, he sighed. "What did the prophecy say about your cloven guide?"

"That you alone knew the way," I recalled. "But you already served that purpose getting us to Palm Springs."

Reluctantly, Grover pulled out his pipes. "I guess I'm not done yet."

"A song of opening?" I asked. "Like Hedge used in Macro's store?"

Grover nodded. "I haven't tried this in a while. Last time, I opened a path from Central Park into the Underworld."

"Just get us into the maze, please," I advised. "Not the Underworld."

He raised his pipes and trilled Rush's "Tom Sawyer." Crest looked entranced. Meg covered her ears.

The cement wall shook. It cracked down the middle, revealing a steep set of rough-hewn stairs leading down into the dark.

"Perfect," Grover grumbled. "I hate the underground almost as much as I hate zoos."

Meg summoned her blades. She marched inside. After a deep breath, Grover followed.

I turned to Crest. "Are you coming with us?"

He shook his head. "I told you. I'm no fighter. I will watch the exit and practice my chords."

"But I might need the uku—"

"I will practice my chords," he insisted, and began strumming a suspended fourth.

I followed my friends into the dark, that chord still playing behind me—exactly the sort of tense background music one might expect just before a dramatic, bloodcurdling fight.

Sometimes I really hated suspended fourths.

37

Want to play a game?
It's easy. You take a guess.
Then you burn to death.

THIS PART OF THE MAZE had no elevators, wandering government employees, or signs reminding us to honk before turning corners.

We reached the bottom of the stairs and found a vertical shaft in the floor. Grover, being part goat, had no difficulty climbing down. After he called up that no monsters or fallen bears were waiting for us, Meg grew a thick swath of wisteria down the side of the pit, which allowed us some handholds and also smelled lovely.

We dropped into a small square chamber with four tunnels radiating outward, one from each wall. The air was hot and dry as if the fires of Helios had recently swept through. Sweat beaded on my skin. In my quiver, arrow shafts creaked and fletching hissed.

Grover peered forlornly at the tiny bit of sunlight seeping down from above.

"We'll get back to the upper world," I promised him.

"I was just wondering if Piper got my message."

Meg looked at him over her blue-taped glasses. "What message?"

"I ran into a cloud nymph when I was picking up the Mercedes," he said, as if running into cloud nymphs often happened when he was borrowing automobiles. "I asked her to take a message to Mellie, tell her what we were up to—assuming, you know, the nymph makes it there safely."

I considered this, wondering why Grover hadn't mentioned it earlier. "Were you hoping Piper might meet us here?"

"Not really . . ." His expression said *Yes, please, gods, we could use the help*. "I just thought she should know what we were doing in case . . ." His expression said *in case we combust into flames and are never heard from again*.

I disliked Grover's expressions.

"Time for the shoes," Meg said.

I realized she was looking at me. "What?"

"The shoes." She pointed at the sandals hanging from my belt.

"Oh, right." I tugged them from my belt. "I don't suppose, er, either of you want to try them on?"

"Nuh-uh," said Meg.

Grover shuddered. "I've had bad experiences with enchanted footwear."

I was not excited to wear an evil emperor's sandals. I feared they might turn me into a power-hungry maniac. Also, they didn't go with my arctic camouflage. Nevertheless, I sat on the floor and laced up the caligae. It made me appreciate just how much more of the world the Roman Empire might have conquered if they'd had access to Velcro straps.

I stood up and tried a few steps. The sandals dug into my ankles and pinched at the sides. In the plus column, I felt no more sociopathic than usual. Hopefully I had not been infected with Caligulitis.

"Okay," I said. "Shoes, lead us to the Erythraean Sibyl!"

The shoes did nothing. I thrust a toe in one direction, then another, wondering if they needed a kick start. I checked the soles for buttons or battery compartments. Nothing.

"What do we do now?" I asked no one in particular.

The chamber brightened with a faint gold light, as if someone had turned up a dimmer switch.

"Guys." Grover pointed at our feet. On the rough cement floor, the faint gold outline of a five-foot square had appeared. If it had been a trapdoor, we would've all dropped straight through. Identical connected squares branched off down each of the corridors like the spaces of a board game. The trails were not of equal length. One extended only three spaces into the hallway. Another was five spaces long. Another was seven. Another six.

Against the chamber wall on my right, a glowing golden inscription appeared in ancient Greek: *Python-slayer, golden-lyred, armed with arrows of dread.*

"What's going on?" Meg asked. "What's that say?"

"You can't read ancient Greek?" I asked.

"And you can't tell a strawberry from a yam," she retorted. "What's it say?"

I gave her the translation.

Grover stroked his goatee. "That sounds like Apollo. I mean, you. When you used to be . . . good."

I swallowed my hurt feelings. "Of course it's Apollo. I mean, me."

"So, is the maze, like . . . welcoming you?" Meg asked.

That would have been nice. I'd always wanted a voice-activated virtual assistant for my palace on Olympus, but Hephaestus hadn't been able to get the technology quite right. The one time he tried, the assistant had been named Alexasiriastrophona. She'd been very picky about having her name pronounced perfectly, and at the same time had an annoying habit of getting my requests wrong. I'd say, *Alexasiriastrophona, send a plague arrow to destroy Corinth, please*. And she would reply, *I think you said:* Men blame rows of soy and corn fleas.

Here in the Burning Maze, I doubted a virtual assistant had been installed. If it had been, it would probably only ask at which temperature I preferred to be cooked.

"This is a word puzzle," I decided. "Like an acrostic or a crossword. The Sibyl is trying to guide us to her."

Meg frowned at the different hallways. "If she's trying to help, why can't she just make it easy and give us a single direction?"

"This is how Herophile operates," I said. "It's the only way she *can* help us. I believe we have to, er, fill in the correct answer in the correct number of spaces."

Grover scratched his head. "Does anyone have a giant golden pen? I wish Percy were here."

"I don't think we need that," I said. "We just need to walk in the right direction to spell out my name. *Apollo*, six letters. Only one of these corridors has six spaces."

"Are you counting the space we're standing in?" Meg asked.

"Uh, no," I said. "Let's assume this is the *start* space." Her question made me doubt myself, though.

"What if the answer is *Lester*?" she said. "That has six spaces, too."

The idea made my throat itch. "Will you please stop asking good questions? I had this all figured out!"

"Or what if the answer is in Greek?" Grover added. "The question is in Greek. How many spaces would your name be then?"

Another annoyingly logical point. My name in Greek was Απολλων.

"That would be seven spaces," I admitted. "Even if transcribed in English, Apollon."

"Ask the Arrow of Dodona?" Grover suggested.

The scar in my chest tingled like a faulty electric outlet. "That's probably against the rules."

Meg snorted. "You just don't want to talk to the arrow. Why not try?"

If I resisted, I imagined she would phrase it as an order, so I pulled forth the Arrow of Dodona.

BACKETH OFF, KNAVE! it buzzed in alarm. *NE'ER AGAIN SHALT THOU STICKEST ME IN THY LOATHSOME CHEST! NOR IN THE EYES OF THY ENEMIES!*

"Relax," I told it. "I just want some advice."

SO THOU SAYEST NOW, BUT I WARN THEE— The arrow went deathly still. *BUT SOOTH. IS THIS A*

CROSSWORD I SEE BEFORE ME? VERILY, I DOTH LOVE CROSSWORDS.

"Oh, joy. Oh, happiness." I turned to my friends. "The arrow loves crosswords."

I explained our predicament to the arrow, who insisted on getting a closer look at the floor squares and the hint written on the wall. A closer look . . . with what eyes? I did not know.

The arrow hummed thoughtfully. *METHINKS THE ANSWER SHALT BEEST IN THE COMMON TONGUE OF ENGLISH. 'TWOULD BEEST THE NAME BY WHICH THOU ART MOST FAMILIAR IN THE PRESENT DAY.*

"He sayeth—" I sighed. "He says the answer will be in English. I hope he means modern English and not the strange Shakespearean lingo he speaks—"

'TIS NOT STRANGE! the arrow objected.

"Because we don't have enough spaces to spell *Apollonius beest thy answereth.*"

OH, HA-HA. A JEST AS WEAK AS THY MUSCLES.

"Thanks for playing." I sheathed the arrow. "So, friends, the tunnel with six squares. *Apollo.* Shall we?"

"What if we choose wrong?" Grover asked.

"Well," I said, "perhaps the magic sandals will help. Or perhaps the sandals only allow us to play this game in the first place, and if we stray from the right path, despite the Sibyl's efforts to assist us, we will open ourselves up to the fury of the maze—"

"And we burn to death," Meg said.

"I love games," Grover said. "Lead on."

"The answer is *Apollo*!" I said, just for the record.

As soon as I stepped to the next square, a large capital *A* appeared at my feet.

I took this as a good sign. I stepped again, and a *P* appeared. My two friends followed close behind.

At last we stepped off the sixth square, into a small chamber identical to the last. Looking back, the entire word *APOLLO* blazed in our wake. Before us, three more corridors with golden rows of squares led onward—left, right, and forward.

"There's another clue." Meg pointed to the wall. "Why is this one in English?"

"I don't know," I said. Then I read aloud the glowing words: "'*Herald of new entrances, opener of the softly gliding year, Janus, of the double.*'"

"Oh, that guy. Roman god of doorways." Grover shuddered. "I met him once." He looked around suspiciously. "I hope he doesn't pop up. He would love this place."

Meg traced her fingers across the golden lines. "Kinda easy, isn't it? His name's right there in the clue. Five letters, *J-A-N-U-S*, so it's got to be that way." She pointed down the hallway on the right, which was the only one with five spaces.

I stared at the clue, then the squares. I was beginning to sense something even more unsettling than the heat, but I wasn't sure what it was.

"*Janus* isn't the answer," I decided. "This is more of a fill-in-the-blanks situation, don't you think? *Janus of the double* what?"

"Faces," Grover said. "He had two faces, neither of which I need to see again."

I announced aloud to the empty corridor: "The correct answer is *faces*!"

I received no response, but as we proceeded down the right-hand corridor, the word *FACES* appeared. Reassuringly, we were not roasted alive by Titan fire.

In the next chamber, new corridors once again led in three directions. This time, the glowing clue on the wall was again in ancient Greek.

A thrill went through me as I read the lines. "I know this! It's from a poem by Bacchylides." I translated for my friends: "*But the highest god, mighty with his thunderbolt, sent Hypnos and his twin from snowy Olympus to the fearless fighter Sarpedon.*"

Meg and Grover stared at me blankly. Honestly, just because I was wearing the Caligula shoes, did I have to do *everything*?

"Something is altered in this line," I said. "I remember the scene. Sarpedon dies. Zeus has his body carried away from the battlefield. But the wording—"

"Hypnos is the god of sleep," Grover said. "That cabin makes *excellent* milk and cookies. But who's his twin?"

My heart ka-thumped. "That's what's different. In the actual line, it doesn't say *his twin*. It names the twin: Thanatos. Or *Death*, in English."

I looked at the three tunnels. No corridor had eight squares for Thanatos. One had ten spaces, one had four, and one had five—just enough to fit DEATH.

"Oh, no . . ." I leaned against the nearest wall. I felt like one of Aloe Vera's spikes was making its slimy way down my back.

"Why do you look so scared?" Meg asked. "You're doing great so far."

"Because, Meg," I said, "we are not just solving random puzzles. We are putting together a word-puzzle prophecy. And so far, it says *APOLLO FACES DEATH*."

38

I sing to myself!
Though Apollo is cooler
Like, way, way cooler

I HATED BEING RIGHT.

When we got to the end of the tunnel, the word *DEATH* blazed on the floor behind us. We found ourselves in a larger circular chamber, five new tunnels branching out before us like the fingers and thumb of a giant automaton hand.

I waited for a new clue to appear on the wall. Whatever it was, I desperately wanted the answer to be *NOT REALLY*. Or perhaps *AND DEFEATS IT EASILY!*

"Why is nothing happening?" Grover asked.

Meg tilted her head. "Listen."

Blood roared in my ears, but at last I heard what Meg was talking about: a distant cry of pain—deep and guttural, more beast than human—along with the dull crackle of fire, as if . . . oh, gods. As if someone or something had been grazed by Titan heat and now lay dying a slow death.

"Sounds like a monster," Grover decided. "Should we help it?"

"How?" Meg asked.

She had a point. The noise echoed, so diffuse I couldn't

tell which corridor it came from, even if we were free to pick our path without answering riddles.

"We'll have to keep going," I decided. "I imagine Medea has monsters on guard down here. That must be one of them. I doubt she's too concerned about them occasionally getting caught in the fires."

Grover winced. "Doesn't seem right, letting it suffer."

"Also," Meg added, "what if one of those monsters triggers a flash fire and it comes our way?"

I stared at my young master. "You are a fountain of dark questions today. We have to have faith."

"In the Sibyl?" she asked. "In those evil shoes?"

I didn't have an answer for her. Fortunately, I was saved by the belated appearance of the next clue—three golden lines in Latin.

"Oh, Latin!" Grover said. "Hold on. I can do this." He squinted at the words, then sighed. "No. I can't."

"Honestly, no Greek or Latin?" I said. "What do they teach you in satyr school?"

"Mostly, you know, important stuff. Like plants."

"*Thank* you," Meg muttered.

I translated the clue for my less educated friends:

> *"Now must I tell of the flight of the king.*
> *The last to reign over the Roman people*
> *Was a man unjust yet puissant in arms."*

I nodded. "I believe that's a quote from Ovid."

Neither of my comrades looked impressed.

"So what's the answer?" Meg asked. "The last Roman emperor?"

"No, not an emperor," I said. "In the very first days of Rome, the city was ruled by kings. The last one, the seventh, was overthrown, and Rome became a republic."

I tried to cast my thoughts back to the Kingdom of Rome. That whole time period was a little hazy to me. We gods were still based in Greece then. Rome was something of a backwater. The last king, though . . . he brought back some bad memories.

Meg broke my reverie. "What is *puissant?*"

"It means powerful," I said.

"Doesn't sound like that. If somebody called me *puissant*, I would hit them."

"But you are, in fact, *puissant* in arms."

She hit me.

"Ow."

"Guys," Grover said. "What's the name of the last Roman king?"

I thought. "Ta . . . hmm. I just had it, and now it's gone. Ta-something."

"Taco?" Grover said helpfully.

"Why would a Roman king be named Taco?"

"I don't know." Grover rubbed his stomach. "Because I'm hungry?"

Curse the satyr. Now all I could think of was tacos. Then the answer came back to me. "Tarquin! Or Tarquinius, in the original Latin."

"Well, which is it?" Meg asked.

I studied the corridors. The tunnel on the far left, the thumb, had ten spaces, enough for *Tarquinius*. The tunnel in the middle had seven, enough for *Tarquin*.

"It's that one," I decided, pointing to the center tunnel.

"How can you be sure?" Grover asked. "Because the arrow told us the answers would be in English?"

"That," I conceded, "and also because these tunnels look like five fingers. It makes sense the maze would give me the middle finger." I raised my voice. "Isn't that right? The answer is *Tarquin*, the middle finger? I love you, too, maze."

We walked the path, the name *TARQUIN* blazing in gold behind us.

The corridor opened into a square chamber, the largest space we'd seen yet. The walls and floor were tiled in faded Roman mosaics that looked original, though I was fairly sure the Romans had never colonized any part of the Los Angeles metropolitan area.

The air felt even warmer and drier. The floor was hot enough that I could feel it through the soles of my sandals. One positive thing about the room: it offered us only three new tunnels to choose from, rather than five.

Grover sniffed the air. "I don't like this room. I smell something . . . monstery."

Meg gripped her scimitars. "From which direction?"

"Uh . . . all of them?"

"Oh, look," I said, trying to sound cheerful, "another clue."

We approached the nearest mosaic wall, where two golden lines of English glowed across the tiles:

Leaves, body-leaves, growing up above me, above death,
Perennial roots, tall leaves—O the winter shall not freeze
you, delicate leaves

Perhaps my brain was still stuck in Latin and Greek, because those lines meant nothing to me, even in plain English.

"I like this one," Meg said. "It's about leaves."

"Yes, lots of leaves," I agreed. "But it's nonsense."

Grover choked. "*Nonsense?* Don't you recognize it?"

"Er, should I?"

"You're the god of *poetry*!"

I felt my face begin to burn. "I *used* to be the god of poetry, which does not mean I am a walking encyclopedia of every obscure line ever written—"

"*Obscure?*" Grover's shrill voice echoed unnervingly down the corridors. "That's Walt Whitman! From *Leaves of Grass*! I don't remember exactly which poem it's from, but—"

"You read poetry?" Meg asked.

Grover licked his lips. "You know . . . mostly nature poetry. Whitman, for a human, had some beautiful things to say about trees."

"And leaves," Meg noted. "And roots."

"Exactly."

I wanted to lecture them about how overrated Walt Whitman was. The man was always singing songs to himself instead of praising others, like *me*, for instance. But I decided the critique would have to wait.

"Do you know the answer, then?" I asked Grover. "Is this a fill-in-the-blanks question? Multiple choice? True-False?"

Grover studied the lines. "I think . . . yeah. There's a word missing at the beginning. It's supposed to read *Tomb-leaves, body-leaves*, et cetera."

"Tomb-leaves?" Meg asked. "That doesn't make sense. But neither does body-leaves. Unless he's talking about a dryad."

"It's imagery," I said. "Clearly, he is describing a place of death, overgrown by nature—"

"Oh, now you're an expert on Walt Whitman," Grover said.

"Satyr, don't test me. When I become a god again—"

"Both of you, stop," Meg ordered. "Apollo, say the answer."

"Fine." I sighed. "Maze, the answer is *tomb*."

We took another successful trip down the middle finger . . . I mean, central hall. The word *TOMB* blazed in the four squares behind us.

At the end, we arrived in a circular room, even larger and more ornate. Across the domed ceiling spread a silver-on-blue mosaic of zodiac signs. Six new tunnels radiated outward. In the middle of the floor stood an old fountain, unfortunately dry. (A drink would have been much appreciated. Interpreting poetry and solving puzzles is thirsty work.)

"The rooms are getting bigger," Grover noted. "And more elaborate."

"Maybe that's good," I said. "It might mean we're getting closer."

Meg eyed the zodiac images. "You sure we didn't take a wrong turn? The prophecy doesn't even make sense so far. *Apollo faces death Tarquin tomb*."

"You have to assume the small words," I said. "I believe

the message is *Apollo faces death* in *Tarquin's tomb*." I gulped. "Actually, I don't like that message. Perhaps the little words we're missing are *Apollo faces* NO *death; Tarquin's tomb . . .* something, something. Maybe the next words are *grants him fabulous prizes*."

"Uh-huh." Meg pointed at the rim of the central fountain, where the next clue had appeared. Three lines in English read:

Named for Apollo's fallen love, this flower should be planted in autumn.
Set the bulb in the soil with the pointy end up. Cover with soil
And water thoroughly . . . you are transplanting.

I stifled a sob.

First the maze forced me to read Walt Whitman. Now it taunted me with my own past. To mention my dead love, Hyacinthus, and his tragic death, to reduce him to a bit of Oracle trivia . . . No. This was too much.

I sat down on the rim of the fountain and cupped my face in my hands.

"What's wrong?" Grover asked nervously.

Meg answered. "Those lines are talking about his old boyfriend. Hyacinth."

"*Hyacinthus*," I corrected.

I surged to my feet, my sadness converting to anger. My friends edged away. I supposed I must have looked like a crazy man, and that's indeed how I felt.

"Herophile!" I yelled into the darkness. "I thought we were friends!"

"Uh, Apollo?" Meg said. "I don't think she's taunting you on purpose. Also, the answer is about the *flower*, hyacinth. I'm pretty sure those lines are from the Farmer's Almanac."

"I don't care if they're from the telephone directory!" I bellowed. "Enough is enough. *HYACINTH!*" I yelled into the corridors. "The answer is *HYACINTH*! Are you happy?"

Meg yelled, "NO!"

In retrospect, she really should have yelled *Apollo, stop!* Then I would've had no choice but to obey her command. Therefore, what happened next is Meg's fault.

I marched down the only corridor with eight squares.

Grover and Meg ran after me, but by the time they caught me it was too late.

I looked behind, expecting to see the word *HYACINTH* spelled out on the floor. Instead, only six of the squares were lit up in glaring correction-pen red:

U
N
L
E
S
S

Under our feet, the tunnel floor disappeared, and we dropped into a pit of fire.

39

Noble sacrifice
I'll protect you from the flames
Wow, I'm a good guy

UNDER DIFFERENT CIRCUMSTANCES, how delighted I would have been to see that *UNLESS.*

Apollo faces death in Tarquin's tomb unless . . .

Oh, happy conjunction! It meant there was a way to avoid potential death, and I was *all about* avoiding potential death.

Unfortunately, falling into a pit of fire dampened my newfound hope.

In midair, before I could even process what was happening, I lurched to a halt, my quiver strap yanked tight across my chest, my left foot nearly popping free from my ankle.

I found myself dangling next to the wall of the pit. About twenty feet below, the shaft opened into a lake of fire. Meg was clinging desperately to my foot. Above me, Grover held me by the quiver with one hand, his other gripping a tiny ledge of rock. He kicked off his shoes and tried to find purchase with his hooves on the wall.

"Well done, brave satyr!" I cried. "Pull us up!"

Grover's eyes bugged. His face dripped with sweat. He

made a whimpering sound that seemed to indicate he didn't have the strength to pull all three of us out of the pit.

If I survived and became a god again, I would have to talk to the Council of Cloven Elders about adding more physical education classes to satyr school.

I clawed at the wall, hoping to find a convenient rail or emergency exit. There was nothing.

Below me, Meg yelled, "REALLY, Apollo? You water hyacinths thoroughly UNLESS you are transplanting them!"

"How was I supposed to know that?" I protested.

"You CREATED hyacinths!"

Ugh. Mortal logic. Just because a god creates something doesn't mean he understands it. Otherwise, Prometheus would know everything about humans, and I assure you, he does not. I created hyacinths, so I'm supposed to know how to plant and water them?

"Help!" Grover squeaked.

His hooves shifted on the tiny crevices. His fingers trembled, his arms shaking as if he were holding the weight of two extra people, which . . . oh, actually, he was.

The heat from below made it difficult to think. If you've ever stood near a barbecue fire, or had your face too close to an open oven, you can imagine that feeling increased a hundredfold. My eyes dried up. My mouth became parched. A few more breaths of scalding air and I would probably lose consciousness.

The fires below seemed to be sweeping across a stone floor. The drop itself would not be fatal. If only there were a way to turn off the fires . . .

An idea came to me—a very bad idea, which I blamed on my boiling brain. Those flames were fueled by the essence of Helios. If some small bit of his consciousness remained . . . it was theoretically possible that I could communicate with him. Perhaps, if I touched the fires directly, I could convince him that we were not the enemy and he should let us live. I would probably have a luxurious three nanoseconds to accomplish this before dying in agony. Besides, if I fell, my friends might stand a chance of climbing out. After all, I was the heaviest person in our party, thanks to Zeus's cruel curse of flab.

Terrible, terrible idea. I would never have had the courage to try it had I not thought of Jason Grace, and what he had done to save me.

"Meg," I said, "can you attach yourself to the wall?"

"Do I look like Spider-Man?" she yelled back.

Very few people look as good in tights as Spider-Man. Meg was certainly not one of them.

"Use your swords!" I called.

Holding my ankle with just one hand, she summoned a scimitar. She stabbed at the wall—once, twice. The curve of the blade did not make her job easy. On the third strike, however, the point sank deep into the rock. She gripped the hilt and let go of my ankle, holding herself above the flames with only her sword. "What now?"

"Stay put!"

"I can do that!"

"Grover!" I yelled up. "You can drop me now, but don't worry. I have a—"

Grover dropped me.

Honestly, what sort of protector just drops you into a fire when you tell him it's okay to drop you into a fire? I expected a long argument, during which I would assure him that I had a plan to save myself and them. I expected protests from Grover and Meg (well, maybe not from Meg) about how I shouldn't sacrifice myself for their sake, how I couldn't possibly survive the flames, and so on. But nope. He dumped me without a thought.

At least it gave me no time for second-guessing.

I couldn't torture myself with doubts like *What if this doesn't work? What if I cannot survive the solar fires that used to be second nature to me? What if this lovely prophecy we are piecing together, about me dying in the tomb of Tarquin, does* NOT *automatically mean that I will not die today, in this horrible Burning Maze?*

I don't remember hitting the floor.

My soul seemed to detach from my body. I found myself thousands of years back in time, on the very first morning I became the god of the sun.

Overnight, Helios had vanished. I didn't know what final prayer to me as the god of the sun had finally tipped the balance—banishing the old Titan to oblivion while promoting me to his spot—but here I was at the Palace of the Sun.

Terrified and nervous, I pushed open the doors of the throne room. The air burned. The light blinded me.

Helios's oversize golden throne stood empty, his cloak draped over the armrest. His helm, whip, and gilded shoes sat on the dais, ready for their master. But the Titan himself was simply gone.

I am a god, I told myself. *I can do this.*

I strode toward the throne, willing myself not to combust. If I ran out of the palace screaming with my toga on fire the very first day on the job, I would never hear the end of it.

Slowly, the fires receded before me. By force of will, I grew in size until I could comfortably wear the helm and cloak of my predecessor.

I didn't try out the throne, though. I had a job to do, and very little time.

I glanced at the whip. Some trainers say you should never show kindness with a new team of horses. They will see you as weak. But I decided to leave the whip. I would not start my new position as a harsh taskmaster.

I strode into the stable. The sun chariot's beauty brought tears to my eyes. The four sun horses stood already harnessed, their hooves polished gold, their manes rippling fire, their eyes molten ingots.

They regarded me warily. *Who are you?*

"I am Apollo," I said, forcing myself to sound confident. "We're going to have a great day!"

I leaped into the chariot, and off we went.

I'll admit it was a steep learning curve. About a forty-five-degree arc, to be precise. I may have done a few inadvertent loops in the sky. I may have caused a few new glaciers and deserts until I found the proper cruising altitude. But by the end of the day, the chariot was mine. The horses had shaped themselves to my will, *my* personality. I was Apollo, god of the sun.

I tried to hold on to that feeling of confidence, the elation of that successful first day.

I came back to my senses and found myself at the bottom of the pit, crouching in the flames.

"Helios," I said. "It's me."

The blaze swirled around me, trying to incinerate my flesh and dissolve my soul. I could feel the presence of the Titan—bitter, hazy, angry. His whip seemed to be lashing me a thousand times a second.

"I will not be burned," I said. "I am Apollo. I am your rightful heir."

The fires raged hotter. Helios resented me . . . but wait. That wasn't the full story. He hated *being here*. He hated this maze, this half-life prison.

"I will free you," I promised.

Noise crackled and hissed in my ears. Perhaps it was only the sound of my head catching fire, but I thought I heard a voice in the flames: *KILL. HER.*

Her . . .

Medea.

Helios's emotions burned their way into my mind. I felt his loathing for his sorceress granddaughter. All that Medea had told me earlier about holding back Helios's wrath—that might have been true. But above all, she was holding Helios back from killing *her*. She had chained him, bound his will to hers, wrapped herself in powerful protections against his godly fire. Helios did not like me, no. But he *hated* Medea's presumptuous magic. To be released from his torment, he needed his granddaughter dead.

I wondered, not for the first time, why we Greek deities had never created a god of family therapy. We certainly could have used one. Or perhaps we had one before I was born, and she quit. Or Kronos swallowed her whole.

Whatever the case, I told the flames, "I will do this. I will free you. But you must let us pass."

Instantly, the fires raced away as if a tear had opened in the universe.

I gasped. My skin steamed. My arctic camouflage was now a lightly toasted gray. But I was alive. The room around me cooled rapidly. The flames, I realized, had retreated down a single tunnel that led from the chamber.

"Meg! Grover!" I called. "You can come down—"

Meg dropped on top of me, squashing me flat.

"Ow!" I screamed. "Not like that!"

Grover was more courteous. He climbed down the wall and dropped to the floor with goat-worthy dexterity. He smelled like a burnt wool blanket. His face was badly sunburned. His cap had fallen into the fire, revealing the tips of his horns, which steamed like miniature volcanoes. Meg had somehow come through just fine. She'd even managed to retract her sword from the wall before falling. She pulled her canteen from her supply belt, drank most of the water, and handed the rest to Grover.

"Thanks," I grumbled.

"You beat the heat," she noted. "Good job. Finally had a godly burst of power?"

"Er . . . I think it was more about Helios deciding to give us a pass. He wants out of this maze as much as we want *him* out. He wants us to kill Medea."

Grover gulped. "So . . . she's down here? She didn't die on that yacht?"

"Figures." Meg squinted down the steaming corridor. "Did Helios promise not to burn us if you mess up any more answers?"

"I— That wasn't my fault!"

"Yeah," Meg said.

"Kinda was," Grover agreed.

Honestly. I fall into a blazing pit, negotiate a truce with a Titan, and flush a firestorm out of the room to save my friends, and they still want to talk about how I can't recall instructions from the Farmer's Almanac.

"I don't think we can count on Helios *never* to burn us," I said, "any more than we can expect Herophile not to use word puzzles. It's just their nature. This was a onetime get-out-of-the-flames-free card."

Grover smothered the tips of his horns. "Well, then, let's not waste it."

"Right." I hitched up my slightly toasted camouflage pants and tried to recapture that confident tone I'd had the first time I addressed my sun horses. "Follow me. I'm sure it'll be fine!"

40

Congratulations
You finished the word puzzle
You win . . . enemies

FINE, IN THIS CASE, meant *fine if you enjoy lava, chains, and evil magic.*

The corridor led straight to the chamber of the Oracle, which on the one hand . . . hooray! On the other hand, not so wonderful. The room was a rectangle the size of a basketball court. Lining the walls were half a dozen entrances—each a simple stone doorway with a small landing that overhung the pool of lava I'd seen in my visions. Now, though, I realized the bubbling and shimmering substance was not lava. It was the divine ichor of Helios—hotter than lava, more powerful than rocket fuel, *impossible* to get out if you spilled it on your clothes (I could tell you from personal experience). We had reached the very center of the maze—the holding tank for Helios's power.

Floating on the surface of the ichor were large stone tiles, each about five feet square, making columns and rows that had no logical patterns.

"It's a crossword," Grover said.

Of course he was right. Unfortunately, none of the stone

bridges connected with our little balcony. Nor did any of them lead to the opposite side of the room, where the Sibyl of Erythraea sat forlornly on her stone platform. Her home wasn't any better than a solitary-confinement cell. She'd been provided with a cot, a table, and a toilet. (And, yes, even immortal Sibyls need to use the toilet. Some of their best prophecies come to them . . . Never mind.)

My heart ached to see Herophile in such conditions. She looked exactly as I remembered her: a young woman with braided auburn hair and pale skin, her solid athletic build a tribute to her hardy naiad mother and her stout shepherd father. The Sibyl's white robes were stained with smoke and spotted with cinder burns. She was intently watching an entrance on the wall to her left, so she didn't seem to notice us.

"That's her?" Meg whispered.

"Unless you see another Oracle," I said.

"Well, then *talk* to her."

I wasn't sure why I had to do all the work, but I cleared my throat and yelled across the boiling lake of ichor, "Herophile!"

The Sibyl jumped to her feet. Only then did I notice the chains—molten links, just as I'd seen in my visions, shackled to her wrists and ankles, anchoring her to the platform and allowing her just enough room to move from one side to the other. Oh, the indignity!

"Apollo!"

I'd been hoping her face might light up with joy when she saw me. Instead, she looked mostly shocked.

"I thought you would come through the other . . ." Her voice seized up. She grimaced with concentration, then blurted out, "Seven letters, ends in *Y*."

"*Doorway?*" Grover guessed.

Across the surface of the lake, stone tiles ground and shifted formation. One block wedged itself against our little platform. Half a dozen more stacked up beyond it, making a seven-tile bridge extending into the room. Glowing golden letters appeared along the tiles, starting with a *Y* at our feet: *DOORWAY*.

Herophile clapped excitedly, jangling her molten chains. "Well done! Hurry!"

I was not anxious to test my weight on a stone raft floating over a burning lake of ichor, but Meg strode right out, so Grover and I followed.

"No offense, Miss Lady," Meg called to the Sibyl, "but we already almost fell into one lava fire thingie. Could you just make a bridge from here to there without more puzzles?"

"I wish I could!" said Herophile. "This is my curse! It's either talk like this or stay completely—" She gagged. "Nine letters. Fifth letter is *D*."

"*Quiet!*" Grover yelled.

Our raft rumbled and rocked. Grover windmilled his arms and might have fallen off had Meg not caught him. Thank goodness for short people. They have low centers of gravity.

"Not *quiet*!" I yelped. "That is not our final answer! That would be idiotic, since *quiet* is only five letters and doesn't even have a *D*." I glared at the satyr.

"Sorry," he muttered. "I got excited."

Meg studied the tiles. In the frames of her glasses, her rhinestones glinted red. "*Quietude?*" she suggested. "That's nine letters."

"First of all," I said, "I'm impressed you know that word. Second, context. 'Stay completely *quietude*' doesn't make sense. Also, the *D* would be in the wrong place."

"Then what's the answer, smarty-god?" she demanded. "And don't get it wrong this time."

Such unfairness! I tried to come up with synonyms for *quiet*. I couldn't think of many. I liked music and poetry. Silence really wasn't my thing.

"*Soundless*," I said at last. "That's got to be it."

The tiles rewarded us by forming a second bridge—nine across, *SOUNDLESS*, connecting to the first bridge by the *D*. Unfortunately, since the new bridge led sideways, it got us no closer to the Oracle's platform.

"Herophile," I called, "I appreciate your predicament. But is there any way you can manipulate the length of the answers? Perhaps the next one can be a really long, really easy word that leads to your platform?"

"You know I cannot, Apollo." She clasped her hands. "But, please, you *must* hurry if you wish to stop Caligula from becoming a . . ." She gagged. "Three letters, middle letter is O."

"*God*," I said unhappily.

A third bridge formed—three tiles, connecting to the O in *soundless*, which brought us only one tile closer to our goal. Meg, Grover, and I crowded together on the G tile.

The room felt even hotter, as if Helios's ichor was working itself into a fury the closer we got to Herophile. Grover and Meg sweated profusely. My own arctic camouflage was sopping wet. I had not been so uncomfortable in a group hug since the Rolling Stones' first 1969 show at Madison Square Garden. (Tip: As tempting as it might be, don't throw your arms around Mick Jagger and Keith Richards during their encore set. Those men can *sweat.*)

Herophile sighed. "I'm sorry, my friends. I'll try again. Some days, I wish prophecy was a present I had never—" She winced in pain. "Six letters. Last letter is a *D.*"

Grover shuffled around. "Wait. What? The *D* is back there."

The heat made my eyes feel like shish-kebab onions, but I tried to survey the rows and columns so far.

"Perhaps," I said, "this new clue is another vertical word, branching off the *D* in *soundless?*"

Herophile's eyes gleamed with encouragement.

Meg wiped her sweaty forehead. "Well, then why did we bother with *god?* It doesn't lead anywhere."

"Oh, no," Grover moaned. "We're still forming the prophecy, aren't we? *Doorway, soundless, god?* What does that mean?"

"I—I don't know," I admitted, my brain cells simmering in my skull like chicken soup noodles. "Let's get some more words. Herophile said she wishes prophecy was a present she'd never . . . what?"

"*Gotten* doesn't work," Meg muttered.

"*Received?*" Grover offered. "No. Too many letters."

"Perhaps a metaphor," I suggested. "A present she'd never . . . *opened?*"

Grover gulped. "Is that our final answer?"

He and Meg both looked down at the burning ichor, then back at me. Their faith in my abilities was not heartwarming.

"Yes," I decided. "Herophile, the answer is *opened.*"

The Sibyl sighed with relief as a new bridge extended from the *D* in *soundless*, leading us across the lake. Crowded together on the O tile, we were now only about five feet from the Sibyl's platform.

"Should we jump?" Meg asked.

Herophile shrieked, then clamped her hands over her mouth.

"I'm guessing a jump would be unwise," I said. "We have to complete the puzzle. Herophile, perhaps one more very small word going forward?"

The Sibyl curled her fingers, then said slowly and carefully, "Small word, across. Starts with Y. Small word down. *Near or next to*."

"A double play!" I looked at my friends. "I believe we are looking for *yo* across, and *by* down. That should allow us to reach the platform."

Grover peered over the side of the tile, where the lake of ichor was now bubbling white hot. "I'd hate to fail now. Is *yo* an acceptable word?"

"I don't have the Scrabble rule book in front of me," I admitted, "but I think so."

I was glad this wasn't Scrabble. Athena won every

time with her insufferable vocabulary. One time she played *abaxial* on a triple and Zeus lightning-bolted the top off Mount Parnassus in his rage.

"That's our answer, Sibyl," I said. "*Yo* and *by*."

Another two tiles clicked into place, connecting our bridge to Herophile's platform. We ran across, and Herophile clapped and wept for joy. She held out her arms to hug me, then seemed to remember she was shackled with blazing-hot chains.

Meg looked back at the path of answers in our wake. "Okay, so if that's the end of the prophecy, what does it mean? *Doorway soundless god opened yo by?*"

Herophile started to say something, then thought better of it. She looked at me hopefully.

"Let's assume some small words again," I ventured. "If we combine the first part of the maze, we have *Apollo faces death in Tarquin's tomb unless* . . . uh, *the doorway* . . . to?" I glanced at Herophile, who nodded encouragement. "*The doorway to the soundless god* . . . Hmm. I don't know who that is. *Unless the doorway to the soundless god is opened by*—"

"You forgot the *yo*," Grover said.

"I think we can bypass the *yo* since it was a double play."

Grover tugged his singed goatee. "This is why I don't play Scrabble. Also, I tend to eat the tiles."

I consulted Herophile. "So Apollo—me—I face death in the tomb of Tarquin, unless the doorway to the soundless god is opened by . . . what? Meg's right. There's got to be more to the prophecy."

Somewhere off to my left, a familiar voice called, "Not necessarily."

On a ledge in the middle of the left-hand wall stood the sorceress Medea, looking very much alive and delighted to see us. Behind her, two pandos guards held a chained and beaten prisoner—our friend Crest.

"Hello, my dears." Medea smiled. "You see, there doesn't have to be an end to the prophecy, because you're all going to die now anyway!"

41

Meg sings. It's over.
Everybody just go home
We are so roasted

MEG STRUCK FIRST.

With quick, sure moves, she severed the chains that bound the Sibyl, then glared at Medea as if to say *Ha-ha! I have unleashed my attack Oracle!*

The shackles fell from Herophile's wrists and ankles, revealing ugly red burn rings. Herophile stumbled back, clutching her hands to her chest. She looked more horror-struck than grateful. "Meg McCaffrey, no! You shouldn't have—"

Whatever clue she was going to give, across or down, it didn't matter. The chains and shackles snapped back together, fully mended. Then they leaped like striking rattlesnakes—at me, not Herophile. They lashed themselves around my wrists and ankles. The pain was so intense it felt cool and pleasant at first. Then I screamed.

Meg hacked at the molten links once again, but now they repelled her blades. With each blow, the chains tightened, pulling me down until I was forced to crouch. With all my insignificant strength, I struggled against the bonds, but I quickly learned this was a bad idea. Tugging against the manacles was like pressing my wrists against red-hot griddles. The agony almost made me pass out, and the smell . . . oh, gods, I did *not* enjoy the smell of deep-fried Lester. Only by staying perfectly neutral, allowing the manacles to take me where they wished, could I keep the pain at a level that was merely excruciating.

Medea laughed, clearly enjoying my contortions. "Well done, Meg McCaffrey! I was going to chain up Apollo myself, but you saved me a spell."

I fell to my knees. "Meg, Grover—get the Sibyl out of here. Leave me!"

Another brave, self-sacrificing gesture. I hope you're keeping count.

Alas, my suggestion was futile. Medea snapped her fingers. The stone tiles shifted across the surface of the ichor, leaving the Sibyl's platform cut off from any exit.

Behind the sorceress, her two guards shoved Crest to the floor. He slid down, his back to the wall, his hands shackled but still stubbornly holding my combat ukulele. The pandos's left eye was swollen shut. His lips were split. Two fingers on his right hand were bent at a funny angle. He met my eyes, his expression full of shame. I wanted to reassure him that he had not failed. We should never have left him alone on guard duty. He would still be able to do amazing fingerpicking, even with two broken fingers!

But I could barely think straight, much less console my young music student.

The two guards spread their giant ears. They sailed across the room, letting hot updrafts carry them to separate tiles near the corners of our platform. They drew their khanda blades and waited, just in case we were foolish enough to try leaping across.

"You killed Timbre," one hissed.

"You killed Peak," said the other.

On her landing, Medea chuckled. "You see, Apollo, I picked a couple of highly motivated volunteers! The rest were clamoring to accompany me down here, but—"

"There's more outside?" Meg asked. I couldn't tell if she found this idea helpful (*Hooray, fewer to kill now!*) or depressing (*Boo, more to kill later!*).

"Absolutely, my dear," Medea said. "Even if you had some foolish idea about getting past us, it wouldn't matter. Not that Flutter and Decibel will let that happen. Eh, boys?"

"I'm Flutter," said Flutter.

"I'm Decibel," said Decibel. "May we kill them now?"

"Not just yet," Medea said. "Apollo is right where I need him, ready to be dissolved. As for the rest of you, just relax. If you try to interfere, I *will* have Flutter and Decibel kill you. Then your blood might spill into the ichor, which would mess up the purity of the mixture." She spread her hands. "You understand. We can't have tainted ichor. I only need Apollo's essence for this recipe."

I did not like the way she talked about me as if I were already dead—just one more ingredient, no more important than toad's eye or sassafras.

"I will *not* be dissolved," I growled.

"Oh, Lester," she said. "You kind of *will*."

The chains tightened further, forcing me to all fours. I

couldn't understand how Herophile had endured this pain for so long. Then again, she was still immortal. I was not.

"Let it begin!" Medea cried.

She began to chant.

The ichor glowed a pure white, bleaching the color from the room. Miniature stone tiles with sharp edges seemed to shift under my skin, flaying away my mortal form, rearranging me into a new kind of puzzle in which *none* of the answers was *Apollo*. I screamed. I spluttered. I might have begged for my life. Fortunately for what little dignity I had left, I couldn't form the words.

Out of the corner of my eye, in the hazy depths of my agony, I was dimly aware of my friends backing away, terrified by the steam and fire now erupting from cracks in my body.

I didn't blame them. What could they do? At the moment, I was more likely to explode than Macro's family-fun grenade packs, and my wrapping was not *nearly* as tamper-resistant.

"Meg," Grover said, fumbling with his panpipe, "I'm going to do a nature song. See if I can disrupt that chanting, maybe summon help."

Meg gripped her blades. "In this heat? Underground?"

"Nature's all we've got!" he said. "Cover me!"

He began to play. Meg stood guard, her swords raised. Even Herophile helped, balling her fists, ready to show the pandai how Sibyls dealt with ruffians back in Erythraea.

The pandai didn't seem to know how to react. They winced at the noise of the pipes, curling their ears around their heads like turbans, but they didn't attack. Medea had told them not to. And as shaky as Grover's music was, they seemed unsure as to whether or not it constituted an act of aggression.

Meanwhile, I was busy trying not to be flayed into nothingness. Every bit of my willpower bent instinctively to keeping myself in one piece. I was Apollo, wasn't I? I . . . I was beautiful and people loved me. The world needed me!

Medea's chant undermined my resolve. Her ancient Colchian lyrics wormed their way into my mind. Who needed old gods? Who cared about Apollo? Caligula was much more interesting! He was better suited to this modern world. He fit. I did not. Why didn't I just let go? Then I could be at peace.

Pain is an interesting thing. You think you have reached your limit and you can't possibly feel more tortured. Then you discover there is still another level of agony. And another level after that. The stone tiles under my skin cut and shifted and ripped. Fires burst like sun flares across my pathetic mortal body, blasting straight through Macro's cheap discount arctic camouflage. I lost track of who I was, why I was fighting to stay alive. I wanted so badly to give up, just so the pain would stop.

Then Grover found his groove. His notes became more confident and lively, his cadence steadier. He played a fierce, desperate jig—the sort that satyrs piped in springtime in the meadows of ancient Greece, hoping to encourage dryads to come forth and dance with them in the wildflowers.

The song was hopelessly out of place in this fiery crossword dungeon. No nature spirit could possibly hear it. No dryads would come to dance with us. Nevertheless, the music dulled my pain. It lessened the intensity of the heat, like a cold towel pressed against my feverish forehead.

Medea's chant faltered. She scowled at Grover. "Really? Are you going to stop that, or must I make you?"

Grover played even more frenetically—a distress call to nature that echoed through the room, making the corridors reverberate like the pipes of a church organ.

Meg abruptly joined in, singing nonsense lyrics in a terrible monotone. "Hey, how about that nature? We love those plants. Come on down, you dryads, and, uh, grow and . . . kill this sorceress and stuff."

Herophile, who had once had such a lovely voice, who had been born singing prophecies, looked at Meg in dismay. With saintlike restraint, she did not punch Meg in the face.

Medea sighed. "Okay, that's it. Meg, I'm sorry. But I'm sure Nero will forgive me for killing you when I explain how badly you sang. Flutter, Decibel—silence them."

Behind the sorceress, Crest gurgled in alarm. He fumbled with his ukulele, despite his bound hands and two crushed fingers.

Meanwhile, Flutter and Decibel grinned with delight. "Now we shall have revenge! DIE! DIE!"

They unfurled their ears, raised their swords, and leaped toward the platform.

Could Meg have defeated them with her trusty scimitars?

I don't know. Instead, she made a move almost as surprising as her sudden urge to sing. Maybe, looking at poor Crest, she decided that enough pandos blood had been shed. Maybe she was still thinking about her misdirected anger, and whom she should *really* spend her energy hating. Whatever the case, her scimitars flicked into ring form. She grabbed a packet from her belt and ripped it open—spraying seeds in the path of the oncoming pandai.

Flutter and Decibel veered and screamed as the plants erupted, covering them in fuzzy green nebulae of ragweed. Flutter smacked into the nearest wall and began sneezing violently, the ragweed rooting him in place like a fly on flypaper. Decibel crash-landed on the platform at Meg's feet, the ragweed growing over him until he looked more like a bush than a pandos—a bush that sneezed a lot.

Medea face-palmed. "You know . . . I told Caligula that dragon's teeth warriors make *much* better guards. But *noooo*. He *insisted* on hiring pandai." She shook her head in disgust. "Sorry, boys. You had your chance."

She snapped her fingers again. A ventus swirled to life, pulling a cyclone of cinders from the ichor lake. The spirit shot toward Flutter, ripped the screaming pandos from the wall, and dumped him unceremoniously into the fire. Then it swept across the platform, grazing my friends' feet, and pushed Decibel, still sneezing and crying, off the side.

"Now, then," Medea said, "if I can encourage the rest of you to BE QUIET . . ."

The ventus charged, encircling Meg and Grover, lifting them off the platform.

I cried out, thrashing in my chains, sure that Medea would hurl my friends into the fire, but they merely hung there suspended. Grover was still playing his pipes, though no sound came through the wind; Meg was scowling and shouting, probably something like *THIS AGAIN? ARE YOU KIDDING ME?*

Herophile was not caught in the ventus. I supposed Medea considered her no threat. She stepped to my side, her fists still clenched. I was grateful for that, but I didn't see what one boxing Sibyl could do against the power of Medea.

"Okay!" Medea said, a glint of triumph in her eyes. "I'll start again. Doing this chant while controlling a ventus is not easy work, though, so please, behave. Otherwise I might lose my concentration and dump Meg and Grover into the ichor. And, really, we have too many impurities in there already, what with the pandai and the ragweed. Now, where were we? Oh, yes! Flaying your mortal form!"

42

You want prophecy?
I'll drop some nonsense on you
Eat my gibberish!

"RESIST!" Herophile knelt at my side. "Apollo, you must resist!"

I could not speak through the pain. Otherwise I would have told her *Resist. Gosh, thanks for that profound wisdom! You must be an Oracle or something!*

At least she did not ask me to spell out the word *RESIST* on stone tiles.

Sweat poured down my face. My body sizzled, and not in the good way that it used to when I was a god.

The sorceress continued her chant. I knew she must be straining her power, but this time I didn't see how I could take advantage of it. I was chained. I couldn't pull the arrow-in-the-chest trick, and even if I did, I suspected Medea was far enough along with her magic that she could just let me die. My essence would trickle into the pool of ichor.

I couldn't pipe like Grover. I couldn't rely on ragweed like Meg. I didn't have the sheer power of Jason Grace to break through the ventus cage and save my friends.

Resist. . . . But with what?

My consciousness began to waver. I tried to hold on to

the day of my birth (yes, I could remember that far back), when I jumped from my mother's womb and began to sing and dance, filling the world with my glorious voice. I remembered my first trip into the chasm of Delphi, grappling with my enemy Python, feeling his coils around my immortal body.

Other memories were more treacherous. I remembered riding the sun chariot through the sky, but I was not myself . . . I was Helios, Titan of the sun, lashing my fiery whip across the backs of my steeds. I saw myself painted golden, with a crown of rays on my brow, moving through a crowd of adoring mortal worshippers—but I was Emperor Caligula, the New Sun.

Who was I?

I tried to picture my mother Leto's face. I could not. My father, Zeus, with his terrifying glower, was only a hazy impression. My sister—surely, I could never forget my twin! But even her features floated indistinctly in my mind. She had silvery eyes. She smelled of honeysuckle. What else? I panicked. I couldn't remember her name. I couldn't remember my *own* name.

I splayed my fingers on the stone floor. They smoked and crumbled like twigs in a fire. My body seemed to pixelate, the way the pandai had when they disintegrated.

Herophile spoke in my ear, "Hold on! Help will arrive!"

I didn't see how she could know that, even if she was an Oracle. Who would come to my rescue? Who *could*?

"You have taken my place," she said. "Use that!"

I moaned in rage and frustration. Why was she talking nonsense? Why couldn't she go back to speaking in riddles?

How was I supposed to *use* being in her place, in her chains? I wasn't an Oracle. I wasn't even a god anymore. I was . . . Lester? Oh, perfect. *That* name I could remember.

I gazed across the rows and columns of stone blocks, now all blank, as if waiting for a new challenge. The prophecy wasn't complete. Maybe if I could find a way to finish it . . . would it make a difference?

It *had* to. Jason had given his life so I could make it this far. My friends had risked everything. I could not simply give up. To free the Oracle, to free Helios from this Burning Maze . . . I had to finish what we'd started.

Medea's chant droned on, aligning itself to my pulse, taking charge of my mind. I needed to override it, to disrupt it the way Grover had done with his music.

You have taken my place, Herophile had said.

I was Apollo, the god of prophecy. It was time for me to be my own Oracle.

I forced myself to concentrate on the stone blocks. Veins popped along my forehead like firecrackers under my skin. I stammered out, "*B-bronze upon gold.*"

The stone tiles shifted, forming a row of three tiles in the far upper left corner of the room, one word per square: *BRONZE UPON GOLD*.

"Yes!" the Sibyl said. "Yes, exactly! Keep going!"

The effort was horrible. The chains burned, dragging me down. I whimpered in agony, "*East meets west.*"

A second row of three tiles moved into position under the first, blazing with the words I'd just spoken.

More lines poured out of me:

"Legions are redeemed.
Light the depths;
One against many,
Never spirit defeated.
Ancient words spoken,
Shaking old foundations!"

What did that all mean? I had no idea.

The room rumbled as more blocks shifted into place, new stones rising from the lake to accommodate the sheer number of words. The entire left side of the lake was now roofed by the eight rows of three tile-wide words, like a pool cover rolled halfway over the ichor. The heat lessened. My shackles cooled. Medea's chant faltered, releasing its hold on my consciousness.

"What is this?" hissed the sorceress. "We're too close to stop now! I *will* kill your friends if you don't—"

Behind her, Crest strummed a suspended fourth on the ukulele. Medea, who had apparently forgotten about him, almost leaped into the lava.

"You too?" she shouted at him. "LET ME WORK!"

Herophile whispered in my ear, "Hurry!"

I understood. Crest was trying to buy me time by distracting Medea. He stubbornly continued playing his (my) ukulele—a series of the most jarring chords I'd taught him, and some he must have been making up on the spot. Meanwhile Meg and Grover spun in their ventus cage, trying to break free without any luck. One flick of Medea's fingers and they would meet the same fate as Flutter and Decibel.

Starting my voice again was even more difficult than towing the sun chariot out of the mud. (Don't ask about that. Long story involving attractive swamp naiads.)

Somehow, I croaked out another line: "*Destroy the tyrant*."

Three more tiles lined up, this time in the upper-right corner of the room.

"*Aid the winged*," I continued.

Good gods, I thought. *I'm speaking gibberish!* But the stones continued to follow the guidance of my voice, much better than Alexasiriastrophona had ever done.

"*Under golden hills*,
Great stallion's foal."

The tiles continued stacking, forming a second column of three-tile lines that left only a thin strip of the fiery lake visible down the middle of the room.

Medea tried to ignore the pandos. She resumed her chanting, but Crest immediately broke her concentration again with an A-flat minor sharp 5.

The sorceress shrieked. "Enough of that, pandos!" She pulled a dagger from the folds of her dress.

"Apollo, don't stop," Herophile warned. "You must not—"

Medea stabbed Crest in the gut, cutting off his dissonant serenade.

I sobbed in horror, but somehow forced out more lines:

"*Harken the trumpets*," I croaked, my voice almost gone. "*Turn red tides*—"

"Stop that!" Medea shouted at me. "Ventus, throw the prisoners—"

Crest strummed an even uglier chord.

"GAH!" The sorceress turned and stabbed Crest again.

"*Enter stranger's home*," I sobbed.

Another suspended fourth from Crest, another jab from Medea's blade.

"*Regain lost glory!*" I yelled. The last stone tiles shifted into place—completing the second column of lines from the far side of the room to the edge of our platform.

I could *feel* the prophecy's completion, as welcome as a breath of air after a long underwater swim. The flames of Helios, now visible only along the center of the room, cooled to a red simmer, no worse than your average five-alarm fire.

"Yes!" Herophile said.

Medea turned, snarling. Her hands glistened with the pandos's blood. Behind her, Crest fell sideways, groaning, pressing the ukulele to his ruined gut.

"Oh, well done, *Apollo*," Medea sneered. "You made this pandos die for your sake, for *nothing*. My magic is far enough along. I'll just flay you the old-fashioned way." She hefted her knife. "And as for your friends . . ."

She snapped her bloody fingers. "Ventus, kill them!"

43

Favorite chapter
Because only one bad death
That is just messed up

THEN SHE DIED.

I won't lie, gentle reader. Most of this narrative has been painful to write, but that last line was pure pleasure. Oh, the look on Medea's face!

But I should rewind.

How did it happen, this most welcome fluke of fate?

Medea froze. Her eyes widened. She fell to her knees, the knife clattering from her hand. She toppled over face-first, revealing a newcomer behind her—Piper McLean, dressed in leather armor over her street clothes, her lip newly stitched, her face still badly bruised but filled with resolve. Her hair was singed around the edges. A fine layer of ash coated her arms. Her dagger, Katoptris, now protruded from Medea's back.

Behind Piper stood a group of warrior maidens, seven in all. At first, I thought the Hunters of Artemis had come to save me yet again, but these warriors were armed with shields and spears made of honey-gold wood.

Behind me, the ventus unspooled, dropping Meg and

Grover to the floor. My molten chains crumbled to charcoal dust. Herophile caught me as I fell over.

Medea's hands twitched. She turned her face sideways and opened her mouth, but no words came out.

Piper knelt next to her. She placed her hand almost tenderly on the sorceress's shoulder, then with her other hand, removed Katoptris from between Medea's shoulder blades.

"One good stab in the back deserves another." Piper kissed Medea on the cheek. "I'd tell you to say hello to Jason for me, but he'll be in Elysium. You . . . won't."

The sorceress's eyes rolled up in her head. She stopped moving. Piper glanced back at her wood-armored allies. "How about we dump her?"

"GOOD CALL!" the seven maidens shouted in unison. They marched forward, lifted the body of Medea, and tossed it unceremoniously into the fiery pool of her own grandfather.

Piper wiped her bloody dagger on her jeans. With her swollen, stitched-up mouth, her smile was more gruesome than friendly. "Hi, guys."

I let out a heartbroken sob, which was probably not what Piper expected. Somehow, I got to my feet, ignoring the searing pain in my ankles, and ran past her to the place where Crest lay, gurgling weakly.

"Oh, brave friend." My eyes burned with tears. I cared nothing for my own excruciating pain, the way my skin screamed when I tried to move.

Crest's furry face was slack with shock. Blood speckled his snowy white fur. His midsection was a glistening mess.

He clutched the ukulele as if it were the only thing anchoring him to the world of the living.

"You saved us," I said, choking on the words. "You—you bought us just enough time. I will find a way to heal you."

He locked eyes with me and managed to croak, "Music. God."

I laughed nervously. "Yes, my young friend. You are a music god! I—I will teach you every chord. We will have a concert with the Nine Muses. When—when I get back to Olympus . . ."

My voice faltered.

Crest was no longer listening. His eyes had turned glassy. His tortured muscles relaxed. His body crumbled, collapsing inward until the ukulele sat on a pile of dust—a small, sad monument to my many failures.

I don't know how long I knelt there, dazed and shaking. It hurt to sob. I sobbed anyway.

Finally, Piper crouched next to me. Her face was sympathetic, but I thought somewhere behind her lovely multicolored eyes she was thinking *Another life lost for your sake, Lester. Another death you couldn't fix.*

She did not say that. She sheathed her knife. "We grieve later," she said. "Right now, our job isn't done."

Our job. She had come to our aid, despite everything that had happened, despite Jason. . . . I could not fall apart now. At least, no more than I had already.

I picked up the ukulele. I was about to mutter some promise to Crest's dust. Then I remembered what came from my broken promises. I had vowed to teach the young pandos any instrument he wished. Now he was dead. Despite the searing heat of the room, I felt the cold stare of Styx upon me.

I leaned on Piper as she helped me across the room—back to the platform where Meg, Grover, and Herophile waited.

The seven women warriors stood nearby as if waiting for orders.

Like their shields, their armor was fashioned from cleverly fitted planks of honey-gold wood. The women were imposing, each perhaps seven feet tall, their faces as polished and beautifully turned as their armor. Their hair, in various shades of white, blond, gold, and pale brown, spilled down their backs in waterfall braids. Chlorophyll green tinted their eyes and the veins of their well-muscled limbs.

They were dryads, but not like any dryads I'd ever met.

"You're the Meliai," I said.

The women regarded me with disturbingly keen interest, as if they would be equally delighted to fight me, dance with me, or toss me into the fire.

The one on the far left spoke. "We are the Meliai. Are you the Meg?"

I blinked. I got the feeling they were looking for a *yes*, but as confused as I was, I was pretty sure I was not the Meg.

"Hey, guys," Piper intervened, pointing to Meg. "This is Meg McCaffrey."

The Meliai broke into a double-time march, lifting their knees higher than was strictly necessary. They closed ranks, forming a semicircle in front of Meg like they were doing a marching-band maneuver. They stopped, banged their spears once against their shields, then lowered their heads in respect.

"ALL HAIL THE MEG!" they cried. "DAUGHTER OF THE CREATOR!"

Grover and Herophile edged into the corner, as if trying to hide behind the Sibyl's toilet.

Meg studied the seven dryads. My young master's hair was windswept from the ventus. The electrical tape had come off her glasses, so she looked like she was wearing mismatched rhinestone-encrusted monocles. Her clothes had once again been reduced to a collection of burned, shredded rags—all of which, in my opinion, made her look exactly like *The Meg* should look.

She summoned her usual eloquence: "Hi."

Piper's mouth curved in the ghost of a smile. "I met these guys at the entrance to the maze. They were just charging in to find you. Said they heard your song."

"My song?" Meg asked.

"The music!" Grover yelped. "It worked?"

"We heard the call of nature!" cried the lead dryad.

That had a different meaning for mortals, but I decided not to mention it.

"We heard the pipes of a lord of the Wild!" said another dryad. "That would be you, I suppose, satyr. Hail, satyr!"

"HAIL, SATYR!" the others echoed.

"Uh, yeah," Grover said weakly. "Hail to you too."

"But mostly," said a third dryad, "we heard the cry of the Meg, daughter of the creator. Hail!"

"HAIL!" the others echoed.

That was quite enough hailing for me.

Meg narrowed her eyes. "When you say *creator*, do you mean my dad, the botanist, or my mom, Demeter?"

The dryads murmured among themselves.

Finally, the leader spoke: "This is a most excellent point. We meant the McCaffrey, the great grower of dryads. But now we realize that you are also the daughter of Demeter. You are twice-blessed, daughter of two creators! We are at your service!"

Meg picked her nose. "At my service, huh?" She looked at me as if to ask *Why can't you be a cool servant like this?* "So, how did you guys find us?"

"We have many powers!" shouted one. "We were born from the Earth Mother's blood!"

"The primordial strength of life flows through us!" said another.

"We nursed Zeus as a baby!" said a third. "We bore an entire race of men, the warlike Bronze!"

"We are the Meliai!" said a fourth.

"We are the mighty ash trees!" cried the fifth.

This left the last two without much to say. They simply muttered, "Ash. Yep; we're ash."

Piper chimed in. "So Coach Hedge got Grover's message from the cloud nymph. Then I came to find you guys. But I didn't know where this secret entrance was, so I went to downtown LA again."

"By *yourself*?" Grover asked.

Piper's eyes darkened. I realized she had come here first

and foremost to get revenge on Medea, secondly to help us. Making it out alive . . . that had been a very distant third on her list of priorities.

"Anyway," she continued, "I met these ladies downtown and we sort of made an alliance."

Grover gulped. "But Crest said the main entrance would be a death trap! It was heavily guarded!"

"Yeah, it was. . . ." Piper pointed at the dryads. "Not anymore."

The dryads looked pleased with themselves.

"The ash is mighty," said one.

The others murmured in agreement.

Herophile stepped out from her hiding place behind the toilet. "But the fires. How did you—?"

"Ha!" cried a dryad. "It would take more than the fires of a sun Titan to destroy us!" She held up her shield. One corner was blackened, but the soot was already falling away, revealing new, unblemished wood underneath.

Judging from Meg's scowl, I could tell her mind was working overtime. That made me nervous.

"So . . . you guys serve me now?" she asked.

The dryads banged their shields again in unison.

"We will obey the commands of the Meg!" said the leader.

"Like, if I asked you to go get me some enchiladas—?"

"We would ask how many!" shouted another dryad. "And how hot you like your salsa!"

Meg nodded. "Cool. But first, maybe you could escort us safely out of the maze?"

"It shall be done!" said the lead dryad.

"Hold on," Piper said. "What about . . . ?"

She gestured to the floor tiles, where my golden nonsense words still glowed across the stone.

While kneeling in chains, I hadn't really been able to appreciate their arrangement:

BRONZE UPON GOLD	DESTROY THE TYRANT
EAST MEETS WEST	AID THE WINGED
LEGIONS ARE REDEEMED	UNDER GOLDEN HILLS
LIGHT THE DEPTHS	GREAT STALLION'S FOAL
ONE AGAINST MANY	HARKEN THE TRUMPETS
NEVER SPIRIT DEFEATED	TURN RED TIDES
ANCIENT WORDS SPOKEN	ENTER STRANGER'S HOME
SHAKING OLD FOUNDATIONS	REGAIN LOST GLORY

"What does it mean?" Grover asked, looking at me as if I had the faintest idea.

My mind ached with exhaustion and sorrow. While Crest had distracted Medea, giving Piper time to arrive and save my friends' lives, I had been spouting nonsense: two columns of text with a fiery margin down the middle. They weren't even formatted in an interesting font.

"It means Apollo succeeded!" the Sibyl said proudly. "He finished the prophecy!"

I shook my head. "But I didn't. *Apollo faces death in Tarquin's Tomb unless the doorway to the soundless god is opened by* . . . All of that?"

Piper scanned the lines. "That's a lot of text. Should I write it down?"

The Sibyl's smile wavered. "You mean . . . you don't see it? It's right there."

Grover squinted at the golden words. "See what?"

"Oh." Meg nodded. "Okay, yeah."

The seven dryads all leaned toward her, fascinated.

"What does it mean, great daughter of the creator?" asked the leader.

"It's an acrostic," Meg said. "Look."

She jogged to the upper left corner of the room. She walked along the first letter in each line, then hopped across the margin and walked the first letters of the lines in that column, all while saying the letters out loud: "*B-E-L-L-O-N-A-S D-A-U-G-H-T-E-R.*"

"Wow." Piper shook her head in amazement. "I'm still not sure what the prophecy means, about Tarquin and a soundless god and all that. But apparently you need the help of Bellona's daughter. That means the senior praetor at Camp Jupiter: Reyna Avila Ramírez-Arellano."

44

Ha-ha-ha, dryads?
That's straight from the horse's mouth
Good-bye, Mr. Horse

"HAIL, THE MEG!" cried the lead dryad. "Hail, the solver of the puzzle!"

"HAIL!" the others agreed, followed by much kneeling, banging of spears on shields, and offers to retrieve enchiladas.

I might have argued with Meg's hail-worthiness. If I hadn't just been magically half flayed to death in burning chains, I could have solved the puzzle. I was also pretty sure Meg hadn't known what an acrostic *was* until I explained it to her.

But we had bigger problems. The chamber began to shake. Dust trickled from the ceiling. A few stone tiles fell and splashed into the pool of ichor.

"We must leave," said Herophile. "The prophecy is complete. I am free. This room will not survive."

"I like leaving!" Grover agreed.

I liked leaving, too, but there was one promise I still meant to keep, no matter how much Styx hated me.

I knelt at the edge of the platform and stared into the fiery ichor.

"Uh, Apollo?" Meg asked.

"Should we pull him away?" asked a dryad.

"Should we push him in?" asked another.

Meg didn't respond. Maybe she was weighing which offer sounded better. I tried to focus on the fires below.

"Helios," I murmured, "your imprisonment is over. Medea is dead."

The ichor churned and flashed. I felt the Titan's half-conscious anger. Now that he was free, he seemed to be thinking why shouldn't he vent his power from these tunnels and turn the countryside into a wasteland? He probably also wasn't too happy about getting two pandai, some ragweed, and his evil granddaughter dumped into his nice, fiery essence.

"You have a right to be angry," I said. "But I remember you—your brilliance, your warmth. I remember your friendship with the gods and the mortals of the earth. I can never be as great a sun deity as you were, but every day I try to honor your memory—to remember your *best* qualities."

The ichor bubbled more rapidly.

I am just talking to a friend, I told myself. *This is not at all like convincing an intercontinental ballistic missile not to launch itself*.

"I will endure," I told him. "I *will* regain the sun chariot. As long as I drive it, you will be remembered. I will keep your old path across the sky steady and true. But you know, more than anyone, that the fires of the sun don't belong on the earth. They weren't meant to destroy the land, but to warm it! Caligula and Medea have twisted you into a weapon. Don't allow them to win! All you have to do is *rest*. Return to the ether of Chaos, my old friend. Be at peace."

The ichor turned white-hot. I was sure my face was about to get an extreme dermal peel.

Then the fiery essence fluttered and shimmered like a pool full of moth wings—and the ichor vanished. The heat dissipated. The stone tiles disintegrated into dust and rained into the empty pit. On my arms, the terrible burns faded. The split skin mended itself. The pain ebbed to a tolerable level of I've-just-been-tortured-for-six-hours agony, and I collapsed, shaking and cold, on the stone floor.

"You did it!" Grover cried. He looked at the dryads, then at Meg, and laughed in amazement. "Can you feel it? The heat wave, the drought, the wildfires . . . they're gone!"

"Indeed," said the lead dryad. "The Meg's weakling servant has saved nature! Hail to the Meg!"

"HAIL!" the other dryads chimed in.

I didn't even have the energy to protest.

The chamber rumbled more violently. A large crack zigzagged down the middle of the ceiling.

"Let's get out of here." Meg turned to the dryads. "Help Apollo."

"The Meg has spoken!" said the lead dryad.

Two dryads hauled me to my feet and carried me between them. I tried to put weight on my feet, just for dignity's sake, but it was like roller-skating on wheels of wet macaroni.

"You know how to get there?" Grover asked the dryads.

"We do *now*," said one. "It is the quickest way back to nature, and that is something we can always find."

On a *Help, I'm Going to Die* scale from one to ten, exiting the maze was a ten. But since everything else I'd done that week was a fifteen, it seemed like a piece of baklava. Tunnel roofs collapsed around us. Floors crumbled. Monsters attacked, only to be stabbed to death by seven eager dryads yelling, "HAIL!"

Finally we reached a narrow shaft that slanted upward toward a tiny square of sunlight.

"This isn't the way we came in," Grover fretted.

"It is close enough," said the lead dryad. "We will go first!"

No one argued. The seven dryads raised their shields and marched single file up the shaft. Piper and Herophile went next, followed by Meg and Grover. I brought up the rear, having recovered enough to crawl on my own with a minimum of weeping and gasping.

By the time I emerged into the sunlight and got to my feet, the battle lines had already been drawn.

We were back in the old bear pit, though how the shaft led us there, I didn't know. The Meliai had formed a shield wall around the tunnel entrance. Behind them stood the rest of my friends, weapons drawn. Above us, lining the ridge of the cement bowl, a dozen pandai waited with arrows nocked in their bows. In their midst stood the great white stallion Incitatus.

When he saw me, he tossed his beautiful mane. "*There* he is at last. Medea couldn't close the deal, huh?"

"Medea is dead," I said. "Unless you run away *now*, you will be next."

Incitatus nickered. "Never liked that sorceress anyway. As for surrendering . . . Lester, have you looked at yourself lately? You're in no shape to issue threats. We've got the high ground. You've seen how fast pandai can shoot. I don't know who your pretty allies with the wooden armor are, but it doesn't matter. Come along quietly. Big C is sailing north to deal with your friends in the Bay Area, but we can catch up with the fleet easy enough. My boy has *all kinds* of special treats planned for you."

Piper snarled. I suspected that Herophile's hand on her shoulder was the only thing keeping the daughter of Aphrodite from charging the enemy all by herself.

Meg's scimitars gleamed in the afternoon sun. "Hey, ash ladies," she said, "how fast can you get up there?"

The leader glanced over. "Fast enough, O Meg."

"Cool," Meg said. Then she shouted up at the horse and his troops, "Last chance to surrender!"

Incitatus sighed. "Fine."

"Fine, you surrender?" Meg asked.

"No. Fine, we'll kill you. Pandai—"

"Dryads, ATTACK!" Meg yelled.

"*Dryads?*" Incitatus asked incredulously.

It was the last thing he ever said.

The Meliai leaped out of the pit as if it were no higher than a porch step. The dozen pandai archers, fastest shots in the West, couldn't fire a single arrow before they were cut to dust by ashen spears.

Incitatus whinnied in panic. As the Meliai surrounded him, he reared and kicked with his golden-shod hooves, but even his great strength was no match for the primordial killer tree spirits. The stallion buckled and fell, skewered from seven directions at once.

The dryads faced Meg.

"The deed is done!" announced their leader. "Would the Meg like enchiladas now?"

Next to me, Piper looked vaguely nauseous, as if vengeance had lost some of its appeal. "I thought *my* voice was powerful."

Grover whimpered in agreement. "I've never had nightmares about trees. That might change after today."

Even Meg looked uncomfortable, as if just realizing what sort of power she'd been given. I was relieved to see that discomfort. It was a sure sign that Meg remained a good person. Power makes good people uneasy rather than joyful or boastful. That's why good people so rarely rise to power.

"Let's get out of here," she decided.

"To where shall we get out of here, O Meg?" asked the lead dryad.

"Home," said Meg. "Palm Springs."

There was no bitterness in her voice as she put those words together: *Home. Palm Springs.* She needed to return, like the dryads, to her roots.

45

Desert flowers bloom
Sunset rain sweetens the air
Time for a game show!

PIPER DID NOT ACCOMPANY US.

She said she had to get back to the Malibu house so as not to worry her father or the Hedge family. They would all be leaving for Oklahoma together tomorrow evening. Also, she had some arrangements to attend to. Her dark tone led me to believe she meant *final arrangements*, as in for Jason.

"Meet me tomorrow afternoon." She handed me a folded sheet of dandelion-yellow paper—an N.H. Financials eviction notice. On the back, she'd scribbled an address in Santa Monica. "We'll get you on your way."

I wasn't sure what she meant by that, but without explanation she hiked toward the nearby golf-course parking lot, no doubt to borrow a Bedrossian-quality vehicle.

The rest of us returned to Palm Springs in the red Mercedes. Herophile drove. Who knew ancient Oracles could drive? Meg sat next to her. Grover and I took the back. I kept staring forlornly at my seat, where Crest had sat only a few hours before, so anxious to learn his chords and become a god of music.

I may have cried.

The seven Meliai marched alongside our Mercedes like secret-service agents, keeping up with us easily, even when we left bumper-to-bumper traffic behind.

Despite our victory, we were a somber crew. No one offered any scintillating conversation. At one point, Herophile tried to break the ice. "I spy with my little eye—"

We responded in unison: "No."

After that, we rode in silence.

The temperature outside cooled at least fifteen degrees. A marine layer had rolled in over the Los Angeles basin like a giant wet duster, soaking up all the dry heat and smoke. When we reached San Bernardino, dark clouds swept the hilltops, dropping curtains of rain on the parched, fire-blackened hills.

When we came over the pass and saw Palm Springs stretched out below us, Grover cried with happiness. The desert was carpeted in wildflowers—marigolds and poppies, dandelions and primroses—all glistening from the rainfall that had just moved through, leaving the air cool and sweet.

Dozens of dryads waited for us on the hilltop outside the Cistern. Aloe Vera fussed over our wounds. Prickly Pear scowled and asked how we could possibly have ruined our clothes yet again. Reba was so delighted she tried to tango with me, though Caligula's sandals really were not designed for fancy footwork. The rest of the assembled host made a wide circle around the Meliai, gawking at them in awe.

Joshua hugged Meg so hard she squeaked. "You did it!" he said. "The fires are *gone*!"

"You don't have to sound so surprised," she grumbled.

"And these . . ." He faced the Meliai. "I—I saw them

emerge from their saplings earlier today. They said they heard a song they had to follow. That was you?"

"Yep." Meg didn't appear to like the way Joshua was staring slack-jawed at the ash dryads. "They're my new minions."

"We are the Meliai!" the leader agreed. She knelt in front of Meg. "We require guidance, O Meg! Where shall we be rooted?"

"Rooted?" Meg asked. "But I thought—"

"We can remain on the hillside where you planted us, Great Meg," the leader said. "But if you wish us to root elsewhere, you must decide quickly! We will soon be too large and strong to transplant!"

I had a sudden image of us buying a pickup truck and filling the bed with dirt, then driving north to San Francisco with seven killer ash trees. I liked that idea. Unfortunately, I knew it wouldn't work. Trees were not big on road trips.

Meg scratched her ear. "If you guys stay here . . . you'll be okay? I mean, with the desert and all?"

"We will be fine," said the leader.

"Though a little more shade and water would be best," said a second ash.

Joshua cleared his throat. He brushed his fingers self-consciously through his shaggy hair. "We, um, would be most honored to have you! The force of nature is already strong here, but with the Meliai among us—"

"Yeah," Prickly Pear agreed. "Nobody would bother us ever again. We could grow in peace!"

Aloe Vera studied the Meliai doubtfully. I imagined she didn't trust life-forms that required so little healing. "How far is your range? How much territory can you protect?"

A third Melia laughed. "We marched today to Los Angeles! That was no hardship. If we are rooted here, we can protect everything within a hundred leagues!"

Reba stroked her dark hair. "Is that far enough to cover Argentina?"

"No," Grover said. "But it would cover pretty much all of Southern California." He turned to Meg. "What do you think?"

Meg was so tired she was swaying like a sapling. I half expected her to mutter some Megish answer like *dunno* and pass out. Instead, she gestured to the Meliai. "Come over here."

We all followed her to the edge of the Cistern. Meg pointed down at the shady well with its deep blue pond in the center.

"What about around the pool?" she asked. "Shade. Water. I think . . . I think my dad would have liked that."

"The creator's daughter has spoken!" cried a Melia.

"Daughter of two creators!" said another.

"Twice blessed!"

"Wise solver of puzzles!"

"The Meg!"

This left the last two with little to add, so they muttered, "Yep. The Meg. Yep."

The other dryads murmured and nodded. Despite the fact that the ash trees would be taking over their enchilada-eating hangout, no one complained.

"A sacred grove of ashes," I said. "I used to have one like that in ancient times. Meg, it's perfect."

I faced the Sibyl, who had been standing silently in back, no doubt stunned to be around so many people after her long captivity.

"Herophile," I said, "this grove will be well protected. No one, not even Caligula, could ever threaten you here. I won't tell you what to do. The choice is yours. But would you consider making this your new home?"

Herophile wrapped her arms around herself. Her auburn hair was the same color as the desert hills in the afternoon light. I wondered if she was thinking about how different this hillside was from the one where she was born, where she'd had her cave in Erythraea.

"I could be happy here," she decided. "My initial thought—and this was just an idea—is that I heard they produce many game shows in Pasadena. I have several ideas for new ones."

Prickly Pear quivered. "How about you put a pin in that, darling? Join us!"

Putting a pin in something was good advice coming from a cactus.

Aloe Vera nodded. "We would be honored to have an Oracle! You could warn me whenever anyone is about to get a cold!"

"We would welcome you with open arms," Joshua agreed. "Except for those of us with prickly arms. They would probably just wave at you."

Herophile smiled. "Very well. I would be . . ." Her voice seized up, as if she were about to start a new prophecy and send us all scrambling.

"Okay!" I said. "No need to thank us! It's decided!"

And so, Palm Springs gained an Oracle, while the rest of the world was saved from several new daytime TV game shows like *Sibyl of Fortune* or *The Oracle Is Right!* It was a win-win.

The rest of the evening was spent making a new camp down the hillside, eating take-out dinner (I chose the enchiladas verdes, thanks for asking), and assuring Aloe Vera that our layers of medicinal goop were thick enough. The Meliai dug up their own saplings and replanted them in the Cistern, which I guessed was the dryad version of pulling yourself up by your own bootstraps.

At sunset, their leader came to Meg and bowed low. "We will slumber now. But whenever you call, if we are within range, we shall answer! We shall protect this land in the name of the Meg!"

"Thanks," said the Meg, poetic as always.

The Meliai faded into their seven ash trees, which now made a beautiful ring around the pond. Their branches glowed with a soft, buttery light. The other dryads moved across the hillside, enjoying the cool air and the stars in the smoke-free night sky as they gave the Sibyl a tour of her new home.

"And here are some rocks," they told her. "And over here, these are more rocks."

Grover sat down next to Meg and me with a contented sigh.

The satyr had changed his clothes: a green cap, a fresh tie-dyed shirt, clean jeans, and a new pair of hoof-appropriate

New Balance shoes. A backpack was slung on his shoulder. My heart sank to see him dressed for travel, though I was not surprised.

"Going somewhere?" I asked.

He grinned. "Back to Camp Half-Blood."

"*Now?*" Meg demanded.

He spread his hands. "I've been here for *years*. Thanks to you guys, my work is finally actually done! I mean, I know *you* still have a long way to go, freeing the Oracles and all, but . . ."

He was too polite to finish the thought: *but please do not ask me to go any farther with you*.

"You deserve to go home," I said wistfully, wishing I could do the same. "But you won't even rest the night?"

Grover got a faraway look in his eyes. "I need to get back. Satyrs aren't dryads, but we have roots, too. Camp Half-Blood is mine. I've been gone too long. I hope Juniper hasn't gotten herself a new goat. . . ."

I recalled the way the dryad Juniper had fretted and worried about her absent boyfriend when I was at camp.

"I doubt she could ever replace such an excellent satyr," I said. "Thank you, Grover Underwood. We couldn't have succeeded without you and Walt Whitman."

He laughed, but his expression immediately darkened. "I'm just sorry about Jason and . . ." His gaze fell on the ukulele in my lap. I hadn't let it out of my sight since we returned, though I hadn't had the heart to tune the strings, much less play it.

"Yes," I agreed. "And Money Maker. And all the others

who perished trying to find the Burning Maze. Or in the fires, the drought . . ."

Wow. For a second there, I'd been feeling okay. Grover really knew how to kill a vibe.

His goatee quivered. "I'm sure you guys will make it to Camp Jupiter," he said. "I've never been there, or met Reyna, but I hear she's good people. My buddy Tyson the Cyclops is there too. Tell him I said hi."

I thought about what awaited us in the north. Aside from what we'd gleaned aboard Caligula's yacht—that his attack during the new moon had not gone well—we didn't know what was going on at Camp Jupiter, or whether Leo Valdez was still there or flying back to Indianapolis. All we knew was that Caligula, now without his stallion and his sorceress, was sailing to the Bay Area to deal with Camp Jupiter personally. We had to get there first.

"We will be fine," I said, trying to convince myself. "We've wrested three Oracles from the Triumvirate. Now, aside from Delphi itself, only one source of prophecy remains: the Sibylline Books . . . or rather, what Ella the harpy is trying to reconstruct of them from memory."

Grover frowned. "Yeah. Ella. Tyson's girlfriend."

He sounded confused, as if it made no sense that a Cyclops would have a harpy girlfriend, much less one with a photographic memory who had somehow become our only link to books of prophecy that had burned up centuries before.

Very little of our situation made sense, but I was a former Olympian. I was used to incoherency.

"Thanks, Grover." Meg gave the satyr a hug and kissed him on the cheek, which was certainly more gratitude than she'd ever shown me.

"You bet," Grover said. "Thank you, Meg. You . . ." He gulped. "You've been a great friend. I liked talking plants with you."

"I was also there," I said.

Grover smiled sheepishly. He got to his feet and clicked together the chest straps of his backpack. "Sleep well, you guys. And good luck. I have a feeling I'll see you again before . . . Yeah."

Before I ascend into the heavens and regain my immortal throne?

Before we all die in some miserable fashion at the hands of the Triumvirate?

I wasn't sure. But after Grover left, I felt an empty place in my chest, as if the hole I'd poked with the Arrow of Dodona were growing deeper and wider. I unlaced the sandals of Caligula and tossed them away.

I slept miserably and had a miserable dream.

I lay at the bottom of a cold, dark river. Above me floated a woman in black silky robes—the goddess Styx, the living incarnation of the infernal waters.

"More broken promises," she hissed.

A sob built in my throat. I did not need the reminder.

"Jason Grace is dead," she continued. "And the young pandos."

Crest! I wanted to scream. *He had a name!*

"Do you begin to feel the folly of your rash vow upon

my waters?" asked Styx. "There will be more deaths. My wrath will spare no one close to you until amends are made. Enjoy your time as a mortal, Apollo!"

Water began filling my lungs, as if my body had just now remembered it needed oxygen.

I woke up gasping.

Dawn was breaking over the desert. I was hugging my ukulele so tightly it had left gouge marks on my forearms and bruised my chest. Meg's sleeping bag was empty, but before I could look for her, she scrambled down the hill toward me—a strange, excited light in her eyes.

"Apollo, get up," she said. "You need to see this!"

46

Second prize: Road trip
With Bon Jovi on cassette
First prize: Please, don't ask

THE MCCAFFREY MANSION had been reborn.

Or rather, *regrown.*

Overnight, desert hardwoods had sprouted and grown at incredible speed, forming the beams and floors of a multi-level stilt house much like the old one. Heavy vines had emerged from the stone ruins, weaving together the walls and ceilings, leaving room for windows and skylights shaded by awnings made of wisteria.

The biggest difference in the new house: the great room had been built in a horseshoe shape around the Cistern, leaving the ash grove open to the sky.

"We hope you like it," said Aloe Vera, taking us on a tour. "We all got together and decided it was the least we could do."

The interior was cool and comfortable, with fountains and running water in every room provided by living root pipes from subterranean springs. Blooming cacti and Joshua trees decorated the spaces. Massive branches had shaped themselves into furniture. Even Dr. McCaffrey's old work desk had been lovingly re-created.

Meg sniffled, blinking furiously.

"Oh, dear," said Aloe Vera. "I hope you're not allergic to the house!"

"No, this place is amazing." Meg threw herself into Aloe's arms, ignoring the dryad's many pointy bits.

"Wow," I said. (Meg's poetry must have been rubbing off on me.) "How many nature spirits did it take to accomplish this?"

Aloe shrugged modestly. "Every dryad in the Mojave Desert wanted to help. You saved us all! *And* you restored the Meliai." She gave Meg a gooey kiss on the cheek. "Your father would be so proud. You have completed his work."

Meg blinked back tears. "I just wish . . ."

She didn't need to finish. We all knew how many lives had *not* been saved.

"Will you stay?" Aloe asked. "Aeithales is your home."

Meg gazed across the desert vista. I was terrified she would say yes. Her final command to me would be to continue my quests by myself, and this time she would *mean* it. Why shouldn't she? She had found her home. She had friends here, including seven very powerful dryads who would hail her and bring her enchiladas every morning. She could become the protector of Southern California, far from Nero's grasp. She might find peace.

The idea of being free from Meg would have delighted me just a few weeks ago, but now I found the idea insupportable. Yes, I wanted her to be happy. But I knew she had many things yet to do—first among them was facing Nero once again, closing that horrible chapter of her life by confronting and conquering the Beast.

Oh, and also I needed Meg's help. Call me selfish, but I couldn't imagine going on without her.

Meg squeezed Aloe's hand. "Maybe someday. I hope so. But right now . . . we got places to be."

Grover had generously left us the Mercedes he'd borrowed from . . . wherever.

After saying our good-byes to Herophile and the dryads, who were discussing plans to create a giant Scrabble-board floor in one of the back bedrooms at Aeithales, we drove to Santa Monica to find the address Piper had given me. I kept looking in the rearview mirror, wondering if the highway patrol would pull us over for car theft. That would've been the perfect end to my week.

It took us a while to find the right address: a small private airfield near the Santa Monica waterfront.

A security guard let us through the gates with no questions, as if he'd been expecting two teenagers in a possibly stolen red Mercedes. We drove straight onto the tarmac.

A gleaming white Cessna was parked near the terminal, right next to Coach Hedge's yellow Pinto. I shuddered, wondering if we were trapped in an episode of *The Oracle Is Right!* First prize: the Cessna. Second prize . . . No, I couldn't face the idea.

Coach Hedge was changing Baby Chuck's diaper on the hood of the Pinto, keeping Chuck distracted by letting him gnaw on a grenade. (Which was probably just an empty casing. Probably.) Mellie stood next to him, supervising.

When she saw us, she waved and gave us a sad smile, but she pointed toward the plane, where Piper stood at the base of the steps, talking with the pilot.

In her hands, Piper held something large and flat—a display board. She had a couple of books under her arm, too. To her right, near the tail of the aircraft, the luggage compartment stood open. Ground-crew members were carefully strapping down a large wooden box with brass fixtures. A coffin.

As Meg and I walked up, the captain shook Piper's hand. His face was tight with sympathy. "Everything is in order, Ms. McLean. I'll be on board doing preflight checks until our passengers are ready."

He gave us a quick nod, then climbed into the Cessna.

Piper was dressed in faded denim jeans and a green camo tank top. She'd cut her hair in a shorter, choppier style—probably because so much had been singed off anyway—which gave her an eerie resemblance to Thalia Grace. Her multicolored eyes picked up the gray of the tarmac, so she might have been mistaken for a child of Athena.

The display board she held was, of course, Jason's diorama of Temple Hill at Camp Jupiter. Tucked under her arm were Jason's two sketchbooks.

A ball bearing lodged itself in my throat. "Ah."

"Yeah," she said. "The school let me clear out his stuff."

I took the map as one might take the folded flag of a fallen soldier. Meg slid the sketchbooks into her knapsack.

"You're off to Oklahoma?" I asked, pointing my chin toward the plane.

Piper laughed. "Well, yes. But we're driving. My dad rented an SUV. He's waiting for the Hedges and me at DK's Donuts." She smiled sadly. "First place he ever took me to breakfast when we moved out here."

"Driving?" Meg asked. "But—"

"The plane is for *you* two," Piper said. "And . . . Jason. Like I said, my dad had enough flight time and fuel credit for one last trip. I talked to him about sending Jason home; I mean . . . the home he had the longest, in the Bay Area, and how you guys could escort him up there. . . . Dad agreed this was a much better use of the plane. We're happy to drive."

I looked at the diorama of Temple Hill—all the little Monopoly tokens carefully labeled in Jason's hand. I read the label: APOLLO. I could hear Jason's voice in my mind, saying my name, asking me for one favor: *Whatever happens, when you get back to Olympus, when you're a god again,* remember. *Remember what it's like to be human.*

This, I thought, was being human. Standing on the tarmac, watching mortals load the body of a friend and hero into the cargo hold, knowing that he would never be coming back. Saying good-bye to a grieving young woman who had done everything to help us, and knowing you could never repay her, never compensate her for all that she'd lost.

"Piper, I . . ." My voice seized up like the Sibyl's.

"It's fine," she said. "Just get to Camp Jupiter safely. Let them give Jason the Roman burial he deserves. Stop Caligula."

Her words weren't bitter, as I might have expected.

They were simply arid, like Palm Springs air—no judgment, just natural heat.

Meg glanced at the coffin in the cargo hold. She looked uneasy about flying with a dead companion. I couldn't blame her. I'd never invited Hades to go sun cruising with me for good reason. Mixing the Underworld and the Overworld was bad luck.

Regardless, Meg muttered, "Thank you."

Piper pulled the younger girl into a hug and kissed her forehead. "Don't mention it. And if you're ever in Tahlequah, come visit me, okay?"

I thought about the millions of young people who prayed to me every year, hoping to leave their small hometowns across the world and come here to Los Angeles, to make their huge dreams come true. Now Piper McLean was going the other way—leaving the glamour and the movie glitz of her father's former life, going back to small-town Tahlequah, Oklahoma. And she sounded at peace with it, as if she knew her own Aeithales would be waiting there.

Mellie and Coach Hedge strolled over, Baby Chuck still happily chewing his grenade in the coach's arms.

"Hey," Coach said. "You about ready, Piper? Long road ahead."

The satyr's expression was grim and determined. He looked at the coffin in the cargo bay, then quickly fixed his eyes on the tarmac.

"Just about," Piper agreed. "You sure the Pinto is up for such a long trip?"

"Of course!" Hedge said. "Just, uh, you know, keep in sight, in case the SUV breaks down and you need my help."

Mellie rolled her eyes. "Chuck and I are riding in the SUV."

The coach harrumphed. "That's fine. It'll give me time to play my tunes. I've got Bon Jovi's entire collection on cassette!"

I tried to smile encouragingly, though I decided to give Hades a new suggestion for the Fields of Punishment if I ever saw him again: *Pinto. Road trip. Bon Jovi on cassette.*

Meg bopped Baby Chuck on the nose, which made him giggle and spit grenade shavings. "What are you guys going to do in Oklahoma?" she asked.

"Coach, of course!" said the coach. "They've got some great varsity sports teams in Oklahoma. Plus, I hear nature is pretty strong there. Nice place to raise a kid."

"And there's always work for cloud nymphs," Mellie said. "Everybody needs clouds."

Meg stared into the sky, maybe wondering how many of those clouds were nymphs making minimum wage. Then, suddenly, her mouth fell open. "Uh, guys?"

She pointed north.

A gleaming shape resolved against a line of white clouds. For a moment, I thought a small plane was making its final approach. Then its wings flapped.

The ground crew scrambled into action as Festus the bronze dragon came in for a landing, Leo Valdez riding on his back.

The crew waved their orange flashlight cones, guiding Festus to a spot next to the Cessna. None of the mortals seemed to find this at all unusual. One of the crew shouted up at Leo, asking if he needed any fuel.

Leo grinned. "Nah. But if you could give my boy a wash and wax, and maybe find him some Tabasco sauce, that would be great."

Festus roared in approval.

Leo Valdez climbed down and jogged toward us. Whatever adventures he may have had, he seemed to have come through with his curly black hair, his impish smile, and his small, elfish frame intact. He wore a purple T-shirt with gold words in Latin: MY COHORT WENT TO NEW ROME AND ALL I GOT WAS THIS LOUSY T-SHIRT.

"The party can now start!" he announced. "There's my peeps!"

I didn't know what to say. We all just stood there, stunned, as Leo gave us hugs.

"Man, what's up with you guys?" he asked. "Somebody hit you with a flash grenade? So, I got good news and bad news from New Rome, but first . . ." He scanned our faces. He expression began to crumble. "Where's Jason?"

47

In-flight beverages
Include the tears of a god
Please have exact change

PIPER BROKE DOWN. She fell against Leo and sobbed out the story until he, thunderstruck, red-eyed, hugged her back and buried his face in her neck.

The ground crew gave us space. The Hedges retreated to the Pinto, where the coach clasped Mellie and their baby tight, the way one should always do with family, knowing that tragedy could strike anyone, anytime.

Meg and I stood by, Jason's diorama still fluttering in my arms.

Next to the Cessna, Festus raised his head, made a low, keening sound, then blasted fire into the sky. The ground crew looked a little nervous about that as they hosed down his wings. I supposed private jets didn't often keen or spew fire from their nostrils, or . . . have nostrils.

The air around us seemed to crystallize, forming brittle shards of emotion that would cut us no matter which way we turned.

Leo looked like he'd been struck repeatedly. (And I knew. I had *seen* him struck repeatedly.) He brushed the tears from his face. He stared at the cargo hold, then at the diorama in my hands.

"I didn't . . . I couldn't even say good-bye," he murmured.

Piper shook her head. "Me neither. It happened so fast. He just—"

"He did what Jason always did," Leo said. "He saved the day."

Piper took a shaky breath. "What about you? Your news?"

"My news?" Leo choked back a sob. "After *that*, who cares about my news?"

"Hey." Piper punched his arm. "Apollo told me what you were up to. What happened at Camp Jupiter?"

Leo tapped his fingers on his thighs, as if carrying on two simultaneous conversations in Morse code. "We—we stopped this attack. Sort of. There was a lot of damage. That's the bad news. A lot of good people . . ." He glanced again at the cargo hold. "Well, Frank is okay. Reyna, Hazel. That's the good news. . . ." He shivered. "Gods. I can't even think right now. Is that normal? Like, just forgetting how to think?"

I could assure him that it was, at least in my experience.

The captain came down the steps on the plane. "Sorry, Miss McLean, but we are queued for departure. If we don't want to lose our window—"

"Yeah," Piper said. "Of course. Apollo and Meg, you guys go. I'll be fine with the coach and Mellie. Leo—"

"Oh, you're not getting rid of me," said Leo. "You just earned a bronze dragon escort to Oklahoma."

"Leo—"

"We're not arguing about this," he insisted. "Besides, it's more or less on the way back to Indianapolis."

Piper's smile was as faint as fog. "You're settling in Indianapolis. Me, in Tahlequah. We're really going places, huh?"

Leo turned to us. "Go on, you guys. Take . . . take Jason home. Do right by him. You'll find Camp Jupiter still there."

From the window of the plane, the last I saw of Piper and Leo, Coach and Mellie, they were huddled on the tarmac, plotting their journey east with their bronze dragon and their yellow Pinto.

Meanwhile, we taxied down the runway in our private jet. We rumbled into the sky—heading for Camp Jupiter and a rendezvous with Reyna, the daughter of Bellona.

I didn't know how I would find Tarquin's tomb, or who the soundless god was supposed to be. I didn't know how we would stop Caligula from attacking the damaged Roman camp. But none of that bothered me as much as what had happened to us already—so many lives destroyed, a hero's coffin rattling in the cargo hold, three emperors who were all still alive, ready to wreak more havoc on everyone and everything I cared about.

I found myself crying.

It was ridiculous. Gods don't cry. But as I looked at Jason's diorama in the seat next to me, all I could think about was that he would never get to see his carefully labeled plans finished. As I held my ukulele, I could only picture Crest playing his last chord with broken fingers.

"Hey." Meg turned in the seat in front of me. Despite her usual cat-eye glasses and preschool-colored outfit (somehow mended, yet again, by the magic of the ever-patient dryads), Meg sounded more grown-up today. Surer of herself. "We're going to make everything right."

I shook my head miserably. "What does that even mean? Caligula is heading north. Nero is still out there. We've faced three emperors, and defeated none of them. And Python—"

She bopped me on the nose, much harder than she had Baby Chuck.

"Ow!"

"Got your attention?"

"I— Yes."

"Then listen: *You will get to the Tiber alive. You will start to jive*. That's what the prophecy said back in Indiana, right? It will make sense once we get there. You're going to beat the Triumvirate."

I blinked. "Is that an order?"

"It's a promise."

I wished she hadn't put it that way. I could almost hear the goddess Styx laughing, her voice echoing from the cold cargo hold where the son of Jupiter now rested in his coffin.

The thought made me angry. Meg was right. I *would* defeat the emperors. I would free Delphi from Python's grasp. I would not allow those who had sacrificed themselves to do so for nothing.

Perhaps this quest had ended on a suspended fourth chord. We still had much to do.

But from now on, I would be more than Lester. I would be more than an observer.

I would be Apollo.

I would remember.

GUIDE TO APOLLO-SPEAK

aeithales ancient Greek for *evergreen*

Aeneas a prince of Troy and reputed ancestor of the Romans; the hero of Virgil's epic the *Aeneid*

Alexander the Great a king of the ancient Greek kingdom of Macedon from 336 to 323 BCE; he united the Greek city-states and conquered Persia

ambrosia the food of the gods; it gives immortality to whoever consumes it; demigods can eat it in small doses to heal their injuries

Aphrodite Greek goddess of love and beauty; Roman form: Venus

arbutus any shrub or tree in the heath family with white or pink flowers and red or orange berries

Ares the Greek god of war; the son of Zeus and Hera, and half brother to Athena; Roman form: Mars

Argo II a flying trireme built by the Hephaestus cabin at Camp Half-Blood to take the demigods of the Prophecy of Seven to Greece

Artemis the Greek goddess of the hunt and the moon; the daughter of Zeus and Leto, and the twin of Apollo

Asclepius the god of medicine; son of Apollo; his temple was the healing center of ancient Greece

Athena the Greek goddess of wisdom

Bellona a Roman goddess of war; daughter of Jupiter and Juno

blemmyae a tribe of headless people with faces in their chests

Britomartis the Greek goddess of hunting and fishing nets; her sacred animal is the griffin

cabrito roasted or stewed kid goat meat

caligae **(*caliga*,** sing.) Roman military boots

Caligula the nickname of the third of Rome's emperors, Gaius Julius Caesar Augustus Germanicus, infamous for his cruelty and carnage during the four years he ruled, from 37 to 41 CE; he was assassinated by his own guard

Camp Half-Blood the training ground for Greek demigods, located in Long Island, New York

Camp Jupiter the training ground for Roman demigods, located in California, between the Oakland Hills and the Berkeley Hills

Cave of Trophonius a deep chasm, home to the Oracle Trophonius

Celestial bronze a powerful magical metal used to create weapons wielded by Greek gods and their demigod children

Chicago Black Sox eight members of the Chicago White Sox, a Major League Baseball team, accused of intentionally losing the 1919 World Series against the Cincinnati Reds in exchange for money

Claudius Roman emperor from 41 to 54 CE, succeeding Caligula, his nephew

Commodus Lucius Aurelius Commodus was the son of Roman Emperor Marcus Aurelius; he became co-emperor when he was sixteen and emperor at eighteen, when his father died; he ruled from 177 to 192 CE and was megalomaniacal and corrupt; he considered himself the New Hercules and enjoyed killing animals and fighting gladiators at the Colosseum

Cyclops (Cyclopes, pl.) a member of a primordial race of giants, each with a single eye in the middle of his or her forehead

Daedalus a skilled craftsman who created the Labyrinth on Crete in which the Minotaur (part man, part bull) was kept

Daphne a beautiful naiad who attracted Apollo's attention; she transformed into a laurel tree in order to escape him

Delos a Greek island in the Aegean Sea near Mykonos; birthplace of Apollo

Demeter the Greek goddess of agriculture; a daughter of the Titans Rhea and Kronos

denarius (denarii, pl.) a unit of Roman currency

Dionysus Greek god of wine and revelry; the son of Zeus

Doors of Death the doorway to the House of Hades, located in Tartarus; the doors have two sides—one in the mortal world, and one in the Underworld

dryad a spirit (usually female) associated with a certain tree

Edesia Roman goddess of banquets

Edsel a car produced by Ford from 1958 to 1960; it was a big flop

Elysium the paradise to which Greek heroes were sent when the gods gave them immortality

empousa a winged bloodsucking monster, daughter of the goddess Hecate

Enceladus a giant, son of Gaea and Ouranos, who was the primary adversary of the goddess Athena during the War of the Giants

Erymanthian Boar a giant wild boar that terrorized people on the island of Erymanthos until Hercules subdued it in the third of his twelve labors

Erythraean Sibyl a prophetess who presided over Apollo's Oracle at Erythrae in Ionia

Euterpe Greek goddess of lyric poetry; one of the Nine Muses; daughter of Zeus and Mnemosyne

Feronia the Roman goddess of wildlife, also associated with fertility, health and abundance

Furies goddesses of vengeance

Gaea the Greek earth goddess; wife of Ouranos; mother of the Titans, giants, Cyclopes, and other monsters

Germanicus adoptee of the Roman emperor Tiberius; became a prominent general of the Roman empire, known for his successful campaigns in Germania; father of Caligula

gladius a stabbing sword; the primary weapon of Roman foot soldiers

Golden Fleece the much-coveted fleece of the gold-haired winged ram, which was held in Colchis by King Aeëtes and guarded by a dragon until Jason and the Argonauts retrieved it

Hades the Greek god of death and riches; ruler of the Underworld

Hadrian the fourteenth emperor of Rome; ruled from 117 to 138 CE; known for building a wall that marked the northern limit of Britannia

harpy a winged female creature that snatches things

Hecate goddess of magic and crossroads

Hecuba queen of Troy, wife of King Priam, ruler during the Trojan War

Helen of Troy a daughter of Zeus and Leda and considered the most beautiful woman in the world; she sparked the Trojan War when she left her husband Menelaus for Paris, a prince of Troy

Helios the Titan god of the sun; son of the Titan Hyperion and the Titaness Theia

Hephaestus the Greek god of fire, including volcanic, and of crafts and blacksmithing; the son of Zeus and Hera, and married to Aphrodite; Roman form: Vulcan

Hera the Greek goddess of marriage; Zeus's wife and sister; Apollo's stepmother

Heracles the Greek equivalent of Hercules; the son of Zeus and Alcmene; born with great strength

Hercules the Roman equivalent of Heracles; the son of Jupiter and Alcmene; born with great strength

Hermes Greek god of travelers; guide to spirits of the dead; god of communication

Herophile the daughter of a water nymph; she had such

a lovely singing voice that Apollo blessed her with the gift of prophecy, making her the Erythraean Sibyl

Hestia Greek goddess of the hearth and home

Hyacinthus a Greek hero and Apollo's lover, who died while trying to impress Apollo with his discus skills

hydra a many-headed water serpent

Hypnos Greek god of sleep

Imperial gold a rare metal deadly to monsters, consecrated at the Pantheon; its existence was a closely guarded secret of the emperors

Incitatus the favorite horse of Roman emperor Caligula

Janus the Roman god of beginnings, openings, doorways, gates, passages, time, and endings; depicted with two faces

Jupiter the Roman god of the sky and king of the gods; Greek form: Zeus

Katoptris Greek for *mirror*; a dagger that once belonged to Helen of Troy

khanda a double-edged straight sword; an important symbol of Sikhism

kusarigama a traditional Japanese weapon consisting of a sickle attached to a chain

Kymopoleia Greek goddess of violent storm waves; daughter of Poseidon

La Ventana a performance and event venue in Buenos Aires, Argentina

Labyrinth an underground maze originally built on the island of Crete by the craftsman Daedalus to hold the Minotaur

legionnaire a member of the Roman army

Leto mother of Artemis and Apollo with Zeus; goddess of motherhood

Little Tiber the barrier of Camp Jupiter

Lucrezia Borgia the daughter of a pope and his mistress; a beautiful noblewoman who earned the reputation of being a political schemer in fifteenth-century Italy

Marcus Aurelius Roman Emperor from 161 to 180 CE; father of Commodus; considered the last of the "Five Good Emperors"

Mars the Roman god of war; Greek form: Ares

Medea a Greek enchantress, daughter of King Aeëtes of Colchis and granddaughter of the Titan sun god, Helios; wife of the hero Jason, whom she helped obtain the Golden Fleece

Mefitis a goddess of foul-smelling gasses of the earth, especially worshipped in swamps and volcanic areas

Meliai Greek nymphs of the ash tree, born of Gaea; they nurtured and raised Zeus in Crete

Michelangelo an Italian sculptor, painter, architect, and poet of the High Renaissance; a towering genius in the history of Western art; among his many masterpieces, he painted the ceiling of the Sistine Chapel in the Vatican

Minotaur the part-man, part-bull son of King Minos of Crete; the Minotaur was kept in the Labyrinth, where he killed people who were sent in; he was finally defeated by Theseus

Mount Olympus home of the Twelve Olympians

Mount Vesuvius a volcano near the Bay of Naples in

Italy that erupted in the year 79 CE, burying the Roman city of Pompeii under ash

Naevius Sutorius Macro a prefect of the Praetorian Guard from 31 to 38 CE, serving under the emperors Tiberius and Caligula

Neos Helios Greek for *new sun*, a title adopted by the Roman emperor Caligula

Nero ruled as Roman Emperor from 54 to 58 CE; he had his mother and his first wife put to death; many believe he was responsible for setting a fire that gutted Rome, but he blamed the Christians, whom he burned on crosses; he built an extravagant new palace on the cleared land and lost support when construction expenses forced him to raise taxes; he committed suicide

Nine Muses goddesses who grant inspiration for and protect artistic creation and expression; daughters of Zeus and Mnemosyne; as children, they were taught by Apollo; their names are Clio, Euterpe, Thalia, Melpomene, Terpsichore, Erato, Polymnia, Ourania, and Calliope

Niobids children who were slain by Apollo and Artemis when their mother, Niobe, boasted about having more offspring than Leto, the twins' mother

nunchaku originally a farm tool used to harvest rice, an Okinawan weapon consisting of two sticks connected at one end by a short chain or rope

nymph a female deity who animates nature

Oracle of Delphi a speaker of the prophecies of Apollo

Oracle of Trophonius a Greek who was transformed

into an Oracle after his death; located at the Cave of Trophonius; known for terrifying those who seek him

Orthopolis the only child of Plemnaeus who survived birth; disguised as an old woman, Demeter nursed him, ensuring the boy's survival

Ouranos the Greek personification of the sky; husband of Gaea; father of the Titans

Palatine Hill the most famous of Rome's seven hills; considered one of the most desirable neighborhoods in ancient Rome, it was home to aristocrats and emperors

Pan the Greek god of the wild; the son of Hermes

pandai (pandos, sing.) a tribe of men with gigantic ears, eight fingers and toes, and bodies covered with hair that starts out white and turn black with age

parazonium a triangular-bladed dagger sported by women in ancient Greece

Petersburg a Civil War battle in Virginia in which an explosive charge designed to be used against the Confederates led to the deaths of 4,000 Union troops

phalanx a body of heavily armed troops in close formation

Philip of Macedon the king of the ancient Greek kingdom of Macedonia from 359 BCE until his assassination in 336 BCE; father of Alexander the Great

physician's cure a concoction created by Asclepius, god of medicine, to bring someone back from the dead

Plemnaeus the father of Orthopolis, whom Demeter reared to ensure that he would flourish

Pompeii a Roman city that was destroyed in 79 CE when the volcano Mount Vesuvius erupted and buried it under ash

Poseidon the Greek god of the sea; son of the Titans Kronos and Rhea, and the brother of Zeus and Hades

praetor an elected Roman magistrate and commander of the army

praetorian guard a unit of elite Roman soldiers in the Imperial Roman Army

princeps Latin for *first citizen* or *first in line*; the early Roman emperors adopted this title for themselves, and it came to mean *prince of Rome*

Python a monstrous dragon that Gaea appointed to guard the Oracle at Delphi

River Styx the river that forms the boundary between Earth and the Underworld

Sarpedon a son of Zeus who was a Lycian prince and a hero in the Trojan War; he fought with distinction on the Trojan side but was slain by the Greek warrior Patroclus

Saturnalia an ancient Roman festival held in December in honor of the god Saturn, the Roman equivalent of Kronos

satyr a Greek forest god, part goat and part man

scimitar a saber with a curved blade

shuriken a ninja throwing star; a flat, bladed weapon used as a dagger or to distract

Sibyl a prophetess

situla Latin for *bucket*

Spartan a citizen of Sparta, or something belonging to Sparta, a city-state in ancient Greece with military dominance

strix (strixes, pl.) a large blood-drinking owl-like bird of ill omen

Stygian iron a rare magical metal capable of killing monsters

Styx a powerful water nymph; the eldest daughter of the sea Titan, Oceanus; goddess of the Underworld's most important river; goddess of hatred; the River Styx is named after her

Tarquin Lucius Tarquinius Superbus was the seventh and final king of Rome, reigning from 535 BCE until 509, when, after a popular uprising, the Roman Republic was established

Temple of Castor and Pollux an ancient temple in the Roman Forum in Rome, erected in honor of the twin demigod children of Jupiter and Leda and dedicated by the Roman general Aulus Postumius, who won a great victory at the Battle of Lake Regillus

Terpsichore Greek goddess of dance; one of the Nine Muses

Thermopylae a mountain pass near the sea in northern Greece that was the site of several battles, the most famous being between the Persians and the Greeks during the Persian invasion of 480–479 BCE

Tiber River the third-longest river in Italy; Rome was founded on its banks; in ancient Rome, criminals were thrown into the river

Titans a race of powerful Greek deities, descendants of Gaea and Ouranos, that ruled during the Golden Age and were overthrown by a race of younger gods, the Olympians

tragus (tragi, pl.) a fleshy prominence at the front of the external opening of the ear

trireme a Greek warship, having three tiers of oars on each side

triumvirate a political alliance formed by three parties

Trojan War According to legend, the Trojan War was waged against the city of Troy by the Achaeans (Greeks) after Paris of Troy took Helen from her husband, Menelaus, king of Sparta

Trophonius demigod son of Apollo, designer of Apollo's temple at Delphi, and spirit of the Dark Oracle; he decapitated his half brother Agamethus to avoid discovery after their raid on King Hyrieus's treasury

Troy a pre-Roman city situated in modern-day Turkey; site of the Trojan War

Underworld the kingdom of the dead, where souls go for eternity; ruled by Hades

ventus (venti, pl.) storm spirits

Vulcan the Roman god of fire, including volcanic, and of blacksmithing; Greek form: Hephaestus

Waystation a place of refuge for demigods, peaceful monsters, and Hunters of Artemis, located above Union Station in Indianapolis, Indiana

Zeus the Greek god of the sky and the king of the gods; Roman form: Jupiter

COMING IN FALL 2019

THE TRIALS OF

APOLLO

◄ 4 ►

THE TYRANT'S TOMB

While you wait, enjoy the first book from
Rick Riordan Presents:

Aru Shah and the End of Time

by Roshani Chokshi

In Which Aru Regrets Opening the Door

The problem with growing up around highly dangerous things is that after a while you just get used to them.

For as long as she could remember, Aru had lived in the Museum of Ancient Indian Art and Culture. And she knew full well that the lamp at the end of the Hall of the Gods was not to be touched.

She could mention "the lamp of destruction" the way a pirate who had tamed a sea monster could casually say, *Oh, you mean ole Ralph here?* But even though she was used to the lamp, she had never once lit it. That would be against the rules. The rules she went over every Saturday, when she led the afternoon visitors' tour.

Some folks may not like the idea of working on a weekend, but it never felt like work to Aru.

It felt like a ceremony.

Like a secret.

She would don her crisp scarlet vest with its three honeybee buttons. She would imitate her mother's museum-curator voice, and people—this was the best part of all—would *listen.* Their eyes never left her face. Especially when she talked about the cursed lamp.

Sometimes she thought it was the most fascinating thing she ever discussed. A cursed lamp is a much more interesting topic than, say, a visit to the dentist. Although one could argue that both are cursed.

Aru had lived at the museum for so long, it kept no secrets from her. She had grown up reading and doing her homework beneath the giant stone elephant at the entrance. Often she'd fall asleep in the theater and wake up just before the crackling self-guided tour recording announced that India became independent from the British in 1947. She even regularly hid a stash of candy in the mouth of a four-hundred-year-old sea dragon statue (she'd named it Steve) in the west wing. Aru knew everything about everything in the museum. Except one thing...

The lamp. For the most part, it remained a mystery.

"It's not quite a lamp," her mother, renowned curator and archaeologist Dr. K. P. Shah, had told her the first time she showed it to Aru. "We call it a *diya*."

Aru remembered pressing her nose against the glass case, staring at the lump of clay. As far as cursed objects went, this was by far the most boring. It was shaped like a pinched hockey puck. Small markings, like bite marks, crimped the edges. And yet, for all its normal-ness, even the statues filling the Hall of the Gods seemed to lean away from the lamp, giving it a wide berth.

"Why can't we light it?" she had asked her mother.

Her mother hadn't met her gaze. "Sometimes light illuminates things that are better left in the dark. Besides, you never know who is watching."

Well, Aru had watched. She'd been watching her entire life.

Every day after school she would come home, hang her backpack from the stone elephant's trunk, and creep toward the Hall of the Gods.

It was the museum's most popular exhibit, filled with a hundred statues of various Hindu gods. Her mother had lined the walls with tall mirrors so visitors could see the artifacts from all angles. The mirrors were "vintage" (a word Aru had used when she traded Burton Prater a greenish penny for a whopping two dollars and half a Twix bar). Because of the tall crape myrtles and elms standing outside the windows, the light that filtered into the Hall of the Gods always looked a little muted. Feathered, almost. As if the statues were wearing crowns of light.

Aru would stand at the entrance, her gaze resting on her favorite statues—Lord Indra, the king of the heavens, wielding a thunderbolt; Lord Krishna, playing his flutes; the Buddha, sitting with his spine straight and legs folded in meditation—before her eyes would inevitably be drawn to the diya in its glass case.

She would stand there for minutes, waiting for something... anything that would make the next day at school more interesting, or make people notice that she, Aru Shah, wasn't just another seventh grader slouching through middle school, but someone *extraordinary*....

Aru was waiting for magic.

And every day she was disappointed.

"Do something," she whispered to the god statues. It was a Monday morning, and she was still in her pajamas. "You've got plenty of time to do something awesome, because I'm on autumn break."

The statues did nothing.

Aru shrugged and looked out the window. The trees of Atlanta, Georgia, hadn't yet realized it was October. Only their top halves had taken on a scarlet-and-golden hue, as if someone had dunked them halfway in a bucket of fire and then plopped them back on the lawn.

As Aru had expected, the day was on its way to being uneventful. That should have been her first warning. The world has a tendency to trick people. It likes to make a day feel as bright and lazy as sun-warmed honey dripping down a jar as it waits until your guard is down. . . .

And that's when it strikes.

Moments before the visitor alarm rang, Aru's mom had been gliding through the cramped two-bedroom apartment connected to the museum. She seemed to be reading three books at a time while also conversing on the phone in a language that sounded like a chorus of tiny bells. Aru, on the other hand, was lying upside down on the couch and pelting pieces of popcorn at her, trying to get her attention.

"Mom. Don't say anything if you can take me to the movies."

Her mom laughed gracefully into the phone. Aru scowled. Why couldn't *she* laugh like that? When Aru laughed, she sounded like she was choking on air.

"Mom. Don't say anything if we can get a dog. A Great Pyrenees. We can name him Beowoof!"

Now her mother was nodding with her eyes closed, which meant that she was *sincerely* paying attention. Just not to Aru.

"Mom. Don't say anything if I—"

Breeeeep!

Breeeeep!

Breeeeep!

Her mother lifted a delicate eyebrow and stared at Aru. *You know what to do.* Aru did know what to do. She just didn't want to do it.

She rolled off the couch and Spider-Man–crawled across the floor in one last bid to get her mother's attention. This was a difficult feat considering that the floor was littered with books and half-empty chai mugs. She looked back to see her mom jotting something on a notepad. Slouching, Aru opened the door and headed to the stairs.

Monday afternoons at the museum were quiet. Even Sherrilyn, the head of museum security and Aru's long-suffering babysitter on the weekends, didn't come in on Mondays. Any other day—except Sunday, when the museum was closed—Aru would help hand out visitor stickers. She would direct people to the various exhibits and point out where the bathrooms were. Once she'd even had the opportunity to yell at someone when they'd patted the stone elephant, which had a very distinct DO NOT TOUCH sign (in Aru's mind, this applied to everyone who wasn't her).

On Mondays she had come to expect occasional visitors seeking temporary shelter from bad weather. Or people who wanted to express their concern (in the gentlest way possible) that the Museum of Ancient Indian Art and Culture honored the devil. Or sometimes just the FedEx man needing a signature for a package.

What she did not expect when she opened the door to greet the new visitors was that they would be three students from Augustus Day School. Aru experienced one of those elevator-stopping-too-fast sensations. A low *whoosh* of panic hit her stomach as the three students stared down at her and her Spider-Man pajamas.

The first, Poppy Lopez, crossed her tan, freckled arms. Her brown hair was pulled back in a ballerina bun. The second, Burton Prater, held out his hand, where an ugly penny sat in his palm. Burton was short and pale, and his striped black-and-yellow shirt made him look like an unfortunate bumblebee. The third, Arielle Reddy—the prettiest girl in their class, with her dark brown skin and shiny black hair—simply glared.

"I knew it," said Poppy triumphantly. "You told everyone in math class that your mom was taking you to France for break."

That's what Mom had promised, Aru thought.

Last summer, Aru's mother had curled up on the couch, exhausted from another trip overseas. Right before she fell asleep, she had squeezed Aru's shoulder and said, *Perhaps I'll take you to Paris in the fall, Aru. There's a café along the Seine River where you can hear the stars come out before they dance in the night sky. We'll go to boulangeries and museums, sip coffee from tiny cups, and spend hours in the gardens.*

That night Aru had stayed awake dreaming of narrow winding streets and gardens so fancy that even their flowers looked haughty. With that promise in mind, Aru had cleaned her room and washed the dishes without complaint. And at school, the promise had become her armor. All the other students at Augustus Day School had vacation homes in places like the Maldives or Provence, and they complained when their yachts were under repair. The promise of Paris had brought Aru one tiny step closer to belonging.

Now, Aru tried not to shrink under Poppy's blue-eyed

gaze. "My mom had a top secret mission with the museum. She couldn't take me."

That was partly true. Her mom never took her on work trips.

Burton threw down the green penny. "You cheated me. I gave you two bucks!"

"And you got a *vintage* penny—" started Aru.

Arielle cut her off. "We know you're lying, Aru Shah. That's what you are: a *liar.* And when we go back to school, we're going to tell everyone—"

Aru's insides squished. When she'd started at Augustus Day School last month, she'd been hopeful. But that had been short-lived.

Unlike the other students, she didn't get driven to school in a sleek black car. She didn't have a home "offshore." She didn't have a study room or a sunroom, just *a* room, and even she knew that her room was really more like a closet with delusions of grandeur.

But what she did have was imagination. Aru had been day-dreaming her whole life. Every weekend, while she waited for her mom to come home, she would concoct a story: her mother was a spy, an ousted princess, a sorceress.

Her mom claimed she never wanted to go on business trips, but they were a necessity to keep the museum running. And when she came home and forgot about things—like Aru's chess games or choir practice—it wasn't because she didn't care, but because she was too busy juggling the state of war and peace and art.

So at Augustus Day School, whenever the other kids asked, Aru told tales. Like the ones she told herself. She talked about cities she'd never visited and meals she'd never eaten. If she arrived with scuffed-up shoes, it was because her old pair had been sent to Italy for repair. She'd mastered that delicate condescending eyebrow everyone else had, and she deliberately mispronounced the names of stores where she bought her clothes, like the French *Tar-Jay*, and the German *Vahl-Mahrt*. If that failed, she'd just sniff and say, "Trust me, you wouldn't recognize the brand."

And in this way, she had fit in.

For a while, the lies had worked. She'd even been invited to spend a weekend at the lake with Poppy and Arielle. But Aru had ruined everything the day she was caught sneaking from the car-pool line. Arielle had asked which car was hers. Aru pointed at one, and Arielle's smile turned thin. "That's funny. Because that's my driver's car."

Arielle was giving Aru that same sneer now.

"You told us you have an elephant," said Poppy.

Aru pointed at the stone elephant behind her. "I do!"

"You said that you rescued it from India!"

"Well, Mom said it was *salvaged* from a temple, which is fancy talk for *rescue*—"

"And you said you have a cursed lamp," said Arielle.

Aru saw the red light on Burton's phone: steady and unblinking. He was recording her! She panicked. What if the video went online? She had two possible choices: 1) She could hope the universe might take pity on her and allow her to burst into flames before homeroom, or 2) She could change her name, grow a beard, and move away.

Or, to avoid the situation entirely...

She could show them something impossible.

"The cursed lamp is real," she said. "I can prove it."